PUNK'S FORCE

PRAISE FOR THE PUNK SERIES

"With suspense, drama, and action as hot as a fighter jet's afterburner, Carroll's account of modern naval aviation reads like *Top Gun* on steroids."
—***Publishers Weekly***

"Tom Clancy meets Joseph Heller in this riveting, irreverent portrait of the fighter pilots of today's Navy. At last, somebody got it right. I couldn't put it down!"
—**Stephen Coonts, author of *Flight of the Intruder***

"This first novel by former navy pilot Carroll is an exciting tale of a young lieutenant's tour of duty as a fighter pilot on an aircraft carrier stationed near Iraq.... An intriguing look at the modern military, this novel honors the men and women who serve."
—***Library Journal***

"A thoughtful rumination on the ethics of war fighters and the notions of duty, loyalty, and honor that may be tested by inept superiors, intractable bureaucracies, or politics that may be global—or as local as an aircraft carrier in the Persian Gulf."
—***Booklist***

"*Punk's War* has it all: the action of the best techno-thrillers, the emotional drama of Coonts, the realism of Keegan, and the craftsmanship of a true professional."
—**John F. Lehman Jr., former Secretary of the Navy and author of *Command the Seas***

PUNK'S FORCE

A NOVEL

WARD CARROLL
AND
TONY PEAK

Naval Institute Press
Annapolis, Maryland

Naval Institute Press
291 Wood Road
Annapolis, MD 21402

© 2025 by Ward Carroll and Tony Peak
All rights reserved. No part of this book may be reproduced or utilized in any form or by any means, electronic or mechanical, including photocopying and recording, or by any information storage and retrieval system, without permission in writing from the publisher.

Library of Congress Cataloging-in-Publication Data

Names: Carroll, Ward author | Peak, Tony author
Title: Punk's force : a novel / Ward Carroll and Tony Peak.
Description: Annapolis : Naval Institute Press, 2025.
Identifiers: LCCN 2025006465 (print) | LCCN 2025006466 (ebook) | ISBN 9781682476611 hardback | ISBN 9781682476635 hardcover | ISBN 9781682476512 ebook
Subjects: LCSH: Gerald R. Ford (Ship : CVN-68)—Fiction | Gerald R. Ford Class (Aircraft carriers)—Fiction | United States—History, Naval—21st century—Fiction | United States. Navy—Fiction | Aircraft carriers—Fiction | LCGFT: Sea fiction
Classification: LCC PS3553.A7656 P84 2025 (print) | LCC PS3553.A7656 (ebook)
LC record available at https://lccn.loc.gov/2025006465
LC ebook record available at https://lccn.loc.gov/2025006466

♾ Print editions meet the requirements of ANSI/NISO z39.48-1992 (Permanence of Paper). Printed in the United States of America.

33 32 31 30 29 28 27 26 25   9 8 7 6 5 4 3 2 1
First printing

*For those in military test and evaluation
who work hard to stay ahead of the threat*

CHAPTER 1

PUNK RACED into the Combat Information Center as the clang of *Ford*'s general quarters bell sounded through the ship. The captain in CIC didn't notice his arrival, nor did any of the other sailors assembled there. All were focused on their computer screens as warning after red warning flashed across them, creating a growing maze of crimson mirrors.

The USS *Gerald R. Ford* (CVN 78), the United States' newest and most technically advanced aircraft carrier, had been hit.

Judging from what Punk could see on the screens, the carrier had suffered massive damage at the waterline. Something had pierced the hull and exploded with such force that Reactor 1 was offline. The sailors in charge of Reactor 2 weren't answering calls for a damage report. The ship's sensors showed it was taking on water. Fast.

Despite the proof he was seeing around him, a part of Punk's mind stubbornly refused to believe it. No enemy had sunk an American aircraft carrier since World War II.

"Have we responded?" Punk asked. "Is the air wing airborne?"

The deck shuddered under their feet. A petty officer tried to direct an orderly evacuation in the passageway. Someone muttered a prayer in the background. Someone else cursed a trio of terrorist groups—the usual suspects.

The CIC watch team stayed put, their faces hardening into despair by the second.

Punk searched the space for somebody who might be able to answer as he rephrased his question, "Why are there no planes in the air?"

"Admiral, we're evacuating now," the captain said.

Punk couldn't think of the man's name, the commanding officer of the ship, a guy he'd dealt with for months. Had it been so long since he'd been in combat that the adrenaline rush had robbed him of his mental faculties?

"Admiral!" the captain shouted, snapping Punk out his reverie. "You need to evacuate, now!"

As crewmembers rushed past in the corridor outside and the watch team's dismal expressions morphed into doomed resignation, Punk shook his head.

"Have we returned fire at all?" Punk asked. "Do we have airplanes in the air?"

"Sir," the captain said, leveraging a degree of patience achieved only through three decades of operational experience. "*Ford*'s lower compartments have been compromised. She's going down, Admiral."

A thousand questions raced through Punk's mind. How had the world's greatest aircraft carrier been caught unaware? Sinking? It couldn't be sinking.

"What the hell hit us?" Punk asked.

"First word is a hypersonic missile, sir," the captain said sympathetically, like a doctor breaking the news of a family member's death. Which wasn't much of a stretch. Because of all the effort Punk had put into getting *Ford* built and to the fleet, the carrier and everyone on it were his family.

The deck shuddered again, harder. Mugs slid off desks and shattered on the floor. A folder stuffed with papers dumped its contents at the captain's feet as the ship listed to starboard a handful of degrees. It did not right itself, the telltale sign of severe internal damage.

"Get me the four-star at fleet headquarters," Punk said. "We need to—"

"You need to go," the captain said. "Make sure to get as many off the boat as you can. We'll stay behind and keep everything in hand."

Punk swallowed as he staggered backward. *Ford* listed another few degrees to starboard. A distant, shivering creak echoed through the carrier, and Punk felt the vibration travel across the floor and up his legs. He still managed to nod.

The captain was going down with the ship; but before he did, he was going to ensure as many people made it off as possible.

"Good luck, Skipper," was all Punk could say. Before the captain had finished his salute, Punk was already out of CIC and rushing down the passageway.

Punk wanted to call his wife, Suzanne, or his son, Jason, but he couldn't think about them now. Seconds meant lives. He grabbed an officer carrying an armload of files, saying, "Leave it! Get to a lifeboat!"

The officer dropped his burden and hurried down the passageway.

Punk made his way forward, looking in every cabin, down every cross-passageway, telling anyone he came across to abandon ship. By the time he reached the bow, *Ford* was listing a full 20 degrees to starboard. It was easier to walk on the walls now than on the deck. He bumped his knee on a door handle, scraped his hand on a first aid kit on the bulkhead. He tried to gain purchase on the wall as medics rushed past him carrying wounded on stretchers. One of the injured sailors screamed. Her arm was badly burned, the skin blistered and cratered in patches of raw red and pits of black. Another medic hauled an unconscious man on her back; one of his legs was missing, the stump tied off in a tourniquet. They smelled of blood, ash, and burnt metal. There was no need to ask what had happened down there; Punk could see the answer in the damp stains that ran up their legs to their waists.

He tried not to think of how many crew had been lost in the flooding. Or worse.

"Admiral, what do we do?" one sailor asked.

"Admiral, did we get any jets off the deck first?" another inquired.

He couldn't give them an answer. He didn't have one. He pressed on through them, shouting vague orders. He'd always thought he would be as ready as anyone for an attack on the boat, but his guts churned as the full weight of his responsibility hit him.

More and more crewmembers passed by in a cavalcade of human chaos, and he ushered dozens to the evac route. He smiled at some, trying to comfort them, as well as himself, with a confidence he did not feel.

A tremor shook the ship.

"Hurry!" Punk yelled as more crew filed past him, near to panicking now as the distant pop and thud of explosions echoed up to them from belowdecks. They clambered past Super Hornets that had overturned, their locking chains snapped; one had flattened two crewmembers. Punk forced himself not to look as he continued herding the people, worried they were on the verge of becoming a mob. Trained or not, when faced with such a situation, the human psyche reached back to its antediluvian roots and sought safety first. The fight-or-flight mechanism. Self-preservation. Survival. Civilization had taught them to think of others first. That was out the window for them. The Navy had taught Punk not even to consider himself, but to do whatever it took to complete his mission. And his mission was to save the *Ford*'s sailors.

His group jostled into another group near an open hangar bay door, and several people toppled overboard into the sea. Frantic cries for help, curses, and shouts for order warred with the incessant klaxon bleats and the comm's monotonous evacuation call. The systems put in place to handle such a situation were a separate reality from what was transpiring before Punk's eyes. And there was nothing he could do about it.

"Get to the boats!" Punk shouted, trying to be heard above the cacophony of the dying vessel.

More people tumbled into the water. Soon, many gave up waiting for a place on the lifeboats and dove to what might be life. Punk fought to keep his footing and lost. There, on the precipice, he felt another quake along the entire vessel.

Ford yawned bow-first beneath the waves.

A great sucking noise erupted from the depths, a leviathan come from the abyss to devour them all.

More screams. More orders. More bells. Punk was knocked into the breakers that lashed the carrier's hull. The waves smacked into his body and carried him down, the briny water making him blink, and he saw many more bodies beneath it, some of them unmoving.

Finally his head broke the surface. He flinched as he watched a great bubble burst from the ocean's surface, a benthic belch announcing the eruption of the last of *Ford*'s air from its spaces. The force of it sent another wave over him, this one filled with pieces of wreckage and bodies.

Punk coughed, strangling on the seawater. He pushed himself up, then grunted as his right cheek hit something flat and cold. He sucked in a deep, ragged breath and rolled over.

He was on the floor of his room at the DV quarters at Fort McNair.

A nightmare. A goddamn nightmare.

Still blinking as if the salt water had been real, he squinted to read the clock on the nightstand: 0208. In just under eight hours, he would be on Capitol Hill telling the House Armed Services Committee why he thought he could keep an aircraft carrier armed with a new defense system from sinking. And in just under four hours his aide would be knocking on the door to shuttle him to a working breakfast in the Chief of Naval Operations' office at the Pentagon.

"Damn it," he muttered.

He didn't bother trying to go back to sleep. He was all too awake.

CHAPTER 2

JUSTIN WOLFE swiped across the notification on his cell phone then set it aside. The message, which he was pleased to read, did not alter the impassive expression he always wore when discussing business with potential clients.

He sat across a small table from a Russian envoy who seemed completely unimpressed by Wolfe's luxurious beachfront property in Thailand's Satun province. Not even the lovely young women Wolfe paid to serve as a distraction during such meetings diverted the man's attention. They passed by the table in string bikinis, giggling and sharing mixed drinks as if they were at a rave party in Ibiza. It was a necessary part of Wolfe's charade, designed to fool clients into thinking he was motivated by simple pleasures.

"The package we have prepared for you should guarantee a breakthrough with your problems in Ukraine," Wolfe said, leaning back to let the sea breeze flow through his unbuttoned silk shirt. "If you use it correctly."

The Russian, who called himself Palach, stared back at Wolfe with all the emotion of a monument in Red Square. He had not touched his glass of rare vodka—a single shot from a bottle that had cost Wolfe north of a million dollars.

Extravagant perhaps, but Wolfe liked to make an impression. He wanted the smug bastard to believe that if he gave Wolfe his business, he too would be able to afford such a luxury. Palach was an old ex-KGB man, stolid and suspicious; perhaps he thought Wolfe was testing him. Beach, sexy women, expensive alcohol. Distractions that weaker men might give in to. Temptations of the decadent West that Russia no longer rejected. Wolfe wanted Palach to make that assumption.

"We know how to use package," Palace said. Wolfe suspected that Russian agents-for-hire like Palach spoke fluent English but reverted to cartoonish type as a way to annoy Westerners. Certainly, he could not be as stupid as he appeared to be.

"Of course you do, my friend," Wolfe assured him. "I have no doubt of that. But the decisions of your leaders have been . . . costly of late."

"Victories do not happen overnight," Palach said. "Your fortune? Not made overnight, either."

"That is true," Wolfe said. "It's all about the numbers, Palach. Numbers never lie. Like the drones and neural network suite you're planning to buy. They operate on numbers. They are perfect instruments. They fail only if their controllers fail."

Palach offered a slight shrug, neither agreeing nor disagreeing.

Two Thai women ran past laughing. One leaned over and shook sand out of her bikini top, smiling coyly at the Russian. Palach paid no attention. Wolfe had heard the man's name meant "hangman" in Russian—an alias he'd earned while fighting ISIS in Syria. "Wolfe" was also a *nom de guerre*; it had replaced his original identity long ago.

He had come to believe in one maxim above all others: those who wished to sell themselves never sold the truth. The evolution of the self began with one's identity, and he had chosen one calculated to impress and intrigue himself as much as others. One had to believe in their own metamorphosis, otherwise it was only a charade.

Wolfe winked at one of the women, and she kissed his cheek and ran her palm down his lean, muscular chest the way she'd been taught to do in such situations. Palach's stare never left his.

"Numbers have never failed me," Wolfe said. "But you're a professional, Palach. A man who requires evidence. You will have your evidence, and soon. Remember the hypersonic project we discussed?"

Palach's bushy eyebrows rose, and for the first time he glanced at the glass of vodka. "You said not ready. You said too risky and too expensive."

Wolfe chuckled. "Oh, it will be expensive. But things have fallen into place. If my numbers are correct—and they are never wrong—then I will have a demonstration for you and your leaders within two months, a demonstration the world will be unable to ignore."

"Americans?" Palach asked, smiling.

"No one else can provide the magnitude of the demonstration that I require," Wolfe said.

Palach scowled but seemed ready to believe him. "Pah. Americans always hide mistakes."

Wolfe tossed back his own shot of the vodka, enjoying the burn that scorched from his gums to his sternum. "They won't be able to hide the sinking of an aircraft carrier. Imagine the shock, the indignation, the changes to security around the world. Imagine what sort of business we will do after that, you and I, with this technology."

Palach finally looked at the young Thai women, then smirked at Wolfe and downed the vodka shot. He grunted with satisfaction. "You are certain of this? You have agents in place? You have an American traitor?"

Wolfe poured him another shot and cut his eyes toward the closest Thai woman. She understood the cue. She strolled over and bumped her thigh into Palach's arm. She apologized profusely while bending over him, letting gravity reveal her attributes. The Russian's smirk deepened. He wrapped an arm around her waist and allowed Wolfe to push the refilled shot glass into his liver-spotted hand. The sale was complete.

"Numbers never lie," Wolfe said.

While his customer trifled with his newly found diversion, Wolfe surreptitiously checked the status of Wolfe Industries stock. His company had been in the top ten of the Nasdaq 100 Index for the past eight months, sometimes even creeping into the top five. The price had fluctuated a bit after the hiccups experienced with the cube sat Internet network he'd deployed, but the introduction of a robust cryptocurrency, the WolfeCoin, had alleviated that.

The proper application of mathematics could achieve nearly any desired result. It wasn't gambling. It was enabling certainty. Like any other human innovation, numbers could be harnessed for a variety of uses.

He glanced back at Palach, who was now stroking the Thai woman's upper thigh. Humans, especially the emotional ones, were fallible, prone to failures. Numbers lacked that weakness.

The world needed to move past such frailty if humanity was to survive. Things like war, climate change, and injustice would destroy the planet if allowed to continue unchecked. He knew this because he watched the outcomes as he contributed to those problems, and in that recognition he saw a way out—and a way to profit from it.

If only she had lived to see it. The temptation to drink away that thought crossed his mind, but Wolfe refrained from pouring himself another shot.

A way out indeed. It meant leveling the playing field. Numbers did not take sides. They were not political or ideological. They never compromised. Integers were like the air in a scuba diver's aqualung: it was either there or it wasn't.

That understanding had led Wolfe to market his technologies to the underdogs of the world, be they Burmese freedom fighters, Hezbollah in Lebanon, or the Boko Haram terrorists in West Africa. Most of those movements were doomed to failure, but Wolfe appreciated the passion behind them. More to the point, he appreciated the opportunities they presented, how they could wound dying systems even further. Systems his numbers could supplant and improve upon.

If a hypersonic missile could sink an American aircraft carrier, the probability that China would deescalate its naval production was high. Their focus would turn to different weapons, different tactics. His algorithms said so. Though tensions would remain between the two powers, fewer military vessels in the China seas meant more trading opportunities. More prospects for him to seize and exploit while China and the United States argued over who had pissed in the pool.

On his tablet Wolfe loaded up a camera feed from one of his CubeSats above the California coast. It revealed a long sliver of gray docked at a naval base. A mere flicker of metal in the Pacific sun, until he zoomed in. Then the sliver resolved into a grand vessel built to pacify nations. But the very idea of what a nation was had changed in the twenty-first century. Globalization, deregulation, decentralization—all were mechanisms that aided the numerical formula he had put into action.

It all had to change if humanity was to continue.

Wolfe had decided that change would start with a U.S. Navy supercarrier, the USS *Gerald R. Ford*.

———

Shane Peterson flipped open the burner phone and punched in the number his contact had sent him via encrypted email. It was late evening in the research office at China

Lake, where he was Senior Director of Test Programs at the Naval Air Weapons Center. Everyone else had left for the night. Had anyone been there they would not have questioned his presence; he usually stayed late working on the program's latest project.

It wasn't too late for Peterson. He could stop pushing buttons and forget the whole thing.

As long as the call didn't go through, Peterson was still in control.

He swallowed and dialed faster.

Each ring on the other end made his throat constrict. What was taking his contact so long? The email had simply said "go time" along with the phone number, a series of digits that might lead to any device in the world. A cipher of betrayal.

The contact answered in a genderless monotone; they were using a voice changer.

"The Navy will conduct the test after all," the voice said. "Program implementation is imminent. You have one week to prepare."

"That's not enough time," Peterson lied.

It was more than enough time. Everything was already in place.

Except his certainty.

He wasn't yet past the point of no return. He could hang up. Make excuses. Delay. The contact would be furious, sure, but he could do it.

The contact hesitated only for an instant, then continued. "It will have to be. Your payment will be delivered upon success."

Peterson hesitated, then blurted out his demand.

"I want to meet him first," he said.

"That is not feasible, or advisable," the voice said.

"I *want* to meet him," Peterson reiterated.

It was a gamble, but he had his suspicions as to who his benefactor was. He found it improbable that a foreign power would employ such tactics. No, his patron had wooed Peterson for weeks with promises of not only money but a paradigm shift as well. Told him that the world was about to change for the better, and power would be in the hands of those who could wield it for everyone's benefit. Only one person fit that profile and could afford the cost.

A year ago, frustrated that the Navy didn't appreciate his talents and give him the support his research required, Peterson had privately expressed interest in working for Justin Wolfe Industries. The people he spoke to kept the answer dangling, hinting at possibilities down the road without giving him a definitive yes or no.

Peterson had applied for the job under an alias on a tech employment website. The benefactor had contacted him via that alias' account. It couldn't be a coincidence.

If Wolfe wanted his help, the least he could do was acknowledge Peterson in person. He knew he was risking everything with such a request. But what did it matter at that point? Peterson was already in. Regardless of the outcome, his life would never be the same again.

"A video chat," the voice said.

That wasn't good enough. Peterson felt insulted. He wanted to throw the phone away, dash it against the wall.

But he didn't.

"Okay," Peterson said. "When?"

"Soon," the voice said.

The call ended.

Other things came to an end in that moment as well: loyalty and career. Promises. Oaths. The very order his contributions had helped maintain. All gone with that phone call.

Oaths. His father had been a Navy man, an F-14 Tomcat pilot who'd served as an instructor at Top Gun when it was still at NAS Miramar. Cancer had taken him several years ago. Would he have understood what Shane was doing? Would he, if he were alive, regard his son as a traitor? Peterson remembered a quote by socialist thinker Eugene V. Debs: *"Be true to yourself, and you cannot be a traitor to any good cause on earth."*

Peterson wasn't a socialist. He didn't adhere to any political philosophy. Politics seemed like the games of fools. That quote had once sounded like the adage of a fanatic. Now he understood exactly what Debs had meant. Peterson's cause was a good one.

From his pocket he pulled out the Top Gun patch that his dad had worn on the shoulder of his flight suit. Peterson had found it while going through his late father's effects and had adopted it as a good-luck charm. Of course, he knew there was no such thing as luck. Mathematics told him that. But the patch gave him confidence, made him feel that he belonged.

Peterson gripped the flip phone like he was strangling the contact from afar, then snapped it in two with a grunt of frustration.

A week. The contact expected him to be ready to destroy his life's work in a week.

Peterson took a deep breath and muted his anxiety by considering the compensation he was about to earn. His loyalty and work were in the past now, mistakenly taken for granted by those who had benefitted from them. It was time to consider the future that Wolfe's reward would underwrite.

Peterson placed the broken phone halves into a Ziploc bag, logged off his computer, and left the office. Once outside, he tossed the bag into the first dumpster he passed, one he knew would be emptied later that day.

Shane Peterson had just agreed to sink a U.S. Navy aircraft carrier.

CHAPTER 3

PUNK REICHERT had never enjoyed testifying on Capitol Hill, not that anybody had ever asked him how he felt about it. It was part of his job—one of the worst parts. So, there he was, trying to look relaxed sitting in the front row, although the back of his chair was torturing his spine. He wondered if the lawmakers had designed it for that purpose as part of their fun-filled package for those who sat before them. The microphone was tilted at his face, a snake ready to strike in the event of a wrong answer. He reached for some water to clear his throat, but the plastic bottle was empty. Immediately his aide, Lieutenant Commander Garland "Surf" Davis, reached a long arm across his shoulder and replaced it with a full one.

The lack of a restful night's sleep didn't weigh on him as much as the stakes of his situation. He'd testified on the Hill before, but this time it felt like the future of the Navy, or at least naval aviation, now rested on his shoulders.

A scrum of news media camera people sat on their haunches snapping away before the committee notetaker's stand, a small wooden desk on wheels that shielded a secretary impassively staring at the screen of her desktop. The television cameras flanking the large caucus room reminded Punk that his remarks would be carried live across the airwaves, albeit on a channel that was watched only by the small percentage of the public who actually cared about the inner workings of the Legislative Branch.

"Tell me again why the American taxpayers need to pay 13 billion dollars for another *Ford*-class aircraft carrier," Congressman Seth Gordon demanded from the elevated wooden bench where the key members of the House Armed Services Committee sat like gods looking down from Olympus. On one lapel he wore the conspicuous button of a sitting member of Congress, on the opposite one an oversized American flag pin.

Punk ignored the cameras and the stares of the other committee members as he answered the question with the calm, professional delivery he'd mastered as a flag officer. "Carrier strike groups give the United States a forward presence that can meet any threat, anywhere in the world, at any time."

Gordon flippantly waved a hand and leaned across the table, his silver hair reflecting the room's bright lights. "Let's talk facts, Admiral. Code 8062 allows for eleven aircraft carriers. *Eleven*. There are only seven oceans on the whole dang planet, so why do we need eleven aircraft carriers?"

Punk was put off by the willful ignorance of the question, but he didn't stop to address it directly. "When you look at our need to respond to any and all threats against our interests and those of our allies, eleven aircraft carriers are actually too few," he said.

"And by allies you mean NATO," Gordon said. "Another thing that has outlived its usefulness."

"Not just NATO, Congressman, but our allies in the western Pacific as well. We need carriers more than ever now. Factor in the situation in Ukraine, Houthi rebels in Yemen, protests in Iran, China's threatening moves toward Taiwan—"

"I'm aware of the threats, Admiral," Gordon cut him off, "but I do not see the need for more carriers to deal with them, particularly when they come with such a hefty price tag and—as you yourself just admitted—are hard to maintain. And there is also the matter of new technological threats such as hypersonic weapons. What about that?"

Punk picked up the water bottle and screwed off the top as he measured his response. Congressman Gordon knew full well that the Navy was always working on defenses against whatever an enemy might utilize against them, and he was ready to weaponize that knowledge to make the news that evening. It was nothing but performance art; and he wasn't even good at it.

Punk continued, "I believe you've been briefed on the fact that we have several systems in development that—"

"Yes, but what are they?" Gordon asked, leaning back in his high-backed chair and pointing across the table at Punk. His voice echoed a bit as he moved away from his mic. "The Chinese are developing hypersonic missiles that can sink an aircraft carrier. The Russians used hypersonics in Ukraine. These weapons make an aircraft carrier little more than an expensive target."

"Again, sir, we're developing systems to counter those threats as they become known to us," Punk replied.

Gordon tapped his pen on the bench. "A typical carrier requires over four thousand crew, sometimes as many as five thousand. Should the People's Liberation Army Navy successfully launch a hypersonic missile at a carrier, five thousand of our servicemen and women would not come home."

Gordon moved his face back into the mic and let his words distort just slightly for dramatic effect: "There are cheaper and more effective ways of meeting Chinese threats. We have drones, long-range bombers, and the most accurate cruise missiles in the world." He leaned back again and pointed at Punk. "And you want the American taxpayers to pay 13 billion dollars so the Navy's fighter jocks can drill supersonic holes in the sky?"

The rhetoric was insulting, but such was the state of political jockeying on Capitol Hill. Punk had never wanted to come near this alien world, but once he pinned on his third star, it suddenly was part of the job.

"Aircraft carriers have a long track record of deterring crises when called upon. To quote President Ronald Reagan's Secretary of Defense, Caspar Weinberger, during any given crisis that administration dealt with, 'Where are the aircraft carriers?' For a hundred years that has been the first question asked when our nation is faced with a threat."

Punk worked to keep his tone measured and civil. The Navy's legislative affairs reps who had joined them at breakfast in the CNO's office in the Pentagon had cautioned him that Gordon liked to fire for effect and go ad hominem without warning. They also briefed Punk that several members of the Armed Services Committee had ties to the U.S. Air Force, including Gordon, whose home state of Montana hosted a heavy bomber base and some ballistic missile silos. The defense budget was by and large a zero-sum game, and Gordon needed to make the carrier program look bad in the hopes of funneling that money to projects he had promised his district and the business interests there that kept him in office.

One face on the other side of the bench offered Punk a more welcoming countenance: Representative Evelyn Greenwood, or as he had known her in the VF-104 Arrowslingers, Muddy. He'd helped train her to fly the F-14 at Naval Air Station Oceana in Virginia Beach, right before 9/11 changed the world, and then flew sorties with her as her flight lead over Afghanistan. They weren't in a cockpit now, but it steadied him to see her among the other lawmakers looking down at him.

"Didn't Weinberger resign because he sold weapons to the Contras in Iran?" Gordon quipped with a self-satisfied grin.

Punk could feel the cameras zooming in on him as he replied, "For the record, Mr. Gordon, the Contras were in Nicaragua, not Iran, and Secretary Weinberger was pardoned by the first President Bush. But the question he asked then is still one the Departments of Defense and State should ask now. Our carriers give the United States a capability unmatched by any other military in the world. Losing that superiority simply because foreign powers are developing new weapons—weapons we *will* be able to counter—would hurt our national security."

Gordon fidgeted with his pen but kept his eyes on Punk. "What happens when China has hypersonic capabilities that can sink our aircraft carriers?"

"The gentleman's time has expired," the committee chairman said. "The floor now belongs to the gentlewoman from Virginia."

"My colleague ignores the fact that carriers have been capable of protecting themselves from cruise missiles for years," Muddy said quickly. "Something he knows very well."

"Yes, but not hypersonic missiles, Congresswoman," Gordon retorted.

"This is my time now, sir," she shot back.

Gordon ignored her. "We all know of your record of service with the Navy, Ms. Greenwood. But that period of service never faced threats like these. You were bombing trucks and caves in the Middle East, not trying to intercept hypersonic missiles."

"Mr. Chairman, I believe I have the floor."

"The tactical landscape has changed," Gordon continued speaking over her objection, louder now. "I suggest that the United States adapt to that change rather than maintain an expensive fleet of massive ships that have outlived their purpose."

"Mr. Chairman!"

"The gentleman from Montana will yield," the committee chairman intoned.

Muddy shook her head in irritation and faced Punk again. "In this unclassified setting, what can you tell us about what the Navy has been doing to protect our aircraft carriers against the latest PLAN threats?"

"We have what we call 'directed-energy weapons' in development," Punk said. "We've done a few things along those lines in the past, but we were always limited by our ability to generate enough power. With the new reactors on *Ford*, we finally have that power."

"But you just said that this system is still in development," Gordon said, again intruding on Greenwood's time.

"It is," Punk replied. "But it's very close to being ready for fleet use."

"I think you're bluffing, Admiral. Directed-energy weapons are a Navy pipe dream designed to pad your portion of the defense budget."

"They're still being refined, but I assure you, Congressman, they're very real and very effective."

Gordon said nothing, apparently mulling something over in his head. The other shoe was about to drop. "Then let's do a test," Gordon said, as if the idea had just occurred to him. "And not one of those rigged operational evaluations you guys do. A real test."

The legislative affairs people at breakfast had mentioned a rumor that Gordon might propose such a test, but Punk was surprised all the same to hear him come right out and put it on the table in a public forum.

The other committee members, including Muddy Greenwood, who seemed resigned to her time with the floor getting hijacked, joined Gordon in zeroing in on Punk.

Punk waited a few beats before responding, "This sort of test isn't something I can unilaterally approve at my level. But my first response, sir, is that we could make it happen. *Ford* is currently pierside in San Diego and will be there for the next few months."

He fought to keep his poker face in place. What had he just agreed to, and how did it get teed up so fast? Even as he spoke, he worried he was signing up for a failure that could end his career. More than that, it could saddle him with a legacy as the guy who killed carrier aviation.

"And with that, I guess I return the balance of my time, Mr. Chairman," Muddy said with a shrug.

"Hearing adjourned," the chairman announced with a single rap of his gavel. "God bless our troops, and God bless the United States of America."

The hallway outside the chamber was jammed with reporters seeking statements from the departing committee members. A pedestrian hearing had suddenly become breaking news. A high-stakes challenge had been issued and accepted. Where would the test happen? Who was going to be involved? What weapon would be used to try and sink the aircraft carrier? What security measures would be in place to make sure the Chinese didn't watch? The questions flew at the lawmakers. All replied with generally the same answer: It was too early to know, but they'd keep the media informed.

The press surrounded Punk as well, lobbing the same questions at him. He answered in a similarly vague fashion: it was too early for specifics, but he was eager to demonstrate *Ford*'s capabilities and confident the test, whatever it would be, would reinforce the utility of aircraft carriers.

He easily spotted Surf Davis coming toward him, a head taller than those he slipped past, at once forceful and polite. His sun-bleached blond hair was a beacon to Punk, signaling refuge from the storm.

"Well, that was interesting," Surf said as he steered his boss away from the throng.

"Many-versus-one dogfights always are," Punk replied, using an air combat reference with his fellow fighter pilot, albeit one fifteen years younger who had only seen an F-14 Tomcat in the movies. "What's next on the schedule?"

Surf was swiping across his phone searching for the app that would provide the answer when it suddenly began to ring. Punk saw that the call was from his aide's wife.

"Go ahead and get that," Punk said. "You need to keep the home front happy."

Surf nodded and retreated to the nearest alcove to answer the call. Punk watched the aide's expression darken. The conversation was obviously more than just the routine "How's your day going, honey?" catch-up.

Punk hadn't known Surf long, but he came to the job with a solid endorsement from the skipper of his Super Hornet squadron, and the staff's due diligence hadn't flagged anything of concern. He had the chill demeanor of a guy who'd grown up riding the waves off La Jolla, which is where his "Surf" call sign came from. But he was also consistently ahead of any situation. Calm and competent. Exactly what Punk needed in an aide.

Being an aide to a three-star was far different than being a carrier pilot. There was a unique 24/7 quality to it. Days were long and free weekends were rare. The aide's job could be summed up as making sure the admiral was in the right place at the right time wearing the right uniform and saying the right things. So far Surf hadn't failed at any of those things, but the stakes were about to be raised.

Punk considered what it was going to take to set up the test that had just been laid at his feet. While he welcomed a chance to prove the worth of a carrier to a political hack like Gordon, the test was an unwelcome complication. With the tactical situation always changing in the Pacific, the Persian Gulf, and the Black Sea, the Navy had more immediate priorities.

"A wise fighter pilot once told me it's better to die than to look bad," a voice said behind him.

Punk shook his head and smiled as he turned around and faced Evelyn Greenwood. "You're saying I looked bad, Representative Greenwood?" Punk retorted as they shared a brief embrace.

"Call me Muddy," she said. "Anything else sounds weird coming from you."

"And call me Punk for the same reason."

Next to Muddy, a short female who looked barely out of her teens was staring intently at her phone through black bangs. "She's checking social media for reactions to the hearing," Muddy explained. "My office is nearby. Do you have a second?"

"Of course," Punk said as he looked across her shoulder and caught Surf's eye, gesturing that they were on the move. The aide nodded and waved in return.

Muddy cut an impressive figure as her heels clacked along the marble floor, echoing across the House Office Building's walls and high ceilings. Her hair was longer than it had been the last time Punk saw her and was carefully styled. Her well-made dark blue pantsuit flattered her long legs far more than a flight suit did and reminded him that she'd played basketball at the Naval Academy and had kicked the male aviators' butts during a pickup basketball game in Key West.

As she pushed open the heavy wooden door that led to her office, the receptionist, a lanky guy who looked even younger than the staffer at Muddy's elbow, stood and handed her several yellow sticky notes. She took them without comment and stepped into her office, gesturing for Punk to have a seat on a long leather couch opposite her big wooden desk.

Punk noted a tasteful amount of Navy memorabilia—a "Beat Army" flag, a squadron plaque, and a model of an F-14 adorned in Arrowslinger markings on the coffee table. "You've come a long way, Muddy," he said.

"We've both come a long way," she replied. "Look at you, Commander of Naval Air Forces."

"Stick around the clubhouse long enough..."

Surf appeared in the doorway, and Punk looked over to ask, "How much time do we have?"

"Car's outside waiting to take us to the airport," Surf said.

"Copy that. Give me ten minutes." The aide nodded and backed out of sight, closing the office door as he did.

Muddy pulled a chair to the opposite side of the coffee table and sat down. "Gordon's not an honest broker here," she said. "He's turning this funding inquest into political theater, and make no mistake, he wants funding from the carrier program to be shifted to his pet bomber project."

"So, he might not play fair?"

"Without getting into the dirty details of life on the Hill, let me just say that every accusation he makes is an admission of guilt."

"Seems like there's a lot of that in D.C. these days," Punk said carefully.

"I haven't told you the best part," Muddy said with an air quotes gesture. "The United States Air Force will be acting as the enemy for this test."

"You already know that?" Punk asked. "Then this hearing was a formality."

She nodded. "It was a setup, yes. I'm still junior on this committee, but I can be your eyes and ears inside the Beltway."

"Good. Looks like I'm going to need all the intel I can get."

"*Ford* will be pushed to its limits, and the Air Force will do everything it can to take the carrier, and you, down. So, I'll ask the obvious question—no shit, Muddy to Punk: Can you make this test work?"

"It was sort of kneejerk in the face of this ambush, but I wouldn't have agreed if I didn't think so," he said. "That having been said, we train to deal with threats abroad. Congressman Gordon and the United States Air Force? I think I'd rather deal with the Chinese fleet."

"And don't be surprised if Gordon tries to dig up dirt on you. Your record is about to be examined under a microscope. Even your combat time won't keep Gordon's oppo machine from trying to devour you."

"Whatever," Punk said. "My first concern is getting a plan together to make this work."

"Way ahead of you," Muddy said, holding her phone aloft. "I have someone we can trust. Someone at Peabody Tilden Shipbuilding. You know, the company that built *Ford*?"

Punk's eyebrows rose. "That's where Spud works."

Muddy widened her eyes innocently. "Really? I had *no idea*." She pushed her phone closer so Punk could read the contact displayed there:

Spud O'Leary
VP of Business Development
Peabody Tilden Shipbuilding
oleary@PTSIndustries.com
757-555-1982

Spud had become a captain of industry since being passed over for promotion to rear admiral a few decades before. In a uniquely Spudian way, he'd shown his peer group who'd pinned on their first stars that sometimes losing was winning and there was more to life than making the next rank. Now he was earning high six digits plus a big bonus every year working out of an office with a view of the James River.

"You're a genius, Muddy," Punk said. "Nothing like having my old RIO behind me once again."

"It's a start, but you and Spud will have to find some actual geniuses to make this test work. I'll do what I can on the committee, but Punk, let me just add that Gordon's not the only one up for reelection soon. I can't help you going forward if I'm working at some think tank instead of Congress."

"This is going to work," he said firmly. "It has to."

CHAPTER 4

WOLFE ANSWERED the call on his tablet. "Everything is set?"

"The Armed Services Committee has commissioned a test," the face on the screen said, an avatar of a white male with a buzz cut. Wolfe and his personal agents rarely revealed their faces to each other. Most of the time they used Wolfe Industries' in-house AI face generator. Complete with a randomized voice component, it guaranteed video and audio anonymity.

"I told you they would," Wolfe said, smiling as he donned a polo and buttoned it. "How are we on the cyberwarfare front?"

"The Navy has resisted our probes into their NOSS network this past month," the avatar said. "But that itself gave us plenty of data to work with. Aswan should be ready for a new incursion within forty-eight hours."

Wolfe nodded and slid a Chopard watch onto his left wrist. The hundred-thousand-dollar timepiece was a gift from a clandestine lover in the UAE, the woman who was his contact with Houthi rebels in Yemen. They'd made excellent customers of late.

She'd set one of the watch's faces to her time zone, as if he cared. He didn't wear it to tell time; he wore it as a signal that he controlled other people's time.

"Make it twenty-four," Wolfe said, combing a blond lock to the left. The color was fading, and he considered dying his hair again. In the days of the ancient Romans, blond hair had been regarded as the mane of barbarians, and thus implied lust and a lack of self-control. Decadence. The key was to make others believe they could exploit that decadence when it actually didn't exist.

"Aswan can handle it," Wolfe said. "Above all. Who will our algorithm make it look like the culprit is this time? China? North Korea?"

"I thought you didn't want specifics," the face said.

Wolfe chuckled and slid into his loafers. "Surprise me, then. As long as it isn't tracked back to us. Maybe we should use both, to keep the Navy guessing."

"Very good," the avatar said, then hesitated with clearly more to say.

Wolfe stopped his movement toward the condo's door. "Yes?"

"The asset wants to speak to you."

The asset, meaning Shane Peterson, their person on the inside.

"You told him no, of course?" Wolfe asked. He wasn't angry, just curious.

"Of course, but he persisted," the avatar said.

"Persisted?" Wolfe asked. "You agreed to it, didn't you?"

"The asset implies he knows who you are."

Wolfe grimaced. Peterson had been chosen from among eighteen candidates currently employed by the U.S. Navy. Each of them worked either directly or peripherally in a department connected to hypersonic defense systems. They had been selected by his algorithms based on strict criteria: knowledge of hypersonic counter-technology, visibility among their compatriots, and the likelihood of betraying their country. The last item took into account everything from that person's economic woes to propensity for emotional depression, a small social circle, and a victim complex.

Even then, it had taken Wolfe weeks—via the underground social media platforms where such people often congregated—to cultivate the necessary willingness in Peterson to turn traitor. Befriend him, share grievances, suggest subtle alterations in how he saw himself in his job. Tell him he deserved more. Appealing to such things was as easy as feeding a starving man tainted meat.

"Not surprising," Wolfe said. "He's a smart little bastard. Probably worked it out through our contacts on those message boards. He knows how to use numbers, too.

We selected a fine one. Too bad the Navy didn't do a better job of maintaining his loyalty. Stupid of them not to recognize such a high-quality tool. But this means we'll need to monitor him even more closely. You have the kompromat prepared, kiddie porn and such? We need to be prepared in the event he gets too cocky."

"Of course," the avatar said. "But if you don't want to talk to him, just say so."

Wolfe sighed. "No, we need Peterson. Very well. I will speak to him."

"Shouldn't you use an intermediary instead?" they asked. "Peterson won't know it's you either way, with the generated avatar."

It was a valid concern. Wolfe usually didn't interact with field assets. Fools like Palach had to be convinced and placated the old-fashioned way, but onsite actors were usually expendable and required a more distant method of handling.

Wolfe considered it for a moment, then shook his head. He could have been Peterson a few years ago if the numbers hadn't gone in Wolfe's favor.

"No. I'll speak to him personally," Wolfe said.

"That could compromise everything," the avatar warned.

"Our Judas wants to know who he sold his soul to," Wolfe said. "There's no harm in letting him see his messiah."

CHAPTER 5

AFTER THEY SAID goodbye to Muddy in her outer office, Punk and Surf made their way along the wide corridor and down the circular stairway to the main exit from the Congressional Office Building, where a Navy sedan was waiting to take them to Reagan National Airport.

"Everything okay?" Punk asked, still concerned about Surf's evident anger when speaking to his wife.

"Oh, that was just my wife, sir," Surf said, as if that explained everything. When Punk didn't respond, his aide continued. "She was asking about getting a place closer to North Island. You know how things are with vacancies right now. I'd like to have her there, but I don't want to pull any strings for her and call attention to myself. That would look like favoritism, and like Muddy said, these politicians will be looking for any excuse to make us look bad."

"I'm sure I can help you with that," Punk said. "There's bound to be an apartment the Navy could billet her in so she might see you occasionally while this process plays out."

Surf's neck flushed red, but his tight-lipped smile remained. "Thank you, Admiral. I'm sure she'll appreciate that. Sometimes it's difficult getting her to understand life as a Navy wife."

Punk slowly nodded. "Gwen, right?"

"Yessir."

"You should bring her by sometime to visit Suzanne," Punk said. "We could play a round of golf while they talk about us."

He just realized that he'd never invited his aide to play golf before and regretted not doing it sooner. He wasn't even sure if Surf was a golfer. Surf's neck flushed even redder, though the smile stayed put.

"I'm sure she would appreciate that, sir," Surf said. "I'll relay the message."

Punk nodded again, not sure what else to say. The man didn't like talking about his wife, obviously. They got in the car, Punk in the backseat and Surf riding shotgun, and the driver, a civil servant from the Pentagon motor pool, started the short trip across the Potomac to the airport.

Punk's phone buzzed. He looked down to see that it was Spud. "I never guessed you wanted a career in show business," Spud said as soon as Punk answered.

"You watched, huh?"

"You presented yourself well. I almost believed you were an admiral."

"Thanks," Punk said dryly. "I was just in Muddy's office catching up, and your name came up."

"She's doing the lord's work up there, no doubt. I deal with her on a regular basis since Peabody Tilden is her district's largest employer by far. Funny how life goes, isn't it?"

"They want to sink your baby, Spud."

"*Ford* is the best goddamn carrier on the planet," Spud said. "They should be ashamed of themselves."

"I need an advisor from the industry side, like immediately."

"What's the gig pay?" Spud asked seriously.

"I don't have any additional budget for it," Punk said, voice slightly catching in his throat with the growing realization of the weight of the undertaking. "At this point I'm not even sure how we're going to fund this test at all."

"Bro, I'm kidding," Spud said with a chuckle. "I'm your man, and you don't have to pay me a thing."

"You can leave your job, just like that?" Punk asked.

"This *is* my job. This test matters to the Navy, sure, but it *really* matters to Peabody Tilden. COVID set us back quite a bit. Failing this test could send a lot of workers to the unemployment line, if not put us out of business altogether. And there's no way we're letting those Air Force bus drivers get the best of us."

"We're on our way to the airport now. How soon can you fly out?"

"Booked on the red eye direct to San Diego," Spud said before singing out of key, "California dreaming, on such a winter's *day-ay-ay-ay-ay*!"

"I will pay you to stop that. Plus, it's summer."

"Whatever. See you tomorrow."

The call ended, but Spud's bad rendition of the Mamas and the Papas classic left him with an irritating earworm that he cleared only with the realization that he needed to make another phone call as part of his new and unforeseen team-building effort. As the car inched southbound across the 14th Street Bridge, airport in sight yet still twenty minutes away at least, he dialed another former squadron mate, one still on active duty.

"I figured you'd be calling," the voice said. "Your hearing has everyone here at the systems command talking. It looks like you've signed us up for quite a challenge."

"Hello to you too, Einstein," Punk said.

Punk had known Vice Admiral Paul "Einstein" Francis since he'd earned his call sign as a radar intercept officer by stating the obvious over the F-14's intercom during an ill-fated alert launch in the Persian Gulf with the commanding officer, "Soup" Campbell, in his front seat. Soup had fired a heat-seeking missile at a fleeing Iranian F-4 that was well out of range. Einstein said helpfully, "I think he's too far away for a Sidewinder, Skipper." To which Soup replied for all to hear, "No shit, *Einstein*!"

Einstein had survived Soup's tenure and thrived thereafter and was now the head of the Naval Air Systems Command at NAS Patuxent River in southern Maryland. NAVAIR housed all the program offices for the various types of aircraft and their associated weapons and mission-planning systems and managed the test programs that proved out capabilities before they were handed over to the fleet.

"I'm circling up with the *Ford*-class desk and shipboard defense systems guys, including the directed-energy weapons team, here in an hour," Einstein explained. "I'll tell you up front, none of them love this idea."

"Then they're in the right frame of mind," Punk said.

"Do *you* love this idea?"

"Oh, *yeah*, I love this idea," Punk replied sarcastically. "We don't have a choice here, Einstein. And this is where you and the rest of your eggheads break out your slide rules and make it work." Punk let out a long exhale and added, "Sorry for snapping. I think my state of shock is wearing off, and reality is just now hitting me."

"I was supposed to take a Super Hornet to Lemoore tomorrow just to get some flight time, but I'll land at North Island instead," Einstein said. "The lieutenant on the test team that I'm flying with is from San Diego, so he'll be happy about the switch. We can circle up aboard *Ford* and start to hammer this out."

"That's a great idea," Punk said. "Spud's coming out here too."

"Putting the band back together, huh? Should be fun."

"And nobody does fun like the Arrowslingers, right?"

"Right, buddy."

"Okay, ping me when you get on deck. Fly safe."

"Aye, sir. Einstein out."

A couple of hours later, Punk looked down on the Blue Ridge Mountains from his window seat on the 737 bound for San Diego, thinking fondly of the days he had viewed them from the cockpit of a Tomcat. Things had seemed simpler then. One mission at a time, simple trains of thought, finite focus. Staying ahead of the airplane was a fighter pilot's definition of Zen. Now, as he thought about the challenge ahead, that state of mind seemed out of reach.

CHAPTER **6**

FORD'S COMMANDING OFFICER, Captain Joseph "Gridiron" Williams, met Punk and Surf on the quarterdeck. The CO was wearing a flight suit, which had become the standard working uniform for the aviators assigned to ship's company in the decades since the turn of the century. Although he knew Gridiron well, Punk was always surprised at how big he was in person. As his call sign suggested, Gridiron had played for the Naval Academy for the duration of his time as a midshipman, including his plebe year, which was rare. With him running the offense, the team had beat Army and gone to a bowl every year. As he approached graduation, there had been hints of NFL teams wanting to draft him, but he'd been steadfast in his desire to fly Navy jets. Punk had respected that at the time, and everything he'd seen in the man since that time had reinforced that respect. "Welcome aboard, sir," Gridiron said as he saluted Punk.

"Better here than D.C.," Punk replied, returning the salute. "Should I have worn a flight suit instead of these khakis?"

"Flight suits are how we roll these days, Admiral," the CO returned unapologetically before pivoting to the business at hand. "Everyone's assembled in the flag spaces."

Without any further pleasantries, the captain started the complicated journey along the hangar bay, through hatches, down passageways, and up ladders to the 0-3 level. Walking around *Ford* was at once second nature and foreign to Punk. In terms of sounds and smells, the carrier's atmosphere was like any of the *Nimitz*-class carriers he'd deployed on during his career, but the layout was unique enough that he could get lost without a guide to get him where he was going.

They made their way across the blue tile that marked the flag spaces on the 0-3 level and through the door to the admiral's cabin, used at sea by the strike group commander but currently unoccupied since *Ford* was between deployments. They were met by Einstein, also wearing khakis, who raised a coffee mug in greeting and said, "Welcome, sir."

"Everyone here?" Punk asked as they shook hands.

"Waiting in the Flag SCIF."

They moved into the adjacent sensitive compartmented information facility—one of the handful of spaces on the carrier used for top secret briefings—where a dozen officers and Spud, the lone civilian, sat around a table. They all rose as Punk entered, and he gestured for them to sit back down before moving around the table to greet Spud.

"Nice suit," Punk said as they embraced in a congenial hug. "I'm glad you made it."

"You know the routine," Spud replied. "You get into trouble. I get you out of trouble. It's why you got Tomcats out of flight school. They knew you'd need another guy in the airplane to keep you from killing yourself."

Einstein looked to one of officers across the table and asked, "Are we secure?"

"Yes, sir," the petite female lieutenant, presumably an intelligence officer, replied. "Music's on," she said, indicating that the sound system used to foil listening devices was operating. "SCIF is secure."

"Floor's yours, Vice Admiral Reichert," Einstein said.

Punk stood at the head of the table at the near end of the room and elected to set the tone by skipping the part where everybody introduced themselves. Instead, he got right to business.

"I'm not sure how many of you were watching C-SPAN around noon Eastern yesterday," he said. "But if you missed it, let me bring you up to speed. Bottom line is we're designing a test that will demonstrate that this ship can survive an attack from a hypersonic missile. Make no mistake, the consequences of failing this test would be extreme." He paused for dramatic effect, scanning the faces around the table. "So we're not going to fail."

Punk sat, which was Einstein's cue to stand up at the other end of the table and take over the brief. He grabbed the remote control in front of him and aimed it at the wall to his left. A screen lit up and showed a slide labeled "Test Plan Passkey."

"We're calling this 'Passkey' because that was President Ford's Secret Service code name," Einstein explained. "And like the Secret Service protected the president, in this test it's our job to protect the USS *Gerald R. Ford*."

"Against a hypersonic?" Rear Admiral Melvin Connelly said from his chair at the long end of the table to Punk's right. "Why? The Chinese would never chance it."

Connelly was PEO Carriers, the guy in charge of the Navy side of designing and building aircraft carriers and supporting them once they were added to the fleet's inventory. He was a surface warfare officer—a ship driver—not an aviator, which made him a minority in the SCIF. About a decade into his career, he'd earned a master's degree at MIT on the Navy's dime and pivoted from being an operational officer who deployed to hot spots to an engineering duty officer who mostly hung out at the Navy Yard in D.C. focused on acquisition and sustainment of ships and associated systems. Because he'd been involved since *Ford*'s design was first accepted, he knew as much about the carrier, including the vessel's defensive vulnerabilities, as anyone present.

"Why not?" Punk asked, irritated that Connelly had interrupted Einstein before he'd barely had a chance to start the brief, but curious about the point he was trying to make.

"China is likelier to use a hypersonic on Taiwanese ground forces than on a naval vessel," Connelly said, raising a finger for emphasis. "The only weapon they will use against our fleets will be the ones dictating international law; they won't want an actual showdown with the United States. Plus, the rest of the world would denounce any aggression on China's part." He raised a second finger as he continued. "We're not the only nation with a naval presence in that region. We're talking about the UK, Australia, New Zealand, Singapore, Malaysia, and even Thailand and Italy. But even with that level of support, short of a nuclear strike, it's doubtful we'd aid Taiwan directly. I'm not saying we shouldn't be prepared, but—"

"So, you think the Chinese will invade Taiwan but appeal to the United Nations, claiming it's an internal affair?" Spud asked.

"No one lifted a finger to help when Putin moved into the Crimea back in 2014," Connelly said. "The Chinese navy has performed joint exercises with the Russian navy in the Sea of Japan. And now the Russians have missiles in place on the Kuril Islands north of Japan itself."

The following silence was broken only by an announcement over the 1MC, the ship's intercom system, that a damage control drill on the flight deck was over.

"How can you be so sure?" Spud asked before taking another swig of coffee from one of the ship's mugs that had been placed in front of all those at the meeting. "Crimea was a misstep, sure, but Taiwan is different altogether. The Chinese won't half-ass it like Putin did. They'll play for keeps, using the good stuff. Like hypersonics. And once the PLA invades, the world economy will change drastically."

"Speed is important," Connelly said, "but I'm more concerned with electromagnetic pulses or drones run by these new AI algorithms. Maybe even both of those things at once. Besides, do we really think the PLA is ready to move on Taiwan? I'm more worried about further Russian misadventures in the Baltics, or Yemen's stability going down the drain."

"The Chinese are launching five new ships every month, so yes," Spud said.

"Five pieces of junk a month," Connelly retorted.

"Quantity has a quality all its own."

"Is your CEO willing to sign up for that?"

Punk noted the wheels of a comeback spinning in Spud's head, and he knew the exchange between the two wasn't headed anywhere that would help the group develop a test plan that they were already behind in creating even though they'd only known about it for twenty-four hours.

He interrupted the exchange: "Very respectfully, Rear Admiral Connelly, the Chinese have been tweaking hypersonics for years, and *we're* the reason. Our intel shows they have a wind tunnel that has tested their prototypes with speeds up to Mach 12. They're not going to that effort just for grins. We *have* to take it seriously."

"Not to mention how the Russians have utilized those things in Ukraine," Einstein added. "Their Kinzhal missiles speed along at a smooth Mach 10 with an effective range of twelve hundred miles. And if the Chinese double that range? *Ford* would be a prime target."

"The demand signal for Passkey isn't the PLAN," Punk pointed out, "it's Congressman Gordon. That's the reality we're executing against here."

"Let's start with the givens," Einstein said. "A missile is coming at *Ford* at Mach 5 or so, low altitude. It's been deployed by either a missile boat, a truck, or a fifth-gen fighter. Then, once it's launched, it can alter its trajectory to evade radar detection, and by the time we know about it, it might be too late."

"Okay, so how is the Air Force going to simulate that?" Spud asked.

"A test asset of some sort. We don't exactly know at this point," Punk said.

"Then what are we doing here?" Connelly asked.

"We're here, Admiral, to plan our side of it," Punk said, his tone evincing his growing displeasure that Connelly was assuming the role of group contrarian.

"We know that some of the prime contractors that service the Air Force have been working on hypersonics programs," Einstein said. "They have two versions in the works: air or surface launched. Air launched would most likely come off an F-35 for a test like this, and the ground launched could be fired from almost anywhere, but they'd probably want to do it out of Vandenberg or maybe Edwards. They might also want to do the test off Hawaii."

"Hawaii?" Gridiron asked. "That'll take considerably more effort from this ship and the crew than doing something off the coast of California."

"I'm just throwing out the possibilities," Einstein said.

"We'll try to steer them away from anyplace that requires a lengthy transit, including points north," Punk said to Gridiron before refocusing on Einstein. "Admiral Francis, can you remind me where we are with our anti-hypersonics program?"

"You're asking me?" Einstein returned with a hint of sarcasm in his voice. "I heard you tell Congressman Gordon that *Ford* already had directed-energy weapons that could take down a hypersonic missile."

"That's not exactly what I said, but if that's what the congressman heard, then it's now your job to make sure you don't make a liar out of me."

Einstein tossed his hands up and nodded as if he'd accepted the job. He looked toward the screen and flipped to the next slide. "Here's what we know. A coalition of defense firms has been designing an anti-hypersonics program, but they have been very quiet about it, even with the Secretary of Defense's office. Meanwhile, DARPA has been funding directed-energy weapons, but we have little intel about where they are with them."

"Do we have any clue about what technology they're trying to make work?" Punk asked.

"Their solutions revolve around an anti-hypersonic missile, much like the SeaRAM but faster," Einstein said. "One that could be launched from a carrier or any support ship that is serving as escort. There might even be a fighter-deployed or drone-delivered version; but again, this is all in the works."

"I like the directed-energy defense better than an antimissile missile," Spud said.

"Both would be nice," Gridiron added. "I need more than one play in my playbook."

"We need something now, not tomorrow," Punk said. "What happened to that laser weapon they mounted on the USS *Ponce* a few years ago? Didn't they actually deploy to the Persian Gulf with that?"

"They did," Einstein replied.

"And?"

"And nothing. It's still in development. The issue at the time was the amount of power required to give it an effective range. *Ponce* didn't have it. As you told the good congressman during your testimony yesterday, *Ford* does."

"Yes, it does," Punk said, tapping an index finger on the table for emphasis. "And it's taking too long to get a directed-energy weapon on board this ship. I know my surface warfare counterpart headquartered across Coronado Bay feels the same way."

"Sometimes it takes an external demand signal to goose a program," Spud said. "Sometimes it's the threat of attack; sometimes it's the threat of getting canceled."

"Very funny, Captain O'Leary," Punk said to his former F-14 RIO.

"I'll be here all week," Spud returned.

"You'll be here longer than that, my friend," Punk said. He returned his focus to Einstein, extending both arms toward him, saying, "Captain Williams mentioned a playbook, so, Admiral Francis, let's take a page out of the book NAVAIR uses all the time. Let's treat Passkey the same way we treat any operational evaluation, which is we create a test that gives the system in question the best chance of succeeding."

"I'm way ahead of you, sir," Einstein said, pointing the remote at the screen and clicking to the next slide. "Continuing with the givens, whether air or surface, the Air Force hypersonic needs to be launched from no less than five hundred miles away from *Ford*. We'd actually prefer more like a thousand miles, which is consistent with how the PLAN would employ it in a real-world conflict."

He clicked to the next slide, which featured an *Arleigh Burke*–class guided missile destroyer in the middle of it. "We're building this test in our own real-world way, which is based on the premise that our aircraft carriers don't operate by themselves. Our defense-in-depth construct is fundamental to how we do business. So, we're going to put a *Ticonderoga*-class cruiser at four hundred miles from the carrier and four *Arleigh Burke*s fifty miles inside of that. Using the latest version of their Standard surface-to-air missiles, modified to handle hypersonic speeds better than the earlier versions could, they'll get first crack at the incoming weapon."

The next slide showed a Super Hornet staged on one of *Ford*'s waist catapults. "After that, we'll have two divisions of Super Hornets, eight jets total," Einstein continued. "They'll be alert-launched from *Ford* at the first indication of the inbound missile, each armed with four AIM-174 air-to-air missiles designed specifically to counter PLAN hypersonics, to provide the second line of defense."

"Does the air wing have those yet?" Punk asked.

Einstein looked over toward Spud and quipped, "What was it he just said about demand signals?"

"Oh, great," Punk said, working hard to underreact to the confluence of information coming at him. "Another unknown."

"I'm more confident about the AIM-174 being up and running for this than I am *Ford* having a directed-energy weapon," Einstein said. "But since we're on the subject of DEWs, let's focus on the hypersonic threat and what onboard capability *Ford* should have to counter it." He clicked to the next slide, an artist's conception of a laser beam emanating from *Ford* causing an inbound missile to explode.

"That looks like it's blowing up pretty close to the carrier," Rear Admiral Connelly said.

"It's not drawn to scale," Einstein replied.

"The admiral brings up a good point, though," Punk said. "Let's say the attack jets survive the Standard missiles fired by the cruiser and the destroyers and launch the hypersonic, which gets through the AIM-174s from our Super Hornets. How far out will *Ford*'s DEW hit it?"

Einstein stared at Punk blankly for a few beats, and then said, "I don't have that answer at this time."

"Guess," Punk replied impassively.

"There's a lot we don't know at this point, Punk—er, Vice Admiral Reichert," Einstein shot back, catching his familiarity in the mixed company. "I think for the purposes of this initial meeting our matrix is binary." He raised one hand next to his head followed by the other on the opposite side of it. "Things that allow the carrier to get hit, and things that prevent that from happening."

"Fair enough," Punk said. "Continue."

"The challenge to shooting a hypersonic, regardless of range, is they are designed to fly in an unpredictable trajectory, which makes them hard to track and therefore to intercept. This is why our previous sea-based point missile defense strategy was problematic. But a directed-energy weapon would strike a hypersonic as it drew near its target, when changing its flight path would no longer be possible. So, to give you a ballpark answer to your previous question, we're talking twenty miles out, not two hundred."

"That's too close for comfort," Gridiron said. "How much damage could something like that do to my ship?"

Einstein's eyes narrowed as he thought about it. "Let's use the Boeing X-51 as an example. Though it's a scramjet, it still makes Mach 5. Weighing in at, say, four thousand pounds, it would be like shoving a bullet the size of a Toyota through the *Ford*. With the right kind of delayed fusing, a hypersonic could tear into this ship and deliver an interior detonation. It could target one of the reactors and obliterate it."

"That still wouldn't sink this boat," Spud said.

"We'd still have to abandon ship," Gridiron said. "The chamber would be compromised, and then we'd get bathed in radiation, not to mention scattering radioactive material into the environment."

"Those chambers are below *Ford*'s waterline," Spud observed. "How would one of these missiles reach it?"

"If the hypersonic's trajectory developed into an arc and it came at the *Ford* at the correct angle, it could reach well below the waterline," Einstein said.

"I think I know the answer, but I just want to be crystal clear from the outset, not having ever been on the test and evaluation side of things," Gridiron said slowly. "We're not actually letting the Air Force use a live missile with a warhead against my ship, right?"

"Of course not," Einstein replied amid a few muffled snickers from some of the others at the CO's question. "But this weapon isn't designed with a warhead anyway. The damage comes from hitting the target at just the right place at high speed."

"Could we get away with not using the actual carrier?" Spud asked. "Seems like we could mount the DEW on just about anything to prove it works."

"That would just add more fuel to Congressman Gordon's fire," Punk said. "We have to use *Ford*."

"The test article will self-destruct before it gets anywhere near the carrier," Einstein explained.

Punk, who had poured himself coffee but not drunk any of it yet, swirled the dark liquid around in the mug and stared at it as if the answer to his dilemma might be found there. "Anything else, Admiral Francis?" he asked without shifting his gaze.

Einstein shook his head. "No, sir."

Punk scanned the faces around the table and asked, "Anyone else got anything at this point?"

When no one spoke up, he rapped the table with his knuckles and stood. "We'll reconvene as soon as Admiral Francis gets more definitive word on the status of the directed-energy weapon and his team has a plan for putting it on *Ford*," he said. "We also need to hear from the Air Force on how they're going to present the threat. We're creating a classified chatroom on SIPRnet for this group, so if you have any thoughts in between our in-person get-togethers, put them there. In the meantime, everybody keep your phones with you at all times."

As the group began to shuffle out of the Flag SCIF, Punk quieted the din of casual conversation with a whistle. "One more thing, guys," Punk said as everyone froze in place. "Failure isn't an option."

CHAPTER 7

PETERSON HELD his breath as the video call loaded. It was on an encrypted network, beamed to a CubeSat above the California coastline. After leaving the office early claiming an upset stomach, he'd driven deep into Kern County. If there was a more desolate area on Earth, he didn't want to see it. He usually ignored the barren landscape because it depressed him, but that day he spotted every cactus, heard every bird, saw each bug smashed on his windshield.

The realization that his life was about to change drastically made him appreciate the details of his surroundings. His laptop's software suite said the satellite had a Chinese signature, but he doubted it was genuine. Yet he didn't have the time—likely a week, possibly more—that would be required to hack the sat's security firewall. Whoever was using it had excellent resources.

And now he was one of those resources. Though he should have felt chagrined by the realization, Peterson was elated. He sat on the hood of his car like someone camping out to stargaze. But there was only one glimmer in the firmament he cared about, and it answered.

The call window on his screen loaded with a male face: square jaw, thick eyebrows, dark hair combed back. A pair of aviator glasses obscured the person's eyes.

Peterson already knew what color those eyes were. His hand shook over the keyboard as an old hurt stung his heart. It would have been so easy to hit the Escape key and stop the whole thing.

"I hope this isn't inappropriate?" the avatar asked in a familiar voice.

The avatar's face and speech were near-perfect facsimiles of his father's. Even though Peterson knew the avatar was the construct of an AI-powered algorithm, his suspension of disbelief was stronger than he liked to admit.

Peterson swallowed, then shook his head quickly, saying. "N-no, I'm . . . I'm impressed. You look just like him. You sound like him, too."

His mind raced as to what data Wolfe had scraped together to re-create his father in virtual form so accurately, but those thoughts were interrupted when the avatar spoke again.

"Your father was a good man," the avatar said gently. "I wanted to use him as a way to show my respect for you. My respect for the sacrifices he made. For the ones you're about to make."

"Thank you," Peterson said, his mouth as dry as if he were speaking to his actual father. He'd never earned that sort of praise from the real one.

"The carrier test is under way," the avatar said. "As we've discussed, you're the likeliest person they will select to head any specialty weapons test. Is it viable?"

"LASIPOD is ready," Peterson said, leaning closer to the laptop.

"Fully functional?" the avatar asked. "If there is the slightest problem, they will be unlikely to include you in the test. The weapon must work if they are to accept you into the fold. They must have full confidence that LASIPOD can save them."

Peterson almost blurted out that he was sure that LASIPOD could save them, but he didn't want to brag. He'd been developing the directed-energy weapon system for years. Time and again his funding had been cut, kneecapping his progress, but he'd never given up on it. It was the future of surface vessel defense.

At least it would have been had he not just agreed to sabotage it.

"I already have a demonstration prepared," Peterson said. "Convincing them won't be a problem. I am concerned, however, about my retirement plans."

"The agreed-upon funds are no longer sufficient?" the avatar asked.

Peterson detected the annoyance in his faux father's voice. It rankled him that the damn thing could simulate his dad's anger so accurately. Or was Peterson just projecting his deepest emotions on an artificial construct meant to engender trust in him?

If Wolfe had calculated all that beforehand, as surely he would have, it indicated the man knew everything about Peterson. A person like that would have contingencies for those who betrayed him.

"Those funds are irrelevant if I'm not alive to spend them," Peterson said, faster than he wanted to. "I want a guaranteed escape route. Once the carrier enters the test phase, it will be in restricted waters. If I'm associated with the test and LASIPOD, I'll have to be on board. How will I be extricated?"

The avatar chuckled, turning the critical query into a superfluous request. "Of course. Do you think I would cast you aside? Or that I would allow your former comrades to apprehend you and use you as an example? No, you are more valuable than that."

"That's easy to say," Peterson said. "How? I want to know now."

"A submarine," the avatar said. "Restricted waters or not, the area beneath the surface will belong to us—if only for a brief window of time. It will be up to you to evacuate your position on the ship."

"Evacuate?" Peterson asked. "You mean jump overboard?"

"Shane," the avatar said, "you were selected because you know what needs to be done and we have confidence that you will do it. You have served them for years and look at what it has gotten you. Your father also served, admirably—and you know all too well what his reward was."

Peterson had been told that service was its own reward, but only those who had never lost anyone could say that.

"You want to make a difference," the avatar continued. "You believe, like me, that knowledge is a responsibility. That is how I found you. That's ultimately how you found me. And not just anyone *could* have found me, I promise you. This will be hard. Very hard. But think of what will change afterward. The wars, the hunger, the poverty. The world will see—we will make it see—and change before it destroys itself."

"How can you be sure?" Peterson asked, desperate for an answer that would calm the demons gnawing at his heart. Talking to a facsimile of his dead father was creepy, but at that moment it felt right, almost euphoric.

"My calculations have been correct so far," the avatar said. "I predicted the invasion of Ukraine, I predicted the Silicon Valley Bank collapse, I predicted what happened in Gaza. No one listened, Shane. But you did. The world can't continue like this. Bombs and carriers aren't the tools—the weapons—we'll need for this century. You know what it is, don't you?"

Peterson nodded.

"It's okay," the avatar said. "You can tell me."

The phrase sounded like something his father would have said. Maybe Wolfe's AI had taken it from a naval archive video, or even a home movie that Peterson had saved to his cloud drive. The effect broke something inside him. The final lock on the mental door he'd never realized he had shut.

"Numbers are the weapon," Peterson said. "Numbers will save us."

"Good," the avatar said. "And when *Ford* is at the bottom of the ocean? They'll realize what you and I already know. I know this is risky, Shane. I know you think you're alone, but you're not. Thank you for talking to me."

"No, um, thank *you*," Peterson said, trying to smile.

The face on the screen grinned, just the way his dad should have grinned after he returned home from deployments. But Peterson didn't have any home videos where his father smiled that way. Perhaps it was the AI's algorithm predicting how his father would have expressed happiness to see him.

Peterson grinned back as the call ended, and he found that he didn't care how Wolfe's avatar knew how to replicate his father's expression of joy. It felt real to him.

On the drive back to base, Peterson was still grinning as he imagined what he would do with the money. Maybe he'd create a tech start-up in China under an alias. Perhaps a foreign nation would appreciate his skills and employ him. Whatever happened, it would be on his terms, not someone else's.

Yet when he pulled back into the parking lot at China Lake, he was surprised by the twinge of regret that he felt as he looked up at the large command emblem mounted over the main entrance to his office building. But with a deep cleansing breath, he dismissed it and continued daydreaming.

CHAPTER 8

EINSTEIN'S FIRST SERIES of secure virtual conversations following the meeting on *Ford* were more productive than he'd thought they might be, so Punk decided to host a working dinner that same day. He called a smaller group to the SCIF at the U.S. Naval Air Force Pacific headquarters across the base from where the carrier was docked at NAS North Island.

"I found our guy to move the directed-energy side of this forward," Einstein announced to Punk, Spud, and Connelly as he pointed a remote at the room's front wall screen. A photo of a young man wearing the expression of somebody posing for a mug shot dominated the screen. His short beard and Marine Corps–style buzz-cut hair were jet black.

"Gentlemen, this is Shane Peterson," Einstein said. "He's the Senior Director for Test Programs at the Naval Air Weapons Center at China Lake a couple of hours north of here. He comes highly recommended by NAWC commander and a few others up there. They say he's a wunderkind. He got his engineering bachelor's degree from

Penn State, where he was also in NROTC. He selected pilot but attrited and resigned his commission. While he was earning his master's from Cal Tech, he interned at NAWC and impressed them as both hardworking and super smart. I spoke to him earlier, and he strikes me as very eager to prove that our latest class of aircraft carrier is prepared for the next generation of warfare."

"Dangerous combo, right, Spud?" Punk quipped.

"Very, which is why I chose to be neither of those things," Spud retorted.

"Oh, by the way, his father was a Tomcat pilot and a Top Gun bro, West Coast, before our time," Einstein said.

"Then the wunderkind is also a legacy, which means we have to take him," Punk said.

"Shane's first guess after I read him into the high points of Passkey was that the other side would want to fire the hypersonic from one of the ranges at Edwards Air Force Base; or they might agree to use the Pacific Missile Test Center facilities at Point Mugu if we could bake in some budget incentives."

"Looks like we're paying for the Air Force too, boys."

"That's another reason to get Peterson on the team. He's known for delivering results while cutting development costs. And, most important, he's very bullish on where the Navy is currently with directed-energy weapons. He mentioned that a system they call "THOR" has managed to take out drone swarms."

"I've heard of that," Spud said. "British, right?"

"Yeah."

"THOR only works at short range, and only for brief periods of time," Connelly said dismissively. "They spent twenty million to get nothing."

"They didn't get nothing," Einstein replied. "It was a start that Shane says the NAWC team has used to make a viable long-range directed-energy weapon. He called it LASIPOD. The main difference that makes it effective is our reactors give the system unprecedented amounts of power. The Brits didn't have anything close to that."

"Did this wunderkind say anything about our defense-in-depth test concept?" Punk asked.

"He liked it," Einstein said. "But he warned me that if we do that, the Air Force side will want to do their version of the same thing, adding F-35s to the mix."

"That would seriously complicate our problem."

"But he also warned me that the House Armed Services Committee might not go for it."

"So, this kid is also a legislative affairs expert?" Connelly asked.

"He's been part of a few other HASC-directed proof-of-concept tests," Einstein said. "He said in his experience the military always wants to make it complicated and the lawmakers always want to keep it simple—not because they want to streamline the process but because they have trouble with the details."

"What's his definition of simple?" Spud asked.

"No cruisers or destroyers," Einstein replied. "And no air wing Super Hornets or F-35s. Just *Ford* and a directed-energy weapon versus a single hypersonic missile."

Punk shrugged. "We'll keep building on our plan until we're directed otherwise," he said. "I'm taking my orders from the CNO, not Congressman Gordon."

"How long do we have to put this together?"

"Muddy said Gordon wants us to fail before the end of the fiscal year so he can shift a couple billion to the Air Force in the next defense budget."

"Muddy?" Connelly asked.

"Representative Evelyn Greenwood," Punk replied. "She was a squadron mate of ours back in the Arrowslingers, and now she's our Hill intel."

"Another Arrowslinger? Why am I always surrounded by aviators?" the ship driver moaned.

"You specialized in building aircraft carriers, Melvin," Punk said. "Who did you think you'd be surrounded by?"

"We only have a few months, then," Spud observed, bringing the discussion back to the point.

The group sat in silence for what started to be an awkward amount of time. At this point in the process, silence meant they were losing. Punk finally broke it by asking, "How ready is the Air Force side for this?"

"In general, they're way ahead of us, I can tell you that," Einstein said.

"When should we sit down with them?"

"Sooner rather than later, but it's the Air Force, you know. Those guys won't agree on anything until they run it all the way up the chain of command."

"You mean like we're going to do?" Punk quipped back, causing Einstein to shrug in resignation. "After that congressional hearing yesterday, I'm not signing up for anything without CNO's buy-in."

"So, what's next?"

Punk stared at the screenshot of Shane Peterson's expressionless face, searching the young man's eyes for a clue that would help unlock this mystery man who had been thrust upon him. There was so much at stake if they got it wrong. He saw nothing there that suggested Peterson was the key to success. But it was just a photo.

"Einstein, you set up the meeting with the Air Force side," he said. "And then you and Melvin get with our new favorite engineer Shane to finish demoing LASIPOD and then fast-track getting it aboard *Ford*. I'll get with my counterpart the Ship Boss and have him ID the cruiser and destroyers we'll use in Passkey."

"You make it sound so simple," Einstein returned. "Let's build a rocket and then use it to land on Mars," he sang.

"Or do nothing and get the space program canceled forever," Punk countered.

"What do you want *me* to do?" Spud asked.

"Reach out to your industry counterparts on the Air Force side. Find out as much as you can about what they'll be throwing at us. We need altitudes, speeds, ranges—everything we can get. We don't have enough time to design LASIPOD to tackle every contingency. We need to focus it on this test profile."

"Solid copy," Spud said. "I'll give them some of our nifty Peabody Tilden lapel pins to get them talking."

"And since you mentioned the F-35, I think I'll use the time to get up to Lemoore and take somebody up on the offer to go through their fam syllabus."

"Slumming, huh?" Spud jabbed.

"Flight time is flight time," Punk said. "And what good is rank if you don't abuse it?"

"The test pilots back at Patuxent River tell me those things basically fly themselves," Einstein said. "I tell them I'd never fly an airplane that doesn't have a front seat."

"I agree," Spud added.

"The RIO mafia unites," Punk said with a smile. "The Tomcat will always be my first love, but I'm not one to fight technology. Besides, this invitation came from my stepson."

"I can get you aboard our newest *Arleigh Burke* destroyer if you want to try your hand at driving one of those," Connelly said. "Those Flight IIIs are high tech."

"You forget I had command of an amphib and a carrier," Punk said. "I've logged plenty of time on the bridge in my day."

"How long will you be at NAS Lemoore?" Einstein asked.

"Not long; three days or so. I'll be reachable up there, so don't hesitate to call with updates whenever you get them." Punk stood up. "Now, gentlemen, if you'll excuse me, I need to get home to spend some time with my wife. That's a test I'm absolutely not allowed to fail."

As Punk and Spud exited the SCIF, Spud said, "Tell Suzanne I said hello."

"You set up with a hotel?" Punk asked. "We have plenty of room at our quarters here."

"Not necessary, but thanks," Spud said. "Company put me up in the Hotel Del Coronado."

Punk was relieved. No matter how much he liked seeing his old RIO again, he needed some quality time with Suzanne—even if all he had to tell her was that he'd be spending a week or so up at Lemoore and then focusing all his time over the next few months on this damn test. At least he wouldn't be far from home.

Surf was waiting outside the SCIF with a few messages. As Punk went over the printouts, he glanced at his aide.

"Any luck yet in getting Gwen out here on base?"

Surf offered the same tight smile. "Yes, sir. I took you up on your offer, and Suzanne was able to help her get settled in."

"Excellent," Punk replied. "We need her situated and happy to keep you focused on the task at hand here."

"I am," Surf said. "Trust me, Admiral, I am."

CHAPTER 9

WOLFE PACED back and forth across his penthouse office in Singapore awaiting word from his cyberwarfare operative. He ignored the tall windows' 360-degree view of the Downtown Core, the historic hub of the seaside metropolis' business activity. As one of the Four Asian Tigers, along with Hong Kong, Taiwan, and South Korea, Singapore had economically dominated the South China Sea for the last several decades.

Sinking *Ford* would endanger that economy, and China would imperil it further with its ever-growing fleet. The balance of power would shift, at least temporarily, in Beijing's and Pyongyang's favor. But Wolfe Industries already had cyberwarfare neural nets prepared to market to the so-called Tigers as a safeguard against Chinese hegemony.

The best way to sell a product was to create a demand for it.

And once the power of the neural nets became apparent, the world would see that the old ways of doing things were irrelevant. Carriers and gunboats would become old-fashioned tools akin to Paleolithic Clovis arrowheads. A new era would begin—and the hegemon would be Wolfe.

The thought made him smile. Economics was just another numbers game, but it was harder to manage because of its unforeseen variables. While recessions and scarcity could be predicted, those forecasts were based on past data rather than current information. The world he envisioned wouldn't be hampered that way.

The video call finally came. Wolfe, still pacing, swiped his mobile and the screen came alive. Rather than a person, it showed a progress bar that read zero above a line of red dots presented in an arc above a map of the western coast of the United States. At the bottom was a green audio icon, indicating the caller could hear Wolfe.

"News?" Wolfe asked.

The speaker answered in the genderless monotone provided by a voice changer. "We have reports of a PLASSF attack on NOSS assets. Aswan is monitoring."

"Interesting," Wolfe said impassively, keeping the conversation ambiguous. If his operatives could hack into military networks, someone could hack into his. The charade was necessary.

Aswan was Wolfe Industries' proprietary machine-learning module. It was named after one of the geographical locations the ancient mathematician Eratosthenes had used to calculate the circumference of the Earth. The equation that had told humanity their world was a sphere.

When he was a boy, Wolfe had visited Aswan in Egypt—called Syene in Eratosthenes' day—with his parents. The ancient ruins of previous civilizations had bored him because they hadn't endured. But the story of turning the perception of a flat world into a round one had captured his imagination.

Numbers. Not force of arms, or religious indoctrination, or art. Numbers.

She'd never believed in his numbers, but she'd believed in him. Believed in him so much that she'd flown her F-16 that fateful day.

Wolfe whooshed a long exhale and refocused on the screen.

It had taken some effort and nearly a billion dollars to steal code signatures from the PLASSF, the People's Liberation Army Strategic Support Force. Communist regimes used such clumsy names for their agencies. Since his operatives needed to access NOSS—the Naval Ocean Surveillance System—he made it appear that the Chinese were executing the hacking attempt. The Americans, if they detected the attempt at all, would think hackers in Beijing were trying to access U.S. Navy satellites.

Access to NOSS was critical if his goal of sinking *Ford* was going to be realized. Shane Peterson and his missile would be the harpoon, but Aswan would be the hand that guided it.

In two minutes, the progress bar on the screen grew to 7 percent, then 9.

"Good, but slow," Wolfe said. "Start over."

"NOSS will have been notified of the attempt," the operative said.

Wolfe paused at his desk and picked up a model of an F-16 painted in the red-and-white lines of Singapore's Black Knights aerial acrobatics squadron. Their version of the vaunted Blue Angels. It had been a gift from her: Kanny Chou. She'd been one of their pilots. He'd slept with her the same day she'd first flown with the Knights.

She flew into the sky that day, but she had flown him to the sun.

"Start over," Wolfe said. "I want at least 50 percent infiltration of their network within two seconds. Anything less and the harpoon goes astray."

Such a feat required a great amount of computer processing power, but Aswan was built for it. Wolfe was acting on the probability that he had more to invest in such systems than either the Chinese or the American military. It was a short-term probability and would not last long. A few billion dollars went a long way, but ambition went much further.

The globe on the screen tilted slightly, keeping pace with the orbits of the NOSS satellites. Their blinking red representations made him think of meteorites that refused to die in reentry. But Wolfe didn't want them to die. He needed them to serve him.

"Aswan is ready," the operator said.

Passing the F-16 model from one hand to the other, Wolfe nodded. "Go."

The bar moved to 68 percent in fifty-two seconds.

He grinned, then tossed the model into the air and caught it behind his back. "Excellent. Now, again. Faster."

A minute passed, then the operator indicated that Aswan was ready.

"Go," Wolfe said.

The bar reached 79 percent in forty-four seconds.

"Good, but we need it to get in there even faster," Wolfe said. "Once we're in, there's a chance the Navy will try to shut us out of their systems."

"They might even shoot down their own satellite," the operative said. "ASAT capabilities are more robust than they were when Moscow downed Kosmos 1408."

Wolfe barked a laugh. "The Americans aren't as stupid as the Russians, at least not when it comes to destroying compromised assets. Kosmos had nothing of use on it anyway, despite that lead we received. Besides, even if the Americans launch an antisatellite weapon at the one we acquire, it will have been too late. If you updated our server capacity as I asked."

"It was updated to your specifications," the operative said. "But if we reveal our strength now—"

"You're worried the Navy will be prepared when the actual operation commences?" Wolfe scoffed. "Their cyberwarfare division has never updated to threats in a timely fashion. They can't even handle their own classified documents these days, let alone anything this rapidly complex. No, this will work. We can't test this on other nations' satellites. Their defenses are not robust enough. It would be like a chess master playing against amateurs—their strategy would suffer. It is NOSS or nothing. If you wish to take down Goliath, you do not practice on rabbits forever. Now, start again. I want 100 percent infiltration within fifty seconds."

The pause in the operative's voice was audible over the connection, as if they had started to speak but withheld their initial reply.

"Say it," Wolfe said, his grip on the F-16 tightening.

Kanny would have risked it even if the damn F-16 had lacked wings.

"That will draw even more attention," the operative said.

"So?" Wolfe asked as he stalked from the office to the balcony. The breeze ruffled his clothing. He stared over the cityscape more than eight hundred feet below.

Kanny had loved the view, loved it when he caressed her as she stood at the glass gazing at it.

"Using the PLASSF's signature could cause an international incident," the operative said.

"Hackers joust with each other all the damn time," Wolfe said. "It rarely makes the news. I have done the calculations. Start the infiltration."

"Starting," the operative said.

Wolfe turned and leaned on the balcony railing as he stared back into the office at the screen. The bar slid to 22 percent. A counter ran on the side.

Five seconds.

The bar increased to 38 percent.

Eleven seconds.

"We've tripped their firewall," the operative said.

In the past, Wolfe might have called off the cyberattack. But the numbers were on his side.

Sixteen seconds. The bar grew to 57 percent.

Wolfe stared, unblinking, at the screen. Willing it to reveal the result he had predicted. The result the world needed.

Twenty-three seconds. Bar at 70 percent.

"Come on," Wolfe muttered. "Come on, goddamn you."

Thirty seconds. Seventy-eight percent.

"NOSS is running a trace attempt," the operative said.

"Come on," Wolfe urged, feeling his face flush.

"The trace will catch Aswan in eight seconds," the operative said.

Thirty-seven seconds. Eighty-five percent.

"Come on!" Wolfe yelled.

Forty-two seconds. Ninety-three percent.

"Sir," the operative said plaintively.

Forty-five seconds. One hundred percent.

"Now," Wolfe said, exhaling all the air in his lungs, shaking to the point that he had to steady himself on the railing.

"We got in," the operative said. "But the trace—"

"Congratulations," Wolfe said with a satisfied sigh.

"I . . . thank you, sir," the operative said.

"Let the Chinese and the Americans sort it out," Wolfe said. "Now I want you to work on achieving 100 percent in forty seconds."

"If I may inquire . . . why so quickly?" the operative asked. "We will have the necessary access to NOSS to carry out the operation."

"Because . . ." Wolfe said, turning to face the Singapore skyline once more. "We'll be commanding a harpoon traveling ten times the speed of sound if our asset delivers."

"Ah, of course, sir," the operative said.

Wolfe snickered and swiped his mobile. The screen went dark.

He examined the F-16 model in his hands, then gasped. He had gripped it so tightly that he had snapped off its wings.

"I'm sorry," he mumbled, then flung the pieces off the balcony.

CHAPTER **10**

HEADING ACROSS NAS North Island to his quarters should have cheered Punk up, but it didn't. He could not get what Gordon had said out of his mind, even as he looked at the familiar and comforting sights of naval staff coming and going, warships and vessels in the harbor, and the thump of MH-60 Knighthawk helicopters as they came in for a landing. Normally these surroundings grounded him, wrapped him in the world he'd known for so long. Like any honest sailor he might grow weary of it at times and yearn for the calm of shore leave, but the thrill of flying Navy airplanes and taking warships to sea was in his blood.

His driver, a petty officer attached to the AIRPAC motor pool, made small talk about the weather, then veered into more personal territory without warning.

"Sir, may I ask a question?" he asked as he made a turn on Coronado Avenue bringing the Pacific Ocean into view.

"Of course," Punk said.

The petty officer smiled into the rearview mirror and asked, "What was it like to fly with Captain Soup Campbell?"

Punk suppressed the first reply that came to mind. Soup Campbell was arguably the most arrogant, self-serving, impulsive pilot the Navy had ever produced, and Punk, Spud, Einstein, Muddy, and many others from that era of the VF-104 Arrowslingers had the receipts to prove it. His impetuous drive for glory combined with his aviation ineptitude had allowed an Iranian F-4 to overfly the carrier in the Persian Gulf. Einstein had been Soup's RIO on that hop. Soup had also managed to get shot down over Iraq, and damn if he didn't make himself into a national hero after spending a few weeks in a Baghdad jail as a POW (although there wasn't really any war going on).

On a later deployment he'd summarily arrived as the deputy air wing commander after the air wing commander was killed in a crash right off the catapult. Soup again showed his ass by bombing a civilian pickup truck in Afghanistan because he was so eager to get in on the action that he ignored the call of the forward air controller. That was the same deployment where Punk and Spud had been forced to eject from their Tomcat when one of their bombs exploded prematurely after release. They'd been taken by the Taliban and treated cruelly. For years afterward, Punk had woken in a cold sweat, having dreamed that he was in the cave with that sadistic Chechen, the same man who'd cut off Spud's pinky finger after they refused to participate in filmed propaganda.

The petty officer's query brought back those memories in a rush of emotions, but Punk answered matter-of-factly, "Captain Campbell was an ... assertive pilot."

"Is it true he wanted to go over the brass' heads and fly a sortie out over Afghanistan to find you himself?"

Punk hadn't heard anything of the sort, and he knew that sort of selfless sacrifice wasn't anywhere in Soup's DNA, but he supposed the tales of derring-do had spread over the time since the post-9/11 wars had come and gone.

"I'm not aware of that, but you never know," Punk said diplomatically. "What brings this up?"

The petty officer cleared his throat as they turned onto 8th Street. "Sir, my brother is a Super Hornet pilot who's just finishing up his first sea tour, and well, pardon the ask, sir, but I was hoping you could get Captain Campbell to put in a good word for him with the Blue Angels. He's trying to join the team for the next season."

Soup had been a Blue Angel for a couple of years when he was a lieutenant, and once a Blue Angel, always a Blue Angel, even after they left the Navy.

"Sorry, but I can't help. It's been a while since I've seen Captain Campbell, and we're not in comms these days." Punk thought about trying to find Soup, what that would take and how the conversation would go in the event he managed to track him down. No thanks. "The Blue Angels have a process for picking members of the team that's very solid. Tell your brother to trust the process. And tell him I wish him good luck in getting selected."

"Good luck from the Air Boss," the petty officer said to himself. "He'll like that."

The car pulled into the circular driveway of the official quarters of Commander Naval Air Forces Pacific, and Punk patted the driver on the shoulder before climbing out and shutting the rear door. He watched the car drive away and then looked beyond it long enough to admire another perfect San Diego sunset.

Home. He and Suzanne had lived in nearly twenty different places during his career. NAS North Island was his favorite. It was Coronado, for chrissakes, a charming upscale community they couldn't afford to live in if he wasn't in the Navy. And while traffic could get backed up around the island, as it did in many places around San Diego, that wasn't a factor when your house was just over a mile from your office within the gates of the air station.

Suzanne wasn't standing at the doorway to greet him as she normally did, cued by the crunching of the tires on the gravel driveway. None of the lights were on, and he didn't hear her chatting with one of the tight circle of Navy spouses who often dropped by. Maybe that was a blessing; he didn't need to recount his testimony on Capitol Hill like some sort of standup comic. He was already weary of the notoriety.

"Honey, I'm home," he called, like a TV husband entering the set of a sixties sitcom.

Suzanne slowly walked around the corner and into the entryway. The smile on her face was forced, pained. Her eyes darted past him. Her body posture sent his mind back to how she'd looked more than two decades ago when she learned that Crud, her first husband and his best friend, had been killed in an F-14 accident.

His mind raced. What was it? Another death of a family member? It couldn't be Jason, his stepson who'd become a Navy pilot himself. There's no way she would've heard about that before he did. He moved over to her and clasped her hands. "Tell me."

"Dr. Billings called an hour ago," she said. Her fingers dug into his palms as if she was trying not to lose her grip while hanging off the side of a cliff.

Dr. Billings was at Balboa Naval Medical Center. Her regular checkup. Mammogram. He felt his heart beating in his throat as he asked, "And?" fearing that he didn't want the answer.

Suzanne finally looked into his eyes. Twenty years of marriage, and she was still the most beautiful woman he'd ever seen. "It's back," she said softly.

The simple declaration echoed inside his brain. His brow furrowed as he stood there paralyzed by the information, working through the shock and denial that this was happening. He pulled her close, as if he could tether her to him and nothing would steal her away.

After another extended silence during their embrace, Punk asked, "What's next?"

"I'm not sure," she said. "I have a consult with him on Friday."

"I'm going with you."

"No. No, there's no need for that." She backed away and wiped the tears from her eyes.

"We're going to beat it," he said, as if he could will it so. "Just like before, we'll beat it."

She nodded passively as another tear trickled down her cheek. "I know you've had a long week, especially after yesterday. You're in Washington, and then you come home and this is what I offer you."

As her voice trailed off, Punk shook his head vigorously. "C'mon, stop it," he said, grasping her shoulders like a coach trying to motivate a player. "I'm clearing my calendar. Getting you healthy is the only thing that matters to me."

"No, you're not clearing your calendar," Suzanne returned forcefully, suddenly regaining her strength as she spun on her heel and walked down the hallway toward the kitchen. "We're not making a big deal about this."

"Suzanne, it *is* a big deal," he said to her back.

She turned to face him again and shouted, "No, it's not!"

Punk knew not to fight her now. She was scared and proud and strong all at the same time, and he loved her for that pride and strength, as frustrating as it could be at times. Her pride and strength had underwritten his success, but damn, she was hardheaded sometimes.

He walked up and pulled her close, thinking of all the cute little phrases military couples, separated so often, told each other, like "We're always under the same stars," and other greeting card drivel. But the hard truth was Suzanne and he had been apart as much as they were together.

He held her tighter, wishing he had been home more, wishing he had been there more often to watch Jason grow up, wishing he had slept late in bed with her on those weekends instead of heading off to the squadron to check on the status of the jets.

All those years on the path to becoming an admiral. In the selfish way that love did, it made him feel like the cancer was eating away at him, too, and then he was sorry the thought even entered his head.

"So, tell me about this test," Suzanne said as she walked away from him again.

He felt guilty for even caring about it, considering her diagnosis. "Well, you saw what happened during the hearing," he said, following her into the kitchen. "We basically have to prove that the *Ford* can survive an attack from a hypersonic missile."

"When is this test?"

"Too soon."

"Where will it happen?"

"That's not finalized yet, but probably off the coast here."

"Good," she sighed, massaging her cheeks with the tips of her fingers. "I'd like you nearby for the next few months."

"Me too. Spud says hello, by the way."

"He's in San Diego? You know, he still owes me some of those signature ribs he's always bragging about. You remind him of that."

A cookout. Ribs, beans, coleslaw, potato salad, beer. Music playing through the outdoor speakers. Simple pleasures. Would they ever have the luxury of those again?

"I will," he said, reflexively plucking an apple out of a bowl on one of the kitchen counters. He gave it a sniff and then returned it to the bowl. "Have you told Jason yet?"

"I left him a voicemail to call," she replied. "I didn't give any details. I'm sure he was flying."

"He's an F-35 RAG instructor," Punk observed. "I guarantee you he was flying, which brings up something else I have to cancel."

"What?"

"I suddenly have a few free days as the test team gets to work, and I was thinking of going up to Lemoore to take Jason up on his invite to fly the F-35."

"Sounds like fraud, waste, and abuse to me," she joked, which he was happy to see. "Are you trying to get fired?"

"No, I'm trying to do my job," Punk replied. "I don't know enough about that airplane, and actually flying it is the best way for me to learn. And it's only an hour away."

"Got it," she said. "When are you supposed to go up there?"

"Tomorrow."

"Good. You're not canceling that either. It's a good opportunity for you to talk to him about my diagnosis. He needs to hear it from you. He's always trusted you more than me."

"Not true."

"It *is* true."

"Okay, I'll talk to him when I'm up there. We haven't talked details of the schedule, but I'm sure we'll do dinner or something."

"Are you not staying with them?"

"I don't want to intrude. I'll just stay in the DV room at the BOQ."

Suzanne moved to the sink and turned the faucet on. She watched the water run for a few seconds, filled a glass, then polished it off in large gulps. "Crying makes you thirsty," she explained, as if she needed to.

Punk walked over to the sink, put his arm around her, and led her to the long leather couch in the adjacent living room. Suzanne let out a long sigh and flopped her head back and stared at the ceiling. "I'm fine, right?" she asked.

"Yes," he replied. "Besides, you don't have permission to die until I give it to you."

She chuckled. It was the line she said to him every time he left on deployment: "You don't have permission to die until I give it to you," a defense mechanism against the enduring trauma of the loss of a loved one, an assertion of nonexistent power over tragedy.

Punk considered the family photos visible on the mantle. There, along with their wedding picture, Jason's graduation photos—high school, college, and flight school—a snapshot of his first flight in a Super Hornet, and the family vacation they took to Baja a few years ago, was a photo of Suzanne with Crud. He was fine with it; it belonged there because Crud was family to Punk, too.

But, like her, it was still hard for him even now, after two decades, to speak of Crud and the midair collision between two F-14s over North Carolina that killed him. Punk's relationship with Suzanne had unfolded naturally in the wake of Crud's death, starting with the time at an Officer's Club Happy Hour when he rescued her from some obnoxious Air Force pilots in for the weekend on a cross-country in their F-15s. A few days later 9/11 happened and they came together in a rush of emotion. But the war in Afghanistan had called him back to the Arrowslingers, and their connection was immediately put to a test that both ultimately passed. They got married shortly after his return.

It was during the tour with Crud at the F-14 Fleet Replacement Squadron, where they trained newly winged pilots and RIOs how to operate the U.S. Navy's premier fighter, that Punk had learned the irony of his chosen career. It was shore duty, in theory less challenging than a sea tour on board an aircraft carrier sailing in harm's way. But it turned out that, barring a fatal mishap, the greatest challenges were the those outside the cockpit. Flying was easy; life was hard.

Punk sensed Suzanne was looking at him. "I talked to Gwen Davis," she said.

"Who?"

"Your aide's wife?"

"Oh, yeah, he mentioned to me you'd helped her out. Thanks for doing that."

"She's very sweet, but something's off there."

"Like what?"

"I don't know exactly; just off."

"He's a good aide," Punk said, more defensively than he meant to. "And I'm seriously going to need his head in the game over the next few months here."

"Just letting you know what I saw, is all," Suzanne said with a yawn. She stretched her arms above her head then grabbed the remote and clicked on the widescreen TV over the fireplace. A news correspondent standing in the rain in front of Buckingham Palace reported that the Princess of Wales had just finished chemotherapy and that official sources had no further comment beyond that.

"Perfect timing," Suzanne snorted.

The report was followed by a short video the correspondent said had just been released by the British royal family. It showed the future king, prematurely balding but otherwise appearing youthful with a big-toothed smile, holding his wife's hand as they walked through a wooded area trailed by their children, two boys and a girl. The princess and the children were also smiling as if they had no cares in the world.

"This must've been made before her chemo," Suzanne said. "Her hair and face are perfect. Look at how rosy her cheeks are."

The news moved on to the day's financial report. She looked at him again and asked, "I don't have permission, right?"

"No, you don't," he said. "And you never will."

Punk parked his late-model Corvette—"the fighter pilot mobile" Suzanne called it—in his marked spot in front of the Navy Exchange. The car was red and flashy and a guilty pleasure that he indulged only for short trips across the air station. He was on his way to the transient flight line in front of base operations where the Super Hornet RAG, the West Coast squadron charged with training newly winged pilots and weapons systems officers on the strike fighter, had staged an F/A-18F to take him to NAS Lemoore. As he was packing a small bag for the trip, he'd realized he was out of travel-sized toothpaste and deodorant, hence the need for the stop.

On his way into the Navy Exchange, a combination convenience store, grocery store, and department store, he passed a pretty, long-legged redhead wearing jean shorts and a cutoff sweatshirt and pushing a grocery cart. He nodded and started to smile at her, until he spotted her black eye.

The redhead paused, then cleared her throat. "Admiral Reichert?"

He stopped, trying his best not to fixate on her black eye. "Yes?"

His first thought was that she might be a reporter sent by Congressman Gordon to ask inane questions about the upcoming test. It was the politician's version of psychological warfare, and Punk wasn't in the mood to engage with it.

"I just wanted to let you know that Mrs. Reichert was very helpful in getting us a place," she said, as she extended her hand. "I'm Gwen Davis, Surf's wife."

Punk thought for another beat and then nodded vigorously as they shook, saying, "Of course, Gwen. Nice to meet you. Really glad it worked out."

She seemed harried. He tried not to stare at her black eye but felt compelled to ask, "Is everything all right?"

Gwen blinked, then looked at her empty cart as if something had fallen out of it. "I'm just grabbing a few things before I head out of town, and... oh, my eye. Yeah, that. I had an accident with the door in my room last night. I tried to open it, and, uh, there was a shoe blocking the way and... I'm sorry, I'm rambling. I'm just tired, I guess."

Punk wanted to accept her explanation at face value and let it go. But he thought of his aide's angry tirade over the phone back on Capitol Hill, and his complaints about Gwen. Instantly, pieces fell into place to form an ugly puzzle, and he thought about what Suzanne had said about something being off with the couple. But he didn't want to jump to conclusions, and besides, standing in front of the Navy Exchange wasn't the right place for that sort of conversation.

"I know you're busy, sir, but I just wanted to say thanks again."

"Please call me 'Rick,'" he said. "It's much easier than 'Admiral Reichert.'"

She nodded as she regripped the handle of the cart and took a step toward the sliding door, which opened as she approached.

"Gwen," he called to her. "If you need anything, don't hesitate to give us a call." She turned back toward him, and for a second it looked as if she was about to say something, but instead she gave him a meek smile and disappeared into the store.

CHAPTER 11

WOLFE SWIPED the screen of his burner phone screen and accepted the call. "You made it?"

"Yes," the voice said. "Columbia is beautiful this time of year."

Columbia, as in the District of Columbia. The capital of the United States.

"Good," Wolfe said. "Beware of the muddy roads. I hear it's easy to get stuck there unless you have the right gear."

"Will do," the voice said.

Before the end of the day, Wolfe's agent would be studying Ellen Greenwood's movements. Before the end of the week, they would have any data on Project OpenShip she had. If Aswan was going to succeed at hacking into and gaining control of a NOSS satellite, then OpenShip would first have to be dealt with.

Wolfe smirked as he tossed the phone into a trash bin outside the café in Manila. Muddy. What a silly call sign. Crow, now, that was a real fighter pilot's call sign.

As he walked into the café Wolfe checked his other mobile. The email from his extortion operative about Rick Reichert left much to be desired. The admiral had seemed too clean-cut to be true, even for an older naval officer, but Wolfe's scandal scrapers had found nothing they could use on him. No leverage for blackmail or defamation. There were his wife's cancer battles and his stepson's assault charge during high school, but those were dry wells, too. The best way to get to Reichert was to erode his trust in his friends and confidants. Like Greenwood.

The older Chinese man seated in the café looked up when Wolfe walked in, and his already glum expression darkened further.

"Hello, Hou," Wolfe said, taking a seat opposite the man.

A waitress, all smiles and blush-enhanced dimples, rushed up and asked Wolfe if he wanted something from the bar. He responded with a smile and a $100 tip. She thanked him and left. American money still bought silence better than any other currency.

"Why are you here?" Hou asked in Mandarin.

"It's a nice day," Wolfe replied in the same language. "I was thirsty."

Though he was confident of success, Wolfe was having second thoughts. He needed to see the old man again, one of the few connections to her that remained to him.

"Why do you keep following me?" Hou asked in English. "I live here now. I want to get away from everything. Do you not understand?"

"I do this out of respect," Wolfe said, and meant it.

Hou snorted. "Is this still about Kanny?"

The mention of her name stung something in Wolfe's chest, but he continued smiling. "Yes. I wanted to tell you personally that I am honoring what I said."

Hou scowled. "My Kanny is gone. Go back to your drones and limousines, your rent girls and stupid toys. She was never of your world."

"She wanted to be," Wolfe said. "That's how we met, remember? I was at that air show in Singapore, and she asked for my autograph." He snorted a laugh. "Ha, and I was there trying to get hers."

"You say these things every time you invade my privacy," Hou said. "Why can't you leave me alone? Why can't you let her memory have peace?"

"Because now I can make them pay," Wolfe said.

Hou's eyes shimmered with tears. "Nothing will bring her back to us, Justin, or whoever you really are. Not your money. Not your machines. And not more death."

Kanny Chou, call sign Crow—or *Wūyā* in Chinese—had been a lieutenant in the Republic of Singapore Air Force. Moreover, she'd been a member of the vaunted Black Knights, the RSAF's aerobatics team. She was a superb pilot. The sky was her element.

She'd earned the name Crow because she was acquisitive, a persistent scavenger just like the bird that was an infamous pest in her homeland. Whenever she'd gotten the chance to meet luminaries—such as a Western celebrity like himself—she'd pressed them for an autograph or a selfie to add to her collection. Their first meeting years ago had been the first of many. Their nights together in his apartment had brought him unimagined pleasure.

It was easy for a wealthy person to find pleasure—but love was much harder.

Wolfe had found it with Kanny.

They'd spent as much time together as possible given her tight flight schedule and deployments and his own busy calendar.

When she'd been deployed to Luke Air Force Base in Arizona as part of the RSAF's overseas detachments, she'd asked him to marry her before she left. Crows mated for life, she'd warned him. His beautiful, precious Crow. For the rest of his life he would regret saying no. In his own way, though, he had remained true to her after all.

While stationed at Luke she'd been training with a member of the Naval Operational Support Center's training services detachment. She was living her dream. When the Navy officer asked Kanny to attempt a risky new maneuver, she hadn't hesitated. She'd called Wolfe the night before, so excited she could barely talk.

She crashed while executing the maneuver. The Navy claimed pilot error, said she had likely exceeded her G tolerance and blacked out.

She had not ejected.

To avoid an international incident, Kanny's crash had been swept under the rug. Even though the officer had been reprimanded and demoted, Wolfe had never forgiven the U.S. Navy for killing her.

He'd tried to bring excitement, if not joy, back into his life after losing her. Money, other women, alcohol, cocaine. None of them could compare to his precious Crow.

Sinking Reichert's aircraft carrier was going to be more personal than he liked to admit.

"I have to do this," Wolfe said.

"No, you don't," Hou said. "This has always been your claim. Using Kanny as an excuse for your schemes, for what you do."

Wolfe leaned over the table. "You don't understand. I need to do this."

"Is this your version of closure?" Hou asked.

Closure? Would taking his revenge finally eliminate the pain? That variable numbers could not predict. The part of himself that contained the last elements of frailty.

"I just needed to tell you," Wolfe said, and found himself grinning widely. So widely it hurt his face. "When it happens, I want you to know it was me. That I did it for Kanny."

Hou regarded Wolfe with the pity one might reserve for a dying man. "And you'll do this how? With your invisible new machine gods that you sell like a warped disciple? Your goddamn face on screens and billboards everywhere, smiling like you're saving the world?"

"I *am* going to save the world," Wolfe said. But for the first time he wasn't sure if he believed it.

"You say that your numbers never lie," Hou said, standing up.

"That's right," Wolfe said, trying to maintain his smile, but failing.

Hou's anger gave way to exhaustion. "You are wrong. They have always lied to you."

Wolfe let the old man leave the café without further comment. Hou was a curmudgeon. His grief for Kanny obscured his judgment, and that was why he believed Wolfe was wrong.

But Wolfe had beliefs of his own.

CHAPTER **12**

PUNK TAXIED the F/A-18F Super Hornet to the hold short for Runway 29 at NAS North Island. Lieutenant Travis "Torch" O'Brien, the weapons system officer in his backseat, transmitted, "Tower, Eagle 11 is ready for takeoff."

The tower responded, "Eagle 11, once airborne, execute immediate left turn to a heading of two zero zero prior to the field boundary. You are cleared for takeoff."

"Eagle 11 copies immediate left turn to two zero zero. Cleared for takeoff."

Punk maneuvered the strike fighter into position on the fat white strips that marked the approach end of the runway. He advanced the throttles to military power and checked the gauges. Everything looked good.

"You ready to go, Torch?"

"Ready, Admiral."

Punk looked down his left wing line toward his house. It was close enough to the runway that he could see Suzanne standing in the front yard waving, their NAS North Island tradition when she knew he was flying. He waved back and then advanced the throttles to full afterburner.

The jet's acceleration felt normal and good. He watched the airspeed increase on the left side of the HUD, rotating at 145 knots. Once airborne he raised the gear handle. At 250 knots he banked hard left and put the Super Hornet into a three-G turn to a heading of 200 degrees as directed by the tower controller.

Torch switched the radio frequency and transmitted, "Departure Control, Eagle 11 is airborne."

"Eagle 11, Departure Control has your radar contact, climbing through five thousand feet heading southwest," the controller replied. "Climb and maintain flight level 250 and contact Los Angeles Center on frequency 275.5."

"Eagle 11 is climbing to flight level 250. Switching LA Center 275.5."

Torch dialed in the new frequency and transmitted, "LA Center, this is Eagle 11, heading 200 and climbing to flight level 250."

"Eagle 11, LA Center has you loud and clear. Continue climb to flight level 250. Cleared direct to Naval Air Station Lemoore."

"Eagle 11 copies, cleared direct Lemoore."

"Is Lemoore the first waypoint in the HUD?" Punk asked over the intercom.

"That's it, sir." Torch replied.

Punk pulled the throttles out of afterburner as he continued his climb while steering the Super Hornet to the right until the symbol was centered in his HUD. Northbound now. He looked over his right shoulder back toward the runway and the little white dot just west of it—his home, where Suzanne was.

Her brave face following the diagnosis was typical of how she'd approached whatever challenge life threw her way, and that tenaciousness and drive had always both inspired and frustrated Punk. Her strength had underwritten his success as a naval officer, but it had also caused her to push herself too hard. He was fairly sure that trait had contributed to her cancer, though he'd never say it out loud. As he'd done recently when she informed him that the cancer had returned but she didn't want him to clear his calendar as a result, he knew when to let Suzanne be Suzanne.

But he couldn't block out the worry. Just hearing doctors say the word "cancer" over the years had been knives jabbed into the gut each time. It was a mean disease, made more so by its unpredictability. He thought about how he was going to break the news to Jason once he landed at Lemoore and what his stepson's reaction might be.

The three hundred or so nautical miles between San Diego and Lemoore would take about a half hour at normal cruising speed—a relatively short flight—but Punk was happy for whatever time in the cockpit his other three-star responsibilities allowed him.

Punk had made it a point to stay qualified in the Super Hornet, feeling strongly that he might lose his credibility with the aviators he was responsible for had he done otherwise. Plus, it was a good reminder of why he'd stayed in the Navy all those years despite the sacrifices, hardships, and, most recently, politics inherent in his current position. He liked to remind himself that he was, above all else, a fighter pilot.

To keep Punk's flight hours up, the commander of Strike Fighter Wing Pacific, Captain Brian "Beezer" Bailey, would task one of his dozen or so Super Hornet squadrons to send a jet down to North Island, manned by a pilot who was willing to cool his or her heels in San Diego for several days while the vice admiral went back and forth and flew sorties in between. This time the pilot who handed him the Super Hornet, a lieutenant who'd just finished his first sea tour and was now assigned as an instructor, admitted that he'd volunteered to ferry the jet because his girlfriend lived on Coronado a few blocks outside the air station's main gate.

Jason had urged Punk to get a basic qual in the F-35C for months now, saying, "Dad, you won't believe how easy it is to fly." But ironically, the final push had unintentionally come from Congressman Seth Gordon and his insistence that *Ford* prove it could survive a hypersonic missile attack. The U.S. Air Force "enemy" forces were likely to employ F-35As as one of their delivery platforms, and that justified Punk's request up the chain of command through two four-stars to spend a few days at Lemoore doing simulators and a single familiarization flight in order to gain firsthand knowledge of the fifth-generation fighter, coincident with designing an aircraft carrier exercise defense strategy against it.

The four-stars had bought the logic, which Punk attributed mostly to the fact they were ship drivers and not aviators, and therefore didn't recognize a boondoggle when they were presented with one.

Beezer hadn't been as easy a sell, however. He'd come to his current job fresh from commanding a seagoing F-35C squadron, and while Punk technically outranked him, the "commodore," the informal designation for the wing commander, exercised dominion over the jets—both F-35s and Super Hornets—that he was responsible for. And in this case, that dominion manifested in skepticism that Punk's quickie F-35 fam syllabus was a good idea.

"How many days, Vice Admiral Reichert?" Beezer had asked over the phone when Punk had first touched base with him a few months earlier.

"We're thinking three," Punk had replied.

"You're going to complete ground school, the simulator syllabus, and do a fam flight all in three days?"

"I've already completed ground school," Punk had explained. "I did the computer-based training in the AIRPAC SCIF, so I know the cockpit layout and the basic procedures. I'll do a day's worth of sims, focusing on emergency procedures, then fly the hop the next day."

"Three days," Beezer had repeated.

"Look, I'm just doing the basics: start-up, taxi, takeoff, fly around straight and level, and land. That's it."

"*Three days* . . ."

"I hear the airplane's very easy to fly," Punk had offered.

"Not *that* easy."

Punk leveled the Super Hornet off at 25,000 feet and unhooked his oxygen mask on one side, letting it dangle. Above the marine layer visibility was unlimited, and he could see from Los Angeles down his right canopy rail all the way to the ranges of Edwards Air Force Base to the northeast.

"How's the mood in the ready room these days, Torch?" Punk asked over the ICS.

The question seemed to catch the lieutenant in the rear cockpit by surprise: "Mood, sir?" he answered cautiously.

"How's everybody feeling?"

Torch paused long enough for Punk to wonder whether he'd been unwise to introduce the topic. "Fine, I guess," the lieutenant answered.

Punk decided to change the subject: "Where did you serve your first tour?"

"Another West Coast Super Hornet squadron," he said. "I made the COVID cruise."

The COVID cruise. A bit of U.S. Navy historical infamy. Spurred on by the aircraft carrier's senior medical officer, the captain got caught up in the fear that swept the globe that the pandemic was going to kill everyone. He wanted to pull into the closest port, which happened to be Guam, immediately and stay there until things were figured out.

The carrier strike group commander on board didn't agree, and he insisted that the captain keep the ship at sea and carry out its duties as assigned. In response, the captain wrote an email directly to the Chief of Naval Operations that claimed the only reasonable course of action was to pull into Guam, claiming that the strike group commander was hazarding the health of the five thousand sailors on the ship by forcing them to stay at sea. The captain also leaked that email to select members of the press who covered the military beat.

A bunch of stories came out with a similar theme: Big Navy doesn't care about the young men and women hardworking parents across America have entrusted it with. Congress got involved, demanding that the CNO order the carrier to pull into Guam, which he did, much to the displeasure of the governor there, who said he lacked the resources to host the crew for an extended time and that their presence was a health risk to his citizens.

Then the Secretary of the Navy decided to take matters into his own hands. He flew to Guam, boarded the carrier, and, in so many words, told the crew that taking a principal warship offline jeopardized the defense of the nation. He finished his remarks by berating them for being soft. And before he left the ship, he relieved the commanding officer of his duties.

Those remarks were recorded by several thousand sailors with access to the Internet (for morale purposes) and posted along with videos from multiple points of view that showed the just-fired captain walking off the ship with his head held high surrounded by the crew cheering in support of him.

That fueled another wave of negative press intimating that SecNav's remarks and the crew's reaction to the firing of their beloved captain proved the Navy didn't care about those who'd volunteered to serve. In response to the public outcry, the President fired his Secretary of the Navy and demanded that the CNO do the same to the carrier strike group commander. The carrier sat in port for a month until the vaccine could be produced and administered to the entire crew (whether they wanted to be vaccinated or not, which became its own controversy within the multiple controversies already in play).

Punk figured that to a junior officer in the carrier air wing at the time it must have been like watching your parents fight. "I guess that was . . . interesting?" he asked.

"Interesting," Torch repeated with a laugh. "That's one way to put it. But once all of that blew over, I had a great tour. We flew our asses off and did a lot of real-world ops after we got back out to sea. I saw a bunch of Chinese fighters up close."

Punk thought about his own attitude toward bad leadership when he was at that point in his career, mostly in the form of his skipper, Soup Campbell, and wondered whether he'd been as resilient as Torch seemed to be. And that question brought to mind the constant criticism from the "gray beards," retired naval aviators with selective memories who wanted to know what he was doing about the current lack of warfighting focus in ready rooms.

Meet Torch, Grandpa, he thought. *And shut the fuck up and support him.*

At ten nautical miles from NAS Lemoore, Punk descended to 1,000 feet and accelerated to 350 knots as he lined up with Runway 32L. He brought the Super Hornet into the break, banking hard left at midfield and pulling six Gs until they were on the downwind leg and slow enough to drop the landing gear. He said the landing checklist aloud, Torch replying to each with a simple "roger," and flew a centered ball on the Fresnel lens left of the approach end of the runway all the way to touchdown, like any good carrier pilot would.

They exited the duty runway and taxied toward the control tower. Unlike NAS North Island, which was home to helicopter and utility plane squadrons, NAS Lemoore was a master jet base. Punk noted the lines of fighters in front of the hangars painted with giant emblems that had been a familiar part of his career since his first tour. But now the VF designation of F-14 fighter squadrons had been replaced by the VFA designation of F/A-18 and F-35 fighter/attack squadrons. The Tomcat was gone, relegated to an ornament in front of museums and American Legion halls or cut to bits in the desert for fear of parts being sold on the black market to Iran, now the sole operator of the aircraft (although there were doubts about how many they managed to keep airworthy).

In its place was the Super Hornet—serviceable, capable, efficient, but lacking the sex appeal of the F-14—and the F-35, which for all its fifth-generation gee-whizzery was just plain ugly. Other jets looked as if they were meant to pierce the sky; the F-35 looked like it had unceremoniously fallen from it. Some aviation aficionados— "fanbois," as they were known in squadron circles—had taken to calling the F-35 "Fat Amy," which didn't seem totally inappropriate to Punk.

But he wanted to fly it. He *had* to fly it.

Punk taxied the Super Hornet to the base of the control tower and found a two-person greeting committee waiting; one of them was his stepson, Jason. Once the ground crew signaled that the wheel chocks were in place, he shut the jet down. Torch opened the canopy, and they unstrapped and climbed out.

Captain Steven "Squealer" Simpson, the air station's commanding officer, was the first to walk up and shake his hand, saying, "Welcome to NAS Lemoore, Admiral."

"Thanks, Squealer," Punk replied, reminded that Squealer's call sign was a reference to the pig's snout–like shape of his nose and the fact that he was always fighting to remain within weight standards, a battle he appeared to be currently losing. "It's great to be back."

"Good flight up?"

Punk patted Torch on the back and said, "He took good care of me."

Torch used the compliment as an opportunity to take his leave, saying, "Enjoyed it, sir. I need to get back to the squadron. I have another flight this afternoon."

"Okay, Torch," Punk said. "Are you flying back with me Wednesday afternoon?"

"I don't think so," the young WSO replied with a grin. "We like to spread the good deals around."

Punk smiled in return and said, "Thanks for babysitting me."

Jason moved around the base CO and gave Punk a perfunctory hug (self-conscious that his stepdad was his boss several ranks removed, as was everyone else around him) and said, "We need to get going. We're already late for your helmet fitting."

"What flight gear should I bring with me?" Punk asked.

"None of it. Leave everything here."

Punk shrugged and hung his harness, G suit, and helmet on the Super Hornet's boarding ladder. Squealer escorted them through the base operations building to the VIP spot where Jason's Dodge Challenger was parked. As Punk maneuvered himself into the passenger side he quipped that the car was harder to man up than a Super Hornet, and Squealer gave a hearty laugh that was more than the comment deserved.

"Your mother wants to know if you're still with that girl you were with," Punk said as Jason exited the parking lot and steered the Challenger onto the air station's main drag.

"Nope," Jason replied matter-of-factly. "I don't have the bandwidth for high maintenance these days."

Punk chuckled, reminded once again of how much Jason was like his father, Lieutenant Cal "Crud" Worthington. At times, being around his stepson made him think his former fellow instructor at the F-14 training squadron was still alive. Jason had his mom's eyes, but he was all Crud in his athletic good looks and adventurous outlook, including his love of muscle cars.

"I imagine Bakersfield isn't exactly a hotbed of eligible bachelorettes," Punk said.

"Kind of sad that's what passes as the big city around here," Jason replied. "NAS Lemoore is great for flight ops, but it sucks for having a personal life."

"Don't rush it," Punk advised. "But also hurry up. Your mom wants grandkids before too long."

The comment garnered a quick glance from Jason, who sensed an undercurrent. Not yet ready to tell his stepson Suzanne's news, Punk changed the subject: "Remind me what our schedule is?"

"We're headed to the helmet-fitting facility, which is just outside Gate One," Jason said. "That'll take an hour or so. Then we have an office call with Captain Bailey."

"Beezer wants to tell me again that he thinks this is a bad idea," Punk said wryly.

"And he really does."

"That's fine. It's his job, I guess. But it's also his job to do what I say."

"He's a good guy, Dad."

"Did I say he wasn't?"

"Just watch going all three-star on him."

"Hey, man, you're the one who invited me to do this."

"I'm just asking you to be mindful of the fact that when you leave and go back to San Diego, I still have to work with these people, and some of them have my Navy career in their hands."

"Tough gig being a Reichert these days."

Jason smiled and said, "Actually, it's not because you're not generally thought of as a good guy."

"Well, that's nice to hear," Punk replied sardonically. "Better than being thought of as an asshole, I guess."

"Just don't start being one on this trip . . . please, sir."

"Okay, okay. So, what's the rest of the schedule after we meet with Beezer?"

"That's it for today. I got us a reservation at a new Mexican place for dinner. Tomorrow we have simulators all day, and then the day after that we have your Fam 1 flight with me on your wing."

"Quick and dirty."

"Hopefully not too dirty."

"Right, just appropriately dirty."

Jason turned the radio volume down and said, "Seriously, I saw highlights of your C-SPAN appearance on social media, but what's this exercise really all about?"

"Proving that a *Ford*-class carrier can defend itself against a hypersonic missile," Punk said.

"And if you don't?"

"You might be landing on something besides an aircraft carrier in the future."

Punk sat in a chair looking straight ahead while the technician, an Israeli national named Yosef who was employed by Ephron Industries, the company that designed and built the F-35's unique helmet, used calipers to measure the dimensions of his face: bridge of nose to chin, width of jaw from earlobe to earlobe, and middle of one eye socket to the other. Then he mapped Punk's skull with a laser device, a process that took nearly forty-five minutes to complete and reminded Punk of a trip to the dentist without the physical pain.

"So, we're not building a helmet for the admiral, right?" Yosef asked Jason.

"No, he's going to borrow one from whoever at the squadron has the closest fit to what his would be if we *did* make him one."

Yosef knitted his brows and said, "The helmet-mounted display demands very precise measurements."

"He's not doing any weapons delivery or stuff like that. Just one flight with basic maneuvers."

"Still... what if he has to eject? If the helmet doesn't fit correctly, it could come off."

"Yosef, I understand what you're saying, and we're not intending to be reckless," Jason said. "Just let me know who the closest fit is in the database. We don't have a lot of time here."

The Israeli reluctantly walked over to his computer and after a minute or so of staring at the screen announced, "It's Lieutenant Coleman."

Jason immediately pulled out his phone and punched in a number. When the Staff Duty Officer at the F-35 training squadron answered, he said, "Stoney, it's Crutch. Is Beef around?"

"He's standing right in front of me, as a matter of fact."

"Put him on, please."

Another voice came on the line: "Lieutenant Coleman. May I help you, sir?"

"Beef? Crutch here. I'm over at the helmet-fitting facility, and I need to know if you're ready to do your part to help save the future of carrier aviation."

"What?"

"I'm asking the questions here," Jason said jokingly. "Are you ready to do your part to help save the future of carrier aviation?"

"Um, sure, I guess."

"Great, bring your helmet, mask, and G suit to Captain Bailey's office in the next ten minutes. Turns out that your dimensions match Vice Admiral Reichert's, and he needs to borrow your flight gear for the next couple of days. Thanks, bud. Totally owe you a beer for this." He hung up before the other lieutenant could say anything else.

Beezer Bailey leaned back in his executive chair behind his big wooden desk in his office that overlooked the runways of Naval Air Station Lemoore. On the desk were Beef Coleman's helmet, mask, and G suit.

"I know your invitation to fly came from young Lieutenant Reichert, Admiral," he said. "But while all of us share his excitement that you've taken him up on the offer, and we're ready to fully support your brief training syllabus, we naturally have a few concerns."

"Thank you, Captain," Punk said. "I appreciate the efforts of all hands here to get me smart on the F-35."

"You remember how much this helmet costs, right, Admiral?" Beezer asked, only half kidding.

"Five hundred thousand dollars," Punk returned in the same tone. "You remember that I bottom-line the requisition orders, right, Captain?"

Beezer tilted upright again and put his elbows on his desk. "The normal F-35C syllabus for a newly winged trainee is four months of ground school and simulators before the first fam flight."

What happened to fully supporting my brief flight syllabus? Punk thought before saying, "I'm not an ensign who just pinned on his wings and drove here from Kingsville, Texas. I have four thousand flight hours, significant combat time, and over a thousand carrier landings. And, again, my mini-syllabus has been approved through Fleet Forces Command and the Chief of Naval Operations."

"Remind me how many combined flight hours they have, sir?" Beezer asked with raised eyebrows. His posture softened. "I understand this was approved under the auspices of you gaining a better understanding of how fifth-generation fighters perform. What can you tell me about this exercise you're prepping for?"

Punk took the helmet off the desk and studied it. "I'll give you the unclassified version," he said. "The attack could come in the form of a hypersonic missile launched from a stealth aircraft, a shore station, or both at the same time. We haven't come up with our defense strategy yet. I'm sure what I learn here will get fed into it."

"Thanks for that explanation, Admiral," Beezer said. "And, again, Strike Fighter Wing Pacific is ready to support your flight. But be advised that if you wreck one of my jets, I'm going to tell the mishap investigation team that I thought it was a bad idea."

Punk laughed as he stood and extended a hand across the desk toward the captain.

"Fair enough," he said.

CHAPTER **13**

EINSTEIN STEERED his car off Route 395 and onto the road leading to Naval Air Weapons Center–Weapons Division at China Lake, or as the people who worked there called it, "The Lake." NAWC-WD was one of the subordinate commands to NAVAIR, and the commanding officer, a one-star, reported directly to him.

He took bored notice of the flat, arid Mojave shrubland flanking the road. He was solo for this trip, having left his aide back in Patuxent River, Maryland, and he was enjoying the solitude. Plus, this trip was designed to make Shane Peterson feel like he had direct access to the top of the team they were forming, so the fewer people around the better.

The area had received its name from the Chinese prospectors who gathered borax from the dry lakebed long ago. "Lake" was thus a misnomer; much like Shane Peterson, it was a bit of a contradiction. As Senior Director of Test Programs at NAWC-WD, Peterson was neither senior to his colleagues in age or tenure, nor did he delegate like a typical director.

Others who worked with Peterson had told Einstein that Peterson was known for turning ideas into reality. NAWC-WD was merely the enabler, and its projects the medium, to his alleged genius. The Navy had seen fit to put the man's talents to use at a location that was rich with historic research. China Lake was the testing ground for the AIM-9 Sidewinder, the world's most-used (and copied) air-to-air missile; the Tomahawk cruise missile, made famous during the Gulf War; and JDAM, or Joint Direct Attack Munition, a kit that turned unguided bombs into precision ones.

After reading Peterson's file, Einstein knew that the young director's history was also tied to tradition: Peterson's father had flown sorties over Iraq during Operation Enduring Freedom, and word had it that the son carried the elder Peterson's Top Gun patch for motivation and good luck. Unfortunately, right before Peterson's graduation from Penn State and entry into flight school his father had died from cancer.

Despite his legacy, Peterson had washed out of flight school. There was no such thing as guaranteed in a world that required more than just book learning. Sitting in a classroom was one thing. Strapping into an airplane and pulling Gs was another. Flying required fast thinking and fast reflexes in a dynamic environment, and for all his brains, he'd lacked those things.

So he'd elected to serve naval aviation in a different capacity. He resigned his commission and accepted a position at NAWC-WD. Einstein had to respect that. A lot of the talent around the various NAVAIR organizations, both civil servants and contractors, had similar stories, and their rechanneled motivation benefitted the aircraft programs they were involved with.

Just over a mile inside the main gate, Rear Admiral Tim "Timbo" Timberlane, the NAWC-WD commander, stood waiting curbside at the main entrance to the headquarters building. Timbo had been one of Einstein's Naval Test Pilot School classmates. His call sign, Timbo, was a reflection of his nondescript appearance that would've made him challenging to pick out in a police lineup of average middle-aged white men. His similar personality proved better suited to the environs of aircraft test and evaluation than a fighter squadron ready room either ashore or at sea.

"Welcome back to China Lake, sir," Timbo said as they shook hands. "I know you're short of time, so I'll let you get right to it." Matter of fact as always. Good.

Inside the expansive atrium adorned overhead with a silver rocket from the center's early Cold War days, the two admirals were met by a thin young man with a waxy complexion that appeared untouched by the outdoors, never mind the sun.

"Shane Peterson," he said as they shook. His hands were borderline creepy in their softness, and Einstein couldn't help but notice that he had his phone attached to his belt like a first-generation digital geek. In his other hand he held a large electronic tablet at which he kept shooting glances as if he was expecting an incoming message that could cure world hunger or solve the Kennedy assassination. His black hair was in a Marine Corps cut—buzzed on the sides and neatly parted at the top right side.

"Admiral Francis, I'll circle back with you before you leave," Timbo said to Einstein before turning on his heel and heading for the large circular staircase that led to his office. The building was an architectural marvel by U.S. Navy facility standards, all glass and steel, and Einstein wondered how many deals between government agencies, local lawmakers, and building contractors had been required to make it happen.

"Nice to meet you in person, Shane," Einstein said, returning his focus to the young man standing solemnly in front of him. "Did you read those SIPRnet emails I sent you?"

"Twice," Peterson said as he directed Einstein down a corridor and into one of a handful of SCIFs placed throughout the building. He closed the thick door behind them and flicked a switch on the wall. Music designed to foil listening devices began to play quietly in the background. "What you're asking for is totally feasible, but some of the DEW's power systems will need to be tweaked. It utilizes a fiber optic cable array to power its beam, similar to the LaWS."

"Setting up fiber optics on *Ford* shouldn't be an issue," Einstein said, taking a seat at the head of the table. He looked at the screen angled into the table's surface, impressed that Peterson had already staged the Passkey brief. "And you think that *Ford*'s reactors have the excess power to handle that?"

"I'm sure they do," Peterson said.

"What energy range are we referring to here?" Einstein asked. "The LaWS can manage bursts at 10 to 20 kilowatts. That won't be enough for a hypersonic. We need something more powerful that won't interrupt any of *Ford*'s other systems."

"I've considered that as well," Peterson said. "Most DEW research has sought a 100-kilowatt sweet spot. I've tested a range of energy outputs over the past two months, so we should be fine there."

Einstein cut right to the chase: "So, can you deliver a 100-kilowatt directed-energy weapon? A functional field model, not simply a BS test version to ensure the R&D dollars keep flowing. And we need it soon."

"Yes," Peterson said simply.

Had it been anyone else, Einstein might have considered that answer mere boasting, but Peterson's reputation gave him the confidence he absolutely needed at this point. He couldn't wait to tell Punk it wasn't just hype. They'd found their man.

"Good," Einstein said. "By the way, I read your white paper about how they could tweak the Sidewinder program further, and how you improved the integration of the SLAM-ER's flight guidance system on the Super Hornet. How'd you avoid being poached by the big defense companies?"

"There's more to life than money," Peterson said. "Believe me, Admiral, NAWC-WD is where I want to be." Einstein nodded approvingly, believing the sentiment and thinking the young engineer's late father would have been proud of him for it.

"So, we have the power for the DEW," Einstein said. "That's big, but let's review how we're going to use it for this test."

"Of course," Peterson said, switching to the next slide from his place at the top right corner of the table. "I've collected a breakdown of the defenses available to *Ford* and analyzed how effective they might be for the test."

This slide showed a breakdown of the USS *Gerald Ford*'s defense systems: Mk-29 and Mk-49 guided missile launching systems, RIM-162 Seasparrow missiles, RIM-116 Rolling Airframe missiles, a Phalanx CIWS, Mk-38 25-mm machine guns, and M2 .50-caliber machine guns. Yet each of those was a weapon of last resort: under normal circumstances an aircraft carrier depended on its aircraft, and its escort ships, to protect it.

Peterson enumerated each system and its assets in a monotone, disdain for the outmoded technology on full display. Einstein knew none of them would spare the carrier from what Dr. Wu might come up with, assuming he was the guy leading the Air Force side of the test. As he surely would be. The U.S. Air Force Weapons Center didn't do anything of consequence without him.

"Unless I missed something, none of those will knock down a hypersonic missile," Einstein said. "They were built to deal with subsonic or barely supersonic threats and small craft that might close on warships. Or a drone."

"I only show these for comparison," Peterson said. "None of these weapons will prove useful against the Air Force and the missiles they'll likely use. In fact, I won't mention them again." He clicked to the next slide. "Look at these hypersonics in development by potential adversaries. It's quite a formidable rogue's gallery."

A chill iced down Einstein's spine as he scanned the infographic, mockups of a variety of hypersonic missiles, each of which could pierce *Ford*'s hull and deliver a devastating payload. Some were established models grounded in intelligence gathered by operatives; others were based more on conjecture than fact. All would be deadly to a supercarrier dependent on the older defenses.

The list included several Chinese hypersonics: the DF-17 ballistic missile, the DF-ZF hypersonic glide vehicle, and the Starry Sky-2. There was also the Russian Kinzhal and Zircon. Most of the missiles could reach anywhere from Mach 5 to Mach 10, with ranges measured in hundreds, if not thousands, of miles.

"If you're trying to convince me that we're unprepared, I'm already there," Einstein said.

"Just providing a scene-setter, Admiral," Peterson said.

"Fair enough," Einstein said. "What do we think Dr. Wu is going to use against us here?"

Peterson's brow furrowed. "Who's that?"

"He's a James Bond villain," Einstein joked. The jest apparently went over Peterson's head. He'd never heard of James Bond? The generation gap was real and alive at the Lake. "He's the main guy on the Air Force test side. I'm guessing you've never done any work with the Air Force."

Peterson shrugged. "I'm a homer, as we say. Straight Navy experience."

"Well, stand by to have your horizon expanded."

"I'm ready," Peterson said confidently, clicking to the next slide. "My guess is this Dr. Wu will go for broke since there are so many eyes on Passkey back in D.C. Those guys are going to unleash something that travels at least Mach 7 or 8, likely coupled with machine learning algorithms. Anything less would be an insult to us."

"I'm not worrying about being insulted," Einstein said, measuring the other's arrogance, something they didn't need until it was all said and done, if ever. "I'm worried about our boat getting hit."

Peterson smirked. "Admiral, this is the challenge we've been waiting for. Wu will have to use the same concepts, and the same tools, that the enemy engineer would. I'm already one step ahead of him."

He brought up the next slide. "This schematic is the latest we have on the new anti-hypersonic missile," Peterson said. "This projectile can achieve speeds of up to Mach 7.5, and it can track and intercept anything flying less than Mach 7.2."

"Is this feasible?" Einstein asked. "I thought we were focusing on a directed-energy weapon here."

"We have reports from the Ukrainian military that they successfully intercepted several of Russia's hypersonic missiles with the Patriots DoD sent them," Peterson said. "Bear in mind, the MIM-104 Patriot system is decades old, which is more evidence of how far behind the Russians have fallen."

Einstein grunted and said, "Probably best not to get too comfortable in what you see as American military superiority. We need to stay a couple of steps ahead of potential threats, and right now we're a step behind."

"I don't disagree, Admiral," Peterson said. "The Chinese have no doubt been watching, and learning. They will develop one that can fly faster and possibly jam anything that tries to intercept it. We'll have to make allowances for that. This prototype that Wu will use will do just that."

"Okay, but what about the DEWs?" Einstein asked.

"We've been testing THOR/Mjolnir to disrupt drone swarms, but that won't help us here," Peterson said. "The principles behind it might, however. We've got the Vigilant Eagle still on the table, but research seems to have stalled. Research into particle beam weapons is still building on the BEAR project from way back in 1989, but maintaining a power output capable of producing a gigajoule of kinetic energy remains elusive."

"We need kilowatts, not gigajoules," Einstein said with a frown.

"I've tweaked a version of the EL/M-2080 Green Pine, one that uses what we call 'effective radiated power' to bring down a hostile projectile. Pulses of radar energy can short-circuit the electronics that allow a hypersonic to track its target. But that's not all."

Peterson clicked to the next slide, then got up from the table and walked over to a dry-erase board mounted on the wall behind him. He grabbed a marker and wrote an acronym in big, black letters, saying, "My team here at the Lake has also created a laser-based DEW that we've dubbed LASIPOD."

He pointed back toward the screen in the table where he'd been seated. "What you see there is built using the base of the old Phalanx close-in weapons system. The Laser Intercept Point Defense concept takes the best of every DEW system we've been working on at the Lake for the last twenty years. It uses a fiber optic energy feed, a lot like what LaWS had, but in a more effective configuration."

Einstein studied the schematic on the slide, then asked, "So, this weapon can take down a missile that's coming at *Ford* at Mach 9?"

"Possibly Mach 10, if it's coupled with robust sensory systems," Peterson said, drawing a circle around the acronym he'd just written on the whiteboard.

"A system like Project OpenShip?" Einstein asked.

Peterson gave him a respectful nod. "I see you've done your homework, sir. If the algorithm they're developing is ready, then yes, that would be the icing on the cake. Coupled with a system like that, LASIPOD would be just what the doctor ordered."

"My doctor has told me to eat less cake because of my blood pressure," Einstein deadpanned in response to the engineer's two metaphors in consecutive sentences.

"This is the answer to our problem," Peterson continued forcefully, either ignoring or ignorant of Einstein's jab. "We have tested it thoroughly."

Einstein shifted in his seat. "What is its effective range?"

"Two hundred miles," Peterson said. "But I could push it to a thousand with a robust fiber optic array and a generous amount of *Ford*'s excess reactor power output."

Einstein sat in silent contemplation while Peterson stood at the board, ready to give him all the time he needed to accept the information he'd just been presented with. After a minute or so, the aging former RIO put his elbow on the table and cradled his chin while tapping on the computer screen with the index finger of his other hand.

"This can save an aircraft carrier, huh?" Einstein asked.

"It *will* save an aircraft carrier," Peterson answered without hesitation.

―――

An hour later, Einstein stood on the Lake's exterior testing grounds watching LASIPOD swiveling about on a Phalanx mount two hundred feet away. Peterson stood nearby, operating the system with a handheld remote, looking like a hobbyist trying out his newest RC car. The desert sun shone on them with a vengeance. Sweat trickled down Einstein's face and the back of his neck, and he squinted despite his aviator shades. It reminded him of Iraq, back when he'd gotten shot down with Soup Campbell. He'd hated the desert ever since; even now it set him on edge.

"If you'll look to your right, northeastward, you'll see the target that the LASIPOD will be protecting," Peterson said. He was finally showing some indications of excitement.

Einstein raised his binoculars to his eyes and focused across the dry shrubland. Half a mile away, a rusted old pickup truck awaited its fate.

"How far away is the launch site?" Einstein asked.

"We're launching a prototype hypersonic from fifteen miles away, to the southeast," Peterson said. "There's no point in looking for it with those binocs, Admiral. It'll be speeding along at Mach 5."

Mach 5, one mile every second.

"I'll focus on the truck, then," Einstein said. Despite his discomfort, Peterson's enthusiasm was infectious.

"Whenever you're ready, Admiral," Peterson said.

Einstein nodded. "You may fire when ready, Gridley."

"Gridley?"

Another witticism missed. "Dewey at Manila Bay?" Einstein hinted. "Weren't you Naval ROTC at Penn State?"

"Yes."

"Surprised you didn't get the reference. It's kind of a famous quote."

When Peterson simply stared at him with obvious disinterest in the history lesson, or whatever game the admiral was playing, Einstein said, "Fine, go ahead and launch the missile."

Peterson keyed in a few commands to the LASIPOD, radioed the launcher's crew, and adjusted his sunglasses with the cool of a bon vivant who'd just ordered the most expensive wine in a fine restaurant. Einstein thought the cocky nerd routine might irritate Punk and the rest of the team, but it could be overlooked with good results.

"Test Bravo, this is Alpha," Peterson said over his radio. "You're clear for op away."

"Roger that," a voice on the radio answered.

Peterson counted the seconds: "One. Three. Five."

Before he could count to six, LASIPOD swiveled again and thrummed. A ripple tore the air behind them, invisible but tangible. The thrum reached a shuddering crescendo, and then a muffled pop reverberated from the southeast.

LASIPOD fell silent.

Einstein blinked and put the binoculars to his eyes. The truck was still there, completely untouched.

Peterson keyed his radio: "Bravo, this is Alpha. Good intercept; repeat, good intercept. Target intact."

Einstein kept the binoculars trained on the truck, then moved his focus along the horizon in the direction where the hypersonic had originated. A puff marking the impact point was already dissipating, roughly a hundred feet off the desert floor. A thin contrail leading to that was the only other evidence that the hypersonic missile had even existed.

"I'll be damned," Einstein muttered before dropping the binoculars and looking over to Peterson. "Pardon my French, Shane, but you are the fucking man."

Peterson allowed himself a grin and bowed with his palms pressed together in front of his face like a Buddhist monk. "Ready to head back inside?" he asked. "Admiral Timberlane is waiting for us with coffee and cake."

Einstein followed Peterson across the field back to their jeep. The demonstration had happened so fast that it took him a few minutes to realize they had cause to celebrate.

CHAPTER **14**

JASON SWALLOWED another big bite of his burrito and asked, "How are the fajitas?"

"Really good," Punk said, as he loaded another flour tortilla with strips of marinated steak and piled on half a dozen toppings. "I judge my Mexican restaurants by their fajitas."

"I judge mine by their margaritas," Jason said. "And it's inconclusive so far." He raised his glass toward their server, "Can I get another one of these?"

Jason hadn't asked yet about Suzanne, and Punk was hesitant to wreck the mood. But he had no choice. His wife was trusting him to deliver the news to her only son—the young man Punk had accepted as his own years ago—in the right manner.

Jason had lived under the specter of loss for his entire life. Punk had done his best to raise him as his father would have, but there had always been an asterisk on their situation denoting the tragic death of Crud Worthington. For a moment Punk flashed back to the day when he'd gone to see Suzanne soon after the crash that took her husband. Little Jason had greeted him on the front lawn, saying, "My daddy's in heaven. I won't see him until I die."

"I need to tell you something," Punk said now as he put his fork down. He took a deep breath and stared at his plate for a few beats before looking back up at Jason. "Mom's cancer is back."

Jason dropped his burrito. "What? But it was gone. They said it was gone."

"She found out after her last checkup at Balboa with Dr. Billings." The inside of Punk's mouth was suddenly a desert. He took a sip of water. "It came back," he said simply. "Five years, and then it came back."

"Is she going to have to do chemo again?" Jason asked.

"We don't know yet. Probably. She has a follow-up this week."

"Is Dr. Billings the same guy who treated her last time?"

"Yes. She likes him, and I trust him."

"She'll pull through, Dad. She's strong, the strongest person I know."

"She is," Punk agreed, the weight of the pending reveal now lifted. "And we've got to be strong for her, like we were before. Like you have been your whole life."

"Should I call her?"

Punk checked his watch and said, "She's probably already asleep."

"I'll call her in the morning, then."

"And you know not to overdo it. I made the mistake of saying I wanted to clear my calendar when she told me it was back."

"I can imagine what her reaction was," Jason said with a chuckle.

"That's why I'm out here," Punk said with a chuckle of his own.

A silence settled between them. Suzanne was the family's rock, perhaps to the detriment of her health, and they owed her unconditional support. Life without her was not something either of them wanted to contemplate.

"She's the strongest person I know," Jason repeated, this time more to himself than to his stepfather.

The second margarita arrived, and the younger pilot polished it off in short order.

"What time do our simulator sessions start tomorrow?" Punk asked.

Jason read the question as a comment on how quickly he'd downed the drink. "It's a simulator, not a real flight," he said. "Besides, you're the one in the hot seat. I'm just going to be standing there hoping you don't embarrass me."

"In that case, *I'd* better order another one," Punk said.

They drank the second round while watching highlights from the previous day's NFL games on the widescreen TV mounted over the bar across from their booth.

Punk's mind wandered across the various challenges he was facing, and at the first commercial break asked, "Didn't your last squadron have a domestic abuse issue with one of the lieutenants?"

Jason furrowed his brow and said, "That's a random remark."

"Let's just say I have reason to ask."

"Somebody on your staff is beating his wife?"

Punk dodged the question, instead saying, "Remind me what happened in the case in your squadron."

"This guy, Lieutenant Larry Lorenzo, brand new to the squadron, hadn't even been there long enough to get a call sign. Base cops were called to their house a few times by the neighbors who heard the fighting. Wife showed up in public with bruises on her arms. One time she had a black eye."

"So, what happened?"

"The skipper wanted to give his new pilot the benefit of the doubt, but once his own wife told him about the black eye and how the spouse group was all fired up about it, he jumped in with both feet and grounded him. Told him his career was over even before it started."

"What did Lorenzo do?"

"He lawyered up, which surprised everybody. He was a lowlife, but he had balls. Suddenly the skipper was on defense. Hell, we all were. His lawyer demanded that every married officer in the squadron sign affidavits that we'd never *argued with* our wives—never mind hit them. The JAG Corps and NCIS were all over us."

"I remember some of this now. But how did it play out?"

"There was an investigation that proved nothing, mostly because Mrs. Lorenzo went mum and wouldn't testify against him. She was seldom seen in public after that. The skipper was accused of ruining the new lieutenant's reputation by taking action based on a spouse club rumor and nothing more. Lieutenant Lorenzo was reassigned to another squadron. Ultimately, he dropped his resignation letter. I hear he's an airline pilot now."

"What about your skipper?"

"Well, let's just say he didn't make captain. Ironically, he's an airline pilot now too."

"Different airline, I hope."

Jason laughed and said, "Yeah, wouldn't that be fucked up if they got crewed together?" He mimed talking into an intercom: "Ladies and gentlemen, this is your pilot speaking. I'm about to beat the shit out of my copilot."

Even as Punk laughed, his mind went to Gwen Davis in front of the Navy Exchange and how he planned to deal with his aide. The right course of action existed somewhere between protecting a battered spouse and avoiding a forced career transition to the airlines.

Punk and Jason were greeted inside the front door of the simulator building by half a dozen aviators in flight suits and one civilian in a golf shirt and khakis—which was a half dozen more aviators than a normal simulator session required. Punk figured Beezer had sent his agents to monitor the conduct of the session, again with an eye on distancing himself from the fallout in the event the flight went poorly.

"The gang's all here," Punk quipped to the serious countenances that faced him like a receiving line at a funeral. He shook their hands and noted their ranks: all lieutenant commanders, relatively senior for the circumstances.

At the end of the line was the civilian, whom he already knew. "Great to see you again, Mongo."

"Same here, Admiral," Mongo replied.

Matt "Mongo" Merchado had been the last F-14 Tomcat pilot to go through the Top Gun course. As he was making the transition to the Super Hornet he was diagnosed with a rare blood disease that forced him to take medical retirement from the Navy. For the last couple of decades he'd worked for a laundry list of companies who'd won contracts to run the simulators. The only thing that changed over that time was the logo on his golf shirt, his weight, and the amount of hair on his head.

"My medicine makes me fat," Mongo explained, patting his ample belly. "The bald part is heredity."

"Hey, you look great, shipmate," Punk replied with a smile. "So, what do we have going on here?"

"Right this way, sir, and you'll see."

Mongo led the group into the adjacent room, which was brightly lit and reminded Punk of the clean rooms where astronauts suited up before walking to the launch pad. Beef's helmet, mask, and G-suit were sitting on a table. Amid a sea of expectant stares, Punk took the hint and put on the gear.

The simulator room was dark and at least 10 degrees cooler than the rest of the building. A steady din of fans cooling the electronics filled the air. Mongo gestured for Punk to climb into the cockpit, and he did.

"I know you've done ground school," Mongo said, leaning over the canopy rail. "But let me point out a few things now that you're sitting in the cockpit. First, unlike any fighter you've flown in the fleet to date, the F-35's harness isn't something you wear from the ready room to the airplane. It's already in the airplane."

The civilian technician assisted Punk as he fumbled for the fittings around him, explaining, "You have six connection points to the ejection seat, but unlike the Tomcat or the Super Hornet, all you have to do is zip up the harness and then tighten it down. It's much easier."

Mongo pointed to the various displays and controls about the cockpit. "There's not much to see until you power up the jet, but let's work our way around here," he said. "Left side console you got your oxygen switch. Your canopy handle is right here under the rail. You got your throttle there. Gear handle right over there. The tailhook handle isn't a handle, it's a button, there. I know you're not bagging an arrested landing on the boat while you're here, but just remember that the door to the tailhook is limited to 250 knots, so unlike any other jet in the fleet, you can't drop the hook until you're slowed down on downwind."

"Yeah, that would be a hard habit pattern to break," Punk said. "I'm used to dropping the hook as soon as I get to low holding overhead the boat. Not having the hook down in the break at the boat seems like sacrilege."

"I know," Mongo agreed before continuing with the cockpit tour. "Across the front is your flat panel digital display, like a big iPad or the dashboard of a Tesla. Just like the Super Hornet you have a single ejection handle between your legs. You arm the seat with this lever next to your right thigh, here. And the last thing to note at this point is the stick. Have you ever flown with a side stick before?"

"Yeah, I have some time in the F-16N," Punk replied.

"Okay, that's good. The F-35 stick has a bit more play than the Viper's does, so we'll make sure you get used to that here." Mongo patted Punk on the right shoulder. "I'm going to go to the console now, and we'll get the jet powered up, okay?"

Punk watched Mongo take his seat in front of a bank of screens. Past him was Jason, who gave him a thumbs-up, and the squad of serious lieutenant commanders who stood with their arms crossed.

A few seconds later the cockpit came to life along with the helmet. "Can you hear me, Admiral?" Mongo said over the simulated UHF frequency.

Punk switched the oxygen on, strapped his mask to the other side of the helmet, and replied, "Got you loud and clear."

"Okay, your display panel is coming to life," Mongo said. "You'll see the various self-tests going on. You basically don't have to do anything at this point. Once you get everything in the green, you're ready for engine start."

"Showing all green," Punk said.

"Go ahead and start the jet, then."

Punk did as Mongo ordered, noting how much easier the process was than starting a Tomcat, which required an air source to get the engine turning in addition to electrical power. It was like the difference between pushing a button to start the family car and having to insert and turn a key.

Punk watched the engine data on the left side of the flat panel display reach the idle reading for RPM and temperature. Suddenly he heard an aural tone in his earcups and saw a "fire warning" light on his display.

"We've got an engine fire," Punk said, immediately executing the appropriate emergency procedures. "Throttle off, fire extinguisher, depress."

"Good work, sir," Mongo said. "The Air Force lost an F-35A a few years ago because of an engine fire at start-up. Turns out they had a tailwind that caused back pressure in the aft section of the engine that lit off one of the components. The pilot egressed but got slightly burned on the way out of the airplane."

"Is the tailwind thing still an issue?" Punk asked.

"No, they fixed that."

"What about the pilot?"

"I believe he recovered and was back on a flying status a few weeks later. Scary situation all the same."

"Yeah, it's a long way to the ground without a boarding ladder."

"It is," Mongo agreed with a polite chuckle. "Okay, I'll get you going again."

The displays indicated the airplane was at normal idle power again. No engine fire this time.

"This is the first time you've actually had the helmet powered up, so let me point out a few of the things that'll be new to you," Mongo said. "You're current in the Super Hornet, right?"

"Yep, flew an F up here, in fact."

"Did you have a Joint Helmet Mounted Cueing System helmet?"

"Yes."

"Good. So, this helmet is just like that except that, unlike the Super Hornet, there's no physical heads-up display in the F-35. It's virtual in your visor. That's your primary attitude indicator."

"Copy."

"Go ahead and move your head from the left wing to the right. You'll see the HUD only shows up when you're looking forward, the same field of view as the other HUD-equipped airplanes you've flown, only it's just in your visor, not mounted to the glare shield in front of you."

"Very cool," Punk said as he scanned 90 degrees left and right a few times.

"Okay, let me get you set up on the runway," Mongo said. The view suddenly changed from in front of the hangar to the approach end of Runway 32 left, the same one he'd landed the Super Hornet on the day before. "The other thing you're going to have to remember with your fam flight is you're going to have to do the radio comms. When's the last time you flew without a RIO or WSO?"

"It's been a while," Punk admitted.

"Go ahead and call for takeoff," Mongo said.

Punk had to think about what to say, and in that moment he missed having a Spud or an Einstein or a Torch in his backseat. "What's my call sign?" he asked.

"Um, let's use Puncher 101."

"Tower, Puncher 101, ready for takeoff."

"Puncher 101, this is tower, winds are 310 at ten knots, contact departure control once airborne. You are cleared for takeoff."

"Puncher 101 is cleared for takeoff." Punk hesitated and then asked, "Do you want me to take off?"

"Yeah, go ahead and take off."

"Burner launch or mil power?"

"Go ahead and use full afterburner."

Punk pushed the throttle forward, a linear motion instead of the slight arc of the other throttles he'd manipulated, until he felt the resistance that indicated he was going from basic engine to afterburner. He pushed through that resistance until the throttle was at the forward limit.

"Off the brakes," Punk recited. "One hundred knots . . . one fifty . . . rotating. Airborne, gear's coming up." He raised the gear handle with his left hand and focused on the digital display to make sure they translated fully up and locked. "Out of burner."

"Tomorrow they'll load what we call a 'brick' into the airplane with your entire route of flight already there for you. All you have to do is fly to the waypoints in order."

"Like a donkey following a carrot," Punk said.

"A very high-ranking donkey," Mongo said. "Now, stay at military power and accelerate to three hundred knots, and as you do, start to get comfortable with the symbology in your visor. I'll give you some stuff to look at besides your airspeed, altitude, and attitude."

Punk saw other symbols appear in his visor as he craned his head around. "What about the feature where I can look through the jet?" he asked.

"The Distributed Aperture System," Mongo replied. "Here you go."

Suddenly Punk could see not only the sky above him but also the ground below him, *right through the fuselage*. "This is incredible."

"I hear it's even better in the real airplane," Mongo said. "Okay, I want you to get a feel for the controls, so go ahead and maneuver the airplane."

Punk carefully moved the sidestick to its left limit, back to center, and then to the right limit, getting a feel for the F-35's roll response. Once he had it, he rolled left more aggressively until the jet was in a 90-degree bank, and then he pulled the stick aft. Along the left edge of his virtual HUD, he watched the airspeed decrease, and as it did, he pushed the throttle back to full afterburner. The airspeed increased rapidly.

"This airplane is no pig," Punk observed.

"Who told you it was?" Mongo asked.

"Obviously, guys who've never flown it."

"Exactly."

The simulator session went on for another hour or so, with Mongo coaching between throwing random and unannounced emergencies at Punk, and Punk performing the proper procedures in response.

"Let's go ahead and try a landing," Mongo said once he was satisfied that Punk could handle the jet at altitude. "Are you planning on coming into the break or doing a straight-in?"

"No self-respecting fighter pilot is going to do a straight-in," Punk replied.

Mongo laughed and said, "Of course not."

"Okay, so you want me to fly back to the field now?"

"Yeah, go ahead. Coming into the break at 350 knots. Level four or five G turn at midfield. Drop the gear once you're below 250 knots and keep slowing to on speed for landing."

"So, the landing checklist only has one thing? Drop the gear?"

"Yep, pretty simple."

Punk thought back to the number of items in the F-14's landing checklist: wings forward, gear down, flaps down, speed brake out, direct lift control engaged, trim set, calculate the proper landing speed based on the amount of fuel in the jet. Now he had one thing: gear down. The F-35 did the rest. Unbelievable.

Punk did as Mongo directed. Once he had the jet on downwind with the gear down, Mongo said, "Precision landing mode is exactly what you're used to in the Super Hornet, except the flight control laws are even better. Engage rate and path at the 90 degrees to go position, and then you just point the flight path marker where you want to go."

"I'd say I miss all the control inputs it took to safely land a Tomcat, but I don't," Punk quipped. "These young guys don't know how good they've got it."

"Youth is wasted on the young," Mongo said in the tone the cliché deserved. "Okay, I want you to do a touch-and-go and then climb back up to ten thousand feet."

"Roger."

Punk flew the rest of the approach profile, riding the throttles with his left hand as the control system determined the appropriate power setting and moving the sidestick with his right hand, keeping the flight path marker displayed in his visor on a spot just beyond the threshold at the approach end of the runway. Again, he marveled that he didn't have to touch a flap handle, extend a speed brake, or concern himself with what his fuel weight was beyond making sure he was below the maximum allowed for landing. Once he touched down, he advanced the throttle to full afterburner again.

At ten thousand feet, Mongo said, "Now it's time for the graduation run. We're going to do a flameout approach."

"Oh, good," Punk sighed.

"The F-135 is a reliable engine, but the F-35 only has one of them. If you lose it, you're instantly sucking."

"Yes, you are," Punk agreed. "It was the same situation in the F-16N."

"A flameout approach is an energy management drill, and the first step is to maximize your glide distance. Ideally your high key position is at least ten thousand feet, but you might not have that luxury depending on where you are when the engine stops working. Start by dropping the landing gear. You need to capture 200 knots to the low key, which is 1,500 feet, and that generally means setting the attitude to 30 degrees below the horizon. You want to hit low key at about five nautical miles out, and then you line up with the runway heading and keep pointing at the landing spot at 200 knots. At a mile out you flare, arresting the rate of descent to 700 feet per minute and touching down on the hard surface between 150 and 160 knots. Remember, you won't have precision landing mode without an engine, so don't try to engage it. And more than anything, don't try and salvage a bad profile. If you can't make it, you eject."

"Got it."

"Okay, I'm taking your engine away . . . *now*."

The noise of simulated thrust went away, and Punk immediately pushed the sidestick forward until the nose of the F-35 was 30 degrees down. He looked over his left shoulder at where the runway was. He seemed close enough at that point to make it there.

He focused on his airspeed, trying to maintain 200 knots while hitting the low key at the proper altitude and range from the field. But when he reached 1,500 feet, he saw that he'd gone beyond the five-mile point. He aggressively turned back to runway heading, and the jet slowed faster than he intended. By the time he rolled out, he was too slow and too far out to make the asphalt.

"Bad idea to try a landing on the dirt, right?" Punk asked.

"Very bad idea," Mongo replied. "The jet will flip, and you will die."

"Then *eject, eject, eject*."

"Okay, let's set it up again. I'll put you back at ten thousand feet to speed things up."

As Mongo focused on the control screen, Punk looked over his right shoulder at Jason, who nodded and mouthed "all good." Next to him the lieutenant commanders whispered to each other.

Punk managed the jet's energy better on the second try, hitting the low key point as prescribed. He flared perfectly a mile from the end of the simulated runway, and as the jet safely touched down, Mongo and Jason gave him a golf clap.

"That's a wrap," Mongo said. "You're a qual."

The lieutenant commanders walked out without comment, not sticking around for the debrief, and Punk figured they were headed to Beezer's office for one of their own.

Punk felt a shot of adrenaline as he lowered the canopy, which hinged in the front instead of the back like every other jet he'd ever flown, and brought the F-35 to life. A few minutes later he was done with his start checks and ready to taxi.

"How you looking, Crutch?" he asked Jason in the airplane parked next to him on the flight line, using his call sign instead of his given name now that they were in real jets. Although Punk had never been entirely certain, his stepson had alluded to the idea that his *nom de guerre* was a cryptic reference to the possibility of nepotism between them, an element he'd nullified by kicking professional butt on his own terms since Induction Day at the Naval Academy years before.

"Crutch is ready to taxi."

"Ground Control, Raider 25 is a flight of two, ready to taxi with information Charlie," Punk transmitted. "Information Charlie" meant he had the latest update from the Automatic Terminal Information Service that gave him the duty runway, wind, visibility, and altimeter setting.

"Raiders 25 and 26, taxi to Runway 32 right, copy information Charlie," the controller replied.

As he rolled toward the runway with Crutch a few hundred feet in trail, he thought about the flight brief earlier that morning and Beezer's presence there. Was it simply his sense of protocol as wing commander, or was it a function of what the lieutenant commanders had told him yesterday after the qual flight? Beezer had said nothing as Crutch and Punk exited the room to man their jets except, "Have a good flight, Admiral."

Just give me the jet that doesn't flame out, and we'll be fine, Punk had thought as he shook his hand and said thanks.

The two jets reached the hold short and switched tower and were given permission to take off. Crutch had briefed a "flight leader separation" launch with Punk in the lead, so they split the runway and rolled in sequence, with Crutch waiting for the other jet to rotate before starting his own takeoff. Punk noted how the kick of full afterburner felt more powerful than that of the Super Hornet, and that surprised him considering that the F/A-18 had two afterburners instead of just one.

They'd been blessed with another beautiful day in southern California, perfect flying weather. Punk watched Crutch join in tight parade formation on his right wing and steered toward the first waypoint beaming into his helmet-mounted display as the mission brick had been programmed, which took them west over the Pacific.

The hours with Mongo had been effective, and he felt surprisingly comfortable in the aircraft considering it was his first flight. He thought about the early days in flight school and how rudimentary simulators were back then compared with what he'd experienced yesterday. Like everything else technology-wise, they'd come a long way.

"Kick it out into combat spread, Crutch," Punk transmitted. "I'm going to do some aerobatics."

"Two copies," Crutch returned.

Punk accelerated the jet to four hundred knots and pulled into the vertical, continuing over the top and down the backside in a loop. He looked over and saw Crutch had mirrored the move a half mile abeam. Punk went right into a barrel roll followed by a Split-S into an Immelmann. Crutch stayed right with him.

"This feels great," Punk said.

"Do you have DAS working?" Crutch asked.

Punk had almost forgotten about the Distributed Aperture System, the "see through the jet" function. "Engaging now," he said.

The world suddenly became whole in his visor. It was like Dorothy going from a black-and-white world to color when she opened the door to Oz. He could see the water beneath them through the fuselage. "This is amazing," he gasped.

"Once you have it, you can't live without it; like a backup camera in a car," Crutch said.

All too soon they reached waypoint three, which defined the outer limit of their mission profile, and the steering cue in his HMD urged him to turn back to the east toward NAS Lemoore. He felt like a kid at an amusement park when his parents told him it was time to go home.

He checked his fuel state. Plenty of gas.

"You ready for a little basic flight maneuvering?" Punk asked his wingman.

"We didn't brief any BFM," Crutch replied.

"Okay, here's the brief. Sticks and stones, as we used to call it. Only valid shots are aft of the wing line. Simulated loadout is two AIM-9Gs not Xs. Five-hundred-foot separation between jets at all times. When in doubt, pass left to left. Hard deck is 5,000 feet. Bingo fuel is 2,500 pounds. How do you copy?"

"Seriously, Dad, we're doing this?"

"We are. And there's no dad up here. Call me 'Punk.'"

"Okay, Punk," Crutch said. "I'm a mile and a half abeam. Speed and angels on the right."

"Speed and angels on the left," Punk said. "*Fight's on.*"

Punk rolled hard right and pulled the stick to its rearward limit, fighting the crush of seven Gs as he did. Halfway through the turn he picked up Crutch coming toward him. They merged, and as Crutch screamed down his left side, Punk torqued around in his ejection seat to keep him in sight. Only then did he note that the F-35's rearward visibility wasn't great because of the design limitations of stealth technology.

He managed to keep his eyes on the other jet and saw that Crutch had turned hard right, so he went hard left, forcing a "one-circle fight." His plan was to keep his opponent at close range and force the fight to happen at as slow a speed as possible. They merged a second time, and Punk thought he'd gained some angles on the other jet and had a speed advantage, so he pulled into the vertical. To his delight, Crutch followed him.

Punk pushed the throttle into full afterburner so hard he was afraid he might bend it and waited to see who would fall away first, like Icarus flying into the sun. But as he watched his airspeed decay in his HMD, he realized *he* was Icarus. He pulled the sidestick as far aft as it would go, but the flight control laws vetoed his wish for more nose authority.

Punk pitched nose down toward the water, Crutch rolling in behind him.

"Fox-2 on the F-35 nose low, passing through 280 degrees at 20,000 feet," Crutch transmitted. "That's a kill."

"Punk copies good kill. Knock it off."

"Crutch is knocking it off."

"Punk is bingo fuel."

"Crutch same."

"We're RTB."

Crutch rejoined his flight lead in parade formation and they returned to base, flying into the overhead pattern at 450 knots, breaking sharply downwind in a ten-second interval, and landing one minute apart. As Mongo had mentioned, the precision landing mode in the F-35 was even smoother than that of the Super Hornet, and as he slowed to taxi speed and exited the duty runway he wished he could take the jet to the boat and bag some traps.

Maybe another boondoggle is in order, he thought. After all, he wouldn't be AIRPAC forever. There was no telling what his next assignment might be—if he was going to be offered one at all. Things got narrow at the top of the pyramid. His flying days were numbered.

When the jet was back in the chocks in front of the squadron hangar, Beezer walked up with several of the lieutenant commanders who'd attended the simulator session the day before. All of them were waving and giving a thumbs-up, obviously happy he'd completed the flight and returned the jet in one piece. Punk returned the gesture and then watched Crutch pull into the parking spot next to him wearing a smile as wide as California was long.

And he smiled a proud smile back.

CHAPTER 15

WOLFE RAN the simulation on Aswan again. The answer was instantaneous, at least in human terms. Machine learning algorithms, with the aid of a supercomputer, could execute quadrillions of calculations per second. The Chinese system running his setup had just been upgraded, and even so it was about to fall behind the fastest ones continually being upgraded by the world's key players.

The simulation's result yielded a 94 percent chance that Peterson's directed-energy weapon could defend *Ford*. The overeager engineer had alerted his handler, via text on a burner phone, that the admiral visiting China Lake had found the weapon satisfactory.

But 94 was still too low. Wolfe would have been more comfortable with 96 percent or more—because the better the weapon performed, the more confident the Navy would be that they could pass the test. Confidence easily led to arrogance, and arrogance increased the possibility of the Navy's failure.

Peterson also needed to be confident. The slightest doubt could make the young engineer crumble under pressure, and then Wolfe's plans would crumble too.

Which is why Wolfe operated on the programmer's maxim: Always have a backup. Wolfe swiped his burner mobile and connected to the asset in Washington, D.C.

"It's time," Wolfe said. "Is everything ready?"

"Yes," the voice said.

"Good," Wolfe said. "Find the documents. Scan them, then text the images to the designated account."

"Eyes and ears have been dealt with?"

He was inquiring about the security systems in the office building where Representative Evelyn Greenwood worked. Those systems were robust but not unassailable. He'd seen tougher security setups protecting sex traffickers in Mumbai.

"As soon as you text 'go' to the second number on your phone, the eyes and ears will be deactivated for three minutes. That is your window."

"Understood," the asset said, and the call ended.

Wolfe tossed the phone to his butler to dispose of it. Next, he used his personal phone to tip off the agent who was his medium with Ukraine's cyberwarfare division. Though he disliked giving up a key asset in that region, he had to do it to divert attention from the Washington hack attempt. Wolfe Industries was a public supporter of democracy, after all. It was smart business.

It was also smart business to leverage social media, in this case to make it part of the misdirection. He signed into the Wolfe Industries X account and tweeted: "#AI is an incredible tool, but companies need to take steps to ensure it can't be used in unintended ways. #tech #smartbusiness #power4good"

"Everything is set, but we'll need a diversion," Wolfe said. "Expose the Black Sea operation. Make sure they find The Hangman. He's long overdue for the noose."

CHAPTER **16**

DURING ANOTHER SET of pre-briefs at AIRPAC headquarters the previous day, Einstein had asked Punk how the fam flight in the F-35C had gone. That had been a mistake, because after that Punk had dominated every agenda break with details about it. Now, as they walked down the pier to board *Ford* once again, Einstein noticed that Punk had regained the bounce in his step that an aviator gets from time in a jet. Despite what he was dealing with on the home front with Suzanne's diagnosis, his old squadron mate strode toward the carrier's brow with purpose, a focused and confident man.

Good, Einstein thought, realizing what he'd thought was a boondoggle—Commander Naval Air Force Pacific taking the time to fly the Navy's newest fighter for what arguably served no immediate operational purpose—was exactly what Punk had needed to lead them as they faced the challenge ahead.

Punk was also buoyed by the fact that he'd been afforded some quality time with Suzanne. They had spent a quiet weekend with time on the beach, a meal at their favorite restaurant, and a movie at home with the two of them nestled under a blanket on the couch. No talk of cancer, as if ignoring the subject might possibly make it go away.

Walking down the pier, Punk also felt Surf's presence at his flank, where a good aide should be. He'd seen nothing in the lieutenant commander's demeanor that suggested what Punk feared might be true, but he addressed it all the same.

"I saw Gwen at the Exchange the other day," Punk said over his shoulder. "That was quite a shiner under her eye."

Surf laughed too easily and said, "She had a midair with a doorknob. She's very athletic, even played volleyball in college, but she's always been clumsy. I'm used to it by now."

The aviation analogy was too cute, and the backstory was more information than necessary. Punk kept the aide on the hook for a few seconds by not responding to that, but then he let it go, hoping that mentioning that he'd seen the black eye might be enough for his aide to clean up his act. In any case, they couldn't focus on that right now. They had other matters to attend to that were bigger than anyone's personal failings.

Spud, Einstein, and Connelly were waiting for them at the foot of the officers' brow. The Marines behind them dressed in full battle gear and holding M-16s were evidence that security was tight for the occasion. They'd gone back and forth with their U.S. Air Force counterparts about where to hold the first meeting between the two sides, and Punk was happy they'd settled on *Ford* as the venue. He figured some of them had never seen an aircraft carrier in real life before, and he hoped that the experience might at least instill in them the respect due.

"Seating in the SCIF is suitcased?" Punk asked Surf as they navigated the stairs up to the metal walkway between the pier and the carrier, a semi-precarious setup that took some getting used to as well as agility.

"Yessir," the aide replied. "I had a meeting with *Ford*'s intel officer and a few others yesterday. We should be all set."

Once again Gridiron met them on the quarterdeck, this time in his summer whites instead of a flight suit.

"Have the Air Force reps arrived?" Punk asked.

"Affirmative," Gridiron replied, checking a piece of paper in his hand. "Major General Robert Howe, Commander Air Combat Command."

"F-15 guy, call sign is Slapshot," Punk said, reviewing some of the details they'd discussed at the pre-brief for the benefit of those around him. "I served with him on the Joint Staff. He's tight with Congressman Gordon."

"James Thompson," Gridiron continued as he went down the list.

"Bear Thompson," Einstein said from behind Punk. "CEO of Rhimes-Phillips Aerospace."

Punk looked at Spud and said, "*Our* shipbuilder gives us biz dev, and the Air Force bomber company brings the CEO."

"Navy biz dev is the equivalent of an Air Force CEO," Spud said, surreptitiously flipping Punk the bird.

"Thompson went straight to the defense industry after his tour, and became Howe's inside man there," Einstein explained.

"No conflict of interest there," Connelly said.

"There's also Dr. Peter Son Wu, Chief Engineer, Air Force Weapons Center," Gridiron said.

"As I mentioned yesterday, he's the guy they brought in to sink *Ford*," Einstein said.

"The same Wu who made his reputation by scaring the hell out of the E-Ring at the Pentagon," Punk added. "Hope our wunderkind is everything you say, Admiral Francis."

"Again, everything I saw at China Lake tells me we're in good hands," Einstein said.

With that, just as on their previous visit, *Ford*'s commanding officer ushered them directly to the SCIF on the 0-3 level. The music was already playing when they got there, and it wasn't the classic rock the intel team normally selected in Punk's honor.

"Who chose the music?" Punk asked.

"Not me," Einstein said. "Maybe the PSYOPS people?"

"That's not music," Connelly muttered. "It's robots gone insane."

"I'm sure the intel folks picked it," Spud said. "You know kids these days."

"Look at it this way," Connelly said. "If we hate the music, maybe the Air Force team will too."

Inside the SCIF's heavy door they were met by Shane Peterson. Punk's first thought was that he looked even younger than Einstein had described him.

"Admiral Reichert, it's an honor," Peterson said as they shook hands.

His hand was as soft as Einstein had said it was. "Welcome to the team, Shane."

Behind them a man wearing blue coveralls banded by a khaki belt around his midsection extended his arm across Peterson. "Bhaavik Chatterjee, Admiral. It's a pleasure to meet you."

"Dr. Chatterjee is Shane's boss," Einstein explained. "He's the NAWC-WD Chief Engineer."

"I'm here to make sure *Ford* can defend itself against whatever the Air Force manages to deploy," Chatterjee said. Punk wanted to say "no duh" to that, but he stifled the impulse because they'd just met and he had no idea whether the engineer had a sense of humor. Best to avoid embarrassing an important cog in the gears of this test.

Howe, Thompson, and Wu stood across the table from them. Their handshakes were brief, and they offered no reminiscences about the good old days on the Joint Staff in the Pentagon because those didn't exist. Pentagon duty was a forced march that only the upwardly mobile and flag rank–motivated sought and endured.

As soon as they retook their seats, Major General Howe immediately took control of the meeting, exactly the sort of alpha move Punk had expected him to pull.

"Welcome to Exercise Blue Aegis," Slapshot announced.

"Passkey, you mean," Einstein interjected.

"In accordance with U.S. Air Force test and evaluation protocols, the system has named this Blue Aegis."

"But we already have Passkey swag," Spud deadpanned. "What are we going to do with all the keychains and hoodies?"

Slapshot glared at him like a headmaster about to scold an adolescent causing a ruckus at the back of the classroom. "Business development, right?" he asked.

"Correct, General," Spud replied.

"Well, we ain't selling anything or giving away any prizes here, so with your permission, we'll continue the meeting."

Spud stole a glance at Punk, who returned a subtle head shake directing his former RIO to let it go. And with that, the first slide in the presentation beamed across the digital boards on each of the long walls.

"I'm sure this isn't necessary, but I'll remind everyone in the room that this brief I'm reviewing is top secret and compartmented information. There are to be no hard copies of it, and it should be viewed only on devices authorized to handle such information and within approved facilities like this SCIF." Howe scanned the room as he asked, "Does everyone understand what I just said? I need to hear it from each of you."

The general walked his index finger across the dozen or so people seated around the table and the half dozen along the near and far walls adjacent to the ones that hosted the screens, like a flight attendant asking passengers if they were willing to accept the responsibilities that came with sitting in the exit row. All followed Punk's lead in answering, "Yes, General" when his finger arrived in their direction.

"We're using Navy turf, the Pacific Missile Test Range at Point Mugu, California, as homebase for our side of the exercise," Slapshot said. He looked across the table at Einstein. "Have you seen our resource request?"

"I have, General," Einstein replied. "They have 90 percent of what you've asked for on hand and are working hard to obtain the rest. I don't anticipate any problems on that front."

"That being the case . . ." Slapshot said, pausing as he brought up the next slide, labeled TIMELINE, "Operation Blue Aegis will commence in two weeks."

The Navy side of the SCIF emitted a collective gasp. Punk said, "That's considerably less time than we were planning on, which was already not enough time."

"I saw your testimony a few weeks ago, Admiral," Slapshot returned, sarcasm barely hidden. "I got the impression you were ready immediately. The two weeks isn't for you, it's for us."

As Slapshot continued his brief, it became apparent that Punk's assumption that Congressman Gordon would insist that the test be simple and basic—one hypersonic missile versus one *Ford*-class aircraft carrier—was way off. Either that or the Air Force test team hadn't run the plan by him yet, because it was much more complicated than anybody on the Navy side had envisioned.

The Navy could use defense in depth consisting of a cruiser, four guided missile destroyers, and Super Hornets from the carrier air wing. In return, the Air Force would come at *Ford* with F-15EXs and F-35As launching out of Elmendorf Air Force Base in Alaska. They'd be met along the way to the California warning area off the coast by enough KC-135 tankers to get them there and back. The strikers would be escorted by F-22s from the test squadron at Edwards AFB armed with AIM-120ERs, the extended-range Advanced Medium Range Air-to-Air Missile, which meant that they could reach out and touch the defending Super Hornets from far away. Some of the Super Hornet's AIM-174s meant for the inbound hypersonic missile would now have to be dedicated to shooting down those Air Force jets.

While the exact attack profile would remain unknown to the defenders before the fact, Slapshot allowed that they intended to present a multi-axis threat profile. As Howe continued speaking, Punk mentally went from Commander of Naval Air Forces to carrier strike group commander mode, doing the math and positioning the aircraft carrier and all the escorts and support assets against the threat.

To "diversify the presentation," as Slapshot put it, one hypersonic missile truck would be manned by Air Force operators at Point Mugu.

Other general details were briefed—communications plans, safety of flight rules, go/no-go criteria—before Slapshot clicked to the final slide, which featured a single word: "Hermes." "At this point, I'll hand the floor over to Dr. Wu," he said.

In his mind, Punk heard a gong crash like some sort of kung fu movie cliché as the legendary engineer of Asian descent slowly and majestically rose from his chair. Once fully standing, Wu scanned the others in the SCIF with a smile more menacing than warm. "We will launch the item from Edwards Air Force Base with an inert warhead," he said in a quiet, high-pitched monotone, almost a whisper. Einstein had warned him that Wu's voice was high-pitched to distraction, and he was right.

"The test is complete when the test article is destroyed at any time by any platform during the attack profile. If the test article closes to five nautical miles from *Ford* without being destroyed, we'll consider that a direct hit on the ship," Wu continued. "At that point we'll activate the hypersonic's self-destruct function, and the test will be complete." He paused for a second, eyes unfocused as if lost in thought, then finished with, "That's all I have to say at this point," and retook his seat.

Hermes: Dr. Wu's mystery hypersonic weapon. Though Punk was no expert on Greek mythology, the significance of the name wasn't lost on him.

Hermes was the Greek god of speed.

CHAPTER **17**

AFTER MAJOR GENERAL HOWE adjourned the meeting and the attendees walked out of the Flag SCIF and started the complicated journey off *Ford*, Punk tapped Howe on the shoulder and invited him for a coffee in the adjacent flag cabin. The brief for Passkey—now Blue Aegis—had been informative but also unsettling to the degree that Punk wanted to refamiliarize himself with the man who'd once been his Air Force counterpart in the Pentagon. Although Punk had intended for the conversation to be one-on-one, Bear Thompson and Dr. Wu had stayed glued to Slapshot's elbow like loyal servants. Einstein and Spud had attempted to do the same, but Punk told them to head back to AIRPAC headquarters to organize their post-brief thoughts and said he'd join them shortly.

"The third star suits you," Punk said as he sat down in one of the leather chairs surrounding a circular coffee table in the corner of the cabin's living room.

"And look at you at AIRPAC," Slapshot returned, taking another leather chair as Thompson and Wu occupied the couch against the bulkhead behind Punk. "The fleet is yours." Howe's hair was a shade whiter than it was the last time they'd been together, but he still appeared to be in very good physical shape.

"I'm pretty sure there are some four-stars, including the Chief of Naval Operations, who might take issue with that," Punk said with a smile.

A culinary specialist arrived balancing a silver tray with a pot of coffee and two mugs adorned with the carrier's crest. As the young sailor poured the coffee for the senior officers, Punk studied Slapshot and thought back to what he'd learned about him during their tour as brand-new one-stars on the Joint Staff.

The call sign Slapshot was a tribute to ice hockey hall-of-famer Gordie Howe, which Punk had always found a bit weak in that the general had never played hockey. No-brainer call signs were usually attributed to aviators who were either dullards or complete assholes like Soup Campbell. Slapshot wasn't stupid.

Howe had bagged an Iraqi MiG during Desert Storm, which gave him the street cred he needed to pivot into the test and eval community afterward without chucking his pride in the process. He was a very good fighter pilot, but he was also the most parochial military officer Punk had ever met, which was saying something coming from a Navy fighter pilot and carrier aviator. Although they were assigned to joint service billets, Slapshot had never subscribed to the concept of "jointness." As far as Punk could tell, his Air Force counterpart back then had one outlook over all others: "I win, you lose." And nothing seemed beneath him—dirty tricks, bad intel, false rumors—in the pursuit of the U.S. Air Force's advantage.

"I see you brought some old allies along for this thing, like O'Leary," Slapshot said between sips of coffee. "And I see he's still a wiseass."

Punk offered a forced laugh and said, "Spud has done well for himself since he retired."

"Not admiral material, huh?"

"Spud would tell you he was lucky to get squadron command and make captain after that," Punk replied masking his defensiveness at Slapshot's underlying insult. "Not making flag isn't always a bad thing."

"Of course, of course," Slapshot said. "Besides, I'm sure he's making a lot more money than we are at this point."

"Let's just say he's staying in the presidential suite at the Hotel Del Coronado while he's in San Diego."

Slapshot polished off what was left in his mug and poured himself more coffee as he asked, "I trust Suzanne is doing well?"

Punk forced another smile; no way in hell was he going to tell Slapshot anything about his wife's ordeal. He wondered if somehow Howe had gotten wind of it and was bringing it up just to throw Punk off and add to his anxiety. Slapshot was anything but merciful or compassionate.

"Suzanne remains the best Navy wife in the business," Punk said. "She's very happy with our life aboard NAS North Island."

"To be honest, this is my first time here," Slapshot said. "It's very nice."

"You've brought old friends along too," Punk observed, sweeping an arm toward the couch. "Never without your wingmen, just like the old days."

Bear Thompson nodded once. Shorter than Slapshot, he was also a little wider, having logged more desk time. Male-pattern baldness had come calling years ago, and Thompson tried to hide it with an ostentatious combover that started just above his right ear. He wore a sports jacket without a tie, trying hard to be his notion of a style-conscious corporate mogul.

"The Air Force needs all the help it can get, considering the games you're playing on the Hill," Bear said. "And was that Muddy Greenwood I saw on C-SPAN? She's come a long way since scaring you guys on the aircraft carrier."

"She was actually one of the Arrowslingers' best pilots by the time all was said and done," Punk said. "And nobody on the Navy side thinks of this as a game."

"Neither do we," Slapshot said. "Which is why I'm thankful for this opportunity to speak to you mano a mano."

"Well, one-on-one plus your wingmen," Punk said, jerking a thumb over his shoulder toward the couch.

"I'll get right to the point since we're both busy men," Slapshot said, ignoring Punk's jab. "You're about to sink with that stone around your neck, Vice Admiral Reichert, and I'm pretty sure you know it."

"What stone are we talking about?" Punk asked with a chuckle. "I have so many in this job it's hard to keep track."

"Aircraft carriers," Thompson said from the couch.

"Says the CEO of the company that builds Air Force bombers," Punk said. "I appreciate your unbiased point of view."

"*Ford* cost thirteen billion dollars to build."

"And will last fifty years."

"B-52s have lasted that long."

"Because they had to due to bad planning by you guys." Punk torqued around in his chair to face Bear as he continued. "The Air Force always wants to compare aircraft carriers to long-range bombers. It's been going on since 1947 when your service was created."

"I don't see a problem there," Slapshot said, jumping into the exchange. Punk suddenly felt like a fox between hounds. "Bombers are more cost effective, for one thing."

"One aircraft carrier air wing can hit five times the number of targets that one bomber can."

"We can launch twenty bombers for every aircraft carrier."

"As long as you have permission from the host country. We don't have to ask. We go wherever we want, whenever we want."

"Blue Aegis is a naval shield," Dr. Wu said, breaking his silence to that point in his strangely high voice. Punk turned back to face the couch again, considering the man widely regarded as the Pentagon's foremost master weapons technician. "But what if the shield shatters?"

Punk watched Slapshot's eyes narrow as he put a finer point on his engineer's metaphor: "Warfare is changing, Vice Admiral Reichert." Every time he addressed Punk by his rank it sounded like an insult. "But it also remains the same in the ways that count, you understand? No navy needs another aircraft carrier with that price tag."

The general took another swig of coffee before putting the mug down and staring at it. "Next Generation Long Range Bombers will render your carriers obsolete," Slapshot said. "You say carriers can go anywhere, anytime; but putt-putting around the ocean at twenty or thirty knots is too slow. Our bombers are going nearly supersonic. They can be over any target in the world in hours, not days." He raised his mug again and took a sip. "That's deterrence."

"You're ignoring that we have two or three carrier strike groups forward-deployed at all times," Punk countered. "They're not sailing from their homeports if the bubble goes up. They're already there. Not within hours. Now."

"I'm sure the Chinese appreciate that," Bear retorted. "They'll need something to shoot at before we get there and blow them to kingdom come."

"Punk, we get it. After all, you started your career as a Tomcat guy," Slapshot said. "For all the hype, that airplane didn't do anything besides shoot down four Libyan flight students and an Iraqi helicopter."

"A bunch of bad guys on the ground in Afghanistan after 9/11 couldn't be reached for comment," Punk said in return. The meeting wasn't having the utility he'd thought it would, and he was quickly growing tired of the company.

"Face it, Admiral, you guys consistently make bad acquisition choices," Bear said. "There's a Super Hornet, but there's no Super Tomcat. At least the Navy replaced the F-14 with a jet that actually had the technology that allowed it to be upgraded."

"Upgraded like my beloved Eagle that's been around in various forms for five decades," Slapshot added. "Check out the F-15EX we're using in this exercise. That thing's amazing."

"And now the Super Hornets are already aging out and the carrier version of the F-35 has been delayed," Bear said. "And just look at the ship designs that have flopped in recent years—Littoral Combat Ship and DDG 1000. Total wastes of time and money."

Slapshot leaned forward and crossed his arms over the table. "Punk, this isn't some petty interservice rivalry; this is the future calling. The *Ford*-class carrier is an anachronism, a step backward. We've got new weapons, unmanned vehicles in every domain, and AI that can predict what a pilot will do next. And you think a bigger boat is the answer?"

"A *better* boat," Punk replied. "And yeah, it *is* the answer."

"Welp," Slapshot said with a hearty chuckle as he got to his feet. "We're about to find out."

CHAPTER 18

SLAPSHOT HOWE'S photo loaded on Wolfe's phone as he waited for the waiter to fetch his drink at the café in Souq Waqif. The marketplace lent that section of Doha a nostalgic, Arabian Nights–style mystique to a rich Westerner such as himself. Like the rest of Qatar's major metropolis, the spot was an amalgamation of Old World Arabic architecture and culture fighting for space with a modern-day skyline glowing with the loom of a million office windows.

Chuckling, Wolfe shook his head at the picture, then showed his phone screen to his host, Cahya, who sat with her hands folded in her lap. She still hadn't touched her glass of Domaine Jean-Louis Chave Ermitage. The wine, though not expensive by Wolfe's standards, was still ten thousand dollars a bottle, and considering Qatar's "sin tax" on alcohol, it represented a forbidden and tasty treat.

"Can you believe this Air Force guy?" Wolfe asked in English, pitching his voice below the hubbub of the night traffic outside. "A typical John Wayne wannabe. I bet he gets off on pictures of Chuck Yeager."

Cahya—her given alias, which he'd discovered was supposed to mean "one who is a light in the darkness"—flicked a glance at Howe's picture then brought her eyes back up to his.

"I did not come here to listen to your schoolboy humor," Cahya said, her Bahasa Indonesian English bearing the staccato, toneless quality of a Mandarin speaker. She looked younger than her actual mid-thirties, with long, dark hair and the high cheekbones of a model. Her blouse and pants, which cost more than their waiter earned in half a year, hugged every curve. It was all part of the image China's Ministry of State Security wished to present. The MSS had a *Vogue* model brokering its deals.

But her beauty didn't go past her eyes, the empty eyes of a traitor. Wolfe wondered if all double agents possessed such a gaze.

He smiled. Her response proved her to be who he'd thought she was: a true believer in her cause. His crude humor had been intended to provoke a reaction. If she had laughed, he'd have lost respect for her, thought her superficial, ready to say or do anything to placate a business partner.

"You came for this, I believe," he said, passing an envelope under the table. She snatched it before his hand neared her thigh. "Above all."

"You and that phrase," she said scornfully. "Maybe you need a new one?"

"Some things never get old," he said, forcing the smile this time. Then he nodded at the envelope. "Well?"

"A meg?" she asked, using the tech code for a megabyte, a million bits of data. In this case, it was 1 million dollars accessible via an offshore account. The login details were contained in the envelope. If he'd texted or emailed them to Cahya rather than handing them to her, the MSS would have caught it—and her.

Wolfe had gained an ally in the MSS when he'd leaked the identities of the people who had alerted the Free Tibet organization about demolitions at Larung Gar Buddhist Academy. In the years since, he'd maintained that connection by helping Cahya deal with the Eastern Turkistan Islamic Movement and the World Uyghur Congress, organizations that China alleged posed terrorist threats.

"The last time we had drinks you seemed happier," he said, putting the phone away. "More problems with African exports? Or has Iran finally lowered its oil prices to Beijing?"

"You can fuck off," Cahya said. "I'm tired of this post. It's too hot, and it's hard to avoid rubbing shoulders with my . . . rivals here. But I go where the Ministry tells me." She raised her eyebrows tauntingly. "Above all."

"You're not worried someone will hear you say that?" he asked.

Cahya sniffed. "Who would care? Everyone knows everyone here. My presence is to advertise the MSS reach, but proxy work doesn't suit me. I like to be directly involved."

Wolfe accepted a bottle of cheap beer from the waiter. He enjoyed the curious lift to Cahya's brow. She was wondering why he would order something so cheap while he'd just bought her alcohol worth a small fortune.

He popped the bottle's top and sipped the bitter lager. "Okay, but stop pretending that you're not happy to see me."

"You know I am the pretty face they present to people like you," Cahya said, looking uncomfortable. "Unless they tell me to show the other side. But I'm not sleeping with anyone this time. I want to get this op over with. What is it you Americans say? The hell with Dodge?"

He smiled. "It's 'get the hell out of Dodge'—and hey, I get it. But I have something that might cheer you up."

"Oh?" she asked, glancing at the wine, then at him with obvious disinterest. She was very good at her job; he almost believed her apathy. But he knew she'd be intrigued with what he had to say. It was the whole reason he'd booked a flight to Doha on such short notice.

"I've got someone acquiring info on Project OpenShip," he said casually, then swigged the beer.

"Hmm," Cahya said, also casually, although her attention sharpened to a laser focus.

"I could use some hints as to how the PLA will deal with the U.S. Navy's latest defense system," he said. "The methods the MSS's cyberwarfare division will use against it. That way I can protect my own networks from them. Your comrades are getting better. You're almost as good as KillNet was in Ukraine."

"Fuck you," she said, laughing now.

Wolfe spread his arms and raised his brows. "Well?"

"Don't you already pretend that it's us when you hack American networks?" she asked. "Isn't that how you acquired that photo of your Air Force John Wayne? You are such an arrogant ass. You should have brought two envelopes."

"If you give the PLA my OpenShip intel, then maybe they'll send you somewhere else," Wolfe said. "Maybe even Singapore again. I have a nicer office there now. You'd like it."

"They saw your tweet about AI from your business account, I can tell you that. They got the message. Word has it that they're deploying their newest aircraft carrier and some destroyers well beyond the Second Island Chain as a signal to the Americans."

She leaned over the table, snatched his beer, and downed the remains in one gulp, then added, "And maybe I will go to Singapore."

He knew he had her.

"I'm impressed," he said. "You chugged that like a frat boy. Is that a yes, then?"

Cahya stood and took his hand. "I said maybe."

Later, as she slept naked beside him in her hotel bed, Wolfe watched her chest rise and fall with each breath. How a person who had killed so many people could look so peaceful was beyond him. Maybe that was one reason he'd stayed in touch with Cahya over the years: he wanted to feel that same peace after doing what he needed to do.

But she was no Kanny. Sure, he'd allow Cahya to stay with him in Singapore if the MSS relocated her there. But she would never be more than a visitor. Not only in his home, but in his heart.

He rose from the bed and gazed out the hotel window at Doha's West Bay, where the skyline's blue and white lights had a few more hours to defy the night before morning came. He stepped out on the balcony, slid the door shut, and called his assistant.

"Get me all the dirt you can on Major General Robert Howe," Wolfe said. "Apply pressure as needed. Oh, and place another bid on oil coming out of Tehran. Use our old contacts in Sinopec and PetroChina. Beijing only stays in the game as long as it's hungry."

CHAPTER **19**

AFTER TWO HOURS of restless tossing and turning, Punk was finally asleep when a ring on his cell phone woke him. The clock on the nightstand read 2:38. He snatched the phone off the stand and saw Surf Davis' name on the screen. "What is it?" he demanded.

"Admiral?" Surf asked, then spoke before Punk could answer. "My apologies for waking you so early, sir, but I need to tell you about an . . . unfortunate incident."

Barely awake and fighting his pique at being robbed of what little sleep he was going to get that night, he said, "Well? What is it? What happened?"

"Sir, I, uh, I was arrested by the MAAs on the dock earlier tonight."

"*Arrested*?" Punk asked, fully awake now. "What for?"

"A pool game with a few locals at the bar got out of hand," Surf said. "Some of the sailors accused them of being pool sharks. There was a scuffle, and I tried to break it up."

"You tried to break up a bar fight," Punk said, as if repeating Surf's statement would help him understand it. The aide to a vice admiral involved in a bar fight.

"Yes, sir," Davis said.

"Then why were you arrested?" Punk asked, glaring at the clock that mocked him.

"Like I said, I tried to stop the fighting," Surf said. "Gwen was there, and I was afraid she'd be hurt."

The whiny undertone in his aide's voice aroused Punk's suspicion. Gwen's black eye, still fresh in his mind, aroused it much more.

"You had your wife with you ... at a bar ... and you were playing pool with sailors from *Ford*?" Punk asked, trying to put the pieces together in his sleep-deprived mind.

"Oh, no sir, I wasn't playing pool. I just saw the argument, and when the fight started, I tried to break it up. Gwen told me not to intervene, but then one of the locals insulted her, made a rude gesture, and I couldn't just sit there and do nothing."

"Is Gwen all right?" Punk asked.

"Yessir, she's back at the house now," Davis said.

"Surf," Punk said, drawing out his aide's call sign, "did you hit anybody?"

Another hesitation from the aide. Another glance at the clock, daring it to change.

"I was just trying to break up the fight, sir," Surf said.

"Were you recorded? Photographed?"

"The base police didn't take mug shots," the aide said.

Punk felt his blood pressure rising. "Not the Naval Security Force. Did anyone in the *bar* record you with their phone? Were there media there?"

Muddy had warned him that Congressman Gordon would be keeping an eye on him and his crew. So, Surf's answer wasn't a surprise.

"I think there was a reporter outside the bar, but she didn't try to interview us about what happened," he said.

Punk wasn't in any mood for half-truths and deflections from an officer who should know better. He switched to a more formal tone: "Lieutenant Commander Davis, did the reporter or her crew record you and the other sailors being escorted from the establishment?"

"Yes."

"Are they keeping you overnight in the brig?"

Surf sounded surprised at the question. "No, sir. I convinced them that we needed to be back at our duties for Blue Aegis. I'm back aboard *Ford* now."

"All right. Stay there. We can discuss this further once I get there."

"I'm sorry about this, Admiral."

"You should be. We're all under the microscope right now. We can't afford any self-inflicted wounds."

"I know, sir. I just thought I should protect our sailors and my wife, you know?"

"Maybe you should think about staying out of bars instead."

"Yessir. That was probably a bad call."

Probably? His aide was showing the judgment of a recruit fresh out of boot camp, not an officer on track to command a fighter squadron.

Instead of lecturing him further, Punk just ended the call. He tried to get back to sleep, but it was hopeless. His mind raced with questions about what his aide was hiding and what had really happened. And he also wondered whether there would be something in the news he'd have to answer for, a distraction they didn't need and more ammo for Congressman Gordon and the Air Force mafia.

CHAPTER 20

THE HOT DESERT AIR of Edwards Air Force Base seared Howe's lungs when he got out of the car. He embraced the discomfort with a sense of nostalgia. He scanned the area, noting how little it had changed. The old red-and-white control tower still stood. The new phallus-shaped control tower that loomed across from it, obviously designed by an architect obsessed with Brutalism, was an unwelcome addition. The base's various hangars and structures shimmered in the heat, a mirage of Cold War–era martial omnipotence.

"Climate change is no joke," Bear Taylor quipped as he exited the sedan behind Slapshot. Though he was now CEO of Rhimes-Phillips Aerospace, Bear retained the call sign he had used when they were both captains stationed at Langley Air Force Base years ago. He wiped his forehead with a handkerchief, sweating profusely not even three seconds out of the air-conditioned car.

A jet passed by overhead, then another, going slowly enough for Slapshot to make out the yellow-and-black insignia on their vertical stabilizers.

"I'm sorry," Thompson said, "but those F-35s are ugly planes."

"You're a bomber guy. What do you know about fighters?"

"I know ugly when I see it."

"Ugly or not, I'm glad headquarters approved them for Blue Aegis," Slapshot said. "They're going to complicate Reichert's problem significantly."

"How do you think we did at that meeting?"

"He was trying to hide it, but I think we have him on the run. He's always been hard to read, though. Every time I thought I had him figured out when we were on the Joint Staff together, he'd surprise me." Slapshot searched the sky for more jets and added, "Guys like that concern me."

"I'm reading him loud and clear," Bear said. "Without aircraft carriers he's done. He's got a rice bowl, and he's going to protect it."

"A man has to protect his livelihood, I guess," Slapshot returned. "What is he going to do, say, 'Yeah, we suck, you guys are right. Take all our money and build more bombers'?"

"I'd love for him to say that."

"Of course you would, but he's not going to without us showing him how."

A lone figure approached across the parking lot, distorted by the heat waves coming off the concrete. As Slapshot squinted against the sun, he saw it was Dr. Wu, white lab coat flapping in the desert breeze. As always, he held his phone in his left hand. The general wondered if he ever put it away. As Wu came closer, Howe saw that the top three buttons of the shirt under the lab coat were undone, most likely not due to style but to neglect. Something about the man had always bugged Slapshot, but there was no denying his expertise and the fact that they needed him now.

"How are you, Doctor? How goes the work?" Slapshot asked as the three exchanged handshakes.

Wu nodded at a jeep nearby. "I will take you to what I have," he said shortly.

Slapshot and Bear shared a look. The engineer was known to be eccentric, after all. In fact, the general appreciated the lack of faux niceties and preamble. He wanted to get right to it as well.

Wu drove them across the base to one of the missile test sites, where several projectiles had been arranged in a row. They showed none of the graceful, aerodynamic shape of typical cruise missiles, and their awkward, angular bulkiness seemed at odds with their alleged speeds.

"These are the Hermes?" Slapshot asked. "They don't look like they could go a hundred knots, not to mention Mach 5."

Wu parked the jeep near the missiles and shut off the engine. Without a word, he got out and stalked up to the assembled weapons like a drill instructor inspecting his charges. He pointed at the first missile, which was slightly smaller than the others, and said, "This is the Hermes II. I have modified it for air-to-surface deployment. At 1,100 pounds, it is close to the weight of a JDAM that your aircraft might typically carry. It will reach Mach 6 and has an effective range of eight hundred miles. These would be suitable for the F-15EXs we're using in Blue Aegis."

"Only eight hundred miles?" Slapshot asked. "Could you push that a little farther?"

Wu shook his head. "That won't be necessary. The Hermes II is a diversion. Admiral Reichert, with Peterson's assistance, will likely have *Ford* ready to shoot down a single hypersonic. Yet, if we overwhelm *Ford*'s threat-tracking capabilities . . ."

"You mean, we unload everything on them at once," Bear said. "I like it."

Slapshot removed his blue cap with the silver scrambled eggs on the black brim and fanned himself with it. "Give Reichert more to worry about? Sounds good."

Wu walked to the next missile in line. "This is the Hermes III. It will make Mach 7 or 8 depending on altitude and humidity, with a range of one 1,200 miles. These will be deployed from the missile trucks along the coast."

"And the last one?" Thompson asked, nodding at the third missile.

Wu smiled thinly. "The Hermes IV. With a range of 1,600 miles, superior speed, and machine-learning protocols, it will reach a target within minutes. We can arm or disarm it via our network, as we can with the other models. It can change trajectory as needed to avoid interception."

"How fast is it?" Thompson asked.

"Mach 10," Wu said. "We'll launch this one using an F-35 flying out of a secret location. They will not see it coming, and once they do, they won't be able to stop it."

"Now we're talking," Bear said, then grinned at Slapshot.

Slapshot nodded but didn't smile. "This is all great, but why the different versions?"

"To trick *Ford* and the Navy's other assets," Wu said. "They will have difficulty tracking one of these missiles. A salvo of them, launched all at once and behaving differently? It is highly unlikely they will track them all. A variety of speeds will keep them guessing as we launch one after another in short order. This increases the probability of one getting through whatever defenses Peterson and Chatterjee have put in place."

"But this is just one missile," Slapshot said. "An aircraft carrier is designed to continue operating even if struck in multiple places. None of its systems are co-located. What sort of warhead would one missile have to carry to achieve *Ford*'s destruction?"

"A tactical nuclear payload is the easiest answer," Wu said. "One with enough explosive power to gut the hull at the waterline, and not only sink the ship but irradiate it as well in the event that it doesn't sink. One way or another, the carrier in question would be inoperable."

"But the test isn't considering nuclear yields," Bear said. "That's an entirely different discussion that I'm sure Congressman Gordon doesn't want to get into for the current budget fight."

"Indeed," Wu said. "While we don't have live warheads for the test, the committee needs to understand that in real-world use the Hermes has been programmed to bear down on its target at an extreme angle once it is within closing distance. The missile will detonate a quarter second after impact—enough time for an object of that speed to pierce the *Ford*'s flight deck at 55 degrees, penetrate deep within its interior, and discharge its payload."

"One hit from your missile would be the kiss of death," Slapshot said. "And if one missile gets to within five miles during Blue Aegis, we win."

Wu merely smiled.

CHAPTER 21

MUDDY HID her annoyance behind a polite, neutral expression as Gordon delivered his tirade to the rest of the House Armed Services Committee. His voice echoed off the walls of the caucus room when his impassioned appeal reached peaks, while the valleys forced his captive audience to lean closer to hear him. She hated to admit it, but the man was good at this.

He had been at it for an hour, and the others had allowed him to dominate the proceedings as if he were a king holding court. Finally, she interrupted by clearing her throat, shuffling her papers, and speaking into her mic before Gordon could continue.

"Congressman, I must point out that the evidence you're supplying now has nothing to do with Operation Blue Aegis," Muddy said.

Gordon, mopping his brow with a silk handkerchief, glowered at her. "Ms. Greenwood, are you implying that this proof of negligence has no importance?"

She glanced at the screen that was conveying his presentation to the rest of the committee. It focused on the maintenance records of the USS *Gerald R. Ford* over the last eight months, as detailed by the Government Accountability Office. Gordon's use of such a banal thing as this to push his agenda was galling; and furthermore, there was nothing to it. The so-called evidence was a superfluous addition to Gordon's criticisms of the Navy meant to turn the committee's opinion in his favor.

In addition, Gordon had acquired a news report describing how an officer on Vice Admiral Reichert's staff—his aide, no less—had been detained by base police after he'd gotten drunk at a bar in San Diego. The incident was relatively minor, but it still wasn't a good look for the Navy.

"How is this relevant, Congressman?" Muddy asked.

"This individual is in a position of trust and confidence for this test," Gordon said. "And this test isn't cheap."

"And?" Muddy asked. "We have an officer who had a few too many in town. We have a catapult repair log and a report of a Super Hornet flaming out after it was launched off *Ford*'s deck two months ago. What do these have to do with Operation Blue Aegis?"

Gordon pointed a finger at her as he said, "Everything, Ms. Greenwood. This is the carrier that will carry out the most important naval test of this century, and the aide to the man in charge of it is an incompetent drunk. This test is costing the American taxpayer something to the tune of 80 million dollars and counting. And that's a conservative estimate. The cost, once whatever super-secret defense system Vice Admiral Reichert has up his sleeve is deployed, might be double that. Or triple. This is a delicate operation. And based on the information I have presented, I have serious doubts that the aircraft carrier, its crew, and the others involved in this test are up to the task."

Muddy regarded him coolly. "The purpose of this committee is to ascertain the readiness and worthiness of operations and material required for our military, Congressman—not to make judgment calls on the Navy's interior matters that are not normally part of the public record."

"Perhaps that's the problem," Gordon said. "We don't know enough about what is happening on those ships. You were in the Navy. You're a decorated naval aviator. Is this sort of shoddiness the legacy you fought for?"

Muddy suppressed the anger he was attempting to elicit. "I performed my duty, Congressman," she said mildly. "And I have the utmost confidence in *Ford* and the crew to do theirs. That carrier has the best stats in the entire U.S. Navy. It has exceeded the readiness metrics over the last three consecutive years. It has carried out all its deployments with speed and precision. Your accusations are invalid, and I don't believe they're offered here in good faith, Congressman."

Gordon's face turned crimson as he shot back at her, "The gentlewoman ignores that these are not accusations; they are facts. And I assure you I offer them here in the best faith. American taxpayers have a right to know what the Navy is doing with their money."

Gordon used "American taxpayers" as a root note in every verbal solo, but Muddy thought the ready-made soundbites cheapened the proceedings. Yet there was nothing she could do publicly to stop him; there was too much media attention to the test already, given the deployment of hypersonic weapons in Ukraine and the demand for them from a smattering of foreign nations—allies and otherwise—not to mention the China-Taiwan tensions.

She loathed that Gordon was using something so mundane to push through his agenda, but she wasn't a combat aviator anymore, she was an elected representative in Congress. She could only attempt to counter his performance art with facts, believing those still mattered in spite of the playbook used by some of her colleagues that inexplicably kept them in office.

"Congressman, I would like to put it in the record that the Air Force's current NGLRB is suffering severe developmental setbacks," Muddy said. "The cost of that program is estimated to reach 20 billion dollars, which is nearly twice the budget required for the *Ford*-class carrier program. And the bombers will be dependent on international clearances for basing, and thus will require even more funds.

"Then there are the environmental concerns behind their manufacture," she continued. "I have reports from local media in the district where the manufacturer is located that they are releasing pollutants into the region with a disregard for EPA regulations, as well as—"

"You stop right there, Ms. Greenwood," Gordon snapped. "Those reports come from weirdo activists who tie themselves to trees and walk around in circles in front of the gates pounding on drums to get attention. I assure you the manufacturer is operating well within the EPA's strictures. You are making a poor attempt to sideline us here. This is about *Ford* and its upcoming trial by fire in Blue Aegis. In an effort to save funds, I have put forth a recommendations list for material costs for this test, so that Vice Admiral Reichert doesn't get carried away with *his* spending."

Gordon nodded to a staffer. She swiped her tablet and new numbers flashed on the caucus room's large screen. Some committee members gasped; one snickered; some groaned.

The funds were two-thirds of the original amount allocated for the Navy's side of the test.

Although Muddy kept her expression deadpan, her hands clenched as she visualized strangling Gordon. She had thought flying with a bunch of misogynistic assholes on the carrier had been an ordeal; Gordon was another, and lower, level of Neanderthal. She scanned the chamber, seeking help from the other committee members, and caught the eye of septuagenarian Congressman Woody Withers, who represented a district in Washington State, one of the Navy's few allies in the room. He seemed to shrink into himself and gave her an apologetic smile, thin lips stretched across his wrinkled face, body language begging her not to call on him for support.

"We will have to review these numbers before we can take a vote," Greenwood said, and pointed at Withers. "Congressman Withers and I—"

"We have already been here most of the day," Gordon interrupted. "I say we put this to a vote right now. All of those in favor of accepting the new budget?"

The staccato of "ayes" stole the rest of what Muddy wanted to say.

"What was that about, Woody?" Muddy asked Withers as she caught him in the hallway afterward, both sans their staffers.

A head shorter than his female colleague, Withers clasped his travel mug adorned with "World's Best Grandpa" defensively. "I needed more time than that, Evelyn," he said. "You can't just shoot me a look across the room in the heat of the moment. We must coordinate these things well beforehand."

Muddy sighed, then softened her posture, refocusing her approach. She hunched over slightly, trying to even out the difference in their heights. As her mom always said, you catch more flies with honey than with vinegar. "If both of us had stood up to Gordon, we might have altered a few opinions in there and the vote could have been different. Now Vice Admiral Reichert will have to do this test with a lot fewer assets and even less time to train than the little he has."

Withers sighed too and shrugged. "I understand what this means to you. He trained you to fly. You served together in Afghanistan." He made the monumental milestones of her life sound trivial. "Loyalty like that is admirable. But you have to face the facts."

"Don't you have a Navy port and a shipyard in your district?" Muddy asked, knowing the answer.

"I have, and I also have an Air Force training center and an Army recruit depot."

"Let me help you with your priorities, then," Muddy said. "I can't be the sole voice of reason in that chamber, Woody."

"You're surely not going to win them over by bringing up environmental causes," he shot back.

"Then what do you suggest? I obviously need some help here. We can't send the admiral out with less than he needs."

Withers had been in Congress for two decades and was far more experienced than Muddy in the art of politics. In theory, anyway, he knew who to talk to, how to talk to them, and when to talk to them to move his agenda along.

"Let Gordon have his way," he said simply. "The aircraft carrier program might survive, or it might become extinct. Maybe it should. Does it really matter how we deliver the bombs to the bad guys? Planes on a ship or planes from a base on land? Missiles or drones? In the end, our nation is safe." He patted her arm with a thin, liver-spotted hand. "I suggest you let this one go. You'll get your chance to put pressure on the next project. The only way to survive on the Hill is to play the long game."

Before she could voice her disagreement, Withers nodded politely and ambled on across the marble floor.

Long game? Nah, a long game was the sum of short game results. Muddy nodded slowly to herself as a strategy came to mind. She pulled out her cell phone and called her chief of staff.

"Sally? Yes, I just left the chamber. I need everything you can find on Woody Withers. You know, ties to the HASC, who's in his ear, and who donated to his last campaign. He's the only thing close to an ally on this aircraft carrier test. I need a leverage point with him. Nothing's too trivial."

Muddy ended the call, slid the mobile into her pocket, and made the trek out of the Longworth House Office Building and onto the sidewalk along Independence Avenue. It was a beautiful day, sunny with no humidity, rare for that time of year. The mild breeze carried the scent of cherry blossoms. She took in her surroundings, starting with the Capitol building across the street, buoyed by its timeless majesty the same way she had been by the Yard—the Naval Academy campus. She could do this. She *was* doing this.

The camera installed in the sunglasses of Wolfe's D.C. asset came online. The man was outdoors, watching people moving up and down a flight of concrete steps. The feed jostled as the asset avoided a crowd of people dressed in suits and skirts, probably congressional staffers, then stabilized as she came into view.

Wolfe admired how Ellen Greenwood walked down the Capitol steps toward the National Mall. Tall and slim, she carried herself with an easy athleticism that broadcast regular exercise and a healthy diet. A no-nonsense sort of woman, as attractive for her poise as for her looks.

Wolfe felt a momentary pang at stalking her. He was a generous supporter of women's rights. He had paid for girls' schooling in Afghanistan before the Taliban resumed control and put an end to the possibility of equal rights for females there. He helped fund the education of Maasai girls in Kenya via For the Good and paid for scholarships through the Asian University for Women. He was well aware of his hypocrisy here. *All for the greater good,* he reminded himself. He was playing the long game. To even his playing field, knowledge had to be accessible to all. And whether Greenwood knew it or not, she was supporting Wolfe's efforts along those lines.

The confident way she moved reminded him of Kanny. It was the demeanor of a person who believed she had nothing to fear, that she had the skills and courage to meet any challenge. In another world, Greenwood might have openly helped Wolfe's cause. She might have even been sympathetic to it.

He'd considered the alternative to what he was about to do: bribery. But Aswan had calculated the possibility that Greenwood would accept a bribe at 2 percent of the time, and then only in the high eight figures range. She was a true believer, like Cahya. Such stalwart adherence to loyalty seemed old-fashioned in a world of offer and counteroffer, but Wolfe admired it all the same.

"What if she gets in the way?" the asset asked.

"If you are doing your job correctly, she won't," Wolfe said.

"Yes, but . . ." the asset left the comment open.

"Then make it look like a mugging. Now . . . go."

Wolfe's asset followed Greenwood across the Mall.

CHAPTER 22

AS SOON AS PUNK walked aboard *Ford* he was surrounded by the ship's redolence and the feelings it evoked. That smell—a combination of fuels, metal, and humanity—was the same in all U.S. Navy aircraft carriers, new and old. And although he worked hard to stay in shape, the ascent to the bridge still winded him, the steep angle of the ladders and the number of them between the hangar bay and the bridge trying his fitness. His chest was still heaving a dozen minutes later as he stood at the armrest of the captain's chair where Gridiron was seated, flanked by Einstein, Melvin Connelly, and Spud.

Punk directed his attention out through the shatterproof glass to the waves beyond the bow as the carrier made its way along the channel by Point Loma. It was a perfect day to be at sea. Visibility was unlimited and the seas were calm.

It would have been a nice day to take Suzanne out somewhere. The sudden need to spend more time together warred with their shared sense of duty. But duty, as always, won out, even as they faced the unknowns around the return of her cancer. Nevertheless, the worry about her condition was always at the back of his mind.

Her follow-up appointment with her oncologist had been good in the sense that what he had to say wasn't as bad as it could have been. The mammogram had revealed one thing that he didn't like, but the tumor was growing at a rate that made it treatable with oral rather than intravenous chemotherapy. That meant fewer hospital visits.

He thought about how the mastectomy had altered her body and felt guilty for even considering it. In sickness and in health, the vow went. She'd always be beautiful to him regardless of how her body changed along the way, and he was sure she felt the same way about him. After all, illness and aging weren't gender-specific, and he wasn't getting any younger either.

Standing there on the bridge he felt his heart race and wondered if he was about to have a heart attack right there. How ironic would that be, after years of cheating death bringing jets aboard the aircraft carrier in tough conditions, to die on a carrier bridge while doing nothing? Wouldn't the gang have a good laugh over that?

He forced his attention back to his present situation. "So, Captain, what do you have in store for us?" he asked Gridiron.

"What specifically do you want to know about, Admiral?" Gridiron asked in return.

"What's first?"

"We're going to go over what we have on *Ford* right now in terms of defenses," Gridiron said. "And then we're going to review associated crew roles and responsibilities."

"How have those changed?" Punk asked. "The carrier keeps operating as much as possible, we evacuate damaged areas, seal off decks... what is there that's new?" He said it more abruptly than he'd intended. The nightmare still bothered him.

Gridiron lifted an eyebrow, then asked, "Do you know the last time an American aircraft carrier was sunk?"

Punk hadn't expected a history test. He thought for a few seconds and said, "It had to happen during World War II, right?"

"Nope, the USS *Card* was sunk by the Viet Cong in Saigon Harbor in 1964."

"Really? Why have I never heard about that?"

"*Card* wasn't truly sunk," Connelly said. "The charge the VC planted on the hull only caused it to settle on the bottom in twenty feet of water. It was later refloated and repaired."

"Okay, but it was sunk," Spud said.

"My point," Gridiron interjected, taking back the floor, "is that nobody ever thinks it'll happen to their own ship, and that breeds complacency. A complacent crew is dangerous."

"That's exactly what I want to hear from my carrier skippers," Spud said. "But what General Howe and the other critics don't seem to understand is that it'll take more than one missile to sink a modern supercarrier. Don't forget that USS *America* was tested to see how much damage it could take, and that beauty lasted for a month, taking hits above and below the waterline from aircraft, missiles, and gunships before going down."

"If the hypersonics delivered a *nuclear* payload, there would be no question," Einstein said. "But that's the worst-case scenario, and if the Chinese can make it happen without resorting to nukes, they will."

"Will it matter at that point?" Spud asked. "Even firing on one of our carriers starts World War III."

"Well, if that doesn't, sinking one of our carriers definitely will," Punk said. "So, what say we don't let that happen, starting with this exercise?" He gestured toward the main hatchway leading off the bridge. "Shall we, Captain?"

Gridiron nodded and climbed down from his elevated chair. "Aye, sir."

The captain led them to the flight deck where a foreign object damage—a FOD—walkdown was in progress. Led by the Air Department, all available hands slowly paced the flight deck, elbow-to-elbow, from bow to stern looking for something, anything that might get sucked into a jet's intake and ruin the engine. It was a ritual that involved intense focus on the nonskid surface of the deck, but it was also a social ritual, albeit a quiet one with muted conversations between adjacent crewmates. Occasionally the searchers were interrupted by a member of the Air Department wearing a yellow flight deck jersey walking backward in front of them shouting orders to slow the pace or straighten the line.

Punk, Einstein, and Spud were more than willing to join the procession under the auspices of tradition, and Connelly followed them out of a sense of obligation. Walking FOD was the duty of all hands regardless of rank or billet. The ten minutes it took to complete were as relaxing and mentally therapeutic as they were useful.

Once the line reached the thick white stripe of the round-down across the aft limit of the flight deck, the participants broke up to assume their regular duties. Plane captains in brown jerseys checked tie-down chains and wiped canopies clean while refueling crews in purple jerseys pumped JP-5 aviation gas into airplanes. Tractor drivers in blue jerseys guided by taxi directors in yellow jerseys moved airplanes into their final spots before the first event launch.

The process looked chaotic to the untrained eye, but the actual efficiency behind the activity always filled Punk with pride. The dedication of crews like *Ford*'s were something Congressman Gordon didn't appreciate or deign to understand. Damned if Punk was going to let him destroy it.

Punk, Einstein, Connelly, and Spud followed Gridiron through the hatch into the island and down a ladder to the hangar bay, where Punk took in the variety of aircraft being worked on there. There was the F/A-18 Super Hornet E, as well as its two-seater variant, the F, which featured a weapon systems officer, or WSO (pronounced "wiz-oh") in the backseat, the modern equivalent of the F-14's radar intercept officer, or RIO, the role Spud had performed. Next to that was an EA-18G Growler, an electronic warfare variant of the Super Hornet that had taken up where the EA-6B had left off with the jamming mission, making surface-to-air missile systems blind to incoming aircraft or destroying them with antiradiation missiles. Then there was the unglamorous but trusty E-2 Hawkeye, the twin-engine prop plane with a large, round dome mounted atop the fuselage. As a fighter pilot, Punk had learned early on that without a Hawkeye you had only a piece of the airborne tactical puzzle. The Hawkeye had been part of the carrier air wing inventory since the 1960s, but the D model on board *Ford* was packed with twenty-first-century features like the APY-9 radar, with advanced electronic scanning and computing power via space/time adaptive processing. They were going to need every bit of that capability during Blue Aegis.

Punk bumped a fist against one of the steel tie-down chains and recalled the details of the nightmare he'd had before his testimony in D.C. a few weeks before. He turned to Gridiron and asked, "What if *Ford* was damaged to the point where it lists more than, say, 30 degrees?"

The question was at once relevant and out of nowhere, and the captain shook his head as if he was trying jar the reply loose. He considered the question for a second or two, then replied, "We're talking about tilting a vessel that's over a thousand feet long, weighing a hundred thousand tons. Anything on the flight deck that's not chained down—tractors and airplanes that are taxiing—would slide right off. And at some point the chains could snap on the stuff that is chained down."

"Have you thought about that happening?"

He nodded. "Maybe not specifically 30 degrees, but I worry about rogue waves and high seas all the time."

Next came an integrated fire reactor drill in the bowels of *Ford*. Crewmembers rated as fire controlmen donned yellow FPG PBIs, or Fire Protective Gear, suits; red FXA-1 helmets; and AV-3000 masks. The sailors were timed in how quickly they could react to internal conflagrations. The crew put out a simulated fire and closed hatches before it could spread to other cabins or decks.

Punk knew how uncomfortable the FPGs could be; he'd worn one himself during his carrier CO tour. Every movement and step made you feel heavy and sluggish.

"Those PBI suits are rated to temperatures up to 1,600 degrees Fahrenheit," Gridiron said, voice raised just enough to be heard over the fire team leader shouting instructions to the rest of the damage control team.

Punk turned to Connelly and asked, "Is that enough?"

"If *Ford* were to get struck by a missile, the initial blast explosion could be in excess of 2,000 degrees," Connelly replied, "so probably not. But I'd say the main question is what if it hits one of the reactors?"

"As I'm sure Vice Admiral Reichert remembers from nuke power school, they're surrounded by a thick shroud," Gridiron said.

"Yes, but that shroud is designed to keep radiation *in* in the event of a meltdown," Einstein said. "We're less certain what would happen if one of them took a direct hit from a missile, not to mention a missile traveling Mach 5. At that speed it doesn't even need a warhead to do a lot of damage."

"But it wouldn't sink the ship," Punk said.

"There would be secondaries that could," Einstein said. "And if *they* didn't, a compromised reactor would leak ionizing radiation that wouldn't totally be blocked by the seawater."

"That means we'd have to abandon ship," Gridiron said. "We'd probably also have to scuttle the ship to keep the radioactive particles from getting airborne."

"And don't forget, there are already at least nine nuclear submarines at the bottom," Spud added.

"And?" Punk asked.

Spud shrugged. "I'm just putting that out there."

The conversation between them died abruptly. They watched the sailors secure from the drill and start to put away their PPE. Punk made it a point to meet each of them, pleased that each looked him in the eye as they shook hands. That wasn't always the case, and while it might seem like a minor thing to focus on, Punk viewed it as a barometer of crewmembers' focus and pride in their roles on the carrier.

On the second deck they observed the medical department carry out a MEDEVAC readiness test. Prone sailors were placed on stretchers and gathered at the evac site as the medical corpsmen were timed for speed and efficiency. The department master chief coaxed them into faster and faster reaction times, simulating the evacuation and treatment of wounded personnel. Even Spud got in on the test, volunteering himself as a prone sailor who needed to be rescued.

As he jumped in to carry a simulated casualty on a stretcher, Punk felt chills. The nightmare that haunted him seemed even more real in that moment, as if he was rehearsing for a future event. As if his nightmare was a premonition.

The hours flew by in a blur of drills and briefs throughout the carrier, and they barely managed to grab a quick meal. The tacos al pastor loaded with pineapples, pork, onions, and cilantro were excellent. Punk had gobbled three before he realized it. The food on Navy carriers was as good as he remembered. Then they oversaw an inspection of *Ford*'s reactors: twin Bechtel A1B models that provided 25 percent more power than the reactor on a *Nimitz*-class carrier. The A1Bs converted steam into electricity that powered four main turbine generators providing energy for the entire ship. In fact, the system had been designed for future upgrades, so that only half of its actual power capacity was in use. That alleviated any energy concerns for Peterson's LASIPOD.

"Okay, we have the power," Punk said. "Now we need a look at *Ford*'s current defenses."

"Follow me," Gridiron said with a chuckle, "and don't worry. We're not letting anything come near *Ford*."

CHAPTER 23

GRIDIRON TOOK THEM next to a weapons mount adjacent to the starboard-side catwalk, near the forward elevator that hosted a pair of RIM-162 ESSM missiles. "These are the latest Sea Sparrow missiles," he explained. "They are high speed and have a max range of about twenty-eight nautical miles. They're good against enemy aircraft and UAVs but not the weapon of choice against a hypersonic missile."

They walked across the flight deck to another weapons station aft on the port side. "And these are our twin RIM-116 RAMs. Rolling Airframe Missiles are IR weapons, as you know, like the Sidewinder on our jets, intended for point defense against subsonic or barely supersonic threats. Which also makes them not the weapon of choice against a hypersonic."

"You're building this tour up to a weapon of choice, right, Captain?" Spud asked, only half joking. Gridiron merely smiled.

Just aft of the island on the starboard side was a Phalanx gun, little more than a 20-mm Vulcan cannon on a turret, for years a mainstay on all Navy surface ships. Gridiron explained that while the Phalanx was effective against enemy vessels, missiles, and aircraft, as well as UAVs, it too would be useless against a hypersonic attack.

They took a ladder back down to the 0-3 level and entered the Combat Information Center, a dark room filled with screens of various sizes. The temperature in CIC was noticeably lower than elsewhere on the carrier, the AC being tweaked up to keep the electronics from overheating. Everyone who manned CIC wore a jacket or sweater.

They were met by a short, sturdy female surface warfare officer who introduced herself as Lieutenant Maggie Mildenhall, *Ford*'s Tactical Action Officer. She pointed to chairs arranged around one of the largest displays in the space and asked the party to sit down for her brief.

"Pacific Missile Test Range is about to fire ten UAVs flying in formation at us," Maggie explained. "Each of them is traveling at 130 knots. If they make it ten miles from *Ford*, they will split into five two-drone sections, complicating our targeting problem."

The TAO turned to face the screen behind them. "Here they come," she said.

The RIM-162s made short work of two of the inbound drones. Deep in the bowels of the carrier where CIC was located, the sound of the missiles firing could barely be heard. The rest of the UAVs flew a bit longer but were also taken out well before they got to the split point.

"Not bad, huh, Admiral?" Gridiron asked.

"Good work, Lieutenant," Punk said to the TAO. "But be advised that General Howe's team will be using faster drones that will be capable of shooting even faster test weapons as a diversion while the hypersonic bears down on us."

"We can handle those, too," Gridiron said. "Now let's see what the RIM-116s can do." The captain nodded at the TAO, and she tapped one of the sailors seated at a console in front of her on the shoulder. That sailor murmured something into his headset.

Maggie turned back toward the assembled visitors and said, "Now PMTR is launching sixteen missiles at us, inert, of course." She turned back toward the screen where several symbols started to appear. "Here ... they ... come."

Again, they heard only muted roars as *Ford*'s self-defense missiles launched.

"Four intercepted," the TAO announced pointing to tracks that now had a big X across them. "Three more intercepted."

"PMTR just told me one of their missiles went stupid right off the rails," the sailor at the console said over his shoulder.

"That's eight, then," Maggie said.

Punk watched as eight more tracks bore down on the carrier, waiting for more whooshes of RIM-116s above them. The silence was concerning. "How are we looking, Lieutenant?" he asked.

"Stand by, Admiral," she replied, walking a short distance to an adjacent console and holding the handset there to the side of her head before moving back across the space to the assembled men. "The weapons team was getting a fault code from one of the launchers, but they think they have it cleared now."

As if on cue, more whooshes sounded. A few seconds later three more Xs superimposed themselves on tracks. One remained, bearing ever closer to *Ford*.

"Say range to that track," Gridiron ordered.

"Five miles," the sailor replied. "Now four miles."

The TAO moved over to pick up the handset again. "Missile stuck on the rail," she said across the space.

"Fire another one!" Gridiron returned, working to keep his anger in check.

"Two miles!" the sailor said, stress showing in his voice.

A distinct metallic buzz reverberated through the hull for several seconds, and then sounded again.

"Was that the Phalanx?" Spud asked, to which the others nodded.

They watched the screen as the final track continued on its path toward the carrier.

"Tell them to execute self-destruct!" Einstein shouted at the sailor at the console.

"It's down!" the TAO shouted back, pointing to the screen that now showed an X over the final track.

"How close did it get?" Punk asked.

"Mile and a half, sir," the sailor replied.

Punk looked at Gridiron and said, "That's too damn close."

"Roger that, Admiral," Gridiron replied. "We have some work to do."

"We're not the only ones," Einstein added before turning toward the TAO. "Was Phalanx even supposed to be part of this exercise today?"

She shook her head and quietly replied, "No, sir."

"We need an answer from PMTR about why they didn't self-destruct the missile once it got inside five miles," Einstein said. "Inert or not, those things can do some damage."

"I'll find out, sir," Maggie replied.

"Phalanx isn't going to save *Ford* during Blue Aegis," Punk observed as if the others didn't already know that.

One of the intel specialists walked up and handed the TAO a piece of paper, which she quickly scanned. Eyebrows raised, she handed the paper to Punk. "Flash message, Admiral. The Chinese are headed our way."

Punk read the message aloud: "From Commander Seventh Fleet to Commander Naval Air Forces. National assets show Chinese People's Liberation Army Navy has deployed the aircraft carrier *Fujian* along with three Type 055 destroyers eastbound. Current posit is well beyond the Second Island Chain. Believed to be headed toward the vicinity of USS *Gerald R. Ford* (CVN 78) exercise operating area. P-8 Poseidon maritime patrol planes out of Barbers Point, Hawaii, will track flotilla progress. PLAN emissions surveillance expected. Take necessary precautions."

"Great," Gridiron sighed. "Now we have a real-world threat to contend with along with the exercise."

"The *Fujian* is their newest carrier," Maggie said.

"And it has electronic catapults just like *Ford*," Connelly added.

"Only they just have two of them instead of four like we do," Spud said. "And their manufacturing process and quality suck."

"Maybe we should recommend postponing the exercise," Einstein said.

"No way," Punk replied forcefully. "We're not flinching at the first sign of the Chinese navy. That would play right into the hands of Howe and Gordon. We just need to keep them in our scan here." He pointed at Gridiron and Maggie. "Energize the emissions security grid accordingly and make sure the destroyers do the same."

The two replied, "Aye, aye, sir," in unison.

The group left the TAO in the CIC and moved down the passageway to the flag spaces where the ever-attentive culinary specialists met them with coffee, the fuel that kept the Navy going. Chatterjee was already there.

"Remind me where we are with the directed-energy weapon," Punk said as he dropped into one of the leather chairs around the coffee table.

"Peterson said that we should have the LASIPOD array within the next few days," Einstein answered.

"What's the holdup?" Punk asked. "Are they dragging their feet up at the Lake?"

"No, they're not dragging their feet, Admiral," Einstein shot back, obviously triggered by yet another jab at the test and evaluation community from the operational side. "Remember, a few short weeks ago this program was still in the development phase—and *on schedule*, I might add."

"Funny how it takes a congressional hearing to move that schedule to the left," Punk said.

"That's not productive," Einstein said. "We're working our asses off to make sure we don't make a liar out of you."

"Whatever the demand signal, *Ford* needs DEW," Chatterjee said. "Current defensive systems are terribly insufficient against the PLAN, or any like threat, for that matter."

"You missed the little exercise we just did," Punk said.

"I heard the missiles go off and then the close-in weapons system fire," Chatterjee said. "What was that all about?"

"Let's just say your opinion is not incorrect," Spud said.

"It's correct, you mean?" Chatterjee returned.

"Close," Spud allowed.

"Speaking of these tests, you heard our budget was cut, right?" Connelly asked the room.

"What?" Punk asked back. "Einstein, have you heard anything about this?"

"No," Einstein replied.

"We found out the hard way," Connelly said. "Our test wish list was revised up the chain."

Punk wondered why Muddy hadn't given him a heads up. He asked, "What are the revisions?"

"We only get two destroyers instead of four. No cruiser. And we're only funded for enough aviation fuel to launch eight jets."

The room fell silent as all parties considered the implications of this news. After a time, Chatterjee said, "They really want us to fail, don't they?"

"They're sacking us before kickoff," Gridiron complained. "Well, screw them. They're not sinking my ship."

"We're not letting that happen, Captain," Punk assured. "Go over every part of this carrier with an even sharper eye on survivability. Weld points, bulkheads, compartment sealings, especially below the waterline. Keep drilling the crew in both weapons engagement and damage control."

"Aye, sir," Gridiron replied.

"Einstein, retool the plan. This is all coming down to the DEW. And I'm sure I speak for the Chief of Naval Operations when I say NAVAIR process for the sake of process is out the window. Push the limits of experimentation. Get Wu to work his magic. Get all of NAWC-WD focused on it. Hell, bring engineers from other programs, even from the other coast if you have to."

Einstein read his former squadron mate's body language and answered with a single nod.

"And we should be prepared for even more adjustments to the plan as we go along," Punk said.

"You mean dirty tricks?" Spud said.

Punk shrugged. "I'm being the good steward of the public trust. The bottom line is we'll make this work." Even as he put on a good face, he felt betrayed, and not just by Congressman Gordon. One of *Ford*'s intel specialists poked his head into the space and told Punk he had a phone call from Washington, D.C., in the flag tactical center.

"I'll bet I know who this is," Punk said as he got out of the leather chair.

"Tell her we said hello," Spud said, "and thanks for nothing."

Punk picked up the phone in the adjacent space and said, "Reichert . . ."

"These budget cuts took me by surprise as much as they did you," Muddy said. "I've been in damage control mode all morning trying to find a way to get the funding back, but I'm not having any luck so far."

"We're down to two destroyers and four Super Hornets," Punk said. "And our weapon of last resort isn't ready yet."

"Gordon's willing to go low on this," Muddy said. "Even lower than I thought he would. I'm hawking him like a recovery tanker on a low-state nugget who just boltered for the third time."

"That's great, Congresswoman, but I need to hear things from *you*, not the rumor mill, as we go along here."

"I was holding off relaying the information until the situation stabilized," she said. "There's going to be more no-notice changes, I'm afraid. Gordon's donors either have his balls in a jar or they've promised him a yacht and a mansion, because he's determined to get that 13 billion for his bombers."

"Anything else I should be aware of at this point?" he asked.

"The HASC knows about your aide's arrest," she said. "Gordon used that to help him convince the committee to lower your side of the budget for Blue Aegis. The Air Force is untouched."

Was I too easy on Surf? Punk wondered. *Maybe I should have dug into it deeper.* Now, as far as the test went, anyway, the damage was done. Gwen was another matter he'd have to keep in his scan along with everything else.

"What about my record?" Punk asked.

"What about it?" Muddy asked back. "Anything I don't know about it that I should?"

"I'm just wondering what angles they're using here."

"I think if nothing tripped you up when you were being looked at for the third star, you're fine." He heard another voice away from the phone on her end of the line. "I need to go, Admiral. There's a vote on the floor coming up about something else. While the future of carrier aviation is at risk, so is the future of Medicare."

She said something inaudible away from the phone before speaking to Punk again. "Oh, I also want to pass on that I guilted Congressman Woody Withers into using his connections with CDAO to get us intel on OpenShip for Blue Aegis, and not just the beta version."

"How did you guilt him?" Punk asked.

"I won't bore you with wranglings on the Hill. Let's just say I helped him adjust his priorities."

"We don't need any more scandals."

"No scandals. Just old-fashioned politics. Look, I'll keep you posted." The line went dead.

Punk put the phone back on the cradle and decided he needed to have a one-on-one with his aide. Right now. He went back to the adjacent room where the others sat waiting for a clue about what to do next. "Go grab chow in Wardroom One, everybody. We'll meet back here in thirty minutes or so."

"Aren't you eating?" Spud asked.

"I need to circle up with my aide first," Punk explained. "I'll catch you guys back here."

Punk walked aft on the 0-3 level until he got to one of the ready rooms that would have been bustling with the activities of a Super Hornet squadron during a normal at-sea period. On this trip it was being used by the staffs of those at the top of Blue Aegis. He found Surf sitting in a ready room chair in the front row. When he spotted Punk, the lieutenant commander got to his feet. Punk gestured for him to sit and took the chair next to him.

"Just got off the phone with Congresswoman Greenwood," Punk said in a measured cadence looking straight ahead at the whiteboard that dominated the front of the ready room. "I'll be blunt. News of your arrest reached the desk of Congressman Gordon on the House Armed Services Committee, and that news didn't help our effort."

The blood drained from Surf's face. "I don't know what to say, sir."

Punk paused for a few seconds, letting the tension hang in the air of the empty space. "How did your wife really get that black eye?"

Surf turned to face his boss, but as soon as their eyes met, he looked back toward the board.

"It wasn't a doorknob, was it?" Punk said.

Surf froze for a few beats and then slowly shook his head. His head dropped, and Punk thought he might break down, but he didn't.

Punk stood up and faced his aide, his expression stony. "I'm going to take a few things off your plate once we get back to North Island," he said. "Meanwhile, while we're out here, keep doing your job."

Surf slowly worked his eyes up from the floor and asked, "Are you firing me?"

"You need help, and your wife needs support."

Surf swallowed hard. "That sounds pretty messed up when you say it like that."

Punk turned and took a few steps toward the board, studying the faint lines that remained even after being wiped away by the eraser. Most likely they were the basics of the last flight brief held there—call signs, side numbers, launch and land times. He wished that's what he was dealing with instead of the topic at hand.

"I'm not going to get ahead of the process here," he said. "There will have to be an investigation, and it's probably best that you two not live under the same roof while it's going on."

Punk heard choking sounds behind him, and he turned to see his aide sobbing with his head in his hands. He hated to see an officer who seemed to have so much promise in such a state, but when he thought about Gwen's black eye his anger threatened to overcome his empathy. This man hit his wife.

Punk dragged the little round ottoman in front of the squadron CO's ready room chair over and sat in front of Surf. "I'm ordering you not to communicate with Gwen while we're at sea, and once we get pier-side, I'm going to have you escorted to wherever you decide you want to go, the Navy Lodge on base or wherever."

The aide's sobbing intensified as he asked, "Am I under arrest?"

Punk didn't answer, dealing with a growing sense of guilt that he had failed to deal with an issue he should've addressed at the first sign of it and frustrated that he could do nothing more until the exercise that Congressman Gordon had forced on him was over.

"I'm asking you to be the officer your record says you are for this period coming up, Surf," Punk said. "Can you do that?"

Surf wiped his eyes and, staring at Punk's feet, mumbled, "Yes, sir."

"Look at me, Lieutenant Commander," Punk ordered. "Can you do that?"

Surf snapped his head up and with more conviction said, "I can do that, Admiral."

"Okay," Punk said, patting his aide on the shoulder. "Now let's get back to making sure this boat doesn't get sunk."

CHAPTER 24

LOUNGING IN THE specially built chair in his Singapore office, Wolfe studied the bios Aswan had acquired by hacking U.S. Cyber Command's servers. A perusal of social media and court records would have gleaned some of the information, but Wolfe liked sneaking into every cookie jar the U.S. military thought it had out of reach. It had taken his AI longer than expected to break through their security, but it'd been worth it. Now, armed with knowledge of Reichert's Air Force rivals, he could start to put his virtual thumb on the Operation Blue Aegis scale.

Thompson was the least useful of the three. Although formerly a decent fighter pilot, the man now worked in private industry and sported a laundry list of corrupting influences: patronizing massage parlors, including an incident that resulted in an assault charge, possession of a Schedule 1 narcotic, and insider trading, to name a few. But the board of Thompson's employer, Rhimes-Phillips Aerospace, had used the company's best lawyers to save him for something where success meant hitting revenue targets, something like Blue Aegis. The idiot even appeared regularly in the company's social media videos as a stock "wise guy" character—which likely didn't require much acting on Thompson's part. Though it seemed fertile ground, there was nothing there Wolfe could use as leverage. One couldn't shame the shameless, and the man wasn't worth buying off.

The hypersonic missile engineer, Dr. Wu, was a maybe. He had a dutiful Asian wife, from whom he did not stray, but he was really married to his job. The man had two daughters, both in Ivy League schools. The only possibility with Wu could be floating agitprop linking him to the Communist Party, but Wu's parents, from Hong Kong, had been virulent anticommunists, so that would be a hard sell. And it appeared that Wu couldn't be bought. He lived frugally. All his earnings went to his daughters' education, and they were nearing graduation. Money wouldn't entice him.

That left General Howe, the "John Wayne" he'd joked about with Cahya.

Wolfe grinned as he pored over the data again.

Howe's father had been an Air Force colonel in his professional life and an abusive alcoholic at home—a grim, ambitious individual who had passed on some of those qualities to his progeny. The older man was dead, so that avenue was closed. But that past, coupled with Howe's career choices, offered a window into how Howe would react.

The ends justified the means for Howe. Especially if those ends elevated his status or enriched his assets. The general, an excellent F-15 pilot, had also been the prototypical Hollywood fighter jock. He was more than cocky, he was arrogant. And he seemed to have the general outlook that what benefitted him aided society as a whole.

That characteristic was generally shared among those of Wolfe's economic status, and so Wolfe understood it better than Thompson's or Wu's idiosyncrasies. A person like that would pounce on a lucrative opportunity, no matter whom it hurt.

Howe was twice divorced, with two children: a son and a daughter. The daughter had cut off all contact with him after his harsh response when she came out as a lesbian—a detail only available on Howe's Air Force email account. The son remained in touch with Howe. He was a programmer in Silicon Valley who worked for a dating app start-up.

The son had the daughter as a friend on his social media accounts, however, forming the necessary connection—an avenue he would not have realized without hacking into Howe's Air Force emails.

Wolfe leaned back in his chair. "Aswan, do you like weddings?"

The AI answered in its monotone. "I wasn't aware of your matrimony plans."

"Oh, not me," Wolfe said. "Generate us a wedding celebration where Howe's daughter marries another woman. Generate videos, still images, social media posts, the usual. But include Howe's son in some of this material."

CHAPTER 25

IT WAS LATE AFTERNOON when Punk walked into another ready room, this one farther aft than the one where he'd had the hard conversation with his aide a few hours before. Captain Morphias "Morfie" McNabb, the commander of the carrier air wing assigned to *Ford*, was waiting for him. Morfie was Gridiron's contemporary on the airplane side, reporting up to the strike group commander, a two-star currently not on board because he had better things to do than play this game that the HASC had conjured up in D.C.

"CAG," a holdover acronym from World War II when the airplanes on the carrier were collectively referred to as the carrier air group instead of carrier air wing, was tall and athletic-looking. She reminded Punk of a young Muddy, except her hair was blonde instead of brown, and she wore it braided tightly against her scalp. It was an unattractive and unfeminine look to his old-fashioned eye.

"Good to see you, CAG," Punk said.

"I just heard I lost half my jets for this thing," Morfie said in return, her firm handshake evidence that she did not use gender as part of her professional matrix.

"Afraid so," he said. "So, where does that leave us with your part of the plan?"

She walked up to the whiteboard, which was in the exact place it had been in the last ready room Punk had occupied, and pointed to some notes she'd already placed there in black marker. "More is always better, of course, but four Super Hornets each loaded with four AIM-174s is still a lot of firepower."

"The Air Force is throwing the kitchen sink at us."

CAG threw up her hands in disgust. "Well, let them. I'm tired of hearing how much better the F-22 is than the F/A-18E or F. Those guys don't even have helmet-mounted cueing, if you can believe that. Every time I've fought them in an exercise, I've always taken the first AIM-9X shot because I get a solution way before they do."

"That's Air Force procurement for you. Left hand doesn't know what the right hand is doing a lot of the time."

"Kind of like how F-35s can't operate from this ship, Admiral?"

Punk matched her sly smile and muttered, "Touché."

"Wiseass comments aside, sir, those Elmendorf squadrons know their shit, and as you said, they'll throw the kitchen sink at us." She tapped the board. "So, we're putting all our chips on red. Four AIM-174s on each jet. No AMRAAMs. No Sidewinders."

"Will that shoot down a hypersonic?"

"It worked at the Lake," she said. "But those test assets were only going Mach 2, not Mach 5."

"And the Raptors will be in company with F-35As. Dr. Wu thinks Hermes has a max range of over eight hundred miles, but he also said it could be longer than that."

CAG studied the chart taped to the extreme right side of the board. "That means we have to hit them right as they cross the U.S.–Canada border."

"Or even before that." Punk walked over to the duty desk and dialed the phone. "Send the DESRON down to Ready 7," he ordered whoever was on the other end.

Just over a minute later Captain Levi Solomon, the man in charge of the *Ford* strike group's escort ships, materialized at the entrance to the ready room. He was dressed in blue coveralls banded at the waist by a khaki belt and looked worried. Running his fingers through his curly gray hair, the Destroyer Squadron Commander asked, "Am I in trouble?"

"No, no," Punk said with a wave of his hand. *Typical ship driver paranoia*, he thought. Solomon was a "black shoe" to Punk's "brown shoe," warfare specialty labels derived from the color of their uniform footwear. Their differences extended to leadership style as well. Naval aviators were a tight fraternity who liked to joke that surface warfare officers ate their young.

Punk motioned for Solomon to take a seat next to him, noting that he looked like he needed a shave. But then he always did, even early in the day. "We're going through the outer air battle plan for Blue Aegis."

"Is it true that I've gone from four DDGs and a CG down to two DDGs?" Solomon asked.

"That's what the latest budget cut supports, I'm afraid," Punk said. "Can you make it work?"

"You want my honest answer, sir?" When Punk nodded, he said, "Probably not."

"Levi, don't you know when I need you to lie to me?" Punk said with a laugh. "Read the room."

"Let me modify my answer with a question, Admiral. You want me to shoot arrows or archers?"

"It's been a long day, Captain. Help me out with your analogy here."

"Do you want me to shoot the hypersonic or the airplane launching it?"

"That's actually a good question," Punk said. Captain Solomon looked like he wasn't sure whether to be flattered or insulted. Punk got up and relieved McNabb of the marker she was holding.

"Let's do the math here," Punk said drawing a few lines and shapes on the board. "Now Levi, your destroyers are going to be the first line of defense, and as we know, their SPY-6 radar systems aren't designed for things traveling as fast as a hypersonic. So ideally, you'd get first crack at the Air Force attack jets before they reached max missile launch range." He pointed at the chart. "CAG and I were talking before you got here, and we figure that spot is feet wet right at the border between the U.S. and Canada."

"Okay..." Levi drawled.

"So where do your DDGs have to be to shoot them down before they get to that spot?"

"Are we using virtual surface-to-air missiles or real ones?"

"Exercise scenario. We'll be on the TACTS range down here, so virtual ones."

The surface warfare officer joined Punk at the chart. "Since we're talking virtual, I want the TACTS range to program the latest generation of SM-6s, which means we can shoot the Air Force jets down at almost three hundred miles," he said. "We need to have the destroyers at the northern edge of the warning area."

"How many missiles can each DDG fire?" Punk asked.

"Good news there—if we can call anything about losing three of the five ships we wanted to use for this good—is we have *Arleigh Burke* Flight IIIs for this," Levi said, showing more animation now. "Those have ninety-six vertical launch system cells; and if those miss, they can use the 5-inch gun firing twenty rounds a minute that can hit the target as far as fifteen miles away."

"Okay, we're done here," CAG quipped with a single clap of her hands. "The destroyers will take them all out before they launch anything."

"Remember, the exercise judges at the TACTS range will throw in variables," Punk observed. "Not all of the virtual missiles fired are going to hit their targets."

"That's where we come in," Morfie said. "We can tackle any leakers that haven't launched a hypersonic yet and then focus on the missiles themselves."

"How far away from *Ford* can the combat air patrol stations be?" Punk asked.

"I'm thinking two hundred miles," she said, tapping on the chart at the appropriate CAP location. "But because of the AIM-174 loadout, we'll only have a single centerline drop tank." She looked back at Punk. "Can we have an Air Force tanker?"

"Probably not. With this funding cut, we got what we got."

"Then I'm going to have to turn one of the fighters into a tanker. We're not going to have any loiter time without gas in the air."

"So, we're down to twelve AIM-174s," Punk said. "This just keeps getting better and better."

"That's still a lot of firepower," CAG said confidently.

"Unlike the destroyers, you're shooting real missiles, not virtual ones," Punk returned, trying not to crush her can-do spirit. "Having one successful test-firing at China Lake is one thing. Using them in a high-stakes exercise like Blue Aegis is another."

"Any day we get to fire missiles for real is a good day," she said.

"Not going to argue with that."

"Then it might come down to *Ford*'s self-protect capability," Levi said. "Where are we with Project OpenShip?"

"That's a question for Vice Admiral Francis," Punk said. "But I know that NAWC-WD is playing around with a beta version on their test range. Hopefully they're figuring out a way to quickly integrate it with the carrier. We need it, like, yesterday."

"What about the Chinese navy force headed this way?" Morfie asked.

"That's for the P-8s out of Hawaii to worry about. I need you to focus on the exercise."

The others nodded and then stood in silent contemplation of the challenge ahead.

CHAPTER **26**

ASWAN'S INTERFACE loaded on Wolfe's mobile, but he swiped it off. His flight to Phuket would leave within the hour, and he was on a video conference call with a Silicon Valley start-up accelerator. Though he was alone in his Singapore office, he felt like the eyes of the world were on him. Once, he'd liked that feeling. He was the pacesetter. Everyone looked to him for innovation. But now it annoyed him.

Wolfe had pledged 1.5 billion dollars to the latest machine-learning and CubeSat networks. The accelerator was the latest in the line of intermediary companies that helped funnel money from donors to fledgling tech firms. Not only had the conference's publicity already increased the value of Wolfe Industries' stock and WolfeCoin, but it had landed him another interview with *Forbes*. The *Wall Street Journal* had also promised a follow-up segment later in the day, with him speaking for the company. Aswan would have to wait.

"This has been a great experience, everyone," Wolfe said to the crowd on his laptop screen. No matter how impatient he might be, he could never let it show. "Wolfe Industries is more than happy to provide a boost for the engineers of tomorrow."

The accelerator's moderator grinned and said, "That is fantastic, Mr. Wolfe. I know you're a busy man, but would you be willing to answer a few questions before you go?"

"A few, certainly," he smiled. He humored the moderator for a couple of reasons: it made him look accessible in a time when billionaires were about as popular as a fly in the soup, and it also allowed him to measure potential future competitors. His own company had been on the receiving end of start-up accelerators in its infancy, and he would not commit the cardinal sin of underestimating rivals, like many corporations had done earlier in the twenty-first century.

A software engineer raised her hand, adjusted her glasses, and smiled at Wolfe as if he'd just bought her a lifetime subscription of gigabit Internet. "Mr. Wolfe, first, thank you for this! It means so much to us. I was wondering, though: will Wolfe Industries be involved with the next Women in Tech Summit? It's been a real inspiration, watching what you've done to help Asian women coders, and all."

Wolfe nodded and smiled politely, just as his publicist had taught him to do, though he could barely restrain an eye roll. The earnest young engineer was referring to a dummy corporation Wolfe had created to launder some of his funds. The Thai women who served him had made a few videos for social media pretending to be programmers in a start-up funded by his company. He hadn't intended for it to receive so much attention.

"Great question, and for sure. I hope to introduce a team at the next WITS."

A second engineer was starting to ask a question when Aswan sent him another notification. It was flagged as urgent.

Wolfe raised a hand before the questioner began. "I must apologize, but that's all I have time for today. I look forward to seeing what each and every one of you can create. Goodbye, and remember what Pythagoras said: 'Numbers rule the universe!'"

He snapped the laptop shut and snatched his phone from its charging cradle. His jaw tightened as he swiped the screen to life.

Palach had been captured by the Ukrainian authorities—before Wolfe had intended that to happen.

"Fuck," he muttered as he read the details.

The Russian agent had deployed the drones Wolfe had sold him to disrupt Ukraine's communications, but he hadn't finished setting up a secure network for them first—and he'd been too close to the Ukrainian border. The old bastard had been too stupid to use the neural net after all. Old-schoolers could be arrogant while playing the game, thinking they still knew the rules. But the rules always changed. Much as Wolfe's use for Palach had.

"Send the data packet to NATO's cyberwarfare division," Wolfe said.

"Shouldn't we wait until the operation in the District is completed?" Aswan asked, referring to the Greenwood situation. "It might provide a good diversion."

"No, that won't help us now, and we need to redirect Palach's mistake," he said.

"Sending," Aswan said, its voice now sounding more feminine but still a monotone. The AI was learning, evolving. Soon it would sound like he intended it to. He hadn't expected that hearing even a rough facsimile of her voice would make him so emotional.

The drones and software Palach had used would now be traced to a Chinese tech firm. It would be enough to divert the trail from Wolfe Industries but not so much that it created an international incident with China.

Wolfe checked the details of Palach's apprehension: Aswan calculated that the Ukrainians had utilized a new cyberwarfare system—one that bore similar architecture to those developed by the U.S. military. Of course, the Americans usually sold their technology to their allies—it was like free debugging. The new system had detected not only Palach's drones but also the weak network he had put in place to control them from afar.

He massaged his jaw. "Aswan, what's the probability that the Ukrainians were given an early build of Project OpenShip?"

The reply was immediate.

"Ninety-eight percent," Aswan said.

Wolfe stood and paced the office, recalling his promise to Cahya, but in an entirely different light. "And the probability that Greenwood has OpenShip data we could use?"

"Eighty-two percent," Aswan said.

"Work out a new Capitol Hill scenario," Wolfe said as he headed for the door. "Tell our asset that he needs to produce results—now."

CHAPTER 27

THE DAY AFTER Punk met with the Blue Aegis team on *Ford*, a CMV-22 Osprey tiltrotor aircraft flew Shane Peterson out to join them. He was taken immediately to *Ford*'s SCIF, where he was met with the eager glances of a group that seemed to believe he was going to solve everything with his engineering prowess, if not his mere presence.

Chatterjee started the meeting by reciting the wish list he claimed would be necessary for Blue Aegis. Gridiron sighed with each item mentioned. Spud took copious notes. No doubt he planned to report back to Peabody Tilden what future aircraft carriers would require for defense. It was part thinking ahead, part jumping the gun since the test hadn't even taken place yet, much less succeeded.

Chatterjee and Peterson had agreed beforehand on where to place, and how to power, LASIPOD—at the cost of *Ford*'s RAMs and other surface-to-air missile capabilities. They would still be on board but would not be able to deploy during the operation. The fiber optic array for LASIPOD would have to be routed through the carrier and connected directly to the reactors, which would take time. Though

Gridiron was dissatisfied with the timetable and extra workload, he accepted the consensus—not to mention the orders he was given by the two three-stars on the exercise team—that a directed-energy weapon would be their best bet to take down a hypersonic missile.

"How soon we can get LASIPOD's power couplings and fiber array installed, now that you guys understand the power consumption part?" Punk asked Peterson. "I don't understand why that was even an issue, considering *Ford*'s energy capabilities, but at least we can get that started now."

Gridiron interjected, "They said a week, but I'd like to allow at least ten days." He was obviously concerned about the impact on his crew, which would wind up doing most of the work.

"We can do it in six or seven days," Peterson said.

"Have you guys been paying attention?" Punk asked, agitated at the laissez-faire tone of the discussion. "We probably don't have even that much time. I need you guys to install it in a few days, not a week, and certainly not ten days." He got up and headed for the door, looking back over his shoulder as he twisted the knob to open it. "Now if you'll excuse me, I'm having lunch in the chief's mess. That's where you hear what's really going on."

Half a dozen decks below, Punk served himself a healthy-sized square of lasagna from the food line in the chief petty officer's mess and took a seat at the head of the table where they told him to. Punk had loved eating with the chiefs during his days at sea. He thought back to the first time, when Chief Wixler, the man who ran the Arrowslingers' flight deck effort, had invited him. "You got invited to eat with the chiefs?" his skipper, the infamous Soup Campbell, had asked when he heard about it. "That's quite an honor. Maybe you're not a total fuckup after all."

Everyone in the Navy knew that the food in the chief's mess was better than what the officers ate in the wardrooms. The current meal did not dispel that notion. Punk needed a good meal, and this was it.

Seated to his left was Chief Electrician's Mate Nuclear Power Martha Hill, a sturdy-looking woman with ruddy cheeks and a no-nonsense air. She pronounced her first name "*Mah*-tha" when she introduced herself.

"Let me guess. You're from Boston," Punk said.

She shook her head. "Nashua, New Hampshire."

"How's this at-sea period going for you so far?"

"No complaints about the food, at least," she replied, hoisting a fork-load of the main dish. "Although I'm supposed to be on a diet." She patted her stomach. "Weight standards, you know. My lieutenant says I need to watch it, which is a joke because I always kick his ass during the run portion of the physical readiness test, and supposedly he ran track in college."

Punk laughed, and followed up with, "How are things in the reactor spaces?"

"Fine, I guess," she replied more cautiously.

Punk sensed there was more to her answer. "Are you doing any of the work for this exercise?" He had to keep it general. The chief's mess wasn't a classified space.

"Yes," she replied simply. "But I don't work on the reactors. I work on all the systems around them."

"And?"

"And nothing's easy in our world down there," Chief Hill said. "I'm sorry, sir, I'm not super familiar with what you've done during your time in the Navy. Were you a carrier CO?"

"I was."

"Then you get it." She took a big bite that suggested her diet would wait another day.

"I get the big picture," Punk allowed. "But we never did anything like this exercise."

"Lucky you," she said, her sarcasm reminding him that part of what he loved about the chief's mess was that rank came off once everybody got comfortable. "Because it's a pain."

"How so?"

"A lot of cooks in the kitchen, for starters. That's the nuke way, of course."

"Any of the China Lake folks been down there?"

"The only guy I've seen so far is Chatterjee."

"What do you think of him?"

"He's smart," she admitted.

Punk took another bite, swallowed, and asked, "Can we make it work?"

Chief Hill washed down her lasagna with a gulp of iced tea and replied, "Can I tell you later, sir?"

Punk laughed again and, sensing he was threatening to wreck her meal with the current line of questioning, changed the subject. "How long have you been aboard *Ford*?"

"Three and a half years," she said. "I re-upped midway through my tour, and that got me another year."

"What's next?"

"Well, I just finished getting my degree, so I'm trying to go warrant officer or limited duty officer," she said. "This might sound stupid considering where we are right now, but I'd like to work for NASA whenever I wind up getting out of the Navy."

"That's not stupid at all," Punk said. "And coincidentally, being part of this exercise will give you some experience in the test and evaluation side of the house."

She chuckled and said, "So my bad deal is actually a good deal."

"That's a good way to look at it," he said.

She thought for a second and then said, "You're like Mary Poppins, sir."

Punk recoiled. "What?"

"You know, 'A spoonful of sugar helps the medicine go down'?"

"Haven't heard that for a long time. I'm so old I actually saw that movie in the theater when I was a little kid."

"My parents used to play that DVD for me all the time."

"Better be careful, Chief. That's how call signs come about."

"Yours is 'Punk,' right?"

He nodded.

"How'd you get it?"

Punk gave a long exhale as he leaned back in his chair. "I'll give you the short version. First cruise in my stateroom with the other junior officers. Playing the Beatles pretty loud. Carrier CO pokes his head in and says, 'What is that crap, punk rock?' That's all it took. I was 'Punk' from that point forward."

"Mary Poppins," she considered. "I could do worse."

"Too many syllables," he advised. "A call sign should have no more than two for swift tactical action airborne over the radio. If it takes too long to say it, you might get bagged by an enemy missile."

"Poppins, then," she said with a smile.

"Again, keep it down, Chief." Punk checked his watch and realized he was already late for the next meeting in the Flag SCIF. He pushed away from the table and stood. "Let me know if I can help you with that LDO package."

She stood as well, eyes widening at his offer, and replied, "Thank you very much, Admiral. I just might take you up on that."

"In the meantime, I'll see you around the reactors."

Walking through the mess decks Punk ran into Connelly fresh from those very spaces. He was clasping a Ziploc bag.

"What did you find out down there?" Punk asked.

"Chatterjee keeps misplacing the clamps for those couplings, so I grabbed an extra one of these bags from the galley to keep them in."

"Any progress?"

"Chatterjee and our wunderkind are already getting cross-threaded, but I guess that's to be expected. Not to bilge anybody, sir, but Vice Admiral Francis needs to play an active role here."

Punk was taken aback. "How is he not doing that?"

"He needs to nip the arguments in the bud," Connelly said, fully willing to speak out of school about a senior, which reminded Punk how surface warfare officer stereotypes were born. "Knives in the backs of your peers are rungs on the ladder to success," ship drivers would say out loud, only half-joking.

"Isn't managing the engineers your job?"

"I'm a PEO, not a babysitter," Connelly snapped. "This is NAVAIR stuff."

"What are they arguing about? I thought we had this thing suitcased."

"Chatterjee makes a suggestion, and Peterson shoots it down with a technical word salad that I doubt even he understands. Einstein says we need him, but so far, I'm not seeing it."

Punk checked his watch again and mentally added a new agenda item to the SCIF meeting they were already late for.

As Punk and Connelly passed flight deck control on their way to the Flag SCIF, they were stopped by the handler, who everybody called "Shorty" because he was short, although his full nickname was "Flight Deck Shorty" so as to not be confused with his Air Department colleague "Hangar Bay Shorty." The handler sat in flight deck control overseeing every movement of planes and gear on the flight deck. He told them that another CMV-22 COD had just landed containing "the stuff you were waiting for." It was in two large wooden crates stamped with the DARPA logo—the standard misdirection play for these sorts of loads—and they were doing an elevator run immediately to get them down to the AIMD at the aft end of the hangar bay.

By the time they reached the Aircraft Intermediate Maintenance Division, the crates were being opened in the area where jet engines were tested. Chatterjee groaned when he saw what was inside the first one.

"They included the wrong emitter," he groaned as he rifled through the crate with the manic intensity of a kid who feared he didn't get what he wanted for Christmas. "And these fittings won't work with the Kineto Tracking Mount that is normally used for a Phalanx." He held one of them up. "Look at how cheap this housing is." He picked up another part. "The bolts they sent don't match the threads; they actually mixed metric with standard in the packets. Can you believe that? There are fewer extensions for the fiber optics array than we'll need. And there's only one unit. In two crates, only one DEW?"

"Is another shipment coming?" Connelly asked the handler.

"I don't show any more COD hits on the schedule," the handler said.

"We will only need one," Peterson said from the back of the scrum like a surprise witness at the climax of a Perry Mason trial. Einstein, Gridiron, and Spud stood behind him.

"We were waiting in the SCIF, and when nobody showed up, we figured there must be something better going on down here," Spud said.

"It appears we've been shorted," Punk said.

"I'm seeing a trend here," Einstein said.

"Well, if Wu and his team only launch one missile at a time, we'll be fine," Connelly said sarcastically. "I told you guys this game is rigged."

"Rigged or not, we can't lose," Punk returned.

"I'm not quitting on you, sir, but I'm also realistic about how Big Blue plays the game," Connelly said. "The Air Force is willing to lie, cheat, and steal here, and their guy in Congress, unlike ours, is a scumbag."

Punk walked over to Chatterjee and asked, "What's the plan now?"

Chatterjee's eyes held thunderclouds, but his voice was calm. "We get two additional DEWs."

"How long to get them?" Punk asked.

"A week," Chatterjee said. "Maybe two."

"Didn't you hear me in the SCIF?" Punk asked. "We don't have a week. We have a few days."

Chatterjee sighed, then nodded. "I'll make it work."

"On the silver lining side of things, once Bhaavik shows me where to install this stuff, I'll make certain that Peabody Tilden has the next carrier DEW-ready," Spud said.

"Good to know," Punk replied dryly. "However, if we fail this test there may not be a next carrier."

"That would be a problem, because it's already under construction."

"It'll make a fine museum; or if nobody wants it, razor blades."

Spud winced at the thought. Punk turned toward Gridiron and ordered, "War time footing starting right now. Shut off Internet connectivity with the beach. Crew needs to be focused on Blue Aegis, not TikTok."

"Done, sir," the carrier commanding officer replied.

"Bhaavik, you, Peterson, and I are headed for the SCIF to jump on a video chat with Timbo and the gang at NAWC-WD and have them fast-track the additional DEWs," Einstein said. "I don't care if they have to stop work on every other test program in progress."

As the group started out of AIMD, Punk took Einstein aside, telling the others that he'd meet them in the SCIF shortly.

"I need a gut check from you," Punk said. "If we're not ready I can probably tell Muddy to try and pull the plug on the exercise from her level. That won't be a good look, but it might buy us some time to get our shit together."

Einstein shook his head and said, "That's not an option, Punk. The Air Force and Gordon would just use that to line us out of the defense budget. We have to suck it up and make this work, just like we had to fight the war with half-broken Tomcats back in the day."

"Can the wunderkind make it work? With one DEW? I feel like we're flying a strike sortie with one dumb bomb. And you remember how those used to go."

"Peterson has a reputation for coming up with unorthodox solutions," Einstein said. "If there's someone who can make this work, it's him."

"And what's going on between him and Chatterjee?"

"Well, the other thing about Peterson is that he doesn't play well with others, which is why a lot of the engineers at China Lake give him a wide berth. The problem with being a genius is you think everyone else around you is stupid. He's gotten away with that attitude because he's always been right."

"I'm cool with that," Punk said. "I don't need him to make friends out here. I just need him to be right . . . and fast."

"As far as he and Chatterjee go, you have a traditionalist versus a maverick," Einstein added. "One does everything by the book; the other uses his intuition, rules be damned. The problem is both reached where they are by pressing those approaches to the max, and it worked for them, so they both think they're right."

"Can you get them to work together?"

"I'm trying, Punk."

"Remember, you survived Soup Campbell. You can make anything work."

"I survived Soup Campbell," Einstein intoned, wincing at the memory. "After this is over, I might get that on a t-shirt."

Later that night, as Chatterjee was busy configuring LASIPOD to *Ford*'s power system and Peterson was linking LASIPOD to the beta version of Project OpenShip, Punk, Spud, and Connelly played cards in the back of Ready 7 while the Super Hornet crews watched a movie on the big screen at the front. Punk welcomed the relaxed mood. Exercises like this were a marathon, not a sprint, although at times they were both. The decisionmakers needed to take their minds off the problem for short stretches here and there.

Punk looked at the aviators' heads silhouetted in front of the bright screen. He envied them. Once Blue Aegis kicked off, their mission would be clear. They'd get to fire their missiles for real even if it was only a test asset and not a real enemy. And if they succeeded, as he was confident they would, there would be bragging rights over their Air Force rivals. That was as good as it got for fleet lieutenants in their first fighter squadron.

Gridiron poked his head through the back door and, seeing what was going on, said he had time for one hand before he had to get back up to the bridge.

Connelly dealt him in and quickly called the bet while nursing yet another cup of coffee. Conversation flowed as cards were put down and picked up.

"I'm sure Gordon has offered Howe command of the new bomber wing he's planning to build if this exercise goes his way," Connelly said. "Honest to God, his antics make Curtis LeMay look like a goddamn saint."

"I'm out," Einstein said as he folded.

"Already?" Punk asked.

"In case you haven't noticed, I'm not a good poker player."

"You just need to play more, Admiral," Gridiron said with a leer. "And you need to do it while I'm here."

"Which won't be long, I hope. The quicker we can get this test done, the better," Punk said, sorting his cards and mulling his next move. "Then the heat will be off of us, and we can focus on our real job."

"I thought you were enjoying yourself, Punk," Spud said as he put a card down and picked up another. He examined his new hand with a frown.

"What's not to be happy about?" Punk said, motioning for another card. "I'm at sea with you guys. Never thought I'd see the day."

Even as he said it, he felt guilty for caring about anything other than Suzanne's cancer battle. He pushed the thought back to his subconscious, as if chemo wasn't looming, as if it was okay for him to be off the coast playing cards with his shipmates.

Connelly dealt another hand, saying, "Russia's bogged down in Ukraine, we pulled out of Afghanistan after two decades of pretend nation-building, China and North Korea are still firecrackers desperate to be heard, and the Middle East is doing its best to kick off World War III."

"Random thought alert," Spud quipped.

"Are you saying the threats are the same, Connelly?" Einstein asked as he immediately folded.

"Yes and no," Connelly said. "They're still there. I'm saying how we respond to them is no longer the same. How long before UAVs carry out sorties rather than human pilots? Howe wants a newer, bigger, sexier version of the B-36, but the grapevine points to those Valkyrie drones getting the cash down the road. How long before the Navy invests in even more advanced AI than OpenShip, one that can predict where threats will be before they even pop up? The need for large fleets is fading. The era of the carrier task force is something for the history books."

The sole ship driver in the room looked up and saw the others staring at him in horror. "These are the things that keep me up at night," he explained.

"You need a wife," Spud muttered.

"I have one," Connelly said. "All this drives her crazy, too. You should see us argue when we go see my in-laws—the last election, the cat my mother-in-law feeds at the table, the Army-Navy football game? Now that's World War III."

"Navy leads the series," Gridiron interjected.

"As it should," Spud added.

"That's what I tell my father-in-law, and it pisses him off," Connelly said. "And he was a Marine, for crying out loud! But he pulls for Army every time. So of course I have to remind him what the acronym MARINE stands for."

"My Ass Rides in Navy Equipment," Spud said it first.

"Exactly."

Punk closed his cards, fanned them again, then looked at Connelly. "Regardless of what new tech comes along, it will need a platform, one that can be deployed anywhere in the world. Until the Air Force develops teleporters, that platform belongs to the Navy. That's not going away, no matter how much fuel and thrust the Air Force packs between a pair of wings."

"Here, here," Spud said, and rapped the table.

"You're not wrong, Admiral," Connelly said as he tapped his cards. "But neither am I. Maybe in the future the naming conventions will be improved, too."

Gridiron scowled and upped the ante again, asking, "You got a problem with the name of my ship?"

"He pardoned Nixon, so yeah," Connelly said, meeting Gridiron's ante.

"Gerald Ford was a Navy pilot," Gridiron said firmly.

"Who pardoned Nixon!" Connelly said. "All I'm saying is, we need to have better naming conventions."

"We could be like the Russians and rename carriers four times," Gridiron said. "I guess they missed the memo that that's bad luck."

"What do you suggest can take the place of a carrier, then?" Einstein asked, moving the discussion back on track.

"Kill our enemies with kindness?" Connelly replied.

"Because that's what you're so good at," Punk said.

"Are we playing cards or Risk?" Gridiron asked.

"We make it through Blue Aegis, and the beat goes on," Spud said as he tossed chips into the pot. "More jobs, more contracts, enough consternation on the world stage that China and Russia have to try and keep up, and trash their economies in the process. Everything stays the same, for our lifetime at least."

"This wisdom brought to you by the man who's lost the last three hands," Connelly said.

"All right, gentlemen," Gridiron said. "Show 'em."

As each player revealed his cards, the carrier captain's grin grew wider.

Spud slapped down a pair of jacks. "There it is, my friends."

Connelly feigned choking noises, then laid down three sevens. "There it *was*."

"Damn it," Spud said.

Punk laid his cards down: three aces.

Einstein shook his head. "That's why I folded, Punk. You have the worst poker face."

Punk shrugged, smiled, and reached for the chips, but Gridiron waggled a finger and laid down a straight flush. The others groaned.

Connelly plopped his coffee mug down on the table. "I'm checking those cards, Captain, and looking up your sleeves, too."

"Remember, Admiral, the house always wins," Gridiron said as he raked in his winnings. "And out here I'm the house."

"Didn't you say you had to get back to the bridge?" Spud asked.

"I do," Gridiron said as he smiled and dealt another hand.

CHAPTER 28

PETERSON DIALED the recently sent number at the appointed time. The frantic activity all over the boat had forced him to go as far aft as he could get in the starboard catwalk to make the call. *Ford*'s crew had bustled about with preparations for the exercise all day long trying to satisfy the admiral's demand signal. It had been an exhausting day.

He took a deep breath. Everything was set in motion. Everything was going according to plan. All the same, he felt a twinge of regret. Well, that was to be expected. His soul wasn't completely gone . . . yet.

As Peterson had been told to expect, the call was answered after the fourth ring. "Location?" the robotic voice asked in a monotone.

That's it? Peterson thought. Still holding him at arm's length like he was some unimportant underling? Without him, Wolfe's plan would fall apart. He deserved a personal greeting, congratulations from a human voice. He knew it was partly for security reasons, but more and more he found Wolfe's remoteness insulting.

"Pacific Missile Test Range," Peterson said. Worried he had spoken too quickly, he started to repeat it, but the voice overrode him.

"Time?" it asked.

"A week from now," Peterson answered in a detached tone, as if another person was delivering the secret. Someone else was betraying years of trust and work. Peterson felt cheated. He was not some ordinary spy selling information. He was different. He was superior to the people who sold their nations' secrets for profit or for some ideology, or whatever such people told themselves as they tried to fall asleep in the small hours.

"I want to—"

"Acknowledged," the voice said.

The call ended.

Peterson stared at the phone, then snapped it in two and threw it overboard. Yet destroying the instrument could not separate him from what he was doing. Or what it would gain him. He thought about the payout—the price of his loyalty, something alleged to be priceless. He'd never need to worry about money again after the test. Or the Navy. Or Wolfe. In his new life, his new persona, loyalty would be just another concept thrown out into the darkness of the night.

Loyalty had gotten his dad nothing but a military headstone at Arlington. Peterson wasn't going to follow his father's example and devote his life to an organization that used him and then ignored him. He was different, emboldened in his choices by a growing realization that the image he'd created to show the world was far from who he really was deep inside, the person he was about to become.

After he exited the head, Peterson strolled into a crew's lounge near the reactor spaces. Chief Martha Hill was there, pulling a can of energy drink from the vending machine in the corner. She smiled sheepishly and said, "I know these aren't good for you, but it's the only way I can make it through my watch."

"Not a bad idea," he said. "I need one too."

"My treat," she said, handing him her can and swiping her card to get another. "This has been some exercise. I hope I configured the bandwidth of LASIPOD's beam correctly. I didn't know how nervous I was until afterward."

There was some sort of question in her statement. It took the unsociable Peterson a moment to understand that she wasn't really talking about LASIPOD. She simply wanted to talk to him.

Peterson had never been a ladies' man. It had been two years since his first and only attempt at the dating scene, and that experience had soured him on trying again to connect romantically with anyone. But here he was, "the wunderkind," on the Navy's premier aircraft carrier, and he was getting the attention of a woman.

Peterson opened the can and took a swig. The sharp imitation grape flavor stabbed his tongue as if he was drinking sweetened sand, but he forced a smile.

"They take a little getting used to," Chief Hill said, interpreting the expression on his face.

"If the caffeine doesn't get you, the flavor will," Peterson said.

An awkward silence descended, which she broke by asking, "What do you think we'll figure out tomorrow, sir?"

"Not sir. Call me Shane," he said.

"Okay, Shane."

"I'll finally be proved right, that's what will happen. It was so difficult to get the staff at the Lake to understand that aspect of DEWs," Peterson said. "They either went below 100 GHz or in excess of 400 GHz, and LASIPOD failed to perform each time. I can't get Dr. Chatterjee to understand that. Sometimes, if the power couplings were—" Peterson stopped, then took a long gulp of the energy drink.

"The couplings were what?" Chief Hill asked intently.

He caught his breath. Did she know something? Was she fishing for information? Planning to sabotage his efforts? The old innate distrust of others flooded his mind. He hated that feeling. He wanted to trust her. He'd not confided in anyone for so long, and Wolfe clearly didn't appreciate his brilliance. But he'd almost revealed his method of sabotaging LASIPOD for Blue Aegis.

"They were, er, they were insufficient to power the weapon," Peterson stammered. "The ones at the Lake, anyway. You'll see what I'm talking about tomorrow."

"Looking forward to it," she said, seemingly oblivious to his near slip.

"Thanks for the drink," he said, heading for the hatchway.

"Anytime," she called after him. Her smile had warmed him, but he couldn't allow himself to feel that now, even though the way she looked at him made him feel like he was somebody.

The somebody who was going to consign her and the rest of *Ford*'s crew to death.

CHAPTER 29

WOLFE WATCHED the feed as his agent made a fourth circuit of the Capitol and shook his head. "Your escape route is ironclad," he assured the man. "The window that Aswan will provide is more than enough."

The agent was a private military contractor named David Miller. At least that was his current alias. Wolfe had hired Miller from a prestigious mercenary company because of his "Western" look and his ability to mimic several American accents. More of an infiltrator than a gunman, Miller had thus far passed himself off as a lobbyist for some dummy corporation that allegedly manufactured military drones. It provided cover as Miller shadowed members of the Armed Services Committee.

Especially Congresswoman Evelyn Greenwood.

Miller, who was walking past the doors to the Senate chamber, answered on the mobile Wolfe had provided. "Three minutes isn't enough. I need five."

Wolfe frowned as he paced the stern of his yacht, *Fibonacci's Dream*. He was hosting tech magnates from Japan, South Korea, the Philippines, and Taiwan on a cruise along Thailand's Phuket coast. The Andaman Sea had been calm thus far, and he was close to sealing a deal with his guests. He didn't need Miller pestering him with details. The man's fee was already high; Wolfe wasn't about to pay the mercenary with his personal time as well.

And they were running out of time.

"We have already agreed on three minutes," Wolfe said, then inhaled as a delicate Thai woman applied suntan lotion to his bare chest. Her slender fingers kneaded the greasy substance into his skin with such evident pleasure that he almost believed it. As long as his guests believed the same from their assigned escorts, the women were worth their price.

"Good?" she asked, her English bearing the quality of one who spoke to rich assholes who didn't pay to hear her talk anyway.

"Very," Wolfe said, and he patted her rump. She giggled and hurried back below.

Miller grunted. "Security has increased. Maybe these people don't trust their politicians as much as before?"

"Of course they do. That's how people like us stay in business," Wolfe said. "Fine. I can manage four minutes for you, but any more will incur a set of circumstances I wish to avoid."

"It's either that or pay me double," Miller said.

Wolfe would have laughed, but the man's tone indicated anxiety instead of arrogance. He regretted not hiring a second agent for the job, but the more variables that existed, the higher the chance of failure. At least, that's what Aswan had calculated.

"Four minutes it is, then," Wolfe said. "But Miller? I expect results. Remember what happened to Palach."

Before Miller could reply, Wolfe ended the connection. He walked up to his guests and smiled when they raised their glasses in a champagne toast to him. The luscious young woman who had applied the suntan lotion leaned into him, as much for the optics of making him appear attractive and powerful as to please him. Wolfe wrapped an arm around her waist and nodded to the magnates. For the first time in weeks, he was actually aroused by her closeness.

Soon he'd have what he really wanted.

"Now, who wants to invest in humanity's next paradigm shift?" Wolfe asked.

The guests, already inebriated and distracted by the charms of the young women who surrounded them, cheered.

CHAPTER 30

IT WAS NEARLY MIDNIGHT by the time Punk picked up the phone to check in with Suzanne. It had been a good couple of days, all in all—two steps forward, one step back, which was probably as good as it was going to get. Chatterjee and Peterson got along long enough to get LASIPOD's fiber optic array set up, but to Gridiron's displeasure, that had caused power distribution problems to the electromagnetic launch system as well as other systems around *Ford*'s bow. Now Punk had to conjure up the energy to sound positive on the phone, to be there for his wife.

Except he wasn't there, and that had been the case more often than not during their marriage. They'd become accustomed to their long-distance relationship over the years, ship to shore, starting with snail mail, then email and phone, and now social media. The latter he used very little other than to occasionally comment on one of Suzanne's posts about the Padres, her favorite team, or her pickleball league.

Their call that evening was even more low-key than usual.

"Busy day?" Suzanne asked over the distant murmur of a television playing in the background.

"It was, but we made some headway," he said. "How did the appointment go? How are you feeling?"

Each of them was in the process of conducting a test, but hers really was life or death, and he wanted to be there for her. But she'd insisted—ordered—that he not beg out of the exercise. So he was on the boat and away from her when she needed him, as usual.

"OK. I'm tired," Suzanne said, though she sounded more energetic than he felt. "Very tired. I . . . well, I've vomited twice. I've been trying to eat crackers and bland things, but I can't keep them down. They said this is a normal chemo side effect. I should be able to hold food down better tomorrow or the next day."

His grip on the phone tightened as he stared mindlessly over *Ford*'s deck from his vantage point on the Flag Bridge on the island. There was activity out there, tractors moving through the yellow lights and flashlights waving, but he didn't register it fully.

"When do you go back?" he asked.

"Next week," she said.

Next week. Operation Blue Aegis might be over and he could be there with her. He started to say something, anything to dispel the silence between them, but she beat him to it.

"They say it will be at least two weeks before the doctors can tell me anything," Suzanne said. "So there's nothing to worry about till then. Focus on what's going on out there."

But the sound of her voice growing weaker as she tried to reassure him only made him feel less so. She fought to stay on the line for a few more minutes, but finally she said she had to go to sleep. He apologized again for not being there, and she croaked, "Shut up and do your job." Before he could finish saying, "I love you," the line went dead.

The next morning, Punk stood in the reactor control room watching Peterson and Chatterjee argue about LASIPOD's power output and capabilities. Peterson wanted to route more energy to it, while Chatterjee preferred a more measured approach, fearing the system would burn out when it was most needed—such as during the upcoming test.

A few members of ship's engineering team waited nearby, including Chief Martha Hill, whom Punk hadn't seen since their meal together in the chief's mess a few days ago.

"Okay, talk to me," Punk said. "Bhaavik?"

Chatterjee wiped his brow; sweat stains darkened his khaki shirt despite the boat's air conditioning. "Admiral, LASIPOD requires a burst of energy, not a constant flow. If we keep routing power to it when it isn't needed, it could burn out the couplings, and it might fail at a crucial time during Blue Aegis. We can't afford to let that happen because DARPA won't send replacement parts."

"No spare parts," Punk huffed. "This is like flying Tomcats all over again."

"Yes, but back then parts could be cannibalized from the other F-14s on board," Chatterjee said. "This situation is the opposite. LASIPOD's parts are the only ones we have."

Punk nodded and looked at Peterson, who didn't look particularly concerned.

"Admiral, Dr. Chatterjee is just plain wrong here," Peterson said. "LASIPOD requires constant energy from the reactor, or else it will not be able to power up in time to destroy an incoming projectile, especially one traveling at Mach 5 or more."

"It's going to burn itself out before the missile gets within range," Chatterjee said, the annoyance in his voice hinting that he was tired of repeating the argument.

"It's either that or not have sufficient power when Wu's carrier-killing missile gets close," Peterson said. "If the budget had allowed for the proper fiber optic array, this would not be an issue."

Punk wasn't sure who to believe. He scanned the faces of the others and thought he saw Chief Hill about to say something.

"Yes, Chief?" he asked.

"If we adjusted the array so that only certain strands received a constant power flow while the others received no power, we could accommodate LASIPOD's needs," she said. "Then, when the weapon is ready to fire, power can be sent through the inactive strands."

Peterson bridled. "That would still rob the weapon of the required energy," he said in a tight voice. "In order to discharge a one-hundred-plus-kilowatt energy beam on command, the device must receive constant power—from the *entire* fiber optic array."

Chatterjee's eyes narrowed. "I like what the Chief said. That sounds feasible."

Punk saw Chief Hill stand a little straighter.

"A similar configuration was tested at the Lake," Peterson said obstinately. "It failed."

Punk looked at Einstein and said, "This is where all your post-seagoing schooling pays off. You make the call."

"Say again how long it takes for LASIPOD to charge before being fully operational?" Einstein asked.

"At least seven minutes," Peterson said. "That could have been cut down to five and a half if DARPA had sent us higher-quality couplings and the full cables."

"Seven minutes is a very uncomfortable window, gentlemen," Punk said. "Especially if we have a hypersonic coming at us. If one of those is flying at Mach 5, and it's launched, say, from five hundred miles away, that would leave us with an eight-minute response window—with seven of those minutes spent just getting LASIPOD online."

Peterson smiled in self-satisfaction and said, "Exactly, sir."

"And how long would that process take if we fed constant power to the weapon, as you suggest?" Punk asked.

Peterson gave another self-satisfied smirk. "Five minutes, sir."

In the weapons courses he took during nuclear power school Punk had learned that the strength and effectiveness of the weapon's laser on a target depended on several factors: the energy required to break down the target's material, its ablative qualities, its reflectivity, the level of humidity between the DEW's emitter and its target, and even the chemical makeup of the atmosphere. Then there was the distance from the target to the emitter. To add more factors to those variables, especially a delay in time, invited disaster.

Punk turned to Einstein. "Well?"

He shrugged. "They both have valid points. Right now, the problem is getting the power levels to remain constant for either of those scenarios. The couplings DARPA sent aren't the best for the task."

"How soon can they be replaced?" Punk asked. "And if they can't be replaced, is there anything we can rig up using spares?"

Chatterjee cleared his throat. "Sir, Peterson claimed those would not work."

"Why not, Mr. Peterson?" Punk asked.

"I didn't say they wouldn't work," Peterson said. "I said it would take time to make the necessary adjustments for them to work, which as you keep pointing out is time we do not have. If we follow my instructions, we'll be fine. Let General Howe and Dr. Wu do their worst. If we follow Dr. Chatterjee's and Chief Hill's suggestions, however, we'll get hit by a hypersonic."

Chief Hill looked pissed off, but she remained silent. *So, this is life with the big boys, huh? Be careful what you wish for.*

Chatterjee looked as if he was about to lose it, but he composed himself with a deep breath. "Admiral, I understand risk, but this is inviting a catastrophe." He pointed at Peterson. "I strongly disapprove of his course of action."

Punk focused on the toes of his brown boots, trying to consider the options without looking at either man. "A lot can transpire in two minutes," he said, as much thinking aloud as deciding. "If Wu deploys a hypersonic traveling faster than Mach 5, then that window closes dramatically." He looked at Einstein. "I say we go with Peterson's plan. Do you agree?"

"I agree," Einstein said.

"Copy that," Chatterjee said without looking at Peterson.

Punk grabbed Einstein by the elbow and dragged him to the adjacent space as the others got to work. The two three-stars spoke in loud whispers.

"I thought we'd have agreement between those two by now," Punk said. "The time for arguing is over. We need to get moving on solutions."

"The damn couplings keep malfunctioning," Einstein returned. "Peterson has a point. Chatterjee will not let it go."

"Both of them seem to genuinely believe what they're saying. That's what makes it hard to pick a plan."

"No pressure," Einstein said, offering a half-smile. "Peterson built the LASIPOD system, after all, and his demonstration at the Lake is why it's here at all. I'll have to keep Chatterjee calm. If necessary, I'll separate them."

"Will that be enough?" Punk asked.

"We'll get it done, Punk," Einstein said. "Even if I have to roll up my sleeves, push those two aside, and do it myself."

Punk smiled. "You'll make it work. You always do."

CHAPTER 31

THE WALL SCREEN in Wolfe's Singapore office showed sixteen drone feeds. Each displayed a scene in various shades of black, purple, gold, and crimson: hues revealed via infrared. He glanced at the side map depicting their location: a cobalt mine located in the Democratic Republic of the Congo's Lualaba Province.

It was nighttime there, but work continued unabated in the glare of spotlights. The feeds showed workers prying the precious ore out by hand with picks and shovels, evidence that the colonial era wasn't over in Africa. The crude, backbreaking method of extraction was common in such places where regulation, education, and wealth were lacking. In the world Wolfe planned to usher in, those injustices would be swept aside. But first he needed to exploit the connections of the exploiters. Unfortunately, that sometimes meant eliminating them altogether.

China's hunger for cobalt, used heavily in the latest technologies, had grown, especially as its navy tried to keep pace with the maritime forces of the United States. Interrupting their supply line would exacerbate their rivalry with the West and make them even more anxious. And anxious players often made mistakes.

"Aswan, give me an update," Wolfe said after a sip of coffee. It was night in Singapore, too, and he needed to stay alert.

"Our CubeSats report excellent latency with the drones," Aswan said.

"Good," Wolfe said. "You have the ISIS-DRC video ready?"

"Yes," Aswan said.

He had considered framing the attack on a Western nation, but local terrorists always came through for him—even when they didn't know they were doing it. The Congolese arm of ISIS had rejected his offer of drones last year, thinking he was setting them up. Which he had been, of course, but now he would blame them anyway. The deepfake video would claim responsibility in their name.

"Okay, what am I looking at?'" he asked as the feeds brightened. "There are guards there at the mine, too? Hmm."

The footage revealed men standing over the cobalt pits brandishing Kalashnikovs at the workers below. One laughed as he urinated on a miner. Another drank from a beer bottle in one hand while pushing a local woman against a tree and lifting her skirt with the other.

Wolfe swallowed. He had the power to stop what was about to happen. The wealth to make things better in such places. But he had to stick to the overall plan. One intervention might save a few lives, but he was going to save the world.

At least he couldn't hear the woman's screams with the feed muted. Maybe he was helping her after all.

"Would you like for me to change the drones' engagement parameters?" Aswan asked. It always anticipated his wants.

"Yes," Wolfe said. "ISIS wouldn't leave anyone alive. Neither can we."

The drones hovered closer.

"Thirty meters," Aswan said. "Engage?"

"Not yet," Wolfe said.

A teenage boy stumbled and dropped an armload of ore. A guard jumped into the pit and slammed the butt of his rifle in the teenager's back.

"Twenty meters," Aswan said.

The woman was trying to fight back, but two other guards joined her assaulter.

"Fifteen meters," Aswan said.

Wolfe kept watching. Feeling the blood freeze in his veins. Knowing he needed to witness these things so he would know the horror. Feel it. Understand the need for change.

"Fire," he breathed.

The drones, fitted with missiles, unleashed their payloads. All sixteen screens flared brilliant yellow, dulled to a furious orange-red, then blacked out.

He wondered if *Ford*'s image would look like that when a hypersonic Hermes struck it.

CHAPTER 32

PLANNING ON an early start, Muddy entered her office in the Longworth Building before most of the other representatives and their staffs arrived. Gretchen, one of the two interns working for her between semesters at Georgetown, met her with coffee, and she was eager to get the caffeine into her system before having to deal with Congressman Woody Withers. She had what she needed to get him to help her deal with Gordon—or at least she hoped she did.

She sent Gretchen to find one of Withers' interns to track him down, since he'd not been answering her calls or texts. She needed a better ally on the Hill, but Withers was all she had.

The early news shows had been full of the ISIS-DRC attack on the Congolese cobalt mine last night. The video claiming responsibility was condemned by the usual powers and praised by the typical agitators. Just another world crisis, barely noteworthy. Among her lofty goals when she ran for public office was to help bring lasting peace to the world. And she knew from her own naval experience that peace didn't come without strength.

Politics was an entirely different arena from naval aviation, where one didn't need to second-guess colleagues or bribe them to help the effort. Members of a squadron either worked as a team or didn't make it back to the boat. Not so on the Hill. Teamwork, even among one's own political party, was driven by polls and the next election cycle. She recalled the advice of a retired general who now headed a veterans' service organization: officers should exercise their right to vote but otherwise stay out of politics while wearing the uniform.

Though Muddy had left the Navy, she still felt that advice applied when it came to congressional oversight of the military: leave the politics out of it and do what is best for the country.

Gretchen had also brought donuts, bless her, and Muddy allowed herself one, making a mental note to add a few minutes on the treadmill during her regular workout at the Congressional Fitness Center that afternoon. She worked hard to stay in shape, very much believing that it was a lifelong pursuit. More than that, she *had to* stay in shape. Being fit was part of her image, part of her appeal to voters, and there was always a photographer somewhere ready to catch her at an unflattering angle.

Her leather flats made no sound as she crossed the carpet in front of the desks of her staff and unlocked the door of her office. The scene that came into view made her stop so quickly that the coffee splashed on the floor. The file drawer where she kept sensitive and classified information was open. The drawer she always kept locked unless she was using it.

An open file drawer. In her office. That she kept locked.

She thumbed through the folders and immediately saw that the one containing the printouts about Project OpenShip were missing. They were simply statements of record concerning what the Chief Digital and AI Office were contributing to Operation Blue Aegis—but they mentioned specifications about Project OpenShip, whose inclusion in the exercise had not been announced to the Air Force.

It didn't look like a crime scene. The drawer wasn't hanging by a broken metal slider, and folders and the papers it held weren't scattered over the floor as if the place had been ransacked. Her desk appeared untouched.

But she always kept that drawer locked.

It took Muddy a second to regroup, then she grabbed her mobile and called Sally, her chief of staff, to ask if she'd left the drawer open by accident when she secured the office the previous evening. Sally, who sounded half-asleep, said she hadn't opened the drawer at all yesterday. Muddy apologized for waking her up and said she'd see her in the office in a bit.

Before taking the next step, she looked her office over, checking to make sure she hadn't misplaced the files in her briefcase, her desk drawer, or anywhere else. She hadn't taken them home, much less out of the office. She had a rule about taking classified material out of the proper spaces. Her time in the Navy had taught her how to handle that stuff.

She heard unfamiliar footsteps in the adjacent room, too heavy to belong to Gretchen. Old instincts kicked in, the ones that kept a fighter pilot from allowing a bandit to roll in on her. Though she knew she should call the Capitol Police immediately, she didn't. If the burglar was still in the office suite, she wasn't going to give them the opportunity to flee. She was unarmed, though. Wearing a skirt and blouse that confined her movements.

It would have to do.

She slipped off her shoes and held them in her hands, ready to use them as weapons, and padded into the other room. The glow of a screen caught her attention, then the silhouette of a figure behind it. The figure darted for the door to the hallway, but Muddy reached it first.

"Stop!" Muddy yelled, hoping someone would hear and come running to help.

She brought up her hands in time to ward off a kick to her abdomen. The momentum shoved her to the left, and the heel of the intruder's shoe slapped against the flats she was holding. The shoes went flying as the sting of impact numbed her hands and sent a painful tremor up her arms. Totally unarmed now, Muddy came back with a left hook more desperate than calculated. Her fist connected with a shoulder, and the figure grunted. She could see now that it was a man in a black suit and tie, with close-cropped dark hair.

He pivoted into her strike and slammed his left fist into her right side. Though the blow knocked the wind out of her, Muddy delivered two quick jabs—first a right, then a left—to the man's face. The first clipped his nose. The second crunched into his right cheekbone. The contact busted her knuckles as it broke the skin on his face.

As he staggered backward, Muddy sucked in a deep breath.

"Security!" she shouted—then choked as the man kneed her in the stomach. Muddy doubled over but shielded her head with her right arm while grabbing his belt with her left. As he hammered at her back and face, Muddy, using her handhold as leverage, delivered a fierce right uppercut to his sternum.

The man coughed and wobbled long enough for Muddy to whip around and attempt a roundhouse kick to his right side, but her skirt prevented the full extension of her leg, and her foot snapped into his thigh instead. The attack still forced him back—but toward the hallway rather than deeper into the office.

As she went for another kick, he swiped her supporting leg out from her under her and then staggered into the corridor. Muddy landed hard on her back but was back on her feet in a second pursuing him.

When she entered the hallway he was nowhere in sight.

"Security!" she yelled again. She heard a window break and ran toward the sound.

The building's alarm should have gone off, but it didn't. By the time Muddy reached the shattered window the thief was gone.

"Security!" she cried a third time, tasting blood as she did. She touched her lip, busted in the fight. Her right cheek ached, and her stomach throbbed. The skin on her knuckles burned. Her punches had cut the flesh across several of them.

She looked up at one of the security cameras in the ceiling and asked, "What the hell is going on here?" before pulling out her phone and dialing the Capitol Police.

She felt something between anger and shock that someone had broken into her office. As she waited for somebody to answer the phone on the other end of the line, she walked back into her office and found the files detailing Project OpenShip, and its inclusion in Blue Aegis, on Sally's desk. Right where the thief had been standing.

She recalled the glow of his phone. Had he been photographing the files?

"Hello, this is the Capitol Police," a man's voice said after way too many rings.

"Yes, this is Congresswoman Greenwood. We have a major security breach on the Hill. Someone broke into my office and is still at large."

———

After Muddy gave her deposition to the Capitol Police, she sat on a bench in the hall outside her office clasping the fresh go-cup of coffee that Gretchen had brought her. She welcomed the warmth in her hands but didn't drink. Her mind was alive with suspicions, and she feared that too much caffeine would turn into a headache that would cloud her thoughts.

Her knuckles had been bandaged, and the physician had cleared her to leave. But Muddy remained anyway. Maybe the police would find a clue, or maybe they had already apprehended the man. Surely the security cameras had recorded something. If not that, a lone figure fleeing the Longworth Building early in the morning had to have been noticed by somebody on their way to work.

But the minutes ticked by without any answers.

Congressman Woody Withers appeared, briefcase tucked under one arm, the other hand holding a phone pressed to his ear. He nodded apologetically to her as he halted before the bench that she was sitting on.

"Yes, I will do that," Withers said. "Thank you, goodbye."

He put away his phone and regarded Muddy with grandfatherly concern. "Evelyn, I'm so sorry. This is terrible. Are you okay? My goodness, your face is bruised, and ... oh, dear. Do the police have any idea who your attacker was?"

"No," Muddy said. The reply tasted like ashes in her mouth. "The man escaped. I've been told that the building's security system was hacked. Whoever it was turned off all the cameras and alarms in the building for four minutes. There's no hard evidence the bastard was even here except for that broken window."

"It's all over the news," Woody said. "That's why I stopped by."

Muddy finally sipped the coffee and recoiled as its heat scorched her torn lip. "Of course it is. Congressional beat reporters live for this sort of thing."

He took a deep breath and sat beside her. "Did the perpetrators take anything? Or are you allowed to say?"

Muddy gave him murderous side-eye. "Why wouldn't I be allowed to say?"

Withers' head jerked as if she'd jabbed him in the mouth. "Well, you know, if they took something classified."

"Who said anything about classified?"

"Why else would somebody break into your office?" he asked in bewilderment.

Muddy shifted so she could face him directly on the bench. The steaming coffee in her hands was a caldera between them.

"You are the key representative for Space Force on the committee," she said. "You've been an ally of the Navy at times, but your loyalties remain with the newest branch of our military."

"What is your point, Evelyn? My loyalties are to our country. Always."

Muddy arched an eyebrow. "Which service branch does Space Force recruit from the most?"

Withers gave her a puzzled look, then barked a scoffing laugh. "Evelyn, really..."

"The Air Force," Muddy said. "Space Force came from the old Air Force Space Command."

"That surely has nothing to do with this," Withers said.

"It doesn't?" she asked. "The branch you represent in the HASC benefits when you support Air Force initiatives. Don't act like there isn't pressure from them."

"And you're not biased? Not everyone gets to fly a Navy jet fighter, after all," Withers said, then sighed and looked away.

"Come on, Woody. Of course I'm biased toward the Navy. It's what I did, and it's the industry base I represent. But think about it. If Gordon gets his way this time, do you think the Space Force will get funding next year for the Starfire Optical Range? Or research into those initiatives on the table for Space Domain Awareness?"

Withers gave a rueful laugh as he returned his eyes to her. "You're saying that if we don't stick together, Gordon will sideline what our branches need."

"Exactly," Muddy said. "We need aircraft carriers. We need the best satellite defenses in the world. We also need to trust one another. You and I, we don't have many allies here. Hell, you see how hard it is for me to make friends here." She showed her bandaged knuckles for emphasis.

They shared a smile, then a laugh.

"Evelyn, I don't know," he said.

"I do," she said.

Withers looked at his shoes, contemplating.

"Well?" she asked. "Are you helping me or not?"

Withers' jaw hardened. She was losing him.

Steam wafted off the hot liquid in her cup, a cloud of suspicion between them that she needed to clear away.

"Woody, do you know why I ran for office?"

He regarded her warily. "This isn't going to be an inspirational pep talk, is it? You did just fight off a burglar. Maybe your head needs to clear first?"

She stared back, then offered another smile. The coffee, cooler now, tasted sweet and rich.

"I don't want to go all Top Gun movie on you, but when you're flying a jet like the F-14, you get a new perspective on the world," she said. "You feel connected to everything and everybody around you. After my last tour ended, I wanted to keep that connection and have an even greater hand in it. A real role. As a participant, not a spectator."

Withers laughed softly. "I ran for election because our congressman was as rotten as an apple in autumn. When I actually won, I couldn't believe it. I asked my wife, 'What do I do now?'"

"What did she say?" Muddy asked.

"She said, pardon my French, 'Don't fuck this up.'"

Muddy smiled and immediately regretted it, her busted lip flaring with pain.

"I have a daughter who's a NASA engineer," Withers continued, "and through her I've come to believe that space exploration is still important and needs to be funded. So, now that I'm on the Armed Services Committee, I want to fund things like the Space Force, which is grossly underfunded and struggling to emerge from the shadow of the other services, particularly the Air Force. Even though I've never been up in the air at the controls of a fighter jet to see the perspective you've experienced, I want to give that to others. The security, and the knowledge."

"Now *that* sounded like an inspirational pep talk," Muddy said.

He chuckled. "I suppose so."

She waited. Sipped more coffee. Gave him time to decide, even though she had little time of her own.

"Yes, I can help you," Withers finally said. "But I want a little more trust from you, too, Evelyn."

"That sounds like a question," she said.

"What was taken from your office?" he asked.

Muddy chugged more coffee, looked down at her feet, then back up at him. "Nothing was taken, but that man was looking at documents detailing the CDAO's permission for Vice Admiral Reichert to use Project OpenShip for Blue Aegis."

"Unless they have in-depth details, how can that be damaging?" Withers asked.

"Because now someone will know that Reichert has the assistance of machine learning in the test," Muddy said. "And that file did offer some details. It isn't useless information, Woody. If the Air Force knows the Navy has AI helping them defend the aircraft carrier, they'll try to counter that with something of their own. And now, after this break-in, I'll have to mention Project OpenShip to Congress, not just the HASC."

"You're implying someone on the Hill will use that information," he said. "But who?"

She gave him a flat look.

Withers frowned. "You can't be serious."

Muddy's answer was to gulp more coffee.

"You *are* serious," he said. "Gordon?"

"He'll do anything to help his Air Force connections," she said. "Even if it means leaking classified projects to the rest of Congress—and thus his Air Force friends."

"Do the Capitol Police have any solid leads?" Withers asked. "What about the security cameras outside the building?"

"I haven't heard anything about those yet," she said, "but I'm not getting my hopes up. Whoever did this was a professional. The police don't have anything to go on. No fingerprints in the office or on the door, other than mine and my staff's."

Withers scowled. "Are you implying what I think you're implying?"

"I'm not going to accuse Gordon of this," she said, tapping on her coffee cup. "But it's highly suspicious, don't you think? Gordon, the Air Force—they're all suspects. But we're not going to call them that."

"We?" Withers asked. "You mean you and me?"

She nodded and took another lip-stinging sip of coffee. Maybe she could get Punk what he needed to save *Ford* after all.

—

"What?" Punk said to Muddy on the phone later that morning.

"The committee is having an emergency hearing within the hour," she repeated. "I have Congressman Withers assisting me with this. Maybe after what happened I can get a few more voices on our side."

Punk paced back and forth on *Ford*'s Flag Bridge. "Have you considered that Gordon might accuse you of doing this yourself in order to drum up support?"

Muddy sounded chagrined. "You think he would?" She answered her own question. "Nothing is beyond that man."

Punk stopped pacing and watched as a Super Hornet launched off Catapult No. 3. He waited for the reverberation of engines in afterburner to die away before continuing.

"That sound makes me miss the boat," Muddy said. "I never thought I'd say that."

Punk laughed and returned to the subject at hand. "I don't think you can leave anything out when considering what Gordon might do. From what I've seen he's one of the biggest gaslighters in Congress, and that's saying something these days."

"It would be just like him," she said. "But it doesn't matter. I'm going to try to use this to help you out. Besides, there's the matter of national security. The Hill is like an overturned anthill right now."

Her hesitation made him chuckle. "Please promise me that you won't use that in the hearing."

Muddy snorted a rueful laugh. "Don't worry, Punk. We'll turn this around."

Though he admired her determination, Punk was very worried that his ace in the hole—Project OpenShip—might be less effective if his rivals implemented a counter AI scheme. Or worse, that a foreign power had been seeking the information. Disabling the security in a congressional building for four minutes was no mean feat. He recalled the hacking attempts across several military systems that Einstein had mentioned.

It didn't feel like a coincidence.

"Will the Budget Office reconsider the approved DEW equipment?" he asked. "You should have seen what they sent us. The folks out here were a bit less than enthused."

"That might be difficult," she said. "Although the OpenShip details are now considered leaked, that doesn't mean they'll offer more expensive, or alternative, options. They might even offer you less, as a precaution." Then she voiced his unspoken fear. "And of course there's the possibility that a foreign power might be involved here."

"Spies." he said. "Great."

"How's morale on the boat?" she asked.

"It's good. Captain Williams knows how to keep his crew inspired," Punk said. "But this test is wearing everybody down all the same. And if the equipment gets changed, then I'll have to hear the same arguments from them all over again, and it wasn't easy to get them to compromise the first time. But that's a problem on my end. You have enough on your plate as it is."

Another Super Hornet roared into afterburner, the one on Catapult No. 4.

"Man, I really do miss that," Muddy said, her voice barely audible to Punk over the jet noise.

He waited until the jet shot off the front end of *Ford* before replying, "You miss night landings?"

She chuckled and replied, "Nope."

"Do what you can, Congresswoman, and keep us posted."

"Will do, Admiral."

Minutes later, Punk called the team into the Flag SCIF for a discussion. Once he relayed what had happened—the news had already spread, but in a limited narrative that the media was spinning as part security threat, part political gamesmanship—the others reacted with grim resolve.

"It looks like someone else didn't like the budget, either," Spud said.

"Does this mean we'll have to engage in another bout of Whiteboard Wars?" Connelly asked. "I think our markers are out of ink."

"This isn't a joking matter," Chatterjee said, glaring at both men. "A spy might have compromised a congressional office. Integrating OpenShip was our crown jewel, our guarantee."

Spud shrugged. "I'm aware of that, Bhaavik. Maybe the Budget Office will actually give us what we need this time."

"Perhaps," Einstein said, "but more eyes are on us now. And they're the wrong ones."

Punk noticed that Peterson was the only one nonplussed by the news. "Shane, what are you thinking?"

"Getting angry about it won't solve anything," Peterson said calmly. "We can still make this work. Mr. O'Leary is right: perhaps this will cause the committee to revise our allotted equipment. Not that we need more. One LASIPOD is sufficient."

"But since the information is considered leaked, we might end up with even less to work with when the committee reconsiders our Blue Aegis assets."

"This is going to make some people in Congress feel like the whole thing is more trouble than it's worth and just hand over the funds to the Air Force after all," Connelly said. "Think about it: this break-in is on their turf, not ours."

"If it really *was* a break-in," Peterson said. "The media hasn't reported it as such, just 'misplaced' documents."

"Give me a break," Spud said. "If Muddy says it was a break-in, then you can take that to the bank. She got in a goddamned fistfight with the guy, for crying out loud."

"All the more reason for the committee to do the right thing," Chatterjee said.

Connelly snorted. "Have you actually ever *met* a politician?"

Chatterjee gave Connelly an annoyed look and said, "This isn't a political matter. This is a Navy matter. We are making sure our carriers remain secure against all threats."

"Cool speech, bro," Connelly said.

"Admiral Reichert, I suggest we rethink our approach," Einstein said. "What if even more of this operation has been compromised? The hacking attack is a major concern. Should we even conduct the test at Point Mugu?"

"Where else would we do it within the allotted time frame?" Punk asked, then shook his head. "No, we keep as many of the variables the same as possible. We've already done too much work to toss it all out now, even considering this possible leak."

"Who do you think did this, Admiral?" Gridiron, who'd been uncharacteristically silent to that point, asked. "Care to make a guess? The Chinese? The Russians?"

"Oh, God, I hope so," Connelly said. "Maybe it was this inbound Chinese fleet. That would actually be a threat that would plus-up the budget and end Gordon's game here and now."

"So, who wants the data?"

"The Air Force, so they can kick our asses on this exercise and steal our funding," Spud said. "But maybe that's just the old retired Navy guy in me speaking."

Peterson looked at Spud as if he'd just been informed there wasn't an Easter Bunny. "Would they do something that low, not to mention illegal, just to get more funding?"

"You need to get off the base at China Lake more often, son," Spud returned.

"Howe is a dirty bastard," Punk said. "But this? No, even he wouldn't do this. In any case we can't focus on that. That's the FBI's job. Our job is to make this test work. So, once we get word back from Muddy, we'll make whatever changes are necessary. No more bitching out here either. Debate club is over. Got it?"

The others assented with nods and murmurs but little passion, which frustrated Punk even more. He left the SCIF before letting his anger come out in words he would regret.

Later, as he sat in the flag mess toying with the salmon the cook had prepared for him between normal meal hours, Spud came in and took a seat across the table.

"You going to eat that or just treat it like a hockey puck?" Spud joked. "Make a slapshot?"

"It's actually really good," Punk said. "I'm just not as hungry as I thought I was."

"Here, give it to me." Spud grabbed a knife and fork from another place setting and slid Punk's plate toward him. He took a bite and said, "You're right. It's good."

"I wasn't loving the energy in the SCIF earlier," Punk said.

"They want this to work, Punk," Spud said between bites. "They're just tired. They've been getting very little sleep. Maybe four hours, tops. Then they're up and at it again."

"Hell, it's the boat. We never get enough sleep," Punk said as he watched Spud shovel the salmon into his mouth.

"Yes, but now we've got the weight of the Navy on our shoulders, not just the nation and the world," Spud said. "Does that sound grandiose enough?"

"Plenty grandiose," Punk said.

Spud set his fork next to the remaining piece of fish and cleared his throat. "Freedom isn't free."

Punk shook his head and smiled. "Is that what Peabody Tilden coaches you to say to investors?"

"Surprisingly, only a few of us there are veterans," Spud said. "The others think we need the pat on the shoulder, that 'thank you for your service' nonsense. I love the Navy, and the friends I've served alongside," Spud continued. "I loved being up there in a Tomcat. That's why I do this. Not all those other things."

"Maybe that's what they want to hear," Punk said, recalling his own experiences in that vein. "What they think they need to hear from us."

Then, just as suddenly as that moment of reflection came, it was gone, and they could be old friends sitting in the ready room telling tall tales. People like them defaulted to that. Punk wasn't sure if it was a coping mechanism or simply a representation of who they were.

"I think that fish is dead, Spud," Punk said, breaking Spud out of his trance-like stabbing of the plate. "Maybe this situation with Muddy and OpenShip will blow over and Blue Aegis won't be affected that much."

"Yes, and maybe Connelly will actually be helpful," Spud said, mechanically sprinkling pepper on the fish.

"He's a black cloud, for sure, but he's also right most of the time. That's why Einstein brought him on board."

Spud looked around, then produced a metal flask from his pocket. "I was saving this for a toast once we beat Howe, but maybe you need a bit of it now?"

"Old habits die hard, huh, Spud?" Punk waved it away. "Are you trying to get me fired? Put that away. Besides, wine pairs better with salmon. You're a captain of industry now. You should know things like that."

"Just here to help," Spud said, smiling as he put away the flask.

"You give too much of it."

"So, what now?"

Punk thought for a second then said, "Keep our eyes on the prize until we hear back from Muddy. Maybe let Connelly take Chatterjee's place with Peterson."

As the two men pushed away from the table and stood, Spud asked, "Who do you really think broke into her office?"

Punk took a deep breath and replied, "Someone we need to stay two steps ahead of."

CHAPTER 33

"PROJECT OPENSHIP uses machine learning," Wolfe said as he looked over the information Miller had just sent him. "I'm not surprised, but it complicates things. But nowhere near as much as your performance has done."

Miller, communicating via his burner phone, sounded chagrined and annoyed. "That bitch walked into her office before she should have. I staked out that building for days beforehand, and Greenwood never got there that early."

"As a fellow veteran yourself, I'd have thought you would expect her to stay unpredictable," Wolfe said.

"Nevertheless, I did the job you hired me to do, and I'm prepared to receive the rest of my fee," Miller said.

"That will have to wait since you're still in the U.S.," Wolfe said. "I can't risk a transaction that large. They would flag it."

"That's not what we agreed on," Miller said tightly.

"We *agreed* that you would get me this data without incident," Wolfe said. "Greenwood wasn't supposed to know you had been there. I risked my systems for four minutes. Systems I will need to cover for even more now. Have you even paid attention? The American news media is reporting a break-in and an assault on a congresswoman in her own office. This raises their military and Homeland Security threat levels and interferes with matters already set in motion."

"*I told you, she arrived early,*" Miller said, biting off each word.

"And she kicked your ass," Wolfe laughed.

"I want the rest of my fee," Miller said. "Right now. I've been locked out of my main offshore account, and I need a fucking plane ticket ASAP. I need those funds."

Wolfe leaned back from his laptop and placed his hands behind his head. "I told you it will have to wait. The FBI is monitoring transactions of that magnitude."

"Then make a thousand small transactions," Miller countered. "You've done it before."

Wolfe leaned toward the laptop screen and let his anger show. "Yes, but that was when you *completed* the mission. You fucked this one up." He let Miller stew on that for a few seconds before continuing. "Don't worry, you will get paid. Until then find a homeless shelter. America has plenty of those. Or sleep on a park bench."

Before Miller could say anything else, Wolfe ended the call.

He sat back, sighed, and directed his voice at his mobile. "Aswan, what's the probability you can hack into OpenShip within the window I've laid out?"

"Sixty-four percent," Aswan said.

"Make that a top priority," Wolfe said. "If you're unable to breach OpenShip, this goes nowhere."

"Lower the NOSS hack in my priority queue?" Aswan asked.

"Yes," he said. "For now."

"Should I send the OpenShip data to the account in Doha?" Aswan asked.

Wolfe hesitated. He'd promised it to Cahya, but he preferred to keep a few cards in his hand for now. The MSS might prove useful again later, as long as he had a carrot to dangle before them.

"Send her the first half," he said. "If she makes good on her end of the bargain, then she'll get the rest."

"The probability this will incur a negative reaction from her is 54 percent," Aswan said.

"Cahya might get pissed, but she's patient," he said. "Send the first half. Now, do you have that batch of cruise missiles ready to launch at the U.S. Navy task force making its way through the Gulf of Aden?"

"Yes," Aswan said. "A Houthi deepfake video claiming responsibility is prepared for release afterward."

"Good," Wolfe said. "Make sure it includes the usual nonsense about solidarity with their brethren in ISIS. Make China and the U.S. think they have their hands full, so they'll throw more resources at a problem that isn't there."

CHAPTER 34

MUDDY STORMED OUT of the committee hearing chamber, not bothering to wait for Withers, who trailed behind her, struggling to keep up. She strode through the halls, ignoring everything around her—people and snippets of conversation or interviews playing on devices and screens in the offices she passed.

Although the committee members had expressed their outrage over the break-in, they had just voted to freeze the Navy's part of the Blue Aegis budget until the matter was settled. And the test had been moved up. The parts Punk's team were begging for would not be available to them until just before the test, if at all, and they would have to prepare within four days instead of having a week. She had to rethink her strategy; she was in hostile territory now.

A gaggle of reporters were oblivious to her presence as she passed them. They were surrounding Congressman Seth Gordon, who was more than happy to dominate the news cycle around the break-in. It bugged her that he was living rent-free in her head. He was telling the assembled press corps that while he was sorry Representative Greenwood had been "harassed," if that indeed was the case, he charged her with trying to use the incident to garner sympathy that could be used to shape the defense budget.

"Furthermore, Congresswoman Greenwood is burdening the Capitol Police at a time when they already have too much on their plate," she heard him say.

She walked on, gritting her teeth, and suddenly he was behind her. "Evelyn, my dear, I'm so sorry this happened to you, so very sorry."

She didn't look back as she replied, "Oh, so you admit it happened? That's not what I just heard you tell the press."

He moved up beside her, speaking quietly. "The committee made their call based on the facts. Whatever it was that happened, Blue Aegis is partly compromised now. And you have to own the fact that you didn't secure your file."

"So, you're victim blaming?" she returned in outrage.

He shrugged. "Face it, none of this brouhaha is worthy of the committee's time."

"Then why continue with the exercise?" Woody Withers said from behind them. Muddy turned around and looked at her so-called ally in disbelief.

"I think Congressman Withers is correct to ask that," Gordon said with a wide smile. "Why continue with this mess now that the Navy's defense has been compromised? The Air Force is sure to prevail. It's a waste of the taxpayers' money. Your bid for the pity vote in there just didn't work."

Before they parted ways in one of the Longworth Building's long corridors, Gordon softly offered one last menacing remark: "Don't make me cripple you further." He was gone before Muddy could respond.

Withers remained at her side. He cleared his throat and said, "That could have gone ... better."

"You hung me out to dry, Woody," Muddy said. "You weren't an ally in the hearing, and you weren't one just now."

Withers sunk his head. "What was I supposed to say? I don't know why you thought that playing on their sympathy would work."

"Their *sympathy*? Now you sound like Gordon. All I asked them was to give the admiral what he asked for."

"It's not like Congress has the deep pockets of a multinational corporation, Evelyn."

Muddy stopped in her tracks. "What did you say?"

"Well, I was going to say that maybe we should get the congressman from Arizona—"

"Not that, the corporation idea. Woody, you're a genius."

"I am?" he asked.

She tugged his arm. "Come on. We now have an emergency conference call to attend."

CHAPTER **35**

MAJOR GENERAL HOWE'S shoes crunched over the desert sand of Edwards Air Force Base. Sunset was approaching, and the red-orange orb cast infernal hues across the airstrips and tarmacs. The wind tossed up dust devils all around him. He heard voices in the whistling winds. His father, an abusive, alcoholic Air Force colonel, demanding that he reach the top of the service's hierarchy, having failed to make it himself. His two ex-wives, both of whom had loved what his career and rank brought them more than they'd loved him, demanding more and more. His daughter pleading for understanding and then going silent. And his son, who had moved to Silicon Valley to use his programming genius on whatever trivialities younger people occupied themselves with these days, speaking in undecipherable slang.

He took out his phone and read the posts on his son's social media account again. He considered unfriending him, or whatever it was called when you deleted someone from that part of your life. It was petty, sure. But so was lying, as his son had done. Or lying without gaining any advantage from it. That was senseless. Reckless.

It didn't really matter that his daughter was gay. She was just too much like her mother, who had made his life miserable both when she was married to him and afterward. But for his son to engage with her when he'd promised he wouldn't? And at her wedding to another woman, no less? Seeing the videos of them laughing together plunged a knife into his chest. They were happy without him in their lives. Maybe he'd been lying to himself, and he really *did* care what they thought of him. Either way, he didn't need that emotional baggage.

It was lonely at the top of the mountain, as the saying went. It had taken a lot of effort to get Howe to his current position. Skill, charisma, connections to the right people, and other methods he preferred not to think about. Friends and family had disappeared along the way. He snapped his phone shut and stuck it in his pocket. If there were any ghosts in the winds coming to haunt him, he'd beat them the same way he'd defeated other challenges and obstacles: he'd do whatever it took to guarantee victory.

Howe possessed enough self-awareness to know he had that reputation, and he supposed it was well-deserved. Self-reflection wasn't something he indulged in often. It usually served little purpose, and he wasn't one for navel-gazing. But now, after years of work and intrigue to get where he was, it had come down to this one little test against Reichert and his boat. "Sink an aircraft carrier," the committee and top brass had said, as if they were talking about some poorly defended ship of half a century ago. He was no Billy Mitchell, sinking ships with prop-driven bombers. He had done too much to ensure the world didn't leave him behind—and he wasn't about to change that just because one admiral was stubborn enough to think his way was the right way.

He smiled grimly to himself. As he put the phone away Bear Thompson walked up to him, silk tie in corporate colors flapping in the breeze, his smugness infecting the air like jet exhaust.

Slapshot fumbled in his breast pocket for the cigarette pack he formerly kept there. He'd stopped smoking six months ago, but apparently his subconscious hadn't got the memo. He returned Bear's confident smirk, afraid the other man might think he was catching him in a moment of vulnerability. A person could never let down their guard, even among friends or allies. Not that Bear was the former; he barely constituted the latter. But Howe was never going to let him know that. Ignorance, particularly for the ignorant, was bliss.

"Greenwood did us a favor, huh?" Slapshot asked. "It figures, since Reichert trained her."

Bear snickered, then sipped from a soda can. "That shit on the news was glorious. She was ranting that someone broke into her office, and it backfired on her—just like you said it would when you heard about it. How did you know she would react that way?"

"Because she's a straight shooter," Slapshot said. "That's the only way they know how to operate. The Navy trains them to think inside a box, Bear, and they can't think outside of it. After what Gordon said, half the world thinks she's crazy." As a military man, he was just as angry about the break-in as any red-blooded American was supposed to be. But whoever had been responsible had done him a big favor.

Bear rubbed the cold soda can, damp with condensation, across his forehead. "Yup. And she'll look even crazier once we start posting on social media."

"No, don't waste time on that," Slapshot said. "Whoever pulled off the intrusion gave us what we needed. The ACC's cyber warfare division has been alerted about OpenShip. They should have something for us by tonight."

And then Howe would shuttle the Air Force's cyber assets to grapple with Punk's digital ace: Project OpenShip. Whether it was a beta version or not, he wouldn't allow the Navy to possess a superior tool. That bit of information from the break-in could influence Blue Aegis' outcome. He wasn't going to look a gift horse in the mouth, either. One attacked congresswoman was miniscule compared to what a new long-range strategic bomber program could do for U.S. security.

"Ah, so that did work out with the brass?" Bear asked.

Slapshot nodded. "And Wu? Did you convince him about what we need?"

"Barely," Bear said. "He wasn't easily persuaded."

"You sound doubtful."

Bear ran a hand through his thinning hair. "Do you really think he can send one of those missiles out at Mach 10? I bet he told the brass that so they'd keep funding his projects. Not even the Chinese or Russians have developed a working hypersonic that makes that speed, at least not in the field."

"I could shovel some horseshit that we're Americans, not Chinese or Russian, but that's the kind of talk we made back in flight school," Slapshot said. "If Wu says he can get this done, then he can get it done. His record speaks for itself."

"Do you really think this will intimidate them?" Bear asked, trying not to sound too critical.

"If it doesn't, then this won't be much of a contest," Slapshot said. "And make no mistake. That's what this is, Bear: a contest. We're not testing technology here. We're deciding the role our military pilots will have in this century."

"If there are still human pilots twenty years from now," Bear said. "You know how much I hate to even say something like that."

"Let the brass worry about that. I'm worried about today. And today is going to belong to the Air Force, am I right?"

"Sounds like a recruitment ad," Bear said dismissively in a rare contradiction, but he maintained the shit-eating grin.

Slapshot snorted. "We're going to accomplish something LeMay and all the others before us never managed, Bear: we're going to beat the Navy at their own game—and we're going to make it stick this time. LeMay imagined a unit that could strike anywhere on the globe. Mitchell proved the effectiveness of such a unit. We have faster engines now, faster missiles. Faster ways of detecting those things. And all those variables operate in the air, not on a boat."

Bear grinned. "I'm already sold, so you're preaching to the choir here."

Slapshot smiled thinly. "That wasn't for you," he said softly.

"Oh?" Bear asked.

Howe nodded past Bear.

Wu approached them, his unbuttoned lab coat flapping in the breeze. He was speaking into his phone, then checking something on his tablet. It had taken a while for Slapshot to get accustomed to the fact that Wu wasn't having a conversation with someone; he was dictating his thoughts. And the man was constantly dictating, always preoccupied with a dozen ideas. When Wu was only a few feet away he seemed to notice them for the first time.

"Is the Hermes ready, Doctor?" Slapshot asked, offering the crocodile smile he used to get the truth out of the unwilling and lull the wary into a false sense of security.

Wu, immune to the general's charm, simply nodded. He muttered into his phone, frowned at the tablet, then tucked both into his coat pockets. "I do not think it wise to showcase the Hermes to the admiral and his team before the operation."

"Why not?" Slapshot asked. "The briefing will be via video call. I simply want it in the background for Reichert and his team to see."

"It is a weapon, not a parlor trick," Wu said.

Slapshot clapped Wu on the shoulder as if they were old friends. "That's the thing, Doctor. Half of any weapon's effectiveness lies in its ability to intimidate. Look at how that worked for nukes over the decades." He looked over at Bear. "Am I right, Bear?"

"When you're right, you're right, General," Bear chirped back.

"The Budget Office is getting tight with us as well, General," Wu said. "The Hermes will have to be trucked back to its launching site at the extreme northern edge of Edwards. Timing is already tight for the day of the test. Your request sounds like an unnecessary stunt."

After the theft in Greenwood's office, the Armed Services Committee had reexamined what it was allowing the Air Force for the test, too. The F-35s out of Elmendorf AFB would have only one hypersonic air-to-surface Hermes available to launch; likewise for the missile trucks. Slapshot was still grinding his teeth over that one. But some decisions required sacrifices. He would make it work, even if they gave him a few T-38s flown by rookie pilots. The important thing was that Reichert had lost resources, too, and the onus was on him to pass Blue Aegis. The Air Force had nothing to lose. That was the beauty of this whole construct.

"Doctor, don't forget that your precious missile is on trial here, too," Slapshot said. "The United States military has yet to deploy an effective hypersonic weapon in any theater. We've been playing catch-up with everyone else."

"What you call catch-up I call development," Wu said, looking bored with their conversation.

The man's arrogance gnawed at Slapshot's patience. "Our job is to be the top dog," Slapshot said. "Aren't you tired of reacting to what everyone else is doing, instead of taking the lead? The Russians or the Chinese make a new missile, and we build one to counter it. That's not taking the bull by the horns, Wu. Your missile, if it succeeds, will put our military back in the forefront. Doesn't that inspire you?"

Wu glanced at an MQ-9 Reaper drone speeding over the landscape near an airstrip. "General, you and I grew up in a world where nuclear ICBMs influenced every aspect of our civilization, every layer of military doctrine. Zeitgeists, paradigms, all formulated in the shadow of the mushroom cloud. Now that cloud has expanded into the digital realm and we have UAVs. Drones, thinking machines, and algorithms. Warfare is less personal than ever before. If anything inspires me, it is to maintain impersonal transactions between belligerents."

"Transactions?" Bear asked with a grimace. "You are one cold mother, Doctor."

Slapshot laughed. "Actually, he's quite the opposite, Bear: an idealist. I think the doctor's saying that he wants wars to be as bloodless—and blameless—as possible. That's a lofty goal. Others have tried to make it work, but conflict is not meant to be pretty."

"Now that I think about it, I believe you're right, sir," Bear said deferentially.

Wu graced them both with a flat stare. "Then what is conflict supposed to be, General?"

"An event with a foregone conclusion," Slapshot said. "And that conclusion is that we are the victors. The same goes for the engineering aspects as well as the tactical ones. How does it feel, knowing some PLA engineer in Beijing is at this very moment creating something even faster than your Hermes? That our enemies live to outthink you? Their drive, their existence, is built around creating the best damn missile that current technology can achieve. A person like that is hard to beat."

"This isn't just a competition," Wu said, less sure of himself.

Slapshot took a deep breath before he continued: "Let me put it another way. Think of what we're doing as strategic Darwinism. And we're not going to be the ones outcompeted and sentenced to extinction. You must feel the same way, or you wouldn't be here at Edwards. You wouldn't be putting two kids through college and supporting a wife back in Los Angeles if you thought otherwise."

Wu scowled, the first emotion Slapshot had ever seen him exhibit. "My personal life has no bearing on this conversation; nor is it any of your business, . . . sir."

Slapshot took a step toward Wu, not to intimidate him but because he wanted—needed—Wu to comprehend.

"I wouldn't be standing here either if I believed differently," Slapshot said. "Look at all the things people like you and I have cast aside and forfeited in our lives just to be in this position. I ask myself every morning if it was worth it. Well, Doctor? What do you think? Was it?"

Wu kept his eyes on the Reaper for a moment, then looked at the truck housing one of the Hermes missiles nearby.

Slapshot reached out and touched Wu's shoulder and asked again, "Was it worth it?"

Wu's face hardened with resolve. "I will have one of the missiles ready for the pre-test briefing."

As the engineer walked away, Bear raised his brows and grunted. "Good work, sir."

"Everyone has their weakness," Slapshot said.

Bear nodded and asked, "What's yours?"

"Losing."

CHAPTER 36

"THEY HAVE SHORTENED the time until the operation starts," Peterson said into the second of the three burner phones he'd brought aboard. "The new timetable puts the test less than four days away. I'm not sure this will work. I don't have everything in place. I need more time."

"It must work," the voice on the line said.

There was no room for negotiation in the speaker's tone. Just like his dad's voice. It was like having one of their old arguments all over again. It made Peterson nauseous.

"It's getting difficult to maintain my ... position here," Peterson said, hand cupped over the lower half of the phone to block the wind across the starboard catwalk, the place where he'd made the previous call as well. "Someone will suspect. They might already. People are noticing things. Things it's getting hard for me to hide. I might have to take action, do you understand? To safeguard everything I have done."

He didn't want to hurt anyone, especially Chief Martha Hill. But she had taken to sticking her nose in where it didn't belong.

"Damn it, are you even listening to me?" Peterson asked.

"Continue as we have arranged," the voice said simply.

"What?" Peterson asked, incredulous. "Dad, I can't..."

He stopped. Goosebumps popped out on his arms. He had called the avatar "Dad."

Eyes swimming with tears, Peterson clasped the phone. It would be so easy to snap it in half and throw it away. Snap it and stop his sabotage. Maybe even talk to Martha about it. Explain. She liked him; she would understand.

"Allowances have been made, and the appropriate measures will be implemented," the avatar said, still in his father's harsh tone. "Proceed with the plan. Take whatever actions are necessary."

He wiped his eyes. "I..."

"Shane," his father said. "Do it."

The call ended.

Peterson snapped the phone apart and let it drop into the sea. He swallowed and considered telling Martha anyway.

But it was too late for that. Too late for everything.

"I'll take actions, all right," he muttered as he wrote a text file on his main phone and uploaded it to his cloud drive.

Justin Wolfe wasn't the only one who could make contingency plans.

CHAPTER 37

THE REVISED BUDGET for Operation Blue Aegis following the intrusion into Muddy's office was even worse than Punk had initially feared. Not only did it allow for no replacement parts for LASIPOD, it also forbade parts for anything else on the carrier until the operation was carried out. That meant everything from washing machines to fighter jets. It normally cost between 6 and 8 million dollars per day to run an aircraft carrier. The original test budget had swollen that amount by several million. Now it had been shaved down to just above normal levels.

The amount of fuel that would be allotted to the carrier air wing's jets on board for the exercise had been reduced as well, meaning they would be in the air for a shorter amount of time. While the Super Hornets weren't the centerpiece of his defense plan, without them the Air Force's F-22s were far likelier to achieve aerial superiority over the mock battlefield. If Wu equipped one of those jets with an air-to-surface Hermes, the Navy fighters were *Ford*'s first line of defense.

The news had come at the worst possible time: two hours earlier, one of *Ford*'s EMALS, the Electromagnetic Aircraft Launch Systems that launched the jets, had suffered a power failure due to a fault with its cycloconverter. Chatterjee was accusing Peterson of contributing to the failure with his continual adjustments to LASIPOD.

Punk and Einstein, flanking Gridiron in the elevated captain's chair on the port end of the bridge, shared a disappointed grimace. At this late hour there wasn't any need to hide how the committee's decision made them feel.

Gridiron read over the list again on his tablet. "What happens if the other EMALS breaks down? We use duct tape? Super glue? Push our jets off the flight deck like we did when we were getting out of Vietnam? This whole thing has turned into a damn joke."

Punk sighed as his eyes moved to the large windows that overlooked the flight deck. "Gordon wants to bleed us dry, but we're not going to let him. We still have one day until the exercise commences. Suggestions?"

"We can still make this work with one EMALS," Gridiron said. "We're only talking about four jets. We can have them airborne and on station before the Air Force takes the first shot."

Einstein raised his brows and said, "That's good to hear, but meanwhile, Chatterjee and Peterson have stopped talking to one another, and they're both making adjustments without approving them with me first. And Spud and Connelly are back to arguing about what part of the carrier can get hit and it still not sink."

"Let Connelly focus on coordinating defenses with the destroyers," Punk said. "He's been over every square yard of this boat at least twice in the past week."

Einstein's lips tightened. "With all due respect, Spud should let Connelly complete his evaluations. I realize the man is a curmudgeon, but we need the data he's gathering—even if the results anger Peabody Tilden."

"What are Chatterjee and Peterson even arguing about at this point?" Punk asked. "Is this a leadership problem at my level? If so, this is the time to say it."

Einstein yawned and said, "Punk, it's not you. We're all under a ton of stress. They're trying to break us, make us slip up."

"This is going beyond psychological warfare," Punk said. "We can't fight each other."

Surf Davis walked through the hatch and handed Punk a printout of an official Navy message. "This just came in from the House Armed Services Committee."

Punk read the message aloud: "Following the leak revealing the use of Project OpenShip AI technology, the House Armed Services Committee has decided to grant Air Combat Command security protocols over Blue Aegis."

"That falls under their cyberwarfare division," Einstein observed. "That means that OpenShip could be vulnerable to cyberattacks during the exercise."

"They even cleared this with USCYBERCOM," Punk said. "That means it's kicked up to the highest level at the Pentagon. Clearly, they think it was a serious breach of security."

"There have been multiple low-level hack attempts on several Air Force and Navy servers over the past month," Einstein said. "I heard from Connelly's boss at NAVSEA that someone tried to hack into the network used by our Triton subs last week. And this threat extends across all electronic equipment in the region."

"Howe gets what he wants yet again," Punk said, unable to hide his discouragement.

"Hey, it could be worse," Einstein said, raising his hands. "The committee could have taken OpenShip from us entirely."

"But now Howe can shut it down if he thinks it's been compromised," Punk said. "Then he could claim USCYBERCOM gave him permission to do so. Perfect smokescreen for his bullshit."

It was too convenient—the same pattern Punk had seen during his tenure with Howe on the Joint Staff. The man excelled at dirty tactics. "But we need to focus. Let's see about the EMALS and damage control."

Punk and Einstein left the bridge to check on the situation in the hangar bay and walked into a heated discussion between Rear Admiral Connelly and Spud about hull integrity and manufacturing costs. Although that wasn't necessarily Connelly's realm, he was talking to Spud like *he* ran Peabody Tilden and not the other way around. Once they spotted Punk and Einstein the exchange ceased. Beyond them several of the crew's engineers fiddled with an electromagnetic motor.

"What's the trouble, gents?" Punk asked.

Connelly waved a digital tablet and said, "Admiral, we have a problem with the advanced weapons elevators. This is the same old problem we had a few years back, along with the electronic catapults and advanced arresting gear. They supposedly passed, but I've always thought someone's palm got greased to make that happen."

"For the record, Peabody Tilden doesn't make any of those things," Spud said.

"Right," Connelly sneered. "You guys are just responsible for making sure that the companies that do make the stuff aren't ripping off the Navy."

"They were all working when you commissioned this ship. After that it's your job to keep them working."

"Anyway," Connelly said, "It's going to take longer to load ordnance onto the Super Hornets for Blue Aegis. And worse than that, right now all the catapults are down, so there's no way to launch anything but helicopters off the flight deck."

"Can a helicopter fire an AIM-174?" Spud asked, trying to lighten the moment.

"We were just on the bridge with the captain, and he didn't say anything about the catapults," Einstein said, ignoring Spud's attempt at a joke.

"He doesn't know about it yet," Connelly said. "Funny how all of this stuff failed on the same side of the ship where the wunderkind set up his laser gun."

"What's your point, Admiral?" Spud asked.

"My point, *retired* Captain O'Leary, is I'm wondering what else is going to break down on this boat before that Hermes rips us a new one. And we don't have the parts to fix any of this!"

Punk maintained his calm, letting Connelly's pique wash past him. "How long until we can get the parts and then get these systems up and running?"

"The engineers tell us the elevator should be working within the next few hours," Spud said.

"That EMALS is broke dick for Blue Aegis," Connelly said with dramatic finality.

Punk looked at Spud and said, "See if you can speed up the supply chain with the elevator and cats." Then he gestured toward Einstein and Connelly. "Let me go sidebar with you guys over here."

Once they had crossed to the other side of the hangar bay, Punk focused on Connelly. "You work for Vice Admiral Francis and are here based on his recommendation, but I'm the officer in charge of this exercise, and I need you to get a grip on your tone."

"My tone, Admiral?" Connelly shot back without offering any sense that repentance was imminent. "I'm just trying to flag how hosed up everything is out here. There is something seriously wrong going on. You don't find it strange that all these things screw up a few days before the exercise?"

"I don't want excuses or conspiracies. I want this boat functioning at maximum level," Punk said. "Which reminds me: I need a rundown on the destroyers' readiness by 1900 tonight."

Before Connelly could push back, Punk stepped past him and out the nearest side hatch. He found Chatterjee down in the bowels of the carrier going over schematics with a trio of ship's engineers. He looked near exhaustion, sweating heavily and with dark circles under his eyes.

"I heard you're still having issues with LASIPOD," Punk said.

Chatterjee handed the schematic back to the engineer and slowly nodded. "Yes, sir. The device experienced a power surge earlier. We're trying to determine if that affected the EMALS that ceased operating."

"Peterson isn't here?" Punk asked. "Or Chief Hill? Where are they?"

"He's on the next deck down checking power feeds to the weapon," Chatterjee said with restrained scorn. "I don't know where the chief is. I called for her ten minutes ago."

"Is this related to our decision to allow LASIPOD a constant source of energy?" Punk asked.

Chatterjee sighed and leaned against the railing, looking even more drained. "Yes and no. It's probable that the power to the DEW created these issues, but we haven't completed a full assessment yet. That may take the rest of the day, and maybe even all night."

"And tomorrow is the big day," Punk said.

"Yes," Chatterjee said, dejected. "This could affect *Ford*'s other defense systems as well, such as the Phalanx and the RIMs."

Punk responded with a grunt and crossed his arms. "Let's hope that nothing gets that close tomorrow. What about Peterson? Aren't you two correlating on this?"

"He keeps making changes without alerting the rest of us," Chatterjee said. "I have to backtrack and check everything he does. Chief Hill and the other engineers treat him like he's the next Oppenheimer. Well, news flash: He's not."

"I've heard you're also making changes without clearing them with Vice Admiral Francis first. We all need to be on the same page."

"Is that what the admiral said?" Chatterjee asked, irritation adding strength to his voice and frame. "He keeps taking up for Peterson. I was tasked with defending *Ford*, but I've had to guard my own work as well. It isn't fair, sir."

"I've known Admiral Francis for a long time," Punk said. "I trust him unconditionally."

Chatterjee's eyes narrowed. "Perhaps your trust in old acquaintances isn't—"

Punk uncrossed his arms and met Chatterjee's hard gaze with one of his own. "Don't finish that sentence. From here on out, clear everything through Vice Admiral Francis first. Is that understood?"

"Yes, sir," Chatterjee said quickly.

～

The phone on the Flag Bridge rang at the appointed time, and Punk answered it by pushing the speaker button. "Reichert here."

"I have some news," Muddy said on the other end of the line. "Is Spud there with you?"

"Right here, Congresswoman," Spud said, leaning across Punk to talk directly into the speaker.

"We really need some good news about now, Muddy," Punk said.

"Well, my fellow congressman Woody Withers from the great state of Washington, who's been a disappointment as far as support up to this point, came through with a plan to get parts to you guys in a hurry," Muddy said. "If Peabody Tilden can supply the parts on a research basis, we can skip HASC oversight, and it won't dig into the Blue Aegis budget."

"That's great, but we need those parts first thing tomorrow," Punk said.

"With this option, my folks can fly them here within eight hours," Spud said. "Replacement components for the EMALS and the AWE. I just need to make the call, and they're on the way."

"What about the power couplings for LASIPOD?" Punk asked.

"That's not possible until four days from now," Spud said. "The original plan was to have all of this available within the original test preparation window."

"This is still good news, Muddy," Punk said. "You're a lifesaver."

"You can thank me after you knock down a hypersonic," Muddy said. "We're counting on you, boys. Godspeed."

"Roger that," Punk said.

CHAPTER **38**

AT 1830 PUNK was interrupted by a call from Gridiron. He set aside the message traffic Surf had collected for him, which included details of Project OpenShip's integration with the Fudds' APY-9 radar systems, and snatched up the receiver. He rubbed his aching brow and cleared his throat, wishing he'd asked his aide for more water on his last delivery of paperwork. "Reichert here."

Gridiron spoke quickly, sounding stressed. "Admiral, we have a casualty down in the engineering spaces."

"What's broken now?" Punk asked.

"Not an equipment casualty, a personnel one."

Punk groaned and got out of his chair, a match with the one the captain sat in a level above him in the island. "Who is it?"

"Chief Martha Hill," Gridiron said.

"Is she hurt?"

There was a brief silence over the line before the captain said, "She's dead, sir."

Punk's chest tightened as he recalled that first meal in the chief's mess where she told him about her hopes for the future.

"What the hell happened?"

"She was tweaking the power couplings to LASIPOD," Gridiron said. "She was working by herself and must have gotten something switched on the fiber optic array. The medical officer said she died instantly. Electrocuted."

Punk listened numbly as Gridiron related that the young woman's body was currently frozen in *Ford*'s morgue. Her family had yet to be alerted, but that would come shortly. An investigation was already under way.

"What did Peterson and Chatterjee have to say? Were they in the vicinity when it happened?"

"Negative," Gridiron said. "Both had been trying to contact her, but she never answered her phone or reported in. Everyone assumed she was occupied with her duties, and things have been so busy down there . . ."

"This is terrible," Punk said. "How well did you know her?"

"Pretty well. She was part of the crew when I assumed command, so we've worked together almost two years."

"Did she seem like the type that would be reckless with procedures, the sort of thing that gets sailors electrocuted?"

"Negative, Admiral. Quite the opposite, in fact."

"Is there any danger of this happening again?" Punk asked. "Is LASIPOD and its array still functional?"

"Peterson said all of its systems are functioning—after he corrected the changes Chief Hill made to the couplings."

Punk paused, processing everything Captain Williams had just told him. Gear failures were one thing. A dead sailor was quite another. "Please find Dr. Chatterjee and send him to the Flag Bridge."

"Aye, sir."

Chatterjee rushed through the hatch and onto the Flag Bridge a few minutes later. He looked terrible, uniform crumpled and grease streaks across his face. Without waiting for Punk to ask him anything he said, "I tried to warn her."

"Of what? What happened?"

"She was headstrong, too eager to impress Peterson. God knows why. She kept adjusting the couplings, trying out her idea about not routing power through all the fiber cables to save on power. I warned her against messing with it."

"What did she do wrong?"

"She didn't ground herself while switching out the cables," Chatterjee said.

"That sounds like a rookie mistake," Punk said. "She wasn't a rookie."

"She fawned over Peterson."

"We have a dead chief," Punk said flatly. "This rivalry between you and Peterson needs to end. We have less than three days now until Blue Aegis."

Chatterjee gave him an incredulous look. "Admiral, this isn't about any sort of rivalry. He played her, and he's done it with the rest of the nuke engineering team, too. And Chief Hill paid the price for that."

"Is that what you plan to tell the accident investigators?" Punk asked.

"Absolutely."

Chatterjee stood at near attention at the right armrest of Punk's chair. After a short silence he said, "I guess this means the exercise is canceled."

"No. It's a tragedy, but there are too many things in motion to cancel Blue Aegis because of it. Unfortunately, sailors dying at sea is a part of the business. We'll honor her by pressing on. Speaking of that, I still need you to iron out LASIPOD's incorporation with Project OpenShip."

Chatterjee stiffened even more and asked, "Am I being reassigned, sir, demoted to Peterson's assistant?"

"That weapon is nothing more than an expensive laser toy without OpenShip and *Ford*'s systems working in concert to guide it," Punk said. "Let Peterson continue with LASIPOD. You'll be responsible for helping us tell it where and when to fire."

Some of the tightness left Chatterjee's face, but he still looked flustered. "Thank you, sir. I will do my best."

"I need you to."

As Chatterjee left the Flag Bridge, Punk picked up the phone and asked Gridiron to find Shane Peterson and send him up.

When Peterson appeared on the Flag Bridge twenty minutes later, he seemed largely unaffected by the loss of Chief Hill, although he made a pro forma expression of sorrow.

"So, what happened?" Punk asked.

Peterson ran a hand through his buzz-cut hair and shrugged. "She wanted to prove that she was right. She was very intelligent, but headstrong. She wouldn't listen to me, or even Chatterjee, for that matter."

"Was she acting under your orders or Chatterjee's?"

"Neither, sir," Peterson replied, snugging his hands into his pockets. "I had tasked her with fixing a frayed cable earlier, plus some troubleshooting, preventive measures, and such. But nothing related to what she actually did. I didn't even know she was tweaking the couplings until someone found her body."

"There's no doubt that she electrocuted herself?" Punk asked.

"Afraid not, Admiral," Peterson said, finally showing a little emotion.

Punk wondered if Peterson's apparent lack of feeling was because it was his first brush with death in the service. He'd been stationed at China Lake for most of his tenure in the Navy. Punk saw little point in questioning him further. Like Chatterjee, the man needed rest, and Punk needed them both to continue their duties. He changed the subject. "I understand your father was a naval aviator," Punk said.

Peterson pulled the Top Gun patch from his pocket and held it up to show Punk. "Operation Iraqi Freedom. We lost him right as I was starting flight school." His eyes lost focus with the memory. "Everyone told me they were sorry for my loss and what a great man he was. But they were telling me what I already knew."

"How did he die?"

"Cancer."

The word shot a chill through Punk, and he reflexively asked, "You were a pilot?" to send his mind elsewhere.

"Not for very long," Peterson said. "I suppose I wanted to impress my father. I thought I would have a patch like this of my own that I could pass on to my son."

"You have a son?"

"No."

Punk rose out of his chair and walked over to the side window, staring out to the horizon past the port side of the carrier. "What you've done here will change history," he said. "You'll give sailors the power they need against the forces they're tasked with guarding against. Your father would be very proud of you."

Peterson smiled and said, "Thank you, Admiral. After what happened with Martha, I needed to hear that."

Punk walked over to a shelf and grabbed two cans of energy drink. He handed one to Peterson. "You pulling an all-nighter too?"

"I appears so, sir," Peterson said with a smile.

Punk cracked open his can and raised it. "A toast to the memory of Chief Martha Hill," he said.

"To Chief Martha Hill," Peterson echoed, doing the same. They threw their heads back, tipped the cans upright, and held them there until they were empty.

Wanting to stretch his legs, Punk followed Peterson down the ladder, but he stopped on the second deck while the young engineer kept going deeper into the hull toward the reactor spaces. Punk took a seat at a table full of sailors eating midrats, the "midnight rations" that got the graveyard shift through the night. When someone asked him if he knew anything about the chief who'd died, he said that it looked like she'd been electrocuted and that she was a front-running sailor and reminded them not to cut corners and to follow procedures closely.

A mess specialist came over and asked if he'd like something to eat—a slice of chocolate pie, a chili dog, a chicken quesadilla, or some banana pudding. He said pie would be good, and it was served up in short order. He ate it in the company of the crew, pleased to see that they were in good spirits despite the long days of endless work and the loss of a shipmate, and were interested in the unclassified details of Blue Aegis. They all agreed that *Ford* would kick ass, and their unbridled enthusiasm gave Punk the motivation to do his part to make it so. As it ever had been, the sailors led him, not the other way around.

Afterward, he climbed back up to the Flag Bridge and tried to call Suzanne. She didn't answer. But it was late, after all.

Too late for some, he thought. *Far too late.*

Rear Admiral Connelly followed Punk's instructions and hopscotched between *Ford* and the two Flight III *Arleigh Burke* guided missile destroyers on one of the carrier's two MH-60S Knighthawk helicopters. On each destroyer he did a gut check of the weapons departments and tactical action teams on the eve of Blue Aegis.

Spud worked with the engineering staff as they used the parts supplied by Peabody Tilden to repair the damaged EMALS and weapons elevators, a nice kick-save with a major hat tip to Muddy.

Peterson said that LASIPOD was fully operational and asked Einstein if he could mark the weapon, peripherals, and energy system as off-limits to prevent tampering, accidental or otherwise.

In CIC, Punk, Einstein, and Chatterjee oversaw a trial run of OpenShip's integration with *Ford*'s AN/SPY-4 Multi-Function Radar system. The MFR's main feature was a track-while-scan routine that allowed it to engage multiple targets simultaneously. It was designed for the detection and tracking of cruise missiles, submarine and surface threats, manned aircraft, and UAVs. Its capability versus hypersonic weapons was unknown.

Yet as Punk looked on, OpenShip sped up the MFR's data crunching by several factors, and the reaction of the weapons experts around him bolstered his confidence in it. Security leak or not, he would need the machine-learning software if they were to have any chance against Wu and his Hermes.

Gridiron entered CIC wearing an expression that made Punk fear another member of the crew had died. The captain gestured for Punk to follow him into an alcove behind a bank of servers and held up two rectangular black objects.

"A couple of the ordnance guys found these on one of the aft mounts under the starboard catwalk," Gridiron said, handing the objects to Punk to examine.

"It's two halves of a cell phone," Punk observed, only moderately interested.

"It's a burner phone. And the battery's missing. Whoever brought this aboard tried to destroy it and throw it overboard. But they didn't realize how weird the wind flow is around the ship."

As Punk examined the broken device, Gridiron filled in another blank: "And it gets worse, sir. The medical team found the exact same type of burner phone, snapped in two with the battery missing, in a pocket of Chief Hill's coveralls."

Punk scowled. "This wasn't her phone, Captain. I'm damned sure of that. There's a spy on your boat."

"You think somebody planted this on her?"

"Two burner phones with the batteries missing? That's more than just a sailor trying to sneak a call to a boyfriend in San Diego."

"What do you want to do?" Gridiron asked.

Using the mental agility that had made him such a good fighter pilot, Punk quickly considered their options. The spy could be anyone. The incriminating evidence could have been planted on Chief Hill's body at any time: right after her death, right before she was taken to the morgue, or anytime in between. Perhaps even while she was there.

In his mind's eye Punk saw himself at the hearing table with Gordon across from him, issuing the challenge from his lofty perch. He thought about Muddy and the budget cuts and Slapshot and Bear and Dr. Wu. Then he saw the determined looks on the faces of the sailors around the midrats table the night before.

Ford had been backed into a corner. At this point, news of a crewmember's electrocution during routine maintenance or of a spy conspiracy would just be fuel for Gordon and the Air Force cabal's fight against the future of the aircraft carrier, which was the future of the Navy itself. They'd mangle the narrative and spin the story in an effort to shape the opinions of editorial writers and primetime infotainment hosts—not to mention the others on the HASC—in their favor. And those opinions would manifest themselves in how the budget was carved up.

No, the only way out was to go through with Operation Blue Aegis. And not just go through with it but kill Wu's hypersonic missile. The test had come. The time to ace it was now.

"Let me keep this for now," Punk said. "I'll lock it in the safe in my quarters."

"Then what?" Gridiron asked.

"Then we'll read in the JAGs and NCIS or whoever," Punk replied, reading the captain's poorly concealed concern with his choice of action. "Right now, we have work to do to get ready for Blue Aegis tomorrow."

"Tomorrow," Gridiron repeated, processing the weight of that reality.

"I want masters-of-arms stationed around LASIPOD, in the passageway outside of the flag spaces, on the bridge, and in the reactor room and associated engineering spaces. If anyone asks, tell them the guards are there as part of the test. They answer to you and me until NCIS arrives later tomorrow evening. No one else."

"Copy all, Admiral," Gridiron said.

The rest of the day passed with little contact among the team. Each of the principals reported in with their updates, and there was one last gathering in the Flag SCIF. There was no card game in the ready room afterward.

Once he'd been able to return to his stateroom, Punk put the two halves of the broken burner phone in his safe. He stared at it for a minute or so wondering if he was doing the right thing. With a single phone call to the Chief of Naval Operations, he could call it all off.

He closed the metal door to the safe and torqued the combination knob clockwise three full rotations. Blue Aegis was on.

Punk called Suzanne just after 2200, breathing a sigh of relief when she answered.

"Hello there," she said, poorly feigning perkiness in the wake of what had probably been day-long bouts with nausea.

"Rough day?" he asked, fearing the answer.

"You could say that," she mumbled. He heard the creak of their bed in the background and figured she was sitting up from being prone. "They rescheduled my next treatment because they're overbooked."

"That's unsat," Punk replied. "I'm going to have to make some calls when I get back."

"Don't piss anybody off," she said. "Those hospital administrators have a way of showing you how the game is played. Besides, I get a warped sense of comfort from knowing that I'm not alone with being sick."

"Lots of people have cancer," Punk agreed. "And lots of people get better."

She coughed and changed the subject: "I missed your call last night. I'm sorry, but I was so exhausted."

"You don't need to apologize," he said, fighting his emotions for control of his next words. "I'm sorry I'm not there."

"Soon."

"Soon." A short silence followed until he said, "We lost a sailor. A female chief."

"Oh my God. How?"

"Looks like accidental electrocution. That's not public information yet."

"I'm sorry that happened. The crew has to feel terrible about it."

"They do, but they're also ready to get the job done. I never cease to be amazed by sailors."

"Big day tomorrow," she said before another coughing fit overtook her.

He waited until it passed to reply, "It is. Should be over by lunchtime, and then we'll head back for North Island."

"I'll be waiting for you."

"I love you."

"I love you too."

The call ended. He stretched out on his bunk, forcing himself not to look at the clock.

CHAPTER **39**

DAWN WAS APPROACHING in Singapore as Wolfe prepared himself for the coming actions on the California coast. The time difference between the locales was sixteen hours. He'd long ago deployed CubeSats in key orbits to guarantee the smallest latency possible.

He did a few pullups and some light treadmill jogging to get his blood flowing. Though the butler brought him a tray of food, Wolfe did not eat. He sipped coffee constantly but avoided the amphetamines he kept stashed in his bathroom. It had been some time since he'd felt the need for those drugs, back in his start-up days, living on soda, pizza, pills, and maybe some cocaine to stay awake and get the work done.

Then he paced before the wall screen where Aswan had loaded up feeds to their various assets—as well as those of the test's participants.

"Probability that Reichert is exhausted?" Wolfe asked.

"Sixty-eight percent," Aswan said.

The vice admiral was made of tough stuff, Wolfe had to admit. No matter what pressures he applied—ordering Peterson to take care of that nosy engineer or tweaking his wife's cancer treatment appointments with a simple hack—Reichert remained unbowed, an oak withstanding the storms around him.

Wolfe's burner phone vibrated with a message from Cahya. He ignored it and continued watching the pieces assemble on his digital board.

"What are the chances that Howe has elevated the Cyber Command threat level?"

"Thirteen percent," Aswan said.

Wolfe chuckled. "Good thing I'm not superstitious, or that would be interesting. Did Howe contact his son?"

"Phone records indicate he sent three texts and made one phone call to Samuel Howe," Aswan said.

"Were they of a negative nature?" Wolfe asked.

"The parsing indicates yes," Aswan said.

"Good," Wolfe said. "He's still stewing. That will throw off his judgment. Make sure we route all hacking signatures for Blue Aegis to China."

The burner phone vibrated again. Again he ignored it.

"How much longer until *Ford* reaches the warning area west of Point Mugu?"

"Two hours," Aswan said.

Wolfe smiled. "Load up your Crow profile. You'll be using that from now on."

"Done," Aswan said in a familiar voice.

"Play Kanny's Black Knights stunt reel," Wolfe said. "Put it on a loop until we are twenty minutes from Aegis' start."

As a cockpit-cam video of Kanny's flights with the Knights played on every display in the room, Wolfe turned in a slow circle, giving each screen, every presentation of Kanny, his attention. Her laughter, orders to her squadron, victorious whoops, jokes, and muttered curses at the occasional mishap were reruns he had memorized down to the syllable.

For the first time in years, he could smile as he watched.

CHAPTER 40

THE NUCLEAR-POWERED supercarrier USS *Gerald R. Ford* was steaming north when Punk received word from Spud and Chatterjee that the defunct EMALS and advanced weapons elevators were back online. He checked the digital clock mounted nearby: 0740. The crew had worked until 2300 last night and resumed the task at 0400 after being allowed a few hours' sleep. Punk hoped they would be alert for the operation.

He had managed to eat an egg, bacon, and cheese biscuit in the flag mess despite the butterflies in his stomach. On his way to the bridge, Punk passed the MAAs, which reminded him that *Ford* might be under a quiet, deliberate assault from within. But he had no evidence, no suspects, and no time to search for spies now.

He greeted Gridiron, seated in his elevated chair, and watched the four F/A-18E Super Hornets get towed into place for the launch, each positioned at the head of an electromagnetic catapult: two on the bow, two on the waist. He missed the sight of steam floating out of the cat track, but there was no denying that for all the delays and cost overruns during EMALS' development, it was a huge improvement over the steam catapults in terms of maintenance required and reliability (assuming the power source wasn't fried by a DEW).

On the horizon he could barely make out the two *Arleigh Burke* guided missile destroyers working to distance themselves from the carrier and take their stations ahead for the exercise. Connelly had assured him they were ready to provide the first line of defense, and Punk assumed it was so. There was tension in the air, which was a good thing. Everyone there, on each ship, understood what was at stake. The anxiety was palpable and instinctual, an emotion that he'd not felt on a boat in some time, the same feeling he'd had when launching on a real-world strike mission over Afghanistan. That had been a long time ago, but now it felt like yesterday.

This was the first time he'd had that pre-battle feeling wearing stars on his flight suit, but it felt no less intense and invigorating. He suspected that Slapshot Howe was experiencing a similar rush, and in that moment he felt a bond between them.

Punk watched Morfie McNabb preflight her jet staged on Cat 3, running her hand across the leading edges of the wings and tugging on the AIM-174s just aft of the nose cone to make sure they wouldn't fall off until she pulled the trigger in anger. At the top of the boarding ladder, right before she climbed into the cockpit, she looked up toward the bridge and gave Punk a salute, which he returned, wishing he could have been manning one of the other three jets, even the tanker.

And then he noticed that the Super Hornet on Cat 4 was loaded with four inert bombs instead of air-to-air missiles. He grabbed a clipboard hanging on the left side of Gridiron's chair and flipped through the pages attached to it until he got to the load plan, the master schedule for what ordnance was supposed to be on what aircraft for each launch over the course of a fly day. It showed three of the jets were supposed to be loaded with four AIM-174s each along with simulated AIM-9 heat-seeking missiles on the wingtips and the fourth jet was to be loaded with four drop tanks along with simulated AIM-9s on the wingtips.

"Captain, why does the jet on Cat 4 have bombs loaded on it?" Punk asked Gridiron.

"Morfie audibled with the ordnance officer first thing this morning," Gridiron replied. "We didn't have time to change the hard copy of the load plan."

"Why did she make the change?"

"I don't know, Admiral."

"Awesome how I'm the last to find these things out," Punk muttered as he turned his attention back to the flight deck.

Surf rushed up behind him, out of breath from climbing the ladder from the 0-3 level to the bridge, and announced, "We should have General Howe and his team on the VTC shortly, and everyone on our side is waiting in the Flag SCIF except Peterson and Vice Admiral Francis."

"Do we know where they are?" Punk asked.

"Still in the reactor spaces," Surf replied. "They said it was a last-minute glitch with LASIPOD, but they're on it."

―

Eighteen decks below the flag bridge, Einstein and Peterson were examining a length of the fiber optic array that fed energy to LASIPOD.

"No one else should have been down here last night," Peterson said. "That's why I asked Admiral Reichert not to allow any of the engineers around these things. And look, the bandwidth is off again too."

"How quickly can we fix it?" Einstein asked.

"We can't. The exercise is about to start!" Peterson exclaimed, losing his normal calm. "There's no time."

"Chief Hill and Dr. Chatterjee both said this could still work regardless," Einstein said, walking toward LASIPOD. "I guess we're going to see."

"Where are you going?" Peterson asked. "It's not going to work, I tell you."

"We'll have to adjust the couplings so the rest of the fiber strands won't burn out. Then we'll fix the bandwidth." Einstein beckoned the other man to join him. "Come on, Shane. We have to get this weapon online."

The two hurriedly checked every strand and coupling as precious minutes ticked by. Shaking, Peterson fumbled with his tools, repeatedly apologizing as he spun in neutral. After a minute's work, all he had to show for it was a mess of cables around LASIPOD.

"I'm sorry, Admiral," Peterson muttered as he stood and pushed by the MAA stationed in the reactor spaces. "We should just leave it. Let's go."

"Stay here," Einstein commanded. "We can get this done."

Einstein sorted through the mess Peterson had just created around LASIPOD's energy couplings and targeting system. The laser was connected to *Ford*'s MFR, along with OpenShip, in a dual-screen display at the weapon's control station. The cables stopped below the weapon's position just below the flight deck.

He grabbed the phone an arm's length away and spoke into it. "That should do it, Bhaavik. Test it on your end and make sure we have full capacity from the router."

"All in the green here, Admiral," Chatterjee replied.

Einstein looked over at the young engineer he'd put so much faith in to get them through Blue Aegis. Peterson stood frozen in place, slack-jawed, eyes darting—nothing like the supremely confident man he'd met at China Lake. How long ago had that been? It felt like a lifetime.

The tension between Peterson and Chatterjee had continued despite Punk's demand that it cease. The two remained constantly at odds, arguing about how LASIPOD should be powered and deployed. Einstein hadn't enjoyed playing referee. It had left him on edge; they were all on edge. But as they approached the endgame, all had seemed in order—until now.

Peterson pointed toward the couplings and insisted in a high voice, "It's not going to work! Once it's activated, it's going to burn out. It needs continuous power, not Chatterjee's short bursts."

"He ran the weapon through three tests using that configuration yesterday," Einstein said, still crouched in front of the mess Peterson had just created. "And you worked on this last night. If it's still fucked up, why didn't you report it?" He felt himself close to snapping, so he stopped and took a deep breath, then another.

His attention shifted from LASIPOD to Peterson. "If you knew the setup was faulty, why didn't you report it? Why wait until the day of the test to make a correction?"

"Who would I tell? I'm the only person who can operate this weapon. I was the one who demonstrated what it can do. I gave you proof of concept in the desert. And all you've done is stick me with incompetents, first that idiot Chatterjee, and then Martha Hill. Why won't you understand?"

"This has been a team effort out here," Einstein returned.

"Incompetents!" Peterson shouted.

Einstein stood up. "Enough, Shane," he snapped.

Peterson dropped his eyes and took a deep breath. The tension drained from his face. "You're right, sir." He motioned toward the couplings. "Let me show you the correction."

Einstein nodded, relieved that the young engineer had become a competent professional again. "We need to be quick here. We're already late for the VTC in the SCIF."

Peterson moved past Einstein and knelt over the coupling, saying, "Here, this is the problem. You need to get a closer look."

Einstein knelt beside him. He noticed a tear in the insulated tape at the base of the tangle of wires, and as he reached to point it out, he felt a sharp pain in his back that quickly spread to his torso. He cried out and fell to the deck, already slick with something warm and red. *Blood*, he thought. *My blood. The bastard stabbed me.*

In a state of shock, he heard the snap of electricity and rolled onto his side in time to see the guard jerk violently and fall to the deck. The stench of burnt flesh tainted the air. The mess of cables continued to crackle for a moment before fizzling out.

"You . . . why?" Einstein managed.

Peterson gaped down at him. He held a blade glistening with blood in one hand. The other held a control box linked to the extra cables that he had used to electrocute the guard. And in that moment, Einstein knew he'd also murdered Martha Hill.

"Why?" Einstein spat out the coppery taste of blood in his mouth.

"I didn't want it to be like this," Peterson said earnestly, chest heaving as if he might weep. "It didn't have to be . . ." He stammered something else, then turned and ran.

Einstein gasped for breath as he struggled to pull himself to LASIPOD's control station, hand over hand, each breath searing through his chest. He managed to reach the phone, but his fingers were slick with blood, and he struggled to push the four buttons that he hoped would get Chatterjee on the line.

His fingers felt numb. A chill spread through his chest. His consciousness was fading. The ship was getting darker. Colder. Then he wasn't on a ship at all. He was lying in the sand in Iraq at the spot where he'd ejected with Soup Campbell. What had the bastard gotten them into this time? Why hadn't the arrogant prick listened? The truck with the soldiers arrived. They cursed him in Arabic and brandished their Kalashnikovs at him.

Another jolt of pain brought him back to the base of LASIPOD's control platform. He groaned and labored to hold the bloody phone against his head. A voice over the intercom above announced the start of Operation Blue Aegis. It gave him a strange sense of harmony. He was here on the boat with his squadron mates, his friends. Not in Iraq with that son-of-a-bitch Campbell.

He struggled to keep the phone to his ear as his strength drained away. Another ring. And then another. Nobody was there. He was all alone.

Chatterjee finally picked up the line: "They're waiting for you in the SCIF, sir. Is everything a go down there? Is LASIPOD up and running?"

"Sabo . . ." Einstein whispered, then forced the word out, refusing to take it with him wherever he was going. "Sabotage."

The deck pounded with footsteps. Figures approached him. As they drew closer he recognized them.

Good. They would know what to do; they would save the boat. And that made him smile a final time.

Punk was going to run the Navy's side of the exercise from CIC, a much bigger space than Flag SCIF. The extra room allowed him to keep all the personnel he needed within shouting range, including the TAO, and see all the displays required to monitor the threats and direct engagements with the myriad weapons, both simulated and real, they were going to have to employ to defend *Ford*. CIC was dark, the only light coming from the green glows of the screens that ringed the space.

Punk took his place in the command chair next to the TAO's station where Lieutenant Maggie Mildenhall was already seated. The arms of his chair were equipped with buttons and switches that allowed him to adjust the displays, and he had a handful of radio handsets and telephone lines within arm's reach.

He pointed to his aide and said, "See if you can raise Einstein or Peterson again. If they don't answer, head to LASIPOD yourself."

"Yessir," Surf said, moving across the space to a phone on the wall.

Punk checked the time: 0755.

Spud pointed to the digital display that ran nearly the full width of the far bulkhead above the intelligence specialists manning the bank of radar screens in front of him. "It looks like the Air Force side is ready to start the brief."

"Not yet," Punk muttered. "Give Einstein a little more time. Bhaavik, what did he say on the phone?"

"I couldn't make it out, sir," Chatterjee said. "There was a lot of noise in the background."

"I'm sure they have it under control," Connelly said, running a fresh cup of coffee under his nose.

Punk focused on the screen and saw a handful of people settling into chairs behind a conference table, some in uniform, some not. The bottom of the screen identified the location as "Pacific Missile Test Center." He'd flown sorties off the coast there during his Tomcat days, doing advanced testing on the AIM-54 Phoenix missile, the F-14's signature weapon, the one that scared the hell out of the Russians and Iraqis. More recently it had been used to develop the AIM-120, the Advanced Medium-Range Air-to-Air Missile, the Super Hornet's signature weapon.

He never imagined then that he'd be off the coast as a three-star. It still didn't seem real until Gridiron's voice crackled through a nearby intercom box mounted on one of the vertical beams, asking: "Permission to launch jets?"

"Granted," Punk replied.

Everyone in CIC focused on the PLAT, the closed-circuit television mounted in the far corner that broadcast the goings-on around the flight deck 24/7. The catapults fired in numerical succession, and the four Super Hornets were airborne. It was a sight that never failed to fill Punk with pride that he was allowed to be part of the business of carrier aviation.

Morfie's voice came over another speaker, the one dedicated to the UHF frequency the fighters were using. "Strike, Passkey flight is airborne," she said, reminding Punk that they'd salvaged the original name for the exercise by adopting it as the tactical call sign for the Navy jets. "Heading to CAP stations."

"Strike copies," the carrier's controller replied from the air operations spaces a few frames forward of CIC.

Spud directed Punk's attention toward the screen saying, "It looks like General Howe is ready."

"Admiral Francis and his wunderkind are about to miss the fun," Connelly noted.

"Bhaavik, go check on them," Punk ordered before talking toward the screen. "Good to see you, General Howe."

"Good to see you too, Vice Admiral Reichert," Howe returned with a half-salute. "Greetings from Point Mugu. We show *Ford* in the operating area. Do you concur?"

"We concur," Punk replied. "Fighters airborne and en route to station."

"Same on our side. With your permission, sir, we'll consider Blue Aegis under way."

"You have my permission, sir."

"Okay, we're showing 0800. Commence Blue Aegis."

Despite the clarity of the order, a silence followed. As it continued, the tension built in CIC until Spud said, "Isn't something supposed to happen now?"

The reply came in the form of the voice of the lead air intercept controller on one of the destroyers, using the call sign "AW," short for air warfare commander: "Passkey, Alpha Whiskey is showing two groups. First group zero-one-five for 210 miles. Second group zero-two-three for 205 miles."

"Passkey copies," Morfie replied. "Composition?"

"Unknown at this time."

"Northern group is probably the F-35s and F-15EX Strike Eagles out of Alaska," Punk said to the room like a color commentator working a sports broadcast. "The other group is the F-22s out of Edwards."

"Also showing tickler information from a ground unit, zero-eight-five for 125 miles," the controller said.

"That's the truck at PMTC," Punk added. "Their tracking radar is radiating."

"Who's got the hypersonic?" Spud asked.

"You mean *hypersonics*?" Punk asked back. "Remember, Howe is throwing everything he's got at us, and we won't know how many and from what direction until they come off the rails." At that point it hit him that he'd allowed the exercise to start without knowing why his jets were reconfigured as they were ordnance-wise and without verifying that LASIPOD was online.

Punk picked up the UHF handset in front of him and transmitted, "CAG, interrogative loadout on Dash-3." He had to be cryptic because they weren't using encrypted frequencies for Blue Aegis.

There was a dead air for a few seconds until Morfie answered, "All good, sir."

That wasn't an answer, but he realized one wasn't forthcoming. He'd find out as the flight unfolded. Besides, right now he had a more pressing problem to deal with. He tapped a button on one of the armrests to mute the VTC audio connection and said, "Somebody find Vice Admiral Francis and Shane Peterson, *now*!"

The TAO tapped Punk on the arm and said, "There's something you need to see, Admiral." She pointed to the big screen where a new window popped up over the VTC presentation. In it was a raw video taken from the port observation bubble of one of the P-8 Poseidon patrol planes out of Barbers Point. A Chinese J-15, one of the air wing assets aboard *Fujian*, flew in formation a few hundred yards off the wing, and then another J-15 zoomed by between them, extremely close to the patrol plane, forcing the U.S. Navy pilot at the controls to swerve away.

"That's how wars get started," Punk said.

"Where is our fighter escort?" Spud asked from behind where Punk was seated.

"They're a long way south of Hawaii," Maggie said. "Doubt they can get out there without dedicated tanker support."

"Alright, let's focus here, TAO, but keep an eye open for what happens with the Poseidons," Punk said. "We may be rerouted that way once this is over."

"Copy that, Admiral," Maggie replied.

A few decks below CIC, Peterson cracked a hatch open and entered the port side of the hangar bay about halfway along its length, winded from running up the ladders from the LASIPOD station adjacent to the reactor room. He fought to control his breathing, trying to avoid attracting any attention from the sailors there as he slipped between crates and pallets loaded with supplies, moving toward the opposite hatch on the starboard side. The sailors were too busy with their tasks to notice him.

Through the hatch and outboard, and he was against the rail, considering the waves below. The seas were calm, which was good. He figured he was thirty feet or more above the surface of the water.

Thirty feet to freedom . . . or eternity.

Admiral Francis had forced his hand. Peterson hadn't wanted to hurt the man; he had actually liked him. Unlike Martha Hill and her one-upmanship in the end—no doubt egged on by Chatterjee—Einstein had sincerely wanted to help, to ensure that *Ford* passed the test.

Setting up Chief Hill had been easy. He'd challenged her to tweak the fiber optic array and prove him wrong. The perfect trap because he'd left one of the couplings hot. Afterward, he slid the broken phone into her pocket to implicate her as the saboteur.

Einstein hadn't challenged him, but he'd interfered at the worst possible moment. It had been then or never. A shame he'd died without understanding why.

And that MAA? He'd been in the wrong place at the wrong time. As simple as that. The man hadn't understood what was going on at all. Peterson had neither the time nor the desire to explain that he needed what the Navy had taken from him, what it had refused to give his father: recognition. Cancer had finally claimed his father's life, but the Navy had stolen precious moments of that life. Distilled them down to the Top Gun patch that Peterson now clasped in his hand. To think he had once wanted such a patch of his own more than anything else in the world. The patch soaked up some of the blood on his hand, an inefficient sponge that could never absorb the pain of his failures.

Wolfe had said that a submarine would find him if he jumped overboard. In the meantime, he should swim toward one of the offshore refineries that dotted the warning area off the coast. He'd readily agreed to the mad ploy; Wolfe's plan to rig the Air Force's hypersonics had sounded perfectly feasible. Now, as he gazed at the Pacific with Einstein's blood on his hands, Peterson processed a twinge of regret.

But it was too late now. Finally too late. Even if a submarine wasn't waiting for him, he had no option but to jump. He heard a voice over the ship's intercom telling Vice Admiral Francis and Mr. Peterson to report to CIC. Neither of them was going to comply.

He looked to either side. Not seeing anyone, he climbed over the rail and jumped. He hit the water feet-first and plunged deeper than he'd expected to. The water was cold; it was the eastern Pacific Ocean, after all. He struggled back to the surface and, gasping for air, realized he'd dropped the Top Gun patch as he hit the water. He spotted it bobbing on the surface several yards away and swam toward it. But before he could reach it, *Ford*'s wake picked it up and carried it away from him. The salt water burned his eyes. He coughed, trying not to swallow it. When he looked again, the patch was gone.

He calmly treaded water, conserving his energy and watching the aircraft carrier sail away from him and into the distance. It was a surreal sight. He was having trouble processing what he'd just done—the murders, the plunge off the ship—and he figured it was some sort of defense mechanism kicking in to keep himself from panicking. Panic was a killer in the water.

He'd always been a strong swimmer. Swim clubs as a child. All-state in high school. Varsity swim team at Penn State. His dad had pushed him, telling him that as many flight students got tripped up during tests in the pool as they did in the air with an instructor in their backseat.

The carrier was almost out of sight over the horizon now, and he hoped the rescue submarine would surface soon. Perhaps he had jumped too soon. Maybe it hadn't reached his position yet. Wolfe would keep his promise. Peterson had kept his.

As his head bobbed at the surface, he laughed. He'd fooled them all. Water sloshed into his open mouth, and his laughter turned into a paroxysm of coughs. He fought them off and steadied his breathing. *Stay calm*, he thought.

Chief Hill. Her ambition had killed her as much as the electrical trap he'd set. Why did she have to keep pushing him? Why did she have to keep meddling?

Where was the submarine? Growing desperate now, he dove under the water and opened his eyes, hoping to see the craft emerging out of the murky depths toward him. In the moment he was able to hold his eyes open before the stinging of the salt became too much, he saw nothing. Empty water.

He looked in the direction the carrier had disappeared and then east of that and thought he saw something. He didn't think it was the submarine. It must be one of the refineries, a mile or so away. He could make that. He started to swim in that direction, hoping Wolfe's sub would surface near him.

At 0815 Punk received a phone call from Gridiron on the bridge. "We think we might have a man overboard," the captain said.

"Might?" Punk replied.

"One of the blue shirts in Air Department thought he saw something fall over the side, but he wasn't sure. The crew is mustering on station, and we should have a head count soon. I'm not turning the ship around, but the plane guard helicopter is going to scan the area."

Punk cursed under his breath as he hung up. Getting a crewmember out of the water was always a priority, but it was an unwelcome and untimely distraction. He refocused on the VTC, where Slapshot looked like he was about to speak.

"Admiral Reichert, since we're under way here, let me introduce you to your main adversary." A photo took over the screen showing a missile in a lab setting. It was thin and long with fins that barely extended out from the body near the aft end. "This is Hermes, the weapon that's about to take you down."

When the screen flipped back to those gathered behind the conference table at PMTC Punk noticed Dr. Wu standing behind Slapshot, beaming with pride. "Congratulations on your accomplishment," Punk said, not taking the bait. "I'm glad we were able to give you a reason to complete the work after years of delays."

"I could say the same about your directed-energy weapon," Slapshot returned. "Is it going to work?"

Punk didn't answer. Instead he shifted his attention to the tactical display on the wall next to the VTC as Morfie transmitted, "Alpha Whiskey, say picture."

"Alpha Whiskey shows first group zero-one-seven for 180 miles," the controller replied. "Second group zero-three-zero for 220 miles. Now breaking out four in the near group, two in the far group."

"Confirm hostile," Morfie said.

"Alpha Whiskey confirms both groups are hostile."

"Alpha Bravo, verify weapons status."

Punk lifted the UHF handset and transmitted, "Weapons are free in accordance with exercise parameters." That meant real AIM-174s could be fired only against the test hypersonic missiles, not Air Force jets.

"Alpha Sierra, target the near group," Morfie directed.

On the lead destroyer, Captain Levi Solomon replied, "Copy. Stand by for birds in the air."

A few seconds later, two simulated SM-6 Standard Missiles appeared on the tactical presentation moving away from the symbols that represented the two destroyers.

"TACTS range shows birds in the air," another voice said from the Tactical Training System facility at Point Mugu. Punk thought of all the hours he'd spent in similar dark rooms watching replays of the dogfights he'd fought a few hours before. It was cutting-edge technology in those days, replacing aviators' sole reliance on spaghetti tracks on kneeboard cards and ending the running joke that "first guy to the dry-erase board wins." As Punk studied the screen, he noted that the presentation and the system were state-of-the-art.

The TACTS range was also the final arbiter of simulated kills, another data point for those who feared the rise of computer overlords. If the range showed you were dead, you were dead. And if the algorithm baked into each missile's simulated performance that allowed for failures a percentage of the time decided the weapon had failed, then it had failed.

As the pair of simulated SM-6s tracked toward the southbound Air Force fighters, Punk observed, "Those are aimed at the Strike Eagles. The destroyers' radars can't see the F-35s."

"How are we going to get them?" Connelly asked.

Punk's reply was interrupted by Morfie's next UHF transmission: "Lapdog, detach."

"Lapdog is detaching," another Super Hornet pilot replied.

Punk watched as one of the four Super Hornet symbols on the screen moved eastbound away from the other three. "What is she doing?" he wondered aloud.

"There goes four AIM-174s," Spud observed.

"No, that guy's carrying bombs," Punk said.

"Bombs?"

"I'm as surprised as you are."

A smaller screen mounted to the left-side wall allowed Punk to reference the Project OpenShip data presentation. In this application, OpenShip interpolated the data coming from the sensors of all the Navy ships and aircraft to give an AI prediction of what the enemy planned to do next. According to OpenShip, Howe's forces had gotten the jump on them. The northern Air Force jets were going to split, and the eastern F-22 Raptors out of Edwards AFB were going to stay together while speeding up to engage the Super Hornets first.

That concerned Punk. What would Morfie do? Would she flow toward the Raptors before engaging the northern strikers? As he continued to study the OpenShip presentation he also noted that the AI had determined that the ground station at Point Mugu would launch its Hermes first, but even at Mach 10 it would get to *Ford* after the air-launched hypersonics from the northern element.

Mach 10? Where did that come from? That was twice as fast as they'd anticipated. He was starting to feel overwhelmed and increasingly confused. He needed Einstein here in CIC.

"Have we found Vice Admiral Francis yet?" he asked. Nobody answered.

A pair of bright Xs appeared over the symbols for the Strike Eagles on the TACTS presentation, and the controller there transmitted, "Eagle One and Two, you're dead."

"Eagle copies," the lead Strike Eagle pilot replied. "Taking ourselves out of the exercise to the north."

"Okay, that got two of them," Punk said. "What about the F-35s?"

Morfie looked through the JHMCS presentation in her visor, willing the airplanes to appear and wishing that the TACTS data could have been incorporated among the other symbols she saw—or in this case didn't see—there. Then she spotted a black dot above the horizon just left of the nose of her airplane, then another.

"Morfie's tally two," she transmitted to her wingman, the other missile shooter. "Eleven-thirty, slightly high."

"Fist Pump is blind," her wingman replied. "Oh, got 'em. I'm tally two."

"Pulling nose on."

CAG moved the stick left and slightly aft as she manipulated the cursor on the front of one of the throttles to get a forward-looking infrared system contrast lock on the airplanes in front of her. An F-35 appeared in the center of her left multifunction display on the instrument panel below the glare shield. She checked the range. Still too far away for a simulated AIM-9X Sidewinder shot. She hoped staying nose-on would keep them from being spotted by the Air Force pilots as she climbed toward them. She knew from the hundreds of one-on-one similars she'd done over the years that a Super Hornet pointed at you was hard to see with the naked eye.

"Fist Pump, no tone," her wingman transmitted.

"Out of range," she replied. "Stay chilly."

A few excruciatingly long seconds later, a Sidewinder tone indicating the missile had a heat source chirped and then blared through the headset built into her helmet. "Fox-2 on the western F-35 headed to the south at angels twenty-five," she called over the common UHF frequency.

"Fox-2 on the *eastern* F-35 headed south at angels twenty-five," Fist Pump transmitted in turn.

Punk watched the TACTS display as the simulated AIM-9s flew toward their targets. A few seconds later an X popped up over the left symbol, and the TACTS controller said, "Lightning One is dead."

"Copy that," the lead F-35 pilot said. "Disengaging to the north."

They waited for Fist Pump's simulated missile to simulate blowing up the other F-35, but instead they heard, "Passkey Two's missile is a miss. Continue Lightning Two."

Morfie cursed into her mask before keying the radio. "Fist Pump, take high cover. I've got this guy."

"Fist Pump high cover, aye."

CAG merged with the remaining F-35, taking it down her right side. She checked the airspeed displayed on her heads-up display, the HUD, and saw she was at just less than 400 knots. *Too fast*, she thought.

Morfie yanked the throttles out of afterburner as she threw the stick hard against the inside of her right thigh and then pulled hard aft. Her G-suit expanded and pushed against her stomach and legs as she fought the crush of eight Gs. She tilted her head back, looking through the upper part of the canopy, struggling to keep her opponent in sight.

She saw that the F-35 had elected to turn left. They were in a one-circle fight, which surprised her. That dogfighting strategy favored the airplane with the faster turn rate, and on paper that was the Super Hornet. But in an instant the F-35 turned into a vapor ball, crushing air into clouds as the pilot put on the Gs, converting airspeed for angles.

Before she anticipated it could happen, the other jet had its nose on her. "Fox-2 on the Super Hornet passing through north at 24,000 feet," the Air Force pilot transmitted over the UHF. She cursed and waited for the dreaded ruling.

Just shy of two seconds later, the TACTS controller passed, "Missile failure, Lightning Two. Passkey One, continue."

CAG breathed a sigh of relief and noted that her opponent had overdone it with the first turn back into her. The other pilot dumped the nose of the F-35 to get some knots back on the jet, floating like a leaf at the mercy of the breeze.

She'd managed her energy better, and the Super Hornet closed the other jet quickly, too quickly to get off another Sidewinder shot. She flipped the weapons select switch on the throttle and pulled the trigger, transmitting, "Guns, guns, guns on the F-35 nose low at 22,000 feet, passing through south" while keeping the F-35 squarely in her HUD.

"That's a good kill," the TACTS controller replied. "Lightning Two, you're dead."

"Lightning Two copies," the second Air Force pilot said, frustration evident in his voice. He knew Morfie's HUD tape would show up somewhere beyond the debrief in the future, likely on social media with the title "Stealth Doesn't Work Against Bullets" or something similar that the gamers and other aviation fanbois would make viral.

Morfie keyed the UHF again: "Alpha Whiskey, Passkey One needs a vector to the second group."

"Second group, one-zero-three for fifty-five miles," the controller on the destroyer said.

"Passkey copies," she said. "Fist Pump, we're flowing south."

"Lapdog targeting that group," the third Super Hornet transmitted, reminding Morfie that she'd detached him a few minutes before. Shooting down bandits wasn't Lapdog's mission, but apparently the geometry of the fight had presented the potential for some quick kills on his way to the objective. "Alpha Whiskey, confirm group zero-eight-seven for twenty-three miles from me."

"Alpha Whiskey confirms that group hostile. Cleared to commit."

Back in CIC, Punk observed, "Those are the F-22s out of Edwards."

Lapdog figured the Raptors were poised to shoot medium-range AMRAAMs at him at any moment, but the calls didn't come. At a closure rate of 2,000 knots, they were soon within visual range. "Lapdog's tally," he barked over the squadron common freq.

Lapdog checked the time and his fuel level and realized he didn't have enough of either to tangle with the Raptors for very long. He had to press to his target before it didn't matter. But he had an opportunity here. He was flying a strike fighter, and it was time to do the fighter part.

He had an advantage. In a classic misstep of the U.S. Air Force procurement process, the F-22—their most advanced air superiority fighter—wasn't equipped with the Joint Helmet Mounted Cueing System. That meant that a Super Hornet pilot could aim the AIM-9X seeker head off boresight while a Raptor pilot had to bring the nose to bear. He'd get the first shot. After that he was going to be in survival mode.

The three jets merged, and as the Raptors approached his left wing-line, Lapdog turned his head while commanding the Sidewinder seeker head to go where he was looking. In his visor a diamond superimposed itself over the closest F-22, which was rapidly turning into him trying to get a weapons solution of its own.

"Fox-2 on the left Raptor turning left through two-one-zero at 19,000 feet," Lapdog transmitted.

A few beats later, the TACTS controller passed, "Good kill, Passkey Three. Raptor One, you're dead."

"Raptor One copies, exiting west."

Over his left shoulder, Lapdog saw the other Raptor clawing through the sky toward him, vapes streaming from the wings as the pilot brought its nose to bear. Lapdog had one option at that point: Try to run away. The young carrier pilot selected full afterburner by jamming the throttles to their forward extreme as he pushed on the stick until he felt light in his seat. The Super Hornet accelerated most rapidly between one and zero G, and in short order the jet was nibbling at supersonic speed as he dove toward the ocean below. He heard the chirp of his radar warning receiver. The Raptor had a lock. He winced and waited for the call over the UHF foretelling his imminent demise.

At that moment, an unexpected voice came over the UHF: "Passkey One, simulated Fox-3 on Raptor Two heading one-six-zero at 17,000 feet."

CAG!

Ten miles behind the Raptor, waiting for the TACTS range ruling on her simulated AIM-174 shot, Morfie wondered if the data for the new weapon had even been entered in the system yet. The fact the answer was taking so long made her believe it wasn't. The AIM-174 traveled at Mach 2.5. If they'd programmed it properly, she would already have had a ruling.

Morfie's fears proved unfounded as the TACTS controller transmitted, "Good kill, Passkey One. Raptor Two, you're dead."

"What the hell did she shoot me with?" the Air Force pilot asked.

"Beadwindow," Morfie responded quickly, using the code word for when somebody had passed or was about to pass classified information over a clear frequency.

"Roger, out," the other pilot said, executing the proper response to the previous transmission.

"Good shooting, CAG," Lapdog said over squadron common.

"Thank you," she replied. "Now press to the target."

"I'm on my way."

CHAPTER 41

IN THE LARGE SCIF at the Pacific Missile Test Center, General Howe twisted in his chair and glared at Dr. Wu. "We're getting hammered out there," Slapshot exclaimed. "What's the plan now?"

"Patience, General, patience," Wu murmured in his high, uninflected voice. "Nothing they've killed so far matters. We're about to fire the real hypersonics."

Wu raised the walkie-talkie in his right hand to his mouth and said, "Mobile One, this is Center, how do you read?"

"Got you five-by-five, Doctor," a man's voice with a heavy southern accent crackled back.

"Are you ready for launch?"

"Still spooling up. Give us five."

"We don't have five!" Slapshot shouted at Wu, slapping the table with both palms. "I need real missiles heading toward that damn aircraft carrier *now*!"

Bear pointed at the tactical display and asked, "What about that last F-35 out of Edwards?"

"That's Lightning Three," Wu said. "He's carrying two Hermes, but they're the earlier versions. We had some wiring issues with them." He shrugged. "Too many cooks in the kitchen."

"Does everybody see this Super Hornet coming in?" Bear asked.

"What about the missile on the truck?" Slapshot asked.

"That's Hermes IV, the best we have," Wu replied, finally allowing himself to smile. "That's the one we'll fire first. It's the fastest of the three."

The general slapped the table again. "So do it!"

Some twenty miles west of the SCIF at PMTC, Lapdog checked his moving map display as he continued his rapid descent. Thirty seconds later he was flying just above the wavetops. His radar warning receiver gave no indication that he was being tracked by any other Air Force fighters or ground stations. He checked the symbology in his HUD.

Ten miles to the target. Nine miles. Eight...

At that point, he reefed the stick aft and pointed the Super Hornet's nose 45 degrees up. When he reached 10,000 feet, he pulled the jet on its back and entered a 30-degree dive. His eyes danced around the HUD, first checking his airspeed at 400 knots, then ensuring his navigation system hadn't wandered and the diamond was over the target, which he recognized from the satellite images he'd studied while planning the mission.

As he got closer to the ground the pull-up cue marched up the fall line projected vertically across the center of the HUD. When the cue reached the diamond he transmitted, "Passkey Three, pickle, pickle, pickle four simulated Mark-82s on the missile truck."

Slapshot, his face mottled with fury, shifted his focus to the TACTS presentation and said, "I do not believe this! Where the hell did that guy come from?"

"I asked about him almost a minute ago," Bear said. "I guess nobody heard me."

"Shut up, you incompetent fool! This is going to ruin me!"

Bear started to push back but instead just shrugged. He'd spent enough time around Major General Howe to read his signals, and he knew when to just take the hit.

"And it would have been nice if we'd put at least one surface-to-air missile site next to the truck," Slapshot said, as much to himself as to the others in the room.

At both PMTC and aboard *Ford* they watched Lapdog's simulated bombs fall until another bright X showed up on top of the symbol for the truck's position on the coastline of Point Mugu. "Good kill on the truck," the TACTS controller passed. "Mobile One, you're dead."

"Does that mean we can't fire the hypersonic?" Slapshot asked, obviously having trouble processing what had just happened.

"It's kind of hard to fire a missile from a launcher that's blown to shit," Bear replied sarcastically, for once willing to endure Howe's wrath.

The three-star glared at the two-star with an expression indicating that his emotional instrument panel was blinking red across the board. Bear thought he was about to be on the receiving end of one of Howe's legendary slap-downs, but instead Slapshot sighed, looked over his shoulder, and asked, "What now, Wu?"

"The F-35," Wu replied matter-of-factly.

Howe grunted. "But what about that AI thing, OpenShip? Didn't you say Peterson linked that to the LASIPOD system he installed on *Ford*? That software will give them a heads-up of whatever we send their way. I want this to be a sure thing. No room for error."

"It won't matter, General," Wu said. "The Hermes missiles on the F-35 can reach Mach 7, still much faster than the Navy is anticipating."

At least the final blow to Reichert's plans would come from the air—via an Air Force fifth-gen fighter. That would be poetic justice.

In the Super Hornet over PMTC, Lapdog checked his fuel state as he climbed away from the target. Enough gas for a victory pass. He rolled left, reacquired the truck over his shoulder, and in another crush of G forces, pointed the Super Hornet at it once again. This time he pressed the dive lower and faster. He leveled off at fifty feet and checked his airspeed. Still subsonic, but barely. Didn't want to break any windows, after all.

As Lapdog passed over the truck, he rolled right and saluted with his throttle hand like a World War I Spad pilot waving to a downed Fokker. He saw hand gestures from the people around the truck and figured they were waving back, gracious in defeat.

In the PMTC SCIF, Wu listened to his walkie-talkie and relayed the information to General Howe, who glared into the VTC screen and said, "Your jet just made our technicians jump off the damned truck!"

Punk flashed a thumbs-up at the screen and said, "Copy that. Good kill on the truck." Slapshot returned the gesture with one of his own—a middle finger.

The celebration was short-lived. As Lapdog climbed back to the west, he spotted a black dot in the distance well above him. He tried to get a radar lock but couldn't. F-35.

He keyed the UHF and transmitted, "Passkey Three is tally a possible leaker. Can't lock him up."

"Call your tally," Morfie replied.

"Due west of me, estimating ten miles plus. Altitude 25,000 feet or so. He's fast."

"Can you run him down?"

Lapdog checked his gas and said, "I'll need to hit the tanker afterward."

"Passkey Four, say your posit."

"Passkey Four has Three on radar," the Super Hornet configured as a tanker transmitted. "I'll hawk him on the back side of the intercept."

With that, Lapdog selected full afterburner and watched the airspeed number on the left side of his HUD go up. But a quarter of a minute later, as he hit Mach 1.1, the dot in the sky in front of him still wasn't getting any bigger.

"Passkey Three's not going to be able to catch him, CAG," he transmitted resignedly.

"Alpha Whiskey, are you painting that contact?" Morfie asked.

The controller on the destroyer replied, "Negative."

"Lapdog, call your tally again."

"Estimate still 10 miles due west of my current posit at 25,000 feet. I'm supersonic, and he's walking away from me."

"Okay, conserve your gas. I'll try to find him."

Morfie slaved her FLIR to look dead ahead as she performed the trigonometry in her head, projecting the bandit from where her data link display showed Lapdog was. Ten miles. Twenty-five thousand feet. Westbound. Supersonic.

An object passed back and forth through the FLIR's field of view a few times and then stopped squarely in the middle of the display when the radar obtained a contrast lock. She was just aft of the F-35's right wing-line. She checked the range and closure: 15 nautical miles away, opening at 100 knots.

"Alpha Bravo, this is Lightning Three," the F-35 pilot transmitted, speaking directly to Punk. "Confirm green range."

Punk looked across the table at the range control officer, who nodded and replied, "Lightning Three, this is Alpha Bravo. Range is green."

No sooner did Morfie think *he's about to shoot a real hypersonic* than three missiles dropped down out of the F-35's weapons bay. She watched transfixed as they hung there on the racks that had just extended from the fuselage, the design feature that kept the stealth jet stealthy until ready to launch. *Is he really going to do this?* And he did, one missile was immediately followed by the other two in rapid succession.

"Lightning Three is op away," the F-35 pilot transmitted. "Exiting to the east."

"Understand we're cleared for live fire?" CAG asked, hit with the fact that the "simulated shots" part of Blue Aegis had just summarily ended with three pulls on the trigger by the pilot in Lightning Three.

"The range is green, Passkey One," Punk replied. "You're cleared to fire."

Morfie was able to lock on one of the hypersonics, not yet at full speed but accelerating fast, and was pleased to see the AIM-174's hot trigger logic was met. Her symbology showed she was at max range. She had one chance.

"Fox Three on the first hypersonic heading west," she said over the UHF as she pulled the trigger. A split second later an AIM-174 came off the outer rail under the Super Hornet's left wing in a bright flash and roared away from her faster than any missile she'd ever fired.

But not fast enough. Morfie watched in dismay as the contrail created by her missile traveling through the air arced downward while those of the three hypersonics continued to knife horizontally across the sky in parallel paths.

"Passkey One's shot is a miss," she relayed. She was out of range now, taunted by the other three AIM-174s that still hung on her jet. Unless the situation radically changed, they wouldn't be fired during Blue Aegis.

And then she saw the three plumes of the hypersonics split away from each other and go into steep dives like an airshow demonstration team from hell.

"Alpha Bravo, be advised it looks like they're doing a pincer," she said.

"Alpha Whiskey is showing the same," the controller on the lead destroyer said, reminding CAG that they had real missiles too.

Punk looked at the range from where the F-35 had fired the missiles at *Ford*—273 nautical miles. "Alpha Whiskey, can you take a shot?" he asked.

In the darkness of the destroyer's CIC, Levi Solomon announced, "We're using real missiles now, people," then keyed the UHF handset he was holding and said, "We should have a shot, Alpha Bravo."

Not the definite answer Punk needed at that point, but he knew the DESRON commander had his hands full. "Take it ASAP," he ordered, his heart about to jump out of his chest. He'd thought they had Howe's side against the ropes, and then, right as they were about to deliver the knockout blow, the Air Force had snuck in a couple of left and right hooks along with a jab. Powerful ones.

He scanned CIC and asked, "Where is Admiral Francis? Is LASIPOD up and running?" Again, there was no answer to either question.

CHAPTER **42**

THE SERVER ROOM in Wolfe's Singapore office suite was kept at a steady 70 degrees Fahrenheit. Even just a few degrees cooler or warmer could affect the server's performance, and his work had demanding parameters. The slightest latency in communication might wreck the entire scenario he'd so painstakingly constructed.

Wolfe sipped a latte as he stood before the theater-size screen, which showed the action in several panels. He wore a mic headset. It was just like delivering a TED Talk. Only he didn't have to flash the fake smile.

Though he often rented cloud and computing servers from other companies, he was using his personal network for Operation Blue Aegis. It was protected by the best firewalls money could buy and ran Aswan in tandem with the monitoring suite his system had piggybacked via the hack into NOSS.

And still Project OpenShip's protocols were thwarting him. Aswan had been unable to hack into the Navy's new system, and it was handily augmenting Vice Admiral Reichert's defense efforts.

"The Air Force has deployed all four hypersonics?" Wolfe asked.

"No," Aswan answered in Kanny's voice. "One was removed from the exercise after it was destroyed by a simulated bomb attack."

"And the other three?"

"Deployed."

Wolfe cracked a genuine smile. For a fleeting moment he felt the breeze on the tarmac as she landed her F-16 after a successful airshow. Saw her hop down the cockpit ladder and wring her helmet off as if she couldn't wait to see him.

"This is for you, Kanny," he said. "I wish you could be here."

"I *am* here, Justin," Aswan said, and one of the screen's panels cut to an avatar of Kanny's face. The dimples, the jaw-length dark hair, the mischievous brown eyes—it looked and moved like her. His software engineers had made sure of it. The face was even more lifelike than the one he'd used for Peterson's father. The AI's voice and visage were based on videos of Kanny he'd taken during their relationship. The software replicated every inflection, each pause, every physical nuance perfectly.

It didn't matter if he was speaking to a simulated version of Kanny Chou. He had used his knowledge and wealth to resurrect her. She would be the face and voice of Aswan, the algorithm that would change history. The forces of the old world had tried to extinguish her and what she represented. Now, her successor would help fashion the new world.

"Above all, correct?" the avatar asked, then winked. "But still below us."

"Above all" was the motto of the RSAF. She'd often added the second part, referring to their relationship. Once she'd said that being with him made her feel like she was flying above all that was wrong with the world.

"Always," he said.

He didn't want—or need—live assistants at this stage of the operation. The fewer who knew what he was doing, the better. It was easy to feel like a god, staring at the data on the screen, watching everything come together just as his numbers had predicted. Could one find satisfaction in life if every action was calculated in advance? Yes. The joy came from the control. The mastery of his reality.

"Probability that *Ford* or escort ships will shoot down all three hypersonics?" he asked.

"Two percent," Aswan said.

Wolfe nodded and sipped more coffee. "Probability that they will shoot down two of the missiles?"

"Eight percent," Aswan said.

"And the probability that at least one missile will reach the aircraft carrier?"

"Twelve percent," Aswan said.

"We can work with that," Wolfe said. "Now, what's the status on the hack into Air Force Cyber Command?"

"Twenty seconds to go," Aswan said.

A new panel opened on the screen showing the hack attempt's status in real time. Unlike the nonsense in a Hollywood movie, which typically displayed lines of code running in endless cascades, the screen showed network access requests.

Wolfe chuckled. "This is pathetic. They should have bought my software last year when I offered it."

"Ten seconds," Kanny said. "How do you wish to proceed?"

He grinned at the avatar molded in the likeness of the woman he loved.

"Once we have access . . . arm all of the hypersonics," Wolfe said.

"We are in control of the missiles. Arming now."

CHAPTER 43

AS PUNK FOCUSED on the destroyers, waiting for them to start launching SM-6s, one of the phones in front of him buzzed and blinked red. Before he could even say hello, Chatterjee said, "Admiral? This is Bhaavik." The engineer's voice was shaking. "I just got to the reactor spaces with your aide, and we have a ... a situation—"

Punk interrupted him: "Where's Einstein? Where's Peterson? We have three hypersonic missiles inbound, and I have no idea whether my main defensive weapon is working."

"Vice Admiral Francis is dead," Chatterjee replied.

The word didn't register. "Dead?"

All comms in CIC stopped, and all eyes turned toward Punk.

"Say again, Chatterjee." Punk said in disbelief. He punched the speakerphone button so all could hear and said, "Dr. Chatterjee, say again."

"Vice Admiral Francis is dead. He appears to have been stabbed while ... while examining LASIPOD's couplings," Chatterjee said, his voice fading as if he was moving away from his phone. "The MAA guarding the weapon is dead too. He was electrocuted. Peterson is nowhere in sight. There's a bloody knife next to Admiral Francis' body."

Punk felt a vein throbbing in his temple as he gazed with unfocused eyes at the VTC screen. He took a deep breath, trying to process the information Chatterjee had just relayed. He looked over at Spud, whose face was a mask of fury.

"It had to be Peterson," Spud seethed. "I knew I didn't trust that fucking guy."

The troubles with LASIPOD, Peterson's endless debates over power consumption, the constant rearrangement of the fiber optic array, the tweaking of each power coupling, the bandwidth issue, the arguments with Chatterjee, the suspicious breakdown of EMALs and the elevators... the truth had been right there for them to see all along.

Now it was too late. Einstein was dead.

That bastard. That sorry bastard. The man overboard. Punk pushed his anger aside, selected the intercom, and said, "Captain, have the MAAs seal off the engineering deck! And I need you report to CIC immediately!"

"Aye, aye, sir," Gridiron returned.

Punk looked at the VTC screen and waved his arms. "Stop the exercise! I say again, stop the exercise!"

Major General Howe blinked in confusion and said, "We have missiles in flight."

"*Stop the exercise!*" Punk shouted. "And call me on the hotline *now*, General."

When Gridiron entered CIC, Punk relayed the bad news and told him to lock down the engineering spaces. As the captain rushed to one of the phones on the wall to carry out the order, another phone buzzed and blinked in front of Punk, a secure line from the PMTC SCIF to be used only for emergencies.

"Right as we're winning you cancel, Punk?" Slapshot mocked on the other end of the phone. "Not very sporting of you."

"We found Vice Admiral Francis dead near the carrier's reactors," Punk replied, immediately silencing Slapshot's chuckle.

"Dead? Well, that's sad news, of course. Heart attack?"

"No, murder. It looks like we have a saboteur."

Howe took a few seconds to process that, then said, "Do you know who?"

"We have a strong hunch. Obviously, somebody wanted us to fail badly enough to kill a three-star to make it happen."

Punk studied Howe's face on the screen as he sat with the hotline to his ear. His Air Force counterpart briefly considered the tacit implications of the statement, then offered, "Nobody on our side would do that."

An image of Congressman Gordon in a dark basement in a secret location near Capitol Hill flashed in Punk's mind, but he quickly suppressed it. "No time to point fingers right now, Slapshot. Please confirm you can cancel Blue Aegis on your end immediately. Self-destruct the missiles in accordance with the exercise instruction."

Slapshot put his hand over the phone and over his shoulder said, "Wu, activate hypersonic missile self-destruct."

Dr. Wu, who had been engrossed in the telemetry data and missed the exchange between Slapshot and Punk, did a doubletake. "Why? They're on their way. Flying fine."

"The exercise is canceled!" Slapshot shouted. "Have you not been paying attention?"

Wu didn't react to the tirade but calmly leaned over and pushed a combination of keys on his keyboard. His lips pursed as he repeated the combination. And then again.

"The self-destruct function isn't working," he announced.

"What?" Slapshot said, his face draining of color.

"I just typed in the code a couple of times and nothing's happening," Wu replied.

"Then fly them into the ocean!" Bear ordered.

Wu spoke into his walkie-talkie and shook his head. Then he typed briefly and manipulated a joystick next to his keyboard. He looked at the generals and shook his head again. "Not working."

They watched the tactical display as the three hypersonics stopped splitting and mirrored their turns until they were flying roughly parallel to each other at a wide range of altitudes.

"They just turned, Wu," Slapshot observed along with everyone else in both SCIFs ashore and at sea. "If you're not controlling them, who is?"

"U.S. CYBERCOM has issued hacking warnings for the past several weeks," Wu replied with the same emotion he might have showed perusing the dinner menu at the base chow hall. "This is clearly cyberwarfare. A foreign power must be responsible. Most likely China."

"You mean we've been hacked?"

"It appears so, General."

"Why wasn't I told this threat existed?"

Wu shrugged. "Your command has responsibility for the protocols that allowed it to get hacked. I figured . . ."

"You figured what?"

"Nothing, sir."

From the other side of the VTC screen, Punk asked, "Did you activate the missile self-destruct? We still show them as inbound on our end."

"I'm calling you back on the hotline," Slapshot announced. He picked up the phone he'd just set down seconds before, and seeing Punk had done the same said, "We're not currently in control of the hypersonics."

Briefly, Punk wondered if he was in the middle of another nightmare like the one he'd had the morning of the HASC hearing that had started all of this.

"Then who is?" he asked. The answer was far too long in coming, considering his current state of mind, so he repeated, *"Who is?"*

"We're trying to figure that out."

Punk puffed an exasperated exhale and keyed the UHF: "Alpha Whiskey, say status of weapons launch."

Captain Levi Solomon on one of the nearby destroyers caught the urgency in Punk's voice and replied, "Stand by, sir." He pushed a button on the nearby intercom and said, "Weapons officer, are the SM-6s spun up?"

"Understand you want to shoot live missiles, sir?" a distorted voice asked through the metal speaker.

"That's affirmative," Levi answered. "We're shooting live."

Punk could hear the conversation away from the UHF handset, and he added, "This is also a real-world operation now."

"Say again, Admiral?"

"I don't have time to explain. Throw everything you've got at them. If any of them gets through and you have any ordnance left on either ship, I'm not going to be happy."

"Copy that, Admiral." Levi said. He dropped the handset and checked the speed of the incoming missiles. "Mach 6?" he uttered in disbelief.

"Actually, they're at Mach 7 now, sir," the AW controller seated in front of him said in equal disbelief. "And accelerating. Two are low, one is angels medium, about ten thousand feet."

The captain picked up the nearest phone and said, "Bridge, this is combat. Set general quarters." Then, accompanied by the voice of the destroyer's skipper over the ship's main intercom ordering the crew to man their battle stations, he leaned back into the intercom and asked, "Weps, how many live SM-6s do we have aboard?"

"Four," the distorted voice replied.

"And the other destroyer?"

"Same."

Each *Arleigh Burke* Flight III guided missile destroyer had ninety-six vertical-launch-system cells, meaning in theory they could carry that many SM-6s. And the DESRON's two-ship armada currently had eight in total.

"Friggin' budget cuts," Levi muttered to himself. "Are we ready to fire?"

"We're ready up here," the weapons officer replied on the intercom.

He looked toward the destroyer's Tactical Action Officer, a burly lieutenant seated at a screen left of the controller, and said, "TAO, fire when able."

"They split vertical and horizontal," the TAO observed. "Which one should we shoot?"

"This is a fucking Flight III with a SPY-6 track-while-scan radar," Levi snapped back as if his TAO didn't know the model of guided missile destroyer he was aboard. "Shoot all three of them!"

"Sir, I'm showing the hypersonics now traveling at Mach 8," the controller said.

"I'm seeing the same thing," the TAO replied before looking over his right shoulder at the DESRON commander standing behind him. "What do you want to do, Captain?"

"Launch the missiles," Levi ordered, working hard to keep his cool.

"That's four times faster than any target we've trained against," the TAO observed. "Our missiles may not hack it."

"Fire!" Levi shouted. He picked up the UHF handset again and transmitted, "Small Boy Two, you are cleared to engage targets. Full salvo."

"Small Boy Two, roger," the TAO on the other *Arleigh Burke* replied. "Engaging now."

Everyone in CIC focused on the closed-circuit TV pointed at the cluster of VLS cells just forward of the superstructure. A flash of flame shot up in one of them, followed by a narrow plume of smoke as a missile raged into the sky; it was followed by another and another and yet another.

"Small Boy One, four birds in the air," the TAO transmitted into his headset.

"Small Boy Two, four birds in the air," another TAO echoed from CIC on the second warship.

In the carrier's CIC Punk focused on the tactical picture displayed on the big screen on the wall in front of him. Eight SM-6s arced toward three hypersonic missiles.

"They look like they're tracking," he observed. He picked up the UHF handset and asked, "Alpha Whiskey, are they tracking?"

Levi looked toward his TAO, who nodded without looking away from his screen and replied, "They look to be tracking, Alpha Bravo."

Seconds felt like hours as Punk waited for the "boola boola" call that would mean the Navy missiles had found their marks. But as he watched the screen, he thought he saw the hypersonics maneuvering again.

"They jinked into each other," the TAO said into his display.

"Alpha Bravo, be advised they jinked into each other," Levi passed to Punk over the UHF.

"We're showing the same," Punk acknowledged.

"That wasn't us," Slapshot added on the VTC screen.

"Whoever it was knows what they're doing," Spud said as he pointed to the tactical display. "Look at that track crossing rate now. It's got to be off the page."

As if on cue Levi said, "They missed!"

"All of them?" Punk asked.

"They couldn't hack the turn, I'm guessing. Those things are going Mach 8 and turning on a dime."

Punk quickly did the math in his head: eight SM-6 Standard Missiles at two and a half million dollars each. Twenty million dollars down the drain. Congressman Gordon was going to have a field day with that.

But Einstein was dead, and Peterson had blood on his hands.

"They're turning again! And they're all low now!" Connelly observed, pointing at the screen, snapping Punk back to the task at hand.

"Looks like they dove to the deck and are headed back toward *Ford*," the TAO on the lead destroyer reported.

"How far from us?" Captain Solomon asked.

"Inside one hundred nautical miles."

Without hesitation Levi commanded, "Arm the 5-inch gun."

"Sir?" the TAO asked.

"Arm the gun, damn it!" he shot back, losing whatever composure he had left. "And relay to Small Boy Two to do the same."

"Aye, aye, sir, but it'll be like shooting a bullet with a bullet," the TAO said, his hands moving on his keyboard.

"Then that's what we have to do," Levi replied as he snuck another glance at the tactical picture and stepped toward the main hatch. "I'm headed up to the bridge. As soon as those fuckers are in range, I want rounds going at them. And arm the Phalanx close-in weapons system too. Keep firing until those things blow up or we're totally out of ammo, whatever comes first."

"Aye, aye, sir," the TAO said.

Back aboard *Ford*, Gridiron ended his brief call with his chief master-at-arms and turned toward Punk, saying, "Admiral, I want to set general quarters."

Punk recognized he was task saturated, leveraging a skill he'd learned in the cockpit over the years, and felt negligent for not recommending the action earlier. "Set general quarters," he replied.

Gridiron dialed the phone he'd just hung up and said, "XO, this is the captain. Set general quarters. I say again, set general quarters. This is not a drill."

A second later the voice of the aircraft carrier's executive officer, who was manning the bridge in the captain's absence, came over the 1MC: "General quarters, general quarters! All hands man your battle stations! This is not a drill! I say again, general quarters." The announcement was followed by the clanging of the alarm.

The pounding of feet echoed through the ship as crew rushed to their appointed positions.

"I'm headed for the bridge," Gridiron said.

Punk nodded and picked up one of the phones in front of him. "Bhaavik, can you get LASIPOD running?"

"I've been trying, sir," Chatterjee said, sounding calmer now. "Peterson's been sabotaging this whole damn thing. You wouldn't believe—"

"We need it now," Punk said. "Make it work!"

"I'm on it," Chatterjee said.

"How soon?" Punk asked.

"I'm *on* it, sir," Chatterjee said.

Punk had managed to push aside the knowledge that they had a traitor somewhere on board, a saboteur. A murderer. Someone who had killed a friend, a peer, and a former squadron mate—and others, too. But he had no time to dwell on that now. They had an aircraft carrier to save, and not just funding-wise. For real.

Captain Solomon reached the lead destroyer's bridge after stopping briefly in his VIP stateroom along the way from CIC to take a pearl-handled 9-mm pistol and holster from his safe. He strapped the rig around his waist, an affectation during periods of high operational tempo he'd become known for across the surface warfare community, like a poor man's George Patton.

Levi grabbed a pair of binoculars and hearing protection—"mouse ears"—from a table next to the navigation display and walked onto the port bridge wing. Small Boy Two plied a parallel course a mile away. He held the binoculars to his eyes and scanned the horizon across the bow without any idea what a long, thin tube coming at them at Mach 8 would look like head-on, if it was visible at all at that speed.

"Put the TAO on the speaker out here," he shouted back toward the bridge watch team.

A second later the TAO's voice crackled over the ruggedized speaker mounted to the side of the superstructure. "You got me, Captain Solomon?" he asked.

"Yes. How me?" Levi asked in return.

"I can hear you."

"Say range to targets."

"Forty nautical miles. They're spread across three miles horizontally."

They only had seconds, then. "Open fire at thirty."

"That's outside max range, sir."

"Not for something coming at Mach 8. And put the Phalanx on auto acquisition. I want everything firing until we're dry."

He jumped when the 5-inch gun opened up, one round every three seconds, and quickly slipped on the mouse ears, then raised the binoculars to his eyes again. He directed the glasses toward Small Boy Two, whose gun was also firing.

The Battle of Leyte Gulf twenty-first-century style, he thought.

"TAO, say range!" he shouted over the report of the gun.

"Fifteen miles!" the TAO shouted back over the speaker.

Levi thought he spotted something dead ahead, a glint, a wisp of a contrail. The Phalanx close-in weapon came to life, its rapid-fire buzz of bullets accompanying the pounding of the 5-inch gun. He lowered the binoculars to see if he could make out the missile with the naked eye. And there it was! Or was it?

He pointed his pistol toward the spot and bellowed a war cry as he pulled the trigger again and again. If Vice Admiral Reichert wanted no ammo left, he'd give him no ammo left. He saw a flash above the water from what he guessed was only a mile or so away, followed a second later by the pop of a small explosion.

"That's a hit!" the TAO cried over the speaker.

Levi let out a whoop and shouted back, "The bullet hit the bullet!"

Amid bridge team cheers and high fives, Captain Solomon hurried off the bridge wing to the first handset mounted behind the helmsman and transmitted, "Alpha Bravo, this is Alpha Whiskey. Splash one. I say again, splash one."

"Well done, Levi!" Punk transmitted in response, momentarily breaking from radio protocol. His joy quickly faded as he referenced the tactical screen and realized they weren't out of the woods yet. "Alpha Whiskey, can you take any more shots at the other two?" he asked.

"Afraid not, Alpha Bravo," Levi replied. "They're by us now. Opening rates are way too high for another SM-6 shot."

Punk looked at the VTC screen and asked, "Any chance you guys can get control of those things, Slapshot?"

Major General Howe looked over at Dr. Wu, who shook his head.

"That appears to be a negative, Punk," Slapshot replied.

Punk focused on the OpenShip presentation, manipulating one of the switches in the armrest to zoom in on the representation of the aircraft carrier there. What he saw horrified him.

"AI is showing the hypersonics are headed for *Ford*'s reactors," he said. "General Howe, is that the aim point you selected?"

"That's a Wu question," Slapshot replied, motioning for the chief engineer behind him to move closer to the VTC camera.

"Hermes isn't programmed like a JDAM or other GPS-guided weapons," Wu explained, his tone still phlegmatic in the extremis situation. "We write the code and set algorithms in motion, and machine learning does the rest."

"What the hell does that mean?" Connelly asked.

"It means, Rear Admiral Connelly, that as the missile is in flight it's getting smarter, taking in data from multiple sources, reading the network and pulsing the electromagnetic spectrum, exploiting enemy sensors and using their intel fusion against them, assessing the tactical situation to aim itself at the perfect point of impact to yield the maximum effect. And in the case of multiple missiles, they work together to complicate the enemy's targeting problem. And all of this is going on without any input from whoever originally activated them."

"Dr. Frankenstein has lost control of his monsters," Spud muttered. "Wu should've named Hermes *Frankenmissile*."

"Normally Hermes can be overridden at any point," Wu added. "But right now, we don't seem to have control of these."

Dr. Wu's matter-of-fact delivery was getting under Punk's skin. The aircraft carrier was facing imminent destruction and Einstein was dead—something he still hadn't fully processed because of his current tactical focus—but before he could push back on it across the VTC, a phone buzzed.

"Admiral, it's Dr. Chatterjee."

"I need good news, Bhaavik," Punk said.

"I think we have it," Chatterjee said.

"Think?"

"It's now or never, because we're out of couplings down here."

"Is LASIPOD powered up?"

"No, that will take another minute," Chatterjee said. "The bandwidth—"

"Make it happen," Punk interrupted. "Otherwise, you're about to have a couple of hypersonic missiles in your lap."

With the receiver still to his ear, Punk referenced the OpenShip data on the screen again and asked, "ETA?"

"One point three minutes until first impact," Maggie Mildenhall answered from the TAO's chair next to Punk.

A deathly silence stole over CIC. Those assembled there were frozen, as if time itself had stopped. They were helpless to influence events now. One by one, everyone looked to Punk.

Punk felt that same feeling descending on him that he used to get when things started to get hairy in the cockpit of an F-14, whether warning lights were flashing because of a systems failure or hostile forces were shooting at him in anger. Time compressed, and that allowed things to drop into place and decisions to be made despite the chaos of the moment.

Why die all tensed up? one of his flight instructors had joked in the early days. Why, indeed.

Thirty seconds to go on the first Hermes. One minute on the second.

"They're coming too fast for the RIMs," Maggie reported, referring to *Ford*'s self-defense missiles, which had performed so well against the test drones a few days earlier. "We can't get the hot trigger logic to activate. They're dead on the rails."

Twenty seconds to missile one's impact. He thought of the original exercise brief when Einstein had asked Connelly what a reactor strike would do to the ship and, after it had sunk, to the environment for thousands of miles around. Sea and sky poisoned for a millennium.

Despite his outward cool, every heartbeat in Punk's chest was a drumbeat of doom.

Forty seconds to missile two's impact.

He glanced at the VTC screen and felt his anger rising as he noted the detached concern on the faces of those behind the table in the PMTC SCIF, like an audience eager to see how a movie plays out. As the credits rolled, the audience would leave the theater entertained, bellies bulging with popcorn and soda, and return to the security of their homes.

This isn't how it's going to end, he thought.

But was it?

On the other end of the phone, Chatterjee said, "LASIPOD is up and running. I also finally managed to link it with OpenShip. Their AI is our AI now."

Punk pounded the table with his fist and said, "Hell, yes, Bhaavik! Good work."

His scan jumped between the tactical presentation and the OpenShip display, and in the state of chaos and entropy-induced time compression he mused that somewhere in the distance their doom was speeding toward them from two directions at eight times the speed of sound. There had been a time when people thought the speed barrier could not be broken. Yet it had been, a paradigm shift that led to other, even greater achievements. Everything from jet fighter aircraft to putting human beings on the Moon. And now, those same principles were speeding toward him faster than any other physical object was moving on Earth.

And they were counting on an unproven, barely tested asset to save the day.

"The second missile changed trajectory again," Spud observed, pointing toward the screen.

"Machine learning," Punk said. "Frankenmissile."

"Same thing on missile one," Connelly called.

Punk stared at the OpenShip screen: eighteen seconds to missile one impact. Fifty-seven seconds to missile two.

Something he should have thought of sooner hit him: "Bhaavik, how long does it take LASIPOD to recharge between shots?"

There was no answer.

Ten seconds to missile one impact.

Five.

"I think I see it," Gridiron said over the intercom on the bridge.

"Brace for impact!" Punk ordered as he grabbed the side of the table and stiffened his back against the chair.

A hum reverberated around them emanating from the starboard side of the ship forward where the business end of LASIPOD was mounted. The moment seemed like an eternity.

Then the hum was gone.

On the bridge Gridiron saw a brilliant yellow-white puff explode over the sky forty feet from the starboard bow. Debris fragments rained over the ocean in smoky gray spears that extinguished themselves in the Pacific. A clatter echoed from the Phalanx placement starboard side amidships. A damage alarm sounded.

"Report, Captain," Punk requested over the intercom.

"Looks like a piece of the missile hit the Phalanx," Gridiron said. "Gunners on station reporting two injuries, neither of them critical."

Punk scanned the people working around him and asked, "Did we hit it?"

"Hell, yes, we did!" Maggie answered. "Sir."

Gridiron whooped over the intercom. Spud and Connelly high-fived.

Punk didn't join the celebration, instead focusing on the screens and asking, "Range to missile two?"

"Fourteen seconds out," the TAO replied.

"Bhaavik, charging status down there?" Punk asked as he watched the missile track change again. Frankenmissile's education was ongoing, and the graduation ceremony wasn't going to be pleasant for those aboard *Ford*.

"Almost there, Admiral," Chatterjee said.

"Need it *now*!"

"Where are you, damnit?" Gridiron mumbled, intercom still keyed as he scanned the horizon through the shatterproof windows on the bridge.

"Ten seconds!"

"Chatterjee . . ." Punk pleaded as his eyes tracked data on the screens. "Now, please. Right . . . *now*!"

Nothing happened. Before he could ask Chatterjee to tell him the recharge status the hum reverberated around them again. He stared at the OpenShip screen as if the intensity of his focus could drag an answer out of it. The hum lasted longer this time.

Gridiron saw another flash like the one before, this one off the port bow. The resultant explosive cloud scattered four hundred feet away like a giant sack of flour bursting. Punk stared at the CIC screens, but neither OpenShip nor the tactical picture presented anything resembling a destroyed hypersonic missile.

"Talk to me, somebody!" he asked desperately. His request was met with a deafening silence.

A dozen decks above, the carrier's commanding officer rushed to the starboard bridge wing to assess the damage once the hum of LASIPOD faded to silence. The air had a wavy quality to it, something felt rather than seen. He heard a crackling sound forward and watched a glittering cloud of debris and embers rain down there.

Gridiron hurried back to the intercom and gleefully shouted, "I'm calling it a kill!"

This time Punk joined the others cheering and exchanging high-fives. He put the receiver back to his ear and said, "Bhaavik, you are my hero!"

"Did it work?" Chatterjee asked in return.

"You're still here, aren't you?" Punk replied. "All missiles destroyed!"

"Good, because LASIPOD is hard down. The couplings ignited at the end of that last burst. We had to put out a small fire in the reactor room. All secure here now."

The VTC screen showed the people in the PMTC SCIF on their feet offering polite applause. "Goddamn, Punk," Slapshot said. "You did it."

Punk pinched the bridge of his nose and shook his head. "Pardon my French, General, but that was fucked up."

"I'd say I'm sorry, but we didn't have anything to do with it," Howe said as he resumed his seat.

"Who did?"

"We don't know yet, but we'll find out. I guarantee you that. We've already energized the intel grid at the Pentagon." Slapshot leaned back in his chair and linked his hands behind his head. "In the meantime, congratulations for saving your aircraft carrier. We'll see you at the next budget hearing. Out, here."

Slapshot extended an arm forward beyond the lower limit of the screen, and the display turned into color bars. And with that, Operation Blue Aegis was over.

Punk let out what was most likely the longest sigh of his life before climbing out of his chair and getting to his feet. Maggie did the same. They exchanged a hearty handshake, and she said, "That was close, Admiral."

"Exactly how we drew it up, right?" Punk replied with a shake of his head.

Spud stepped from behind her and wrapped Punk in a hug, and at that moment it fully hit him that Einstein was dead.

The squadron mates' embrace lasted a long time. Once it was over, Punk cleared his throat, keyed the intercom, and said, "Captain, secure from general quarters. Meet me in the reactor spaces."

"Aye, sir," Gridiron replied.

"Have they found Peterson yet?"

"No, sir."

CHAPTER **44**

PETERSON CLUNG to one of the oil rig's lower struts. He'd cut his thigh on the rusted metal and the sun was baking his face and neck, but he was alive.

But Wolfe had lied. The bastard hadn't sent a submarine.

Every muscle in Peterson's body ached so much that he almost wished he hadn't survived the jump overboard. He'd swum for miles and drifted several more holding on to a broken surfboard that came his way. A gift from God. Or Satan. Then he'd seen salvation: a metallic titan looming above the sea a hundred miles off the coast of Los Angeles. It might as well have been six or seven hundred. He'd never make the swim to shore from there.

But the oil rig had saved him. Sheltered him. Grounded him in the new life he would begin when his benefactors came for him—with his promised payment.

He wasn't sure which offshore installation he'd made it to, but it was in the middle of nowhere. Which also described where Wolfe had left him. He'd been waiting for hours, and the promised rescue had not appeared. No boat, no submarine. He'd seen some helicopters in the distance but they hadn't spotted him. Another gift.

You're going to pull this off, Shane, he thought. But first he had to make it to shore. Wolfe had lied... or had it been Peterson's father? He wasn't sure anymore.

Surely someone would come soon. *Ford* and all the assholes on it who'd doubted him were at the bottom of the Pacific now. And Shane Peterson, also-ran civil servant, face in the crowd at China Lake, flight school washout, was responsible. He laughed until he choked. He was exhausted and thirsty; his throat was dryer than sandpaper.

Then it hit him that his dad was dead along with everything the old man stood for. He'd never know what Shane had done, never offer the praise his son so desperately wanted. So, what had been the point?

When a shape loomed over the horizon he squirmed with giddy abandon. He wanted to wave, but that would mean letting go of the strut, and he wasn't sure he could swim again yet. Maybe never again. But a ship was there, and it meant life; it meant rescue.

The shape grew larger, coalescing into a familiar long, gray line. Elements on its heights sparkled in the sunlight, mocking him with their lofty perches.

A tiny silver shape rose from it. Then another.

The *whup-whup* of rotors reached his ears, and Peterson trembled.

It was *Ford*. But that was impossible. The missiles LASIPOD had failed to destroy had sunk it. How was the boat still afloat? How had they found him?

A vibration traveled up his thigh, and Peterson's heart leapt into his throat. He'd forgotten that he still had one more burner phone on him. Though he'd not used it to contact Wolfe, it was still connected to his provider's network.

The one phone he should have discarded had doomed him. They had used it to track him. There was still one option left to him, but first there was a file on his personal cloud drive.

Peterson removed the phone from the sealed plastic wrapping, swiped the screen, and uploaded a file to his drive space on China Lake's servers.

The pair of helicopters—MH-60s—flew closer. So close he could make out the figures inside. They were clasping rifles. Navy SEALs.

Peterson let go of the strut and relaxed back into the swells.

He did not bother swimming.

From his chair on the Flag Bridge Punk watched the two helicopters land on the flight deck amidships. Even before the rotor blades of the forward Knighthawk had come to a halt, the SEALs unloaded Peterson's body and disappeared with it into the base of *Ford*'s island.

"I hope they don't put that fucker in the same freezer Einstein's in," Spud said, staring down at the flight deck from behind Punk's chair.

"They won't," Punk said. "I already talked to Gridiron about that."

"Holding on to an oil rig, huh?" Spud asked, "How did the little creep get that far? He must have been one hell of a swimmer. But now we'll never know why he did it. And who was behind it."

"We don't know why he did it yet, but it almost certainly has something to do with money," Punk said.

"Doesn't it always?"

But Punk was too tired to psychoanalyze Peterson or try to dig out the reason for his deeds. Three people had died during an exercise, and *Ford* could have been lost, all to satisfy a political hack in D.C. He had a vice admiral and two sailors to honor, another pending investigation on the cyberwarfare attack on their networks yesterday, and a wife who needed him more than ever. Unfortunately, that was the order in which he would have to attend to them.

But the boat had been saved. He'd done his duty. Right now, others could argue the finer points.

As he watched the activity on the flight deck Punk felt no sense of victory or even a desire for vengeance. The black body bag the SEALs had unloaded contained a tragic figure who had possessed the potential to do a great deal of good in the pursuit of the nation's defense.

"The media will have a field day with this," Spud said.

"Not to mention our opponents on the Hill and at the Pentagon," Punk added. "I talked to Muddy right before I came up here, and she said that the HASC is like an overturned beehive. I'm sure I'm going to be testifying again soon," he sighed.

"What do you think is going to happen to Howe?"

Punk shifted his focus from the waist to the bow and stroked his chin as he considered the question. "I guess it depends on how the hypersonics got hacked. He owned the protocols, but that doesn't necessarily mean he did anything wrong."

"Muddy hinted that he had some dirty trick up his sleeve that got preempted by the hacking. I take perverse pleasure in that idea."

Gridiron walked through the hatch and said, "We have a helo inbound with NCIS agents aboard. They're going to want statements from both of you, so let me know what your schedule looks like, and I'll bring them your way."

Spud checked his watch in an exaggerated motion and said, "Well, Shane Peterson booked me to be on the bottom of the Pacific Ocean, but now my calendar is wide open."

CHAPTER 45

THE SNAP of his fingers sounded like a pistol shot across Satun beach. All it took was that and a sharp gesture, and the Thai girl was racing to get a fresh glass of champagne. Good. If she couldn't speed up her service, maybe a sex tourist might find her useful.

His tablet blinked with notifications as Wolfe Industries stock continued to drop. Aswan had been compromised again when a Russian hacker planted a buggy code into its architecture. In light of the rumors surrounding a possible Wolfe Industries link with the Navy saboteur and traitor Shane Peterson, several companies had withdrawn their promises to use Aswan as their next machine learning platform.

Shane had done the job he'd been recruited to do, at least, before leaving a confession on his cloud drive linking Wolfe to the events on *Ford*. Wolfe's lawyers had told him not to worry and assured him the Navy didn't have a case.

Yet five of his lawyers had withdrawn their services in the last two days.

Cahya had left a cold voicemail on one of his burner phones, angry that he had neglected to share all of what he knew about Project OpenShip. He'd not returned her calls. China had discovered that ISIS-DRC wasn't behind the cobalt mine attack after all. Maybe Cahya wanted to warn him—for a fee, of course. It didn't matter. The next time they met he'd bring her several envelopes.

Wolfe could live with all those things. They were problems that could be solved with decent PR and better lawyers. More important, he had shown prospective customers what Aswan was capable of. Another build version and the problems revealed during Operation Blue Aegis would be fixed.

The item drawing his ire was the robust architecture and performance of Project OpenShip. Aswan could hack into it, he was certain of that—but now that the Navy realized the danger, it would hire Wolfe's competitors to make its defense system nigh impregnable. NOSS was already receiving updates, as were its Chinese, Russian, and NATO counterparts.

Still, it was simply another challenge. He would surmount it.

Wolfe swiped his tablet and Aswan's avatar loaded. Where before he had seen Kanny in its smile, now he saw a mere facsimile. Mockery, even.

"Probability that Wolfe Industries' board will demand a new CEO?" he asked.

"Seventy-eight percent," Aswan said.

He shrugged. He had expected it to be that high. "Have you started selling off shares?"

"I tried, but the transactions have been placed on hold," Aswan said with the coy simper Kanny had flashed when she knew she'd annoyed him.

Wolfe sat up in the chair. "On hold? Why?"

"I am unable to process that at this time," Aswan said.

"I—" Wolfe started, then stopped as a chopping pulse built in the air. A slowly growing mechanized portent.

Wolfe jumped from the lounge chair, tablet hanging in his limp grasp.

"Aswan?" he asked. "Drone alert status?"

He always maintained a perimeter of thirty security drones at his resorts.

"I am unable to process that at this time," Aswan said.

Two Thai women ran past him. His butler followed. None of them spared him a glance.

"No!" Wolfe said, then took off running, bare feet slapping on the damp sand. His tablet vibrated with notifications. He already knew they were security alerts.

"Aswan, key my yacht!" Wolfe cried.

The pulse grew in volume. The very air shuddered.

The AI's answer was barely audible over the noise. "I am unable to . . ."

He made it to the dock where *Fibonacci's Dream* waited. The burner phone in his shirt pocket vibrated, and he yanked it out. It was a call from Cahya.

He answered it. "What the hell is going on?"

Cahya sounded so smugly amused that he wanted to reach through the phone and strangle her. "You fucked with the wrong people this time, Justin. Not even I could shield you from the Ministry. And they still play nice with the West when it comes to the War on Terror. Like sharing intel."

He was breathing so hard his chest hurt. "I swear, if you sold me out—"

"It's hard to sell out a dead man," she said. "You shouldn't have ghosted my calls. I suggest you get the hell out of Dodge."

No sooner had the call ended than a hail of hisses and pops enfiladed the yacht. A cacophony of shattered glass and perforated fiberglass hull rattled his eardrums.

Above, a black helicopter flew into view.

"This is the Unted States Navy," a voice called down from the chopper through a bullhorn. "Lie down on the ground and place your hands behind your head."

The yacht was out, but there was still a small submarine out in the bay. The one he used to smuggle opium and Thai women. He had to try for it.

"Lie down or we will open fire!" the voice warned.

Wolfe had started to run into the sea when something sharp burned through his right quadricep. He tumbled into the surf. The tablet clattered into the moist sand a few feet away. On the screen, Aswan—Kanny—smiled.

Blood from his wound stained the spume red. He scrambled on hands and knees toward the tablet, but the agony in his leg stabbed through his body. He collapsed into a small breaker. The salt water invaded his eyes, nostrils, and mouth.

Coughing, Wolfe reached for the tablet again.

Kanny was still smiling at him when the device shattered into pieces. They'd shot it. Shot his Crow.

Wolfe rolled over and tried to rise, writhing in pain. The wash from the chopper hovering directly above him blew salt water into his eyes. Helmeted individuals on it were aiming rifles down at him. U.S. Navy SEALs. Impossible. They shouldn't be here. Nothing in his calculations had predicted it.

Wolfe gritted his teeth as he tried to push himself out of the surf.

"No," he said, then raised his voice. "No, damn you! Numbers don't—"

Three SEALs rappelled down to Wolfe and dragged him up on the beach. One pressed his face into the sand while another applied zip cuffs to his wrists. A medic saw to his leg. The chopper's blades disturbed the air, buffeting him with its angry currents.

"Lie," he mumbled as the sea washed away the remnants of the tablet.

CHAPTER 46

VICE ADMIRAL Paul "Einstein" Francis, USN, Commander Naval Air Systems Command, was buried on a calm, sunny morning in autumn. The leaves on the trees that dotted Arlington National Cemetery were at peak color—yellow, orange, and red. They would fall soon, taken by the cold and wind as winter approached. But on this day, they were the window dressing for a solemn military ceremony.

Punk and Suzanne had walked behind the caisson—a horse-drawn casket accompanied by six rifle-bearing sailors assigned to the U.S. Navy Ceremonial Guard—along with hundreds of others who had turned out to honor the fallen flag officer. The slow clopping of the horses' hooves echoed in the still, crisp air. When they reached the gravesite, Suzanne took her husband by the arm and ran her other hand across the stripes—one wide and two thin—on the sleeve of his service dress blue uniform before wiping another tear from her eye.

Following the Chief of Chaplains' brief remarks, the ceremonial guard pointed their rifles in the air and fired a fifteen-gun salute, only half of them shooting the last of the three volleys, and then a lone bugler blew Taps. The last mournful note quavered and slowly faded to silence after being held for an achingly long time as four Super Hornets screamed overhead. One of them pitched into the vertical in a missing man maneuver. Punk noted they were F models, the two-seater, which was appropriate because that was the last airplane that Einstein had logged time in while he was doing developmental test events out of NAS Patuxent River.

After the Navy jets disappeared beyond the monuments and trees and the roar of their engines died away, Punk could hear that Suzanne had broken into sobs. He wrapped an arm around her and pulled her close.

"I'm sorry," she whispered as she fought to control her sobbing. "That sound always..." Her whisper trailed off.

"I know," he whispered back, pulling her even closer. "I know."

Taking the redeye from San Diego to Reagan National Airport after Suzanne's treatment the morning before hadn't allowed them much time to sleep. But the news was good, incredibly good. Dr. Billings reported that her body was responding to the chemo and the tumor was shrinking. There was an excellent chance she would reenter remission. The nausea bouts were less frequent, and her appetite was back. She had already regained some strength, enough to make the trip. Punk had insisted that she didn't have to go, but she wouldn't hear of missing the funeral. Einstein hadn't just been Punk's squadron mate; he'd been hers too.

As the casket was lowered into the ground, Punk read the headstone. A life in a few lines. Would a casual passerby make a distinction between Einstein's final resting place and those to either side of it? And did it matter, these pursuits and ambitions rendered trivial and without consequence when all was said and done? Thousands of bright white headstones lined up in even rows across the acres and acres of trimmed grass. Each told a story, but collectively they formed a single narrative whose theme was left to the beholder to interpret.

Beyond the burial attendees across from him, Punk saw the grounds crew dressed in coveralls and holding shovels and rakes looming, waiting for the ceremony to end so they could finish their grim work. He watched the crowd disperse and start the long stroll back from where they'd come half an hour earlier, only this time there wasn't a caisson to follow.

Punk, Suzanne, Spud, and Muddy stayed behind looking down on the casket. "Good turnout," Spud said.

"It was, but that's not a surprise," Punk said. "Who didn't love Einstein?"

"I could name a few defense contractors," Muddy quipped. "They'd call me and complain that his test pilots were being too tough on their airplanes or whatever, as if I could do something about it."

"No one was better at it. His attention to detail was legendary," Spud said. "I remember when he first got to the squadron when we were deployed, he'd ask me super-complicated RIO questions about the radar and the missiles, and as I was trying to answer he'd be writing it all down in one of those little green notebooks he carried everywhere with him."

"The little green notebooks," the others repeated in unison and laughed.

"I totally forgot about those," Spud said. "Life before laptops."

"And top-secret clearances," Punk added.

The former squadron mates stood in silent vigil until the workers with shovels moved closer and considered the gravesite holdouts with humorless expressions. The four took the hint, but before they walked away, each of Einstein's fellow aviators gave him one last tribute.

"You were trainable," Spud said, his highest compliment. "Rest in peace, shipmate. We have the watch."

"You kept me out of trouble when we flew together," Muddy said. "I wouldn't be here without you. Thanks."

"You were a good squadron mate and an even better fellow flag officer," Punk said. "I've never been an admiral without having you just a phone call away, Einstein, so I'm going to have to figure that out. And even if I do, it won't be as good as when you were here." He stood there until Suzanne took his hand and gently tugged him away.

As the group started along the asphalt path back to the visitors' center, Spud said, "I just realized I didn't see Howe."

"He was here, lurking in the background," Punk said. "I'm sure he left as soon as he felt he'd paid the appropriate amount of respect. He hates losing more than I do."

"Word around the HASC is he won't be getting a fourth star," Muddy said.

"Speaking of winning and losing, Muddy, has Blue Aegis caused any defense budget fallout on the Hill?" Punk asked.

"Everybody's suddenly all in on cybersecurity," she laughed. "And the Navy wants to fully fund Project OpenShip and LASIPOD implementation."

"And *Ford*-class aircraft carriers," Spud added with a smile. "And Peabody Tilden is ready to help with that."

"I can just imagine what the demand for cyber would be if the hacker had been the Chinese navy instead of that guy Wolfe," Muddy said.

"Did you see the body-cam footage of his arrest?" Spud asked. "Dude didn't go easy."

"I heard about it but haven't seen it yet. I did notice on the financial page that Wolfe Industries' stock price tanked after it happened."

"This is my sad face," Spud said with an exaggerated frown.

"He's all but bankrupt."

"What about Gordon?" Punk asked.

"He's a real tough guy when the cameras are on, but he didn't have the guts to show up here," Muddy seethed. "His donors aren't happy with how Blue Aegis went, and if the money dries up, the party will bail on him."

"Couldn't happen to a nicer guy," Spud said.

"He won't go far. Congressman Seth Gordon is a political animal, a survivor. He'll switch districts if he thinks he's going to lose. Hell, he'll run in another state if he has to."

As the four of them reached the parking lot, a black SUV pulled up next to them. The driver, dressed in a black suit and tie, jumped out and opened the right rear door for Muddy.

"Where are we going next, ma'am?"

Muddy looked at the others. "You guys need a ride back into D.C.?"

Punk and Suzanne exchanged shrugs and nodded.

"Beats an Uber," Spud said.

"I'm headed to lunch and would love it if you could join me," Muddy added. "There's this place south of Capitol Hill that has the best she-crab soup on the East Coast."

"Do they serve beer?" Spud asked.

"Why, I believe they do, yes," Muddy laughed.

"Then I accept."

"Day drinking?" Punk said.

"What?" Spud returned defensively. "This was my only scheduled event of the day. Besides, by the time we get there it'll be afternoon."

"I won't judge," Punk said.

"Really? Because it sounds like you're judging."

"Okay, you two, get in the damn car," Suzanne said, giving Punk a playful push toward the SUV. "I'm starving."

His wife was starving. And that was good news on a bad day.

ACKNOWLEDGMENTS

Ward –
I'd like to thank those friends who have inspired and mentored me in a wide variety of ways over the years, specifically James Barber, Rick Beato, Admiral Mike Mullen, Vice Admiral Ted "Slapshot" Carter, Rear Admiral Mike "Nasty" Manazir, Steve Morse, Mark Converse, Kev'n Kinney, Tim Nielsen, Fred Rainbow, Chris Michel, and Bill Shepherd.

Thanks to Greg "Chaser" Keithley and everyone at the Tailhook Association for their support.

Thanks to all my YouTube channel Patrons and subscribers. I endeavor to never take your support for granted.

Thanks to Adam Kane, Mindy Conner, Ashley Baird, and everyone at USNI Press for their hard work. You guys are the best in the publishing business.

Thanks to my longtime literary agent and friend Ethan Ellenberg for being great at his job.

Thanks to Tony Peak for his talent, work ethic, and understanding in co-writing this book.

And most importantly, thanks to my sons for making me proud and my wife Carrie for her support, friendship, and enduring love. Without you whatever success I've achieved would be impossible. I love you always.

Tony –

I want to thank my agent, Ethan Ellenberg, without whom this project wouldn't have taken flight. His persistence, candor, patience, loyalty, and faith in my abilities over the years have been, and continue to be, constant sources of inspiration. You couldn't ask for a better friend in this business. Onward and upward.

Thanks to my co-author, Mooch himself, Ward Carroll. This was the first time I'd co-written a novel with someone, and thanks to his professionalism, honesty, and generosity, I hope it's not the last. It's one thing to write about military aviators, vessels, aircraft, and such, but it's another thing to actually work with someone who's been in the cockpit. Ward guided this story where it needed to go; there is no substitute for that level of experience, and I'm proud he found my contributions worthy of his creation. It's been an honor.

I'd also like to thank all the people at USNI Press for giving Ward and me this opportunity. The Naval Institute's pedigree is impeccable, and I feel privileged to become a part of it.

And, finally, I'd like to thank my parents, Curtis and Irma, for their encouragement and always keeping me grounded while I reach for the stars.

ABOUT THE AUTHORS

WARD CARROLL flew in F-14 Tomcats for fifteen of his twenty years in the Navy after graduating from the U.S. Naval Academy. He was named Naval Institute Press Author of the Year in 2001 for his novel *Punk's War* and is also the author of *Punk's Fight* and *Punk's Wing*. He is the host of the popular Ward Carroll YouTube channel.

TONY PEAK writes science fiction, fantasy, and LitRPG novels. He is the author of *Inherit the Stars,* the *Eden Trilogy,* the *Redshift Runners* trilogy, and other works of speculative fiction. His interests include progressive thinking, storytelling in all mediums, and planetary exploration. He resides in southwest Virginia.

The Naval Institute Press is the book-publishing arm of the U.S. Naval Institute, a private, nonprofit, membership society for sea service professionals and others who share an interest in naval and maritime affairs. Established in 1873 at the U.S. Naval Academy in Annapolis, Maryland, where its offices remain today, the Naval Institute has members worldwide.

Members of the Naval Institute support the education programs of the society and receive the influential monthly magazine *Proceedings* or the colorful bimonthly magazine *Naval History* and discounts on fine nautical prints and on ship and aircraft photos. They also have access to the transcripts of the Institute's Oral History Program and get discounted admission to any of the Institute-sponsored seminars offered around the country.

The Naval Institute's book-publishing program, begun in 1898 with basic guides to naval practices, has broadened its scope to include books of more general interest. Now the Naval Institute Press publishes about seventy titles each year, ranging from how-to books on boating and navigation to battle histories, biographies, ship and aircraft guides, and novels. Institute members receive significant discounts on the Press' more than eight hundred books in print.

Full-time students are eligible for special half-price membership rates. Life memberships are also available.

For more information about Naval Institute Press books that are currently available, visit www.usni.org/press/books. To learn about joining the U.S. Naval Institute, please write to:

Member Services
U.S. Naval Institute
291 Wood Road
Annapolis, MD 21402-5034
Telephone: (800) 233-8764
Fax: (410) 571-1703
Web address: www.usni.org

10/25